SLAYING
the
SHADOW
PRINCE

HELEN SCHEUERER

First printing, 2023

Print illustrated paperback ISBN 978-1-922903-08-2

Print hardcover ISBN 978-1-922903-09-9

Ebook ISBN 978-1-922903-00-6

Cover illustration by Natalie Bernard

This one's for you, Fay.

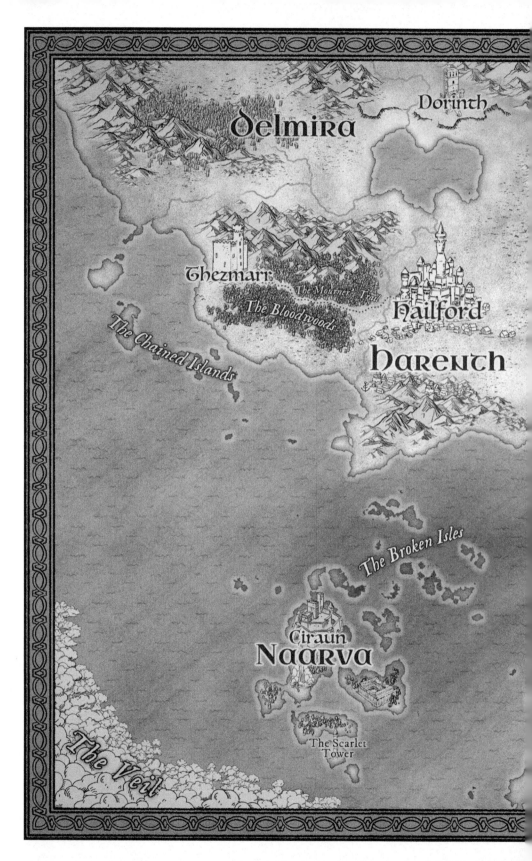

THE MIDREALMS

Darkness came for everyone eventually. But on the darkest night of every month, one of the most elite warriors of the midrealms became a monster. An intoxicating song called to the most primal part of him, buried deep within, and all the colour leached from the world. There was no stopping the change. In a wave, onyx power thrummed through his veins, fracturing the smooth surface of his sun-kissed skin, membranous wings spearing from his muscular back.

In the place of a celebrated Warsword was a deadly master of shadow, talons unsheathing at his fingertips as he wielded wisps of obsidian into the shape of nightmares.

He had been a hero once.

Now, he was cursed with the half-life of a shadow wraith.

I

DRUE

Drue Emmerson patrolled the northernmost point of the fallen kingdom of Naarva and looked into the festering darkness. As she gazed upon the looming clouds and the gathering night, she could scarcely contain her rage. Her homeland, the kingdom of gardens, had once been a place teeming with life and colour, its provinces lush, its gardens overflowing with vibrant blooms and its skies a soaring blue. But that was then.

Now, fear was the constant companion of all those who remained in Naarva, always begging the question: who would be next? The shadow wraiths had taken not only the kingdom's soul, but Drue's mother and brothers as well, leaving only her and her father behind.

She was one of many with such a tale.

The capital, Ciraun, along with the palace within its citadel, had been the first to fall. There had been no sign of the royal family in nearly a year; all the while their people lost their lives and loved ones, one way or another. An entire

I

kingdom was scattered to the wind, with most now living underground or in rural strongholds across the broken lands, constantly on alert for the next attack. Drue's countrymen were still reported missing on a weekly basis and there were rumours of an increasing threat to what little remained of her beloved homeland.

'We shouldn't be out here,' said Coltan, her childhood friend, following her eyeline to the Broken Isles across the seas to the east, and then to the west where the Veil towered. Even from a distance it was a sight to behold: a wall of billowing mist that surrounded all the midrealms, a barrier of protection, so they'd been taught. A shield between the people and the creatures that lurked beyond. A shield that was fracturing.

'*You* shouldn't be here,' Drue snapped, his comment only reigniting her frustration.

'I didn't want you out here alone.'

'I wouldn't have been. If you hadn't messed with the patrol roster, I'd be here with Adrienne.' *And I wish I was*, her clipped words implied. She would choose the company of her best friend and the general of the guerrilla forces any day over the entitled demands of Coltan. What felt like a lifetime ago, Drue had made a mistake with him. They had known each other their whole lives, and thinking he understood the grief she was going through, she had sought comfort in his arms. She'd been paying for that mistake ever since.

'I was just looking out for you,' Coltan said, his mouth downturned.

But Drue didn't have the patience for hurt feelings of his own making. 'You were just sticking your nose in where it doesn't belong. Trying to claim what's not yours to claim.'

Coltan made a noise of disbelief.

Unclenching her jaw, Drue ignored him and scanned the burnished skies again. It was near dusk and she hadn't meant to stay out so late, but the latest less-than-detailed reports from this perimeter had bothered her. She had wanted to check for herself.

Drue was one of the best rangers to have risen from the fall of Naarva. She had shed her noblewoman's skin and shaped herself anew in the wake of all that death and destruction, spitting in the face of laws and tradition.

Her father had too, and as one of the few folk left who knew how to manage such things, he'd taken over the forge of Naarva and the crucial task of hammering the blades of the Warswords. For even amid the fall of a kingdom, the elite warriors of Thezmarr must have their weapons. They were the protectors of the midrealms, the only men capable of slaying a shadow wraith.

But Drue refused to believe they were Naarva's only hope, for they'd failed her people before. She had joined the guerrilla forces as a ranger, hoping one day she might discover the monsters' lair, that she might be the one to set the fucking thing ablaze and watch it burn. But, cloaked in dark magic, it had eluded her for a year.

Drue herself could practically smell a shadow wraith a mile off, and she had no shortage of rage to wield against them. Her hand drifted to the steel cuff at her wrist that she'd forged herself... An experiment that had become her obsession, the thing that filled her mind when the movement of constant travel ceased. She ran her fingertips over its dented surface. She was no master smith like her father, but the cuff wasn't for looking pretty. It sensed the power-hungry magic of the wraiths, warming against her skin when they were near. It was a glimmer of hope, on an otherwise bleak horizon, that there might just be a way to keep the monsters of the midrealms at bay.

'Drue?' Coltan's voice jolted her from her reverie. 'What's that?'

She followed his pointed finger to something in the clouds moving towards them, fast. Her eyes narrowed, her hand shifting to her cutlass, but pausing as the creature came into full view. A sigh of relief whistled between her teeth.

'It's just Terrence,' she replied, not taking her eyes off the wide expanse of those soaring wings closing in. She braced herself for her hawk's landing.

Sure enough, she had to dig her heels into the earth as a powerful gust of wind hit and the bird's talons gripped her shoulder, his substantial weight settling there. Drue found it comforting and reached up to stroke his feathers fondly.

Terrence gave her finger an affectionate nip with his beak before he cast his discerning yellow gaze upon Coltan with unmistakable disdain. Drue loved him for it, especially when it made Coltan yield a step back from her.

The hawk was an impeccable judge of character, to be sure.

'I really wish you wouldn't bring him everywhere,' Coltan muttered.

'Adrienne loves him.'

'Because Adrienne shares your sadistic sense of humour.'

'I have no idea what you're talking about.'

'Please,' Coltan scoffed, starting after her as she continued along the kingdom's perimeter. 'The two of you and that damn bird love ganging up on me.'

'We do no such thing.'

He fixed her with a lingering, longing stare. 'Am I so repulsive to you?' he asked, desperation ringing in his voice.

'I'm not having this conversation again.' Drue's fist clenched around the grip of her cutlass, her knuckles threatening to split. Terrence's claws tightened on her shoulder, as though he too couldn't stand Coltan's constant pestering.

'Drue, please... Just talk to me.'

'I *have* talked to you,' she snapped. 'I have told you time and time again that you have my friendship and nothing more. I have nothing else to give you. You are not entitled to or owed anything more, nor will this constant barrage of pressure from you result in what you want.'

'It truly meant nothing?' he asked.

'It was a night or two of comfort between friends,' Drue replied. 'I told you as much at the time and three dozen times since —'

In a rage, Coltan sent his shield flying. The steel disc clanged loudly as it struck a nearby boulder and bounced off, colliding with several smaller rocks before it rolled onto its face, the sound echoing across the expanse of an otherwise silent land.

Drue's heart had seized, not for fear of Coltan, but for what the rattling noise might draw out from the shadows. She waited a beat, then two, straining to hear anything that might indicate that he'd disturbed something in hiding...

Sensing nothing, she rounded on him. 'You fool,' she hissed, fury bubbling to the surface as she suppressed the urge to swing her blade. Not only was he an entitled, fragile man-child, but he was a fucking idiot as well.

'I didn't —'

She raised a hand to silence him, her scalp prickling.

Something in the air had changed. An unnatural stillness settled over the abandoned, sprawling citadel below.

And as if in answer, the steel cuff warmed against her skin and Terrence let out a sharp cry of warning.

Darkness blocked out the horizon.

Suddenly, the shadow wraiths were upon them.

Membranous wings flared, talons already carving through the air as wisps of onyx power whipped around them, disorientating, alluring.

'Fuck,' Drue shouted, drawing her cutlass and her sword.

Terrence launched himself into the air, and she had to bite back her shriek of fear for him. He was a mighty bird of prey. He could handle himself. Coltan, on the other hand...

'Draw your sword,' she snapped, finding her flint and striking flame to life along her blades.

While she was no Warsword and couldn't slay a shadow wraith to its bitter end, she could fight them off, and there was one thing they hated more than anything: fire.

With her back to Coltan, Drue braced herself for the first assault.

The monsters landed heavily, the earth trembling beneath their claw-like feet. There were seven of them – a bigger swarm than she was used to, but it mattered not, so long as her fire raged hot and her blades were sharp.

The wraiths advanced, their strange, sinewy frames dripping with cursed shadow, their skin almost leather-like, their eyes an eerie clouded blue.

They were not of this world – not anymore.

Magic lashed at her, but she sliced at it like she would a limb, severing it from its source with her fiery steel. She was from a family of blade wielders. Her brothers had trained her well, despite her skirts and jewels, and now... Now she was a force to be reckoned with all on her own.

One wraith screeched as she carved her cutlass across its

wiry arm. The horrific smell of burnt hair singed her nostrils, for that was what these monsters reeked of as they shaped the darkness around them.

Behind her, Coltan shouted, but she couldn't turn her back on the wraith in front of her. The beast towered above her, its body elongated and horrific, eight feet tall, wielding its claws like a puppet master, manipulating the ribbons of power around it, its form taking a familiar shape. The monster's magic picked at the rotting trauma within her, shaping its curse of nightmares into those she had lost, manifesting warped versions of them before her.

'Mother,' Drue wheezed, hesitating just a second as she saw her – a crude imagining of the gentle woman who'd raised her, wrapped in shadow.

Drue lunged, the illusion shattering as she pierced the creature's leathery flesh with the tip of her sword.

But it was not enough. She needed to get herself and Coltan out of there. There was no way they could take on the entire swarm. She couldn't evade the lure of their horrors forever. Dodging another onslaught of lashing shadow, she rolled along the ground, slicing where she guessed the creature's heel tendon would be —

The answering scream confirmed it, black and red blood spurting from the wound.

Drue's hands were growing clammy around the grips of her weapons, but she didn't stop. She delivered an upward cut to another wraith's abdomen, hoping the flames caught alight across its flesh.

'Coltan!' she called, finding her companion further away than she'd realised and surrounded by wraiths.

'Go!' he shouted. 'Let me distract —'

She stopped listening. He was hardly one for heroics.

Instead, Drue ducked and wove her way to him, delivering as much damage to the monsters as she could. All the while, her mind ticking through the options she had.

There weren't many.

She knew the top island of Naarva like the back of her hand, all the nooks and crannies, all the secret passageways the rebels and guerrilla forces had carved out under the noses of the wraiths. But those were no good to them when they were in the thick of a swarm, when Coltan insisted on fighting like a prized idiot. And over her dead body would she lead the monsters back to the citadel.

When she reached Coltan, she noted several lacerations and a scorch mark across his chest. He'd been hit hard... He was panting, raising his sword against an incoming swipe of claws. Drue blocked, swinging her cutlass at the exposed shoulder of another monster.

Above, Terrence shrieked, his wings beating furiously as he aimed his talons for the creatures' clouded blue eyes, clawing viciously, sending one of them stumbling and clutching at its face —

But they were outnumbered and outmatched. Two rangers of Naarva had no chance against seven shadow wraiths from beyond the Veil. Drue desperately scanned their surroundings, looking for anything that might hold them off a little longer, just to give her a second to think —

The thunderous sound of horse hooves vibrated beneath her boots.

Her gaze snapped up to see a pair of mighty warriors leaping from their stallions and into the heart of the fray. In the glowing light of the blazes, the palm-sized totems on their right arms gleamed: a design of two crossed swords with a third cutting down the middle, marking them with the highest honour Thezmarr could bestow.

These were no ordinary warriors. These were *Warswords* of the guild from across the sea.

Drue didn't question it, not then. Instead, she used their arrival and the wraiths' surprise to her advantage, slicing through legs and abdomens with as much force as she could muster, weakening the monsters so that the Warswords might pin them down to deliver swift justice. The warriors lit their swords aflame as well, the larger of the two wielding one in each hand as though the blades were an extension of himself. He moved with such precision and grace that Drue nearly stopped in her tracks to admire him.

The shriek of a wraith brought her out of her near-trance and spurred her into action. She parried and blocked, dodged and advanced, all the while inflicting as much pain and suffering as she could muster. These creatures were the reason her brothers were dead, her mother too, their screams echoing in her nightmares. These beasts of darkness had changed the fate of her entire kingdom and wrought despair upon the people of Naarva. Because of them, she and everyone else she knew on these shores lived a half-life, one cloaked in fear —

An ear-piercing scream set her teeth on edge, and she whirled around to see the Warswords working together to carve out the heart of not one but two wraiths. It was a horrific, brutal act, but when the black masses were cast aside, the monsters moved no more.

Drue allowed herself a moment to catch her breath, gasping in disbelief and awe as the Warswords took on another creature, moving as a single unit, as though they had done this countless times before.

Nearby, Coltan hauled himself to his feet and came to stand at her side, and Terrence landed on her shoulder with a quiet cry, but she didn't dare take her eyes off the wraiths. The Warswords' hands slayed two more, while the remaining three flung out their wings and launched themselves into the sky, leaving near-translucent ribbons of shadow in their wake as they fled.

The Warswords exchanged no words as they lit the carved hearts on fire, before stalking towards Drue and Coltan.

But something tightened in Drue's chest, for there were no more wraiths in sight, and yet... Her cuff was still hot against her wrist.

As the towering Warswords approached, she waited – waited for the air to clear, for the remains of the dead creatures to drift into the wind... She watched as the smoke swept away the scent and ash of the monsters.

And still the heat against her skin lingered.

Still, the cuff sang to her.

Before she knew it, the larger warrior stood before her, a satisfied gleam shining in his hazel eyes. His dark hair was tied up in a knot. Olive skin peeked from beneath his black armour as he sheathed both his swords at his belt.

He offered a blood-stained hand. 'I'm Talemir Starling,' he said with a smile. 'And this is Wilder Hawthorne.'

Drue stared at him. He looked every bit the formidable warrior, every bit the handsome rogue his kind were reported to be: square jaw, corded with muscle...

But even though he smelt like an incoming storm after a drought, she didn't hesitate to thrust her blade to his throat.

For the cuff didn't lie.

And it told her that this man was a shadow wraith.

2
TALEMIR

With her cutlass to his throat, the beautiful young ranger actually *swung her sword at him*. Talemir leapt back in surprise, unsure how he'd managed to offend her so soon. Usually it took a good while for him to get a woman this riled up, but within moments he realised that the fury on her face was not born of a simple slight, but of a hurt so deep it raged white-hot.

He unsheathed his sword in an instant, a thrill surging through him at the new challenge, the pair of them moving so fast that his former apprentice still wore an expression of shock.

Steel met steel, ringing out across the empty lands as he blocked the woman's second strike. He didn't intend to attack, but merely —

Feathers and talons came out of nowhere with a blood-curdling screech, claws as sharp as daggers dragging down his face.

'What the fuck?' He tried to bat back what he realised was an enormous hawk.

'Away, Terrence. He's mine,' the woman commanded, and in a second the bird was gone and she was advancing once more. 'You're one of them,' she spat, whirling on her toes and delivering a surprisingly powerful thrust of her blade.

Her words sent instant dread coiling in his gut, and that strange cuff around her wrist seemed to hum as she pushed forward, but he deflected her attack easily. 'You mean a Warsword?' he asked with mock politeness, sidestepping another lunge. 'I thought that much was obvious.'

She parried, determination and hatred blazing in her ice-blue, kohl-lined gaze. 'A monster.' She feinted right and then struck, but with a downward cut, he knocked her blade aside.

'Talemir?' Wilder's voice sounded a few feet away, more curious than alarmed.

Talemir glanced over his attacker to see his protégé looking bored as he leant against a boulder, the tip of his sword poised at the Naarvian man's throat. 'I thought we were headed to Ciraun?'

'This won't take a minute. I've got it handled,' Talemir called back, returning his attention to the woman just in time for her to deliver a vicious slice to his bicep. Blood trickled, but he barely felt it.

'Do you?' she snarled, forcing him backward, drawing their fight away from the others. 'I know what you are.'

Plastering on his most charming grin, Talemir stepped out of striking range and sketched a bow. 'As I said, Talemir Starling, Warsword of Thezmarr, at your service, lady. Perhaps you've heard of me?' He winked. 'What should I call you, Wildfire?'

The word slipped from his lips before he'd even thought it,

for that was what the woman was – a living flame, both in her violent actions and the streaks of red through her burntumber hair.

'Not that,' she said through gritted teeth, surging towards him again.

This time, their swords met close between their bodies.

'I have to call you something, Wildfire.'

She let out a cry of fury and attacked with renewed rage, her blades blurs of silver in the air before him. It was adorable, really, that she thought she could gain the upper hand against a Warsword. He certainly hadn't survived the Great Rite to be smote by a girl, however pretty, upon the ruins of Naarva. But she clearly sensed something within him, something that, until this point, no one else had... So he let her drive the fight backward, towards the rocky outcrop of the cliffs, so they were out of earshot. He let her hold her blade to his neck, just for a moment.

There was little space between them, and her body heaved with effort as she pressed her weapon to his throat again.

'You're a skilled fighter, I'll give you that,' he told her, utterly calm despite the trickle of blood he felt trailing down his skin. 'Though, you're breaking the laws of the midrealms by wielding that blade.'

Her lip curled into a snarl. 'Women of Naarva learnt long ago to abide by their own laws if they wanted to survive.'

'I can respect that,' Talemir replied. 'If they allowed women warriors at Thezmarr, you'd make a fine —'

'Enough,' she commanded. But her gaze had changed, as had her breathing. She pressed against him, her thigh forced between his, her eyes dipping to his mouth. 'Stop that,' she said.

He frowned. 'Stop what?'

'You're using your dark magic on me, bewitching me with shadows.'

A laugh escaped him. 'What?'

But she'd drawn his attention to it as well, to every part of them that touched. Her body was like a brand on his, awakening something that slumbered deep within.

'You're trying to seduce me into the darkness,' she breathed. 'I can feel it...'

He nearly snorted, but instead he leant in. 'Perhaps you just find me attractive. You wouldn't be the first.'

She blanched.

And that was the signal that whatever this was had gone on long enough. As much as he would have liked to continue rolling around in the dirt with her, he had his orders from the guild. He needed to find and kill the wayward son of the forge master: the man responsible for threatening all that Thezmarr stood for, its very culture and ethos, the protection of the midrealms. The strange buzzing at the woman's wrist told Talemir that the cuff was ample evidence of the man's meddling. There was no doubt it had been made with Naarvian steel.

In three quick manoeuvres, he had her disarmed, her dainty hands trapped in his, her back flush to his chest.

'You were toying with me,' she breathed.

'Only a little.'

'You're a monster...'

Whatever magic that cuff was imbued with – for it had to be the cuff – was powerful and alarmingly effective. There was no trace of doubt in her words. She clearly knew in her bones what he was, which unnerved him. Not even Wilder knew... But she had no proof. Here, he was all man, all warrior, and nothing more.

'I've been called worse,' he allowed. 'Do you yield?'

There was a lingering pause, and he tightened his grip. 'I know what you are, shadow wraith. I will carve out your heart before the end.'

Talemir gave a dark laugh. 'I'd like to see you try, Wildfire. Do you yield?' he asked again.

He felt her against every part of him, stirring something within, and he realised she smelt of lilacs and heather, of a home long forgotten.

'For now,' she said at last.

'Good.' He released her. 'Then you can take us to the forge.'

The woman stiffened. 'What do you want with the forge?'

'Warsword business. Best you don't interfere.'

He could practically hear her grinding her teeth, but the woman seemed to understand that he had her beat and slowly, her blue gaze still searing with rage, she sheathed her weapons. Seething in silence, she led them back down the crest of land to where Wilder waited with their horses, and the other man stood awkwardly, his complexion ashen from his encounter with both wraiths and Warswords. The giant hawk watched from a nearby rock as well, its yellow eyes utterly unnerving. Talemir glared at it, the scratches on his face already itching where the blood had dried.

Wilder handed him his reins. 'What was that about?' he asked under his breath.

'Oh, you know by now I have a tendency to cause extreme reactions in women...' Talemir grinned.

'That's usually after you bed them.'

'What can I say? Perhaps my powers of seduction are stronger in Naarva.'

Wilder snorted. 'She was trying to *kill* you.'

'Some of the best sex starts that way, my young apprentice.'

The younger warrior rolled his eyes in a long-suffering manner. 'I haven't been your apprentice in years. I'm a Warsword now.'

Talemir smirked. He loved baiting the young man. And now more than ever, after the fall of Naarva, after the fall of Wilder's brother, it was an extra joy to see him shed his shell of grief, even for a moment.

'You'll always be my apprentice,' he said, giving his fellow Warsword a gentle shove.

Wilder shook his head and mounted his horse. 'You get more insufferable by the day.'

'You wound me,' Talemir quipped. 'Aren't you forgetting something?'

'What?'

'Well, if we're to reach the forge in the next century, you'll have to make room in that saddle for one more...' Talemir nodded to the scowling Naarvian ranger.

'You can't be serious,' Wilder said, not keeping the disgust from his voice.

'Oh, deadly serious, apprentice. We both know the lady wants to be close to me.'

'I hope she sticks a knife in your back.'

'With a face like that, I might just let her.'

'Insufferable,' Wilder muttered, motioning for the male ranger to approach.

Talemir turned to find the woman closer than he'd realised. She was quiet on her feet. He'd give her that.

'Are you quite done with your dick-swinging?' she demanded, folding her arms over her chest.

He stepped back, presenting the stirrup to her. 'By all means, climb on.'

'You expect me to share a saddle with you? With a fucking shadow wraith?'

Talemir couldn't help but glance towards Wilder, checking that he hadn't heard. 'I don't know where you've got that idea, but I assure you —'

The woman closed the gap between them, her knuckles paling as she clenched her fists around her weapons. 'You may look like a man, but I know better. Don't insult me by saying otherwise.'

'Regardless of what you think, I bear you no ill will. My business is with the forge master. Once that's dealt with, you needn't see me again. But we have to get there first.'

'I can walk.'

'It'll take all night.'

'So be it,' she said, lifting her chin in defiance.

But no, that wasn't how this was going to go. In a single, effortless motion, Talemir enclosed his hands around her waist, the warmth of her skin seeping through her clothes into his palms, and he lifted her into the saddle.

Apparently, only shock stopped her from kicking him in the face, and before she could think better of it, he swung himself up behind her, settling her between his legs. Oh, he could feel the rage rolling off her in waves, but that didn't stop him from appreciating the brush of her soft hair, nor that intoxicating scent of lilac and heather.

A blur of movement to their left caught his eye as he urged his stallion onwards. That damn hawk was back, flying close enough to them that it felt like a warning. But he was a Warsword of Thezmarr. It would take more than some bird to ruffle him.

'What did you say its name was?' he asked the woman, his hands gripping the reins in front of her.

'Terrence,' she said.

'Terrence?' He baulked. 'What sort of name is that for a bird of prey?'

'A perfectly decent one,' she countered coldly.

'Right...' He watched the hawk fly ahead then, dipping in and out of sight. 'What does he eat?'

'Starlings,' she replied, deadpan.

He snorted. For that line alone, under different circumstances he would have courted her. But despite his jesting to Wilder, he was under no illusions about finding passion here. She offered nothing of the sort, or perhaps another form of it entirely – where the tip of her blade kissed the delicate skin of his throat.

As they rode south, Wilder and the other ranger looking equally uncomfortable sharing a saddle to their right, the woman spoke again.

'What are Warswords doing in Naarva?' There was no missing the hatred lacing her question.

'We're here by order of Thezmarr,' he told her.

'You're over a year late.'

He felt, rather than saw, Wilder's attention snap towards her, his rage palpable. 'We were here. We fought. We lost as you lost.'

'I doubt that, Warsword,' she taunted.

Talemir tensed as those words found their mark and Wilder twisted in the saddle, his usually handsome face contorted with unrestrained violence.

'What do you mean by that, ranger?' he bit out.

Talemir didn't blame him. In fact, the same rage simmered in his own veins. Wilder's older brother, Malik, who was also

Talemir's dearest friend, had suffered greatly during the ultimate battle for Naarva. It had been he and Talemir who had fought at the centre of the horrific skirmish, and both had endured a fate crueller than death.

'Wilder,' Talemir barked, sensing that his young protégé was about to do or say something brash. And as much as he wished to throttle the woman for her thoughtless words, he knew better.

But she turned in the saddle, meeting his gaze, her own blue eyes intense with interest, as though she had just pieced a puzzle together. Her attention unnerved him and he pressed his stallion into a canter, so she was forced to face forward. The sooner he and Wilder spoke to the forge master and found his wayward son, the sooner they could leave the festering shithole of Naarva behind.

For it was festering. He had seen it before it had fallen – the kingdom of gardens, it was once called. Both the citadel and the university on the eastern island boasted the most extensive range of blooms the midrealms had to offer. Everything had crumbled after the shadow wraiths broke through the Veil, rendering it nothing more than an overgrown nightmare now. First, his own homeland, the kingdom of Delmira, had been taken... Naarva had followed years later.

He straightened in his saddle as the remains of the citadel came into view.

'You'll direct us to the forge?' he asked.

'If you insist,' she muttered.

'I'd happily enjoy your warm and welcoming company a little longer.'

'Then ride on, wraith. Perhaps the forge master has a special blade for your heart.'

He ignored this, ignored her as they approached the iron doors of the city.

He peered across at Wilder and gave him a subtle nod. For beyond those doors was their enemy: the man who had sabotaged the magical steel source. The consequences of his actions were dire – the weakening of Warsword blades and the consequent strengthening of the shadow wraiths. Talemir himself had sworn to kill the bastard...

Without further comment, the woman nodded to the guards stationed above the gates and directed them through the eerily quiet citadel.

'Where is everyone?' Wilder asked, his brow furrowed.

'Underground,' the woman replied tersely. 'The citadel has been empty for a long time. It's no safer than out in the open. The only thing that operates above ground is the forge.'

Talemir shifted in the saddle, trying to ignore the press of her backside against him. Then, the woman was swinging down from the horse, catching him in the stomach with her boot. He let out a grunt of shock, rather than pain.

'Apologies,' she said, without an ounce of regret. 'You can leave your horses with Brax,' she told them, waving to a youngster who had appeared from the shell of a nearby building. 'It's not far from here.'

Talemir shook his head in disbelief as he dismounted. *This woman... She's something else.*

He stared in awe as that giant hawk soared towards her, landing on her shoulder, its yellow eyes flicking from one man to the next, full of suspicion. The Warswords followed her and her friend down several abandoned alleyways. All the while, Talemir's skin crawled as though he were being watched. No doubt they were. If the survivors of Naarva had sense enough to send rangers to scout the perimeters of their territory, then they'd have sense enough to have people on sentry duty. He'd have wagered that the woman leading them through the empty streets was a leader here. She certainly acted like it.

At last, they reached the forge. It was a simple building at the end of a laneway, but Talemir could hear the strike of a hammer ringing out from within. He knew all too well the calibre of the weapons crafted here, his hands drifting to the grips of his swords sheathed at his sides. Like all Warswords' blades, the iron had been mined from a Naarvian source said to have been created by the Furies themselves with a star shower. The steel forged from such a place was known to be the strongest in all the midrealms, was known to hold the power of the gods. The very same source that was now being threatened by some meddlesome fool.

The woman pushed open the door before them and strode inside, clearly familiar with the blacksmith and his family. 'Fendran!' she called loudly, scanning the somewhat cluttered space around them.

A giant hearth sat in the centre of the forge, with a bellows positioned right beside it. Numerous stands of smithing tools lined the walls, and several long benches, as well as a trough with water for cooling steel, took up the rest of the room. It was sweltering hot, and Talemir could already feel his undershirt growing damp with sweat.

The hammer struck again and his attention cut to the far corner, where a middle-aged man stood tending to the blade of a dagger. Sparks flew as he hit the steel anew.

'What is it?' he near-shouted, not looking up, hammering away at the weapon. He was a muscular fellow, perhaps in his fiftieth year. His beard was scraggly and his face was lined with sweat and grime. He wore a thick leather apron and protective gloves.

'Warswords here to see you,' the woman called, leaning against a nearby bench and crossing her arms over her chest. She looked from the blacksmith to Talemir and Wilder, her gaze filled with disdain.

At last, the man named Fendran glanced up from his work, wiping his brow with the back of his glove, his eyes falling to the Warswords in his forge. Recognition flashed, and he approached them, huffing from the exertion.

'You're a long way from home,' he said by way of greeting. He surveyed Talemir with particular reverence. 'Starling, isn't it?'

Talemir inclined his head.

'I saw you fight in the final battle of Naarva.' He turned to Wilder. 'And you – you could only be the brother of Malik the Shieldbreaker...'

'I am, sir,' Wilder replied stiffly.

But Fendran didn't seem to notice. Instead, he faced Talemir again. 'You have some reputation, even here, even after... everything. I saw the showdown between you and that wraith towards the end of the battle, after Malik was maimed.'

Talemir felt Wilder flinch beside him. Malik had been the best of them. He had not deserved the fate he'd met.

'We thought that wraith had you for a moment there,' Fendran continued, shaking his head as though he were reliving the horror now.

Talemir forced himself to remain stoic, even as the memories came rushing back. He let the panic wash over him as he recalled the wraith's talon-tipped fingers reaching for him, penetrating his chest, the pain searing every inch of his skin as the darkness called to him. Talemir kept his face neutral despite the wave of nausea that gripped him, although his knees buckled beneath him. For a moment, it was as though the change were upon him at the mere memory of it all. Nothing compared to that horror. Nothing compared to the feeling of shedding his humanity and the wraith form taking hold. To the way all the colour seeped from the world and he saw everything in black and white and grey. He'd been trying to find a cure for it ever since, entrusting his secret to one person alone in all of the midrealms: an alchemist called Farissa in Thezmarr.

He tasted iron on his tongue and realised that he'd bitten the inside of his cheek.

Fendran was staring at him expectantly.

Talemir recovered instantly. 'We are here to speak with your son,' he said firmly, leaving out the part about the kill order. 'He has been charged with treason for interfering with the Naarvian steel source. All Warsword blades are connected by its magical properties, and his meddling has left us vulnerable when trying to defend against the shadow wraiths.'

The woman made a noise in her throat, as if she somehow found this amusing. He shot her a warning glare. Ranger or not, this wasn't her concern.

Talemir met Fendran's confused gaze. 'By interfering with the source, your son has endangered us all. He needs to answer for his crimes.'

Fendran's brow furrowed, and he glanced across at the woman who stood picking her nails by the anvil.

'I don't understand,' he said at last. 'What's happened to the source?'

'That's what we're here to find out, but the effects have been felt in the blades of Warswords all over the midrealms. There will be consequences.'

'Who gave you this information? What exactly do you intend to do?'

'It doesn't matter who gave the information,' Talemir said, though he noted the male ranger's defensive change in stance. 'All that matters is that this is dealt with. We cannot have someone interfering with the steel at a time where the weapons of Warswords are all that stand between the midrealms and the shadow wraiths. Our blades have protected the people for centuries —'

'Where is the proof, then?' Fendran argued, pushing his chest out in challenge, even though he had to crane his neck to meet Talemir's eyes. 'Proof that my... son is responsible?'

Talemir ground his teeth. The proof was wrapped around the young woman's wrist. He knew that for a fact, given that he could still feel the damn thing humming in his presence, but that was the problem. If he admitted he could sense the cuff, he was admitting to what he was: a monster. And though he could keep it at bay for now, on the darkest night of every month, there was no stopping it. He became a savage shadow wraith, enraptured by the darkness, by his own power. But that was neither here nor there. He had orders to follow.

'Sir, we just need to speak to your son,' Talemir pressed.

'Speak to him, eh?' Fendran said viciously. 'I have many sons. To which do you refer?'

Talemir exchanged a frustrated look with Wilder, who was growing restless beside him. His protégé wasn't known for his patience, especially after what had happened to Malik. Talemir could hardly blame him, nor could he blame the blacksmith for wanting to protect his child.

Talemir took a deep breath, almost choking on the metallic fumes. 'Your youngest. Drue Emmerson, sir. We need to speak to Drue.'

A grimace wrinkled the man's weathered face, and he pinched the bridge of his nose, as though he'd had this conversation many a time before.

To Talemir's surprise, Fendran turned to the woman, whose kohl-lined blue eyes glimmered with amusement, her fingers casually stroking the feathered chest of that great hawk.

'What's the meaning of this, Drue?' Fendran asked her.

Talemir baulked. *What did he call her?* Surely there was some mistake. She couldn't be —

But the beautiful, fiery woman turned to Talemir, triumph gleaming in her gaze. 'Ah,' she said. 'It would seem I am the wayward son of the forge master...'

She didn't offer her hand, but she sketched a bow, similar to the one Talemir had mocked her with earlier.

'Drue Emmerson, at your service, Warsword.'

3

DRUE

The look on the Warsword's face was priceless. Smiling darkly, Drue pushed off the bench and stalked towards him, hand on the hilt of her cutlass.

The warrior blinked at her. 'You're a forge maiden of Naarva?'

Coltan responded before she could get a word in. 'There's no *maiden* here,' he smirked.

The forge went deadly still for a moment and Terrence let out a warning cry from her shoulder.

Drue shot Coltan a searing look, her grip tightening on her weapon. He took liberties; he insulted her in front of her own father and Warswords of the midrealms... She'd noted his fidgeting as well, a telltale sign that *he'd* been the one to write to the guild at Thezmarr, reporting her supposed wrongdoings. All to curb her behaviour, to control her. He had the good sense to flinch under her and Terrence's glares. She'd deal with him later. Perhaps she'd let Terrence pluck out his eyes.

Now, she turned her focus to the larger of the Warswords. 'I'm a ranger,' she told him. 'And I have no idea what meddling you're talking about.' She hadn't been to the steel source in months. But Talemir Starling kept staring at her cuff, as though the steel around her wrist only confirmed the lies they'd been fed.

However, they both knew that to mention it would draw attention to what he truly was. And though she hadn't seen his claws yet, she had no doubt of the monster that lurked beneath his skin.

I have to kill him, she vowed to herself. But to kill a Warsword in plain sight of another would incite a war. *I have to get him away from everyone.*

She gave him a grin that, in her days as a noblewoman, had infuriated many people. 'You've come a long way for nothing, Warsword. As I said, I'm just a ranger.'

The bastard had the audacity to offer her a lazy smile. 'Oh, I doubt that, Wildfire. I doubt that very much.'

Fury crackled in her veins, heat blooming at her cheeks. 'You know my name now. Use it.'

Another grin answered her. 'I think Wildfire suits you better.'

Gods, she was going to kill him; she was going to carve out his gods-damned heart.

The Warsword she'd heard him call his apprentice cleared his throat and turned pointedly to her father. 'Perhaps you'd be so kind as to show us to a place we can camp?'

Her father waved him off. 'Nonsense. You've travelled far. Let us offer you our hospitality. So long as you mean my "son" no ill will, it would be an honour to host you.'

Drue rolled her eyes. It was just like Fendran to offer people who threatened her a free meal. Her noble-blooded mother had trained him well. The thought of sharing her table with a monster made Drue's blood sing in a rage, but perhaps...

Perhaps let him eat and drink his fill. It might just loosen his tongue, or at least that of his young protégé... She would find out all she could about this half-wraith, half-Warsword... Then, she would strike. She certainly hadn't failed to notice how he'd stiffened at her criticism of the way his guild had handled the fall of Naarva... It was clearly a pain point that she could use against him. So she swallowed her pride and her rage, and followed her father, Coltan and the Warswords to the very back of the forge.

There, they pushed aside a heavy shelf, revealing an arched entrance through the stone wall, and a staircase that descended below. With a rueful glance towards the windows, Drue swiped a torch from the sconce and started down the steps.

While the official fall of Naarva had only been declared six months ago, the kingdom had been under siege for a long time before that. Enough time to allow for its survivors and its most adaptable to turn to the underground vaults of the capital, Ciraun, and create a makeshift subterranean city. No one outside of Naarva knew of it, save for the Warswords who now fell into step beside her.

'You and I still need to talk,' Talemir said in her ear.

'If you say so,' she ground out, trying to storm ahead.

But the elite warrior towering at her side kept up with her pace. With the others in earshot, he didn't press the matter. He clearly didn't want to talk about the magic pulsing from her cuff. Even now it sang in his presence, recognising the shadow power in his veins, recoiling from it.

Drue had known she'd made leaps with her experiment

over the last few months, but the Warsword–wraith proved just how powerful her findings were against his kind. Working on weaponry targeting wraiths had been the passion of her closest brother, Leif. She'd taken up his work after his death, wishing sorely that he was there to see the progress.

Grateful for the silence, she led their small party down the spiralling stairs and through the deep stone passageways, the air becoming cooler as they moved away from the heat of the forge. Terrence remained on her shoulder, his grip tight but not painful, his attention on those around her as sharp as ever.

Talemir Starling... Upon her father's words, she'd finally recognised the name from the list of heroes associated with the most harrowing battles during the kingdom's fall... But how many of the warrior's comrades knew his secret? How many knew that a monster had infiltrated their ranks?

Drue wove them in a few unnecessary loops, her father and Coltan saying nothing as she did so. While her father was determined to host the champions of Thezmarr, she wasn't about to give them a direct map to the heart of her survivors' city.

At last, she reached the end of the passage, pushing open a heavy wooden door with her shoulder. The space beyond opened up into a great subterranean hall – the mess hall, they'd dubbed it. Despite the dim setting, it teemed with light, the huge cavern aglow with dozens of torches and buzzing with as many voices.

'Drue!' a familiar voice shouted.

As her friend Adrienne charged towards her, Terrence took flight, forcing her backward as he launched, soaring for his usual perch above the great oak table. Her back collided with a wall of muscle; gentle hands gripped her shoulders to steady her.

'Easy, there.' Laughter laced Talemir's voice, his tone skittering along her bones and toying with something deep inside her.

But before Drue could shove him away, Adrienne crashed into her, wrapping her in toned arms and squeezing tight. 'We were just about to send some scouts after you,' she said breathlessly, before her whole body tensed at the sight of the Warswords. 'Though I see that would have been unnecessary...' She gave a low, appreciative whistle and twirled a tendril of long blonde hair around her finger. 'Wherever did you find them?'

'Northern watch point,' Drue muttered. 'Fendran fancied adopting them —'

'Well, *thank you*, Fendran.' Adrienne wiggled her eyebrows suggestively.

Drue shook her head. 'Furies save us. Don't go dropping your drawers just yet. I've got to tell you something.'

'How intriguing.'

'Not here, though.'

'Don't keep me in suspense too long,' Adrienne warned. 'You know I'll lose interest.'

Drue sighed, glancing over her shoulder at the Warswords, who were now in deep discussion with her father. 'I know. Let's get some food. I'm starved.'

'Aren't we both?' Adrienne quipped, with a pointed glance at the warriors.

'Good gods, stop that.'

Adrienne laughed. 'I'll stop when I'm dead.'

'Well, that'll be sooner rather than later at this rate.'

'Let's hope so. Things are getting rather dull around here.'

Drue just shook her head again and started for the kitchens. To her dismay, Coltan followed them.

'What do you want?' Adrienne snapped in his direction as they reached the plates. 'I mean, besides messing with my roster?'

Coltan blanched. 'I didn't —'

'Liar.' Adrienne whirled around to face him. 'The next time you mess with one of my guard schedules to feed your own obsessions, I'll hold you down and let Terrence peck you bloody.'

Drue bit back a laugh. Adrienne absolutely *would* do that. She was incredibly protective of her meticulously planned rosters and took her role as general of the guerrilla forces very seriously.

'I...'

'Get out of my sight,' she spat, with a look that invited no challenge.

'Thanks,' Drue murmured, picking up a plate and handing it to her friend.

'He's still giving you grief?'

'Unfortunately. It was his fault we were attacked on the —'

'You were attacked?' Adrienne gaped, all hints of mischief vanishing from her face. 'Why didn't you say?'

Drue ran a hand through her hair, suddenly wary. 'Well, were it not for the Warswords,' she said reluctantly, 'we would have been done for.'

'Then why are we not toasting to their heroics?' Adrienne asked.

'Because...' Drue looked around, checking to make sure that Coltan had indeed scarpered off somewhere and that no one else was in earshot. 'Because one of them is a fucking shadow wraith.'

Adrienne's spoon froze midway into a pot of stew. 'What?'

Drue subtly tapped the cuff on her wrist and flicked her eyes towards the Warsword named Talemir. She had confided in Adrienne long ago about her experiments, and the general fully endorsed her ambitions. Slowly, her friend turned to face the mess hall, her gaze lingering on the large warrior still talking with Fendran.

'You're sure?' Adrienne murmured.

'Positive.'

'That's an interesting development.'

'Interesting? Don't you mean terrifying? The power of a shadow wraith and a Warsword combined? You know they're gifted by the Furies, don't you? Gods-given strength, speed and agility... Some of them are even rumoured to be immortal, Adri.'

'Well... Yes, but...'

'I didn't realise there'd be a "but", General.'

'Well, he's not a wraith now.'

'No,' Drue allowed. 'But mark my words, Adrienne. It's in there. And I'm going to get it to show its claws.'

She drew a sharp breath.

'Do you yield?' he'd asked her atop the cliff, his body pressed to hers.

'For now,' she'd replied. But the word *never* had echoed in her mind. She was going to learn his secrets, draw him out, and destroy him and all his kind. She would do what she had to for the survivors of Naarva, for her family.

'Come on,' Adrienne said. 'Our loitering is drawing attention.'

She was right, so Drue followed her to the long oak table

at the heart of the mess hall, swiping a flagon of wine along the way and settling herself beside her friend.

As soon as they were seated, the usual chaos ensued. As the best ranger and the general of the guerrilla forces, they were in high demand. People flocked to them, asking questions, commenting on their recent accomplishments and just generally wanting to be in their vicinity. Adrienne handled it better than Drue, who, although she had once led the life of a sociable noblewoman, had since found such dealings draining. She kept up appearances, though, understanding that she had earned the respect of her people with her own blood and sweat. She had run out of tears long ago.

The crowd around the young women parted as Fendran led the two Warswords to their table. With a cocky grin, Talemir Starling took up the place opposite Drue, his hulking great frame dwarfing the table and bench.

'This is a sight for sore eyes,' Baledor, her father's friend and right-hand man, announced, seeming to admire the Warswords along with Adrienne. 'The best of both our lands united again.'

'A cause for celebration indeed,' Talemir said wryly, lifting his cup in salute to Drue.

What in the realms was he playing at?

Baledor clapped a hand on the Warsword's shoulder. 'Drue here is our best ranger. She's like a hound on the scent when a wraith is near.'

'Is that so?' Talemir smiled softly.

Drue clenched her jaw.

Beside her, Adrienne sized him up. 'When Naarva fell, the midrealms were no longer safe. Darkness was coming for us all. But Drue helps fight that darkness. Every day.'

'So I've seen firsthand,' he allowed. 'So you have a lot of women here wielding blades?'

Adrienne clicked her tongue in annoyance, mirroring Drue's own feelings. 'That prophecy from years ago was a load of shit and every woman in Naarva knew it the moment Ciraun fell. We've been breaking that law ever since, and fuck anyone who tries to stop us.'

'Hear, hear,' Drue said, clinking her cup against her friend's before turning to the warriors. 'We leave your precious Warsword steel alone, so what have you to complain about?'

'That remains to be seen,' Talemir replied, a glint in his eyes.

'Ladies...' Fendran warned. 'A little less hostility, perhaps?'

Drue waved him off. 'They asked.'

To Talemir's right, his protégé, Wilder, studied her closely before glancing from Drue to Adrienne, as though he'd just realised she was there. His eyes lingered on the blonde general a little longer than necessary.

'We weren't aware that so many people survived the fall of the kingdom,' he said, changing tact and digging into his food.

'Many didn't,' Drue told him, grateful for a new subject. 'Down here, the numbers can feel bigger than they are. Starve-edged despair brought survivors together in this stronghold, but there are those who still dwell in pockets all around Naarva.'

'Both good and bad,' Adrienne added.

Drue glanced at her. 'More news?'

Adrienne gave a stiff nod. 'A report from one of our southern outposts – a gang of raiders attacked a small settlement there.'

'Fuck,' Drue muttered. How there could be Naarvians

attacking fellow Naarvians amid all the other horrors, she didn't understand. But war brought out the darkest parts of humanity, of which there was no shortage, it seemed.

'I know,' Adrienne replied. 'There are more reports of people going missing as well. I've got all our watchtowers manned as of today.'

'Good.' Drue looked around then, scanning the familiar faces for one she did not see. 'Where's Gus?'

Angus Castemont was their shared charge, eleven years old and desperate to join their forces – and every bit the pain in the arse Drue remembered her brothers being at that age.

After they'd died, Drue had kept everyone but Adrienne at arm's length, even her father. But Gus... Gus had wormed his way into her hardened heart. His older cousin, Dratos, had brought him to the safety of the stronghold from the wraith-infested south, another orphan of Naarva... He looked the part, too. Gus was smaller than the average eleven-year-old, forever wearing the same hole-ridden knitted jumper, a mop of curls always falling in his eyes.

Somehow, the world hadn't dimmed the light in the boy.

He'd found Drue on watch one day and, despite her surly nature, had sat down beside her, pummelling her with a barrage of questions she didn't bother answering. Nothing fazed him, though. The kid could talk under water.

Just as Drue had been losing her patience with him, he'd given her a piercing look.

'Do you have brothers and sisters?' he asked, so earnestly that Drue couldn't deny him that one kernel of information.

'I had brothers.'

'I can tell,' he replied proudly.

'Because I'm trying to ignore you?'

'Yep,' he declared. 'I had three sisters. I was in the middle: the big brother and the little brother at once. It was a mess.'

A laugh bubbled out of Drue unexpectedly and she looked upon the boy, all skinny limbs, big blue eyes and matted chestnut hair. 'I know the feeling.'

His lower lip trembled then, and a pang of sympathy shot through Drue. 'Where are they now?'

'Dead.'

She'd figured as much. 'I'm sorry.'

'What about your brothers?'

'Dead.'

The boy nodded in understanding beyond his eleven years. 'Dratos says that anyone can be a family.'

'Does he?'

Gus nodded, picking at his sleeves. 'You just have to feed each other.'

Drue had barked another laugh at that, and decided then and there that she liked the kid.

Young Gus Castemont had grown on her, and Adrienne, ever since. Eager, insistent and infuriatingly charming, he longed to be a ranger like them. They'd agreed to give him small, safe tasks as a squire of sorts.

'I sent him with Dratos for watch training,' Adrienne was saying now, around a mouthful of food.

Drue came back to herself, tense. 'To what tower?' Dratos had been known for his recklessness and carefree nature before he'd taken his orphaned cousin into his care.

Adrienne gave her a knowing smile. 'The first tower. Don't worry, you know I'd never put him in harm's way.'

'I know,' Drue mumbled. 'How do you think he's progressing?' Both she and Adrienne had agreed that Gus was far too young for any formal duties, but he'd hounded them often enough that they'd allowed him to shadow some of the rangers, including his cousin, much to Dratos' annoyance.

Adrienne laughed. 'Slowly. What he lacks in skill, he makes up for with enthusiasm.'

Drue knew that too well. The last time Gus had tried to assist her in the stables, he'd nearly lit the damn building on fire. 'Furies save us.'

'Exactly. But though I'd never admit it to the little bastard... I miss him when he's gone.'

'I could do without the brutal honesty sometimes,' Drue said.

Adrienne chuckled. 'You still not over what he told you on your name day?'

'You would be if someone informed you that you were *getting older but not smarter?*' Drue huffed, detecting Talemir's gaze falling on her once again. Thankfully, there was a brief commotion as Terrence landed atop the table, sending a few empty bowls flying and spilling someone's mead.

'That's hardly hygienic,' Wilder muttered.

To her surprise, Talemir laughed deeply. 'You haven't had a bath in a week. What would you know about hygiene?'

'Piss off.'

Talemir didn't seem fazed in the least. Instead, he watched the bird with an awed but wary expression, following Drue's movements as she fed the hawk a piece of meat from her plate.

'What sort of name is Terrence for a bird of prey, anyway?' he asked, not taking his eyes off them.

Adrienne chuckled. 'Drue's had him since he was a hatchling,' she offered. 'And when he first broke through that egg, he looked like a cranky old man – worse than Fendran and Baledor combined —'

'That's enough out of you, General,' Fendran scolded from a few seats over.

But Adrienne simply grinned. 'Drue and I thought "Terrence" suited him well enough then.'

Terrence's head whipped around, as though the giant bird knew exactly what they were saying.

Talemir laughed, reaching for his drink. 'He certainly scowls like an angry old bastard —'

There was a flash of a yellow beak, and Talemir gave a cry of surprise. A streak of blood smeared across the back of the Warsword's hand and he cursed the hawk, snatching his hand away with a growl.

Drue snorted. 'Terrence has always been an excellent judge of character.'

'I assure you, in this case, he's mistaken.'

Sitting back in her seat, Drue surveyed the warrior with a swelling sense of satisfaction. 'Oh, I doubt that,' she said, echoing his previous words. 'I doubt that very much.'

But to her surprise, the Warsword's gaze flickered with appreciation and that infuriatingly cocky grin returned to his handsome face.

Adrienne elbowed her. 'Shadow wraith or not,' she whispered under her breath, 'you could cut that tension with a knife and spread it on bread.'

'Shut up,' Drue snapped. 'I've got to get rid of him, but I can't do it here...'

'No,' Adrienne agreed. 'But that wouldn't stop the Drue I know.'

Across the table, Talemir watched them as though he could hear every damn word. Drue's eyes met his: warm and hazel, dancing with quiet delight. Beneath the table, she curled her fists as her stomach clenched. He was more than striking, more than handsome; he was beautiful, and that only made matters worse, for what dark danger lurked behind a face that could make her want to melt?

He smiled then, not the cocky grin from before, but a more genuine expression. 'You alright there?' he asked, his voice deep and silken, causing her blood to heat. He seemed to sense the conflict within her.

'Never better,' she managed, averting her gaze.

Elsewhere in the hall, the survivors of Naarva had decided that the visit of two mighty Warswords was cause enough for celebration. Baledor had brought out his old lute and was stringing together an awkward tune, while Coltan had stopped sulking in the corner and was now filling people's cups with a cask of wine he'd found hidden somewhere.

As the music built its rhythm, Drue's feet tapped under the table. Gods, she missed dancing. She had been a glorious dancer once, losing herself to melodies in a grand ballroom, long skirts billowing around her legs as she twirled. Drue had been to many a ball a lifetime ago, all over Naarva, favouring those held at the university on the lower eastern island, surrounded by gardens, thousands of blooms hanging overhead.

Now, she tried to keep the longing from her face as her people took to the pockets of space around the oak table, dancing in pairs, in circles of friends. She watched as several young women lingered nearby, attempting to rally their courage to approach the great Warswords of Thezmarr, both of whom seemed oblivious to their attentions.

Yara, a pretty girl whose family had fled to Ciraun from the south, tapped Talemir on the shoulder, her cheeks flushing as he turned to her.

'Would you care to dance... sir?' she asked, her voice pitching high with nerves.

He actually grimaced before shaking his head. 'Ah... I'm flattered,' he told her kindly. 'But I don't dance.'

'Not even for one song?' Yara asked boldly, her blush deepening.

'Not even for half a song.' But then he clapped Wilder heartily on the shoulder. 'My apprentice here will gladly oblige you, though.'

Wilder shot him a look of furious disbelief, but didn't protest as Yara dragged him to his feet.

'I'm not your fucking apprentice,' the younger Warsword hissed as he was hauled to the makeshift dancefloor.

Talemir laughed.

'That was rather cruel,' Drue commented, watching Wilder try to maintain a respectful distance between himself and the eager women of Naarva.

'Ah, a necessary cruelty,' Talemir replied, sipping his drink and following her gaze. 'He's had a hard time recently. His brother... His brother was injured during the final battle here. Poor lad blames himself.'

'And was he to blame?' Drue asked.

Talemir's gaze snapped to her face. 'Not in the slightest. If there's blame to be had, I lay claim to it.'

The words hung between them, and for a fraction of a second, Drue pitied him. But when his eyes flitted to her cuff, she remembered herself, remembered what he truly was. She turned her attention back to the celebrations. They were a far cry from what the kingdom of gardens had offered prior to its downfall, but there was beauty and earnestness in its simplicity now. All around her, people found small joys where they could. She only wished she could be one of them. But losing her mother, losing her brothers, had stripped her of that. Now, she watched as folk danced, drank and kissed in the dim corners of the hall, her own heart filling with a dark emotion she didn't care to identify.

Her scalp prickled, and she twisted in her seat to spot Coltan peering at her hopefully from across the room. She shuddered. She would never live that poor choice down, it seemed.

'He's in love with you, then...' Talemir stated, nodding to the ranger.

'One of many,' Adrienne declared from her side, the tip of her nose pink from the wine. She slung her arm around Drue's shoulders affectionately.

'That doesn't surprise me,' Talemir replied, the corner of his mouth tugging upward as Drue made to protest.

She didn't appreciate this line of commentary in the least. When her life had comprised balls and feasts, she'd had many nights of passion, but after the kingdom had fallen and she had shed her gowns for leathers and weapons, a night of passion meant something else. It had been Adrienne who had warned her of the way men spoke, of the disrespect that festered among the weaker ones, especially for women in positions of power. Adrienne had told her then to guard her heart, her reputation. That it was better to be known as the formidable ranger than the girl who slept with one.

And then she'd made the stupid choice to give in to Coltan. She had thought he was safe, that as childhood friends they could find comfort with one another. But after a few nights together, he had changed – staking a claim to her he had no right to. And she had vowed not to make that mistake again. She would rather be alone than be owned by someone.

'Let me know if you need me to dispatch him for you,' Talemir was saying.

'We do our own dispatching,' Adrienne quipped. 'But thanks.'

Drue stood, her patience wearing thin at last. 'I'll see to it that you and your friend have rooms for the night and fresh water for bathing. By the sounds of it, you need it.'

'How thoughtful of you.'

'I'm nothing if not thoughtful, Warsword.'

She leant down to whisper to Adrienne. 'Can I trust you to occupy the younger one?'

Adrienne offered a brazen grin. 'He's a little broody for my taste, but I'll consider it part of my official duties as general.'

Drue shook her head. 'Have fun with that.'

'Oh, I intend to,' her friend said with a wink. 'Luck be with you, sister.'

'Not if he's been with you first.'

Without another glance in the Warsword's direction, Drue gave a soft whistle, which brought Terrence back to her shoulder. Then she set out to talk to her father.

DRUE ARRANGED it so that the Warswords were given guest quarters near her own, and then she waited. Sharpening her blades, she sat by the fire until the revelry had died down, until she heard the creak of the door two down from hers. She waited even longer to allow for the bath to be filled, for the Warsword to sink into the false lull of security, and then she crept towards his chambers.

Silent as the dead, she picked the lock and slipped inside.

'Come to kill me, Wildfire?' that deliciously dark voice said from the corner of the room.

There, Talemir Starling's enormous frame took up the entire wooden tub, his torso sprawled above the waterline, muscular arms gripping the sides. His broad bare chest was on display, a series of scars dotted around his heart.

Drue froze. Her eyes locked on his.

Challenge filled that hazel gaze and water poured from his naked body as he stood.

Every thought emptied from Drue's head. The room was instantly too hot, and another heat entirely pulsed between her legs as she took in the mouth-watering sight of him, drank in every glorious inch of him.

Talemir Starling was a figure carved by the Furies themselves and he moved like a graceful predator, stepping from the tub, not deigning to cover himself. Droplets gleamed in the dark trail of hair across his sculpted chest, where a blue jewel rested against his sternum – the only thing he wore. Water sluiced down the rippling plane of his abdomen, across his scar-littered golden skin.

Drue couldn't move, couldn't breathe as his sinful magic caught her in its talons. The urge to move towards him was nearly overpowering; the urge to run her hands across that skin nearly overcame her. Her gaze travelled further south, following the defined V-shaped dip of sinew below his hips, directing her stare to the perfect cock that hung low and heavy between his muscular thighs.

Her breath caught.

And a dark laugh forced her attention upward.

A wicked smile played on Talemir's lips. 'Do I look like a master of shadows to you?' Desire blazed in those hazel eyes, desire that matched her own. Every part of her tightened under that stare. Every part of her sang out to him.

Drue suddenly felt wound too tight, so much so that every

breath that heaved her breasts sent a thrill of need through her, a stark reminder of how much she wanted to be touched, touched by him. A fire had ignited within her.

Still naked, he approached her, leaving a trail of wet footprints in his wake.

As he drew closer, she realised it was a sapphire he wore around his neck, a woman's jewel. Had his presence not been so overpowering, she might have wondered to whom it belonged, but then he was before her, close enough that she could feel the heat of his wet body radiating outward.

'Do you believe me now?' His voice was low, sending a thrill through her very bones.

The longing coursing through her was like nothing she had felt before, a rush of white-hot need that had her taking a step towards him.

But it wasn't real. It was magic. His dark power had come to claim her. There were no shadows, no claws or wings, but he was a monster. She was sure of it.

'No,' she ground out, though her every movement said she didn't care. She fought her desire back, forcing it down. 'My cuff doesn't lie.'

Something in the warrior's eyes shifted, and he reached for a towel, securing it low around his hips in a quick, angry motion. 'So you admit it, then? You've been meddling with the steel source? Don't you realise that all blades from that source are connected? That by interfering with the origin point, with the magic of the Furies, you have weakened the Warsword weapons? The very weapons used to defend the midrealms?'

She scoffed. 'I have done no such thing.'

He ignored her protest, his gaze darkening. 'The darkness grows *because of you*. You have a lot to answer for.'

'*Me?* What about *you?* A shadow wraith masquerading as a Warsword? Is that not more of an insult to Thezmarr?'

He flinched.

There, she thought, *there's that pain point again. Let's see if you come out to play.* She palmed the dagger she'd been hiding in her arm sheath. 'Do your brothers-in-arms know what you are?' she spat. 'Do they know that while they fought back the darkness, one of those monsters was among them? Perhaps you were working with them the whole time. Perhaps it's your shadow side that drew more wraiths to that final battle in the first place. That caused the fall of your friend —'

His expression was changing, the veins around his eyes turning to webs of black.

Drue wasn't done. It wasn't enough. Not yet. 'Perhaps *you* are to blame. Perhaps it is *your* fault —'

Suddenly, she was pressed against the wall.

And darkness exploded.

4

TALEMIR

Talemir Starling became one with the darkness. Every ounce of power he'd been trying to suppress broke free in a violent undoing, shooting through his veins, shadows bursting from his very being. Talons punched through his fingernails, the pain momentarily blinding him while wings speared from the tapered muscles of his back in equal agony and he bit down a roar. Night and rage coiled deep within, tightening around his bones, threatening to snap and forge themselves anew with gloom and despair.

Shadows rippled from him like smoke, taking the form of whatever nightmares haunted the young woman before him, swirling everywhere, taunting her. She had a trembling dagger to his throat, but it didn't matter. The magic within him was so great that one thought from him could see that blade flying in the opposite direction, at the mercy of his shadows.

He commanded a roiling black mass of power. Ribbons of

onyx magic unfurled from him, wrapping around her wrists and easily removing her from his body. Despite the fire in her blue eyes, she seemed suddenly fragile to him, breakable under all that he could wreak upon the realm.

Somewhere within himself, he clawed at the darkness. She'd baited him and he'd fallen for it, let his emotions get the better of him, let his power fester in that bleak recess of his mind until it had become too much, until his true self had broken free. He should have known better. He'd quickly learnt that heightened emotions meant he was more susceptible to losing control... and until now, he'd managed to maintain control. Except for the darkest night of every month – that was when there was no stopping becoming the monster. Then, the darkness called to him and he had no choice but to answer.

Panting, he caught his reflection in her eyes. For the first time, he saw the beast for what it truly was – terrifying, primal and snarling... Uncontrollable. Part man, but just as much, if not more, wraith. His membranous wings flared between his shoulder blades; his talons made marks in the wall, and whips of shadow poured from him like blood from a wound, roiling around them, threatening to snuff out the fire.

But there was something else, he realised as he leant back and surveyed the woman who was flame incarnate... On the other occasions when he'd been in this form, the world had looked different, sapped of life, of colour, drenched in blacks and greys that mirrored the darkness of his own heart. But now...

Drue Emmerson stood before him, soaked in colour, full of life.

Shock rippling through him, his form flickered, his talons

retracting, his wings disappearing. Slowly, the shadows retreated, and he stared at her.

Her breasts heaved as she caught her breath. He was braced over her, his knee planted between her thighs, her hands still in place where his power had held them to the wall. Their bodies were almost flush, close enough that he noticed her thick lashes, the flush across her high cheekbones as she gazed up at him. And her panting... That was no longer from fear, but desire. He felt it too, felt it heating his blood in an entirely unfamiliar way. But Talemir Starling steeled himself.

'A clever trick,' he said quietly. 'That's twice now you've tried to kill me when I've meant you no harm. Next time I won't be so forgiving.'

Hiding his trembling hands, he stepped back from her and waited. He wouldn't let her know just how unnerving the experience had been for him, wouldn't let her know that in a world made black and white, she had been doused in colour.

Drue gaped at him. 'How is this possible?' she breathed at last. 'How can you still...'

'Be me?' he finished for her, plucking his shirt from the bed and tugging it on, hoping that it would hang low enough to cover the bulge of his cock as it strained against the rough fabric of the towel.

'Yes.'

'Believe it or not, I'm still figuring that out.' Talemir sighed, rubbing the nape of his neck, trying to erase the blaze of pain that had ripped through him upon the change. He busied himself with finding his pants and, with his back to Drue, dropped his towel and stepped into them. She'd seen every inch of his front – why not give her a glimpse at the muscled curve of his backside while he was at it?

The sound of her quiet intake of breath was his reward.

Fully clothed now, he turned to face her. 'Decent,' he announced.

'You're the most indecent person I've ever met,' she retorted.

'Why, thank you.' At least she'd called him a person. He took up a place by the fire, stoking it with the poker. 'Now, why don't you tell me what you've been doing to the steel source? Our blades are having less effect against the monsters. They're increasing in numbers. Darkness is spreading – we can see it from Thezmarr.'

Drue crossed her arms over her chest. 'And you think this has something to do with me?'

'Yes. Show me the cuff.'

'No.' She shoved her hands behind her back. 'You think I'd let you anywhere near this thing? You'll destroy it.'

Talemir sighed. He would not take it by force. Not yet, anyway.

'Who told you about it?' she asked.

'My guess is that you already know who.'

'Coltan.'

Talemir nodded. 'Your lover was adamant that you were breaking the laws of Thezmarr and that you put yourself and others at risk.'

'He's not my lover.'

'No?'

Drue shifted. 'Not anymore.'

Good, Talemir almost said aloud. The fragile-egoed boy was no match for the woman before him. Slowly, he watched another realisation dawn on that devastating face.

'You were sent here to kill me...'

Talemir flinched at those words. As soon as he'd

discovered she was his target, it hadn't sat right with him. He'd seen her hatred of the shadow wraiths firsthand, more than once now. How likely was it that someone with that much rage towards them would jeopardise their demise by sabotaging the Naarvian steel source?

'I was,' he allowed. 'But I have a different proposition for you.'

'I don't make deals with monsters.'

'Perhaps not, but hear what I have to say first...'

She waited for him to speak. That was permission enough to forge ahead with the madness that was forming in his head.

'If you're not responsible for the weakening steel source, I need to investigate it myself. I need to find out more about what's making the wraiths stronger and more resistant to our blades.'

'Why? You're one of them. You're more evolved, even. You're probably their fucking leader, about to infiltrate the one safe place Naarvians have left. For all I know, it's *you* causing the chaos.'

'It's not,' Talemir bit out, trying to tame his rising anger. Gods, this woman knew how to rile him. 'I'm doing everything I can to rid myself of this part of me. So if it's not you tampering with the steel source and it's not me leading the army of dark servants, then what's happening? Tell me what you know from your travels, from your time as a ranger. What have you seen?'

She seemed to debate with herself, a muscle in her jaw twitching as she clenched and unclenched her teeth.

Talemir forged on. 'If you want to find your missing people and hunt wraiths so much, then use me. I have a connection to them. I assume you wish to locate their lair? You haven't been able to find it all this time, have you? But where your trail goes dead, perhaps I can help you. And before you start – I have more reason than anyone to hate them, more reason than anyone to want to end them. You now know that better than anyone.'

'You're suggesting we work together...' she chewed out slowly.

'At last, we're on the same page.'

'Hardly. I'm a wraith hunter, you're a wraith. We'll never be on the same fucking page.'

Talemir threw his hands up in frustration, but Drue continued.

'If we are to work together, there will be rules,' she told him.

'Go on...'

'Regardless of your current form, you're a danger. You will stay by me at all times. If I truly am the only one who knows this secret, then you are my responsibility. I'm putting my people in harm's way by welcoming a monster into the fold.'

'Some welcome,' Talemir muttered. 'You think I'd prey upon innocents? I'm a Warsword of Thezmarr.'

'You're a shadow wraith.'

'Have I not proven —'

'You've proven nothing except the fact that you can't control your temper,' Drue snapped. 'Darkness still floods your veins.'

Talemir paced the length of the room in an effort to cool the inferno raging within. 'What do you suggest, then?' he asked through gritted teeth.

'I'll show you the steel source, so you know once and for all that I am no threat to it. Along the way, we can track the missing Naarvians, and see for ourselves what your kind is up to.'

'They're not my kind.'

'The shadows don't lie, Warsword.'

Talemir tensed. 'And you? What is it you get?'

'You'll help me find the wraiths' lair and destroy it.'

Talemir took a deep breath and offered her his hand. 'Then we have a deal?'

Drue stared at it. 'We have an understanding.'

'And you'll keep my secret?' Talemir asked, still holding out his hand. 'Not even Wilder knows. He can't know. He's been through enough.'

'Your friend is no business of mine.'

'So, it's settled then?' He felt exposed with his offered truce hanging between them.

'One more thing,' she said, her hand hovering near his.

'What?'

'You'll stop using your magic on me.'

Talemir frowned. 'What?' he repeated.

Her eyes narrowed. 'You know exactly what I mean. You'll stop using your power to... to make me feel things.'

A slow smile spread across his face and he grasped her warm hand in his, a spark jolting through his whole body. He didn't have the heart to tell her his magic had no such hold over her.

'Then we're agreed?' she asked.

'Agreed.'

She broke their handshake quickly, as though she'd felt that same jolt between them and it had rattled her.

As she gripped the door handle, he spoke once again. 'By all means, Wildfire... You can kill me when this is through.'

'I may just do that, Warsword.' She didn't turn around. 'We leave at first light.'

Talemir Starling watched her go, noting the curve of her backside and the sway of her hips. He dragged a hand through his hair as the door closed behind her, his cock twitching in his pants.

'Fuck...'

5
DRUE

'You're insane,' Adrienne told her back in her quarters.

'I know,' Drue admitted, rummaging through her wardrobe to find her travel pack. Terrence watched her from his perch by the door. He seemed unsettled.

Adrienne wasn't done discussing her antics. 'Making deals with shadow wraiths? That's a new level of crazy, even for you.'

'*I know.*' Drue went to her dresser, one of many items they'd salvaged from the abandoned city and dragged back here.

'I kind of like it, though,' Adrienne quipped, handing her a shirt to pack. 'It's fucking ruthless.'

Drue laughed, some of the tension leaving her shoulders as she did. She hadn't realised how tightly wound she still was. At the thought, the fresh memory of Talemir Starling in wraith form came flooding back, his wings outspread behind his carved torso, those ribbons of shadow gripping her wrists and pinning her to the wall, all-powerful. He could have killed her with a swipe of those talons, with a lash of that black power. And yet... desire pulsed between her legs. She cursed him silently, stuffing another spare shirt into her pack, unable to stop the image of his naked body flooding her mind —

Adrienne was staring at her, noting the look she hadn't wiped from her face. 'Did something happen?'

Drue flushed. 'No.'

'You're sure?'

'I'm sure.'

'You're mighty defensive...'

Drue heaved a sigh. 'And you're a mighty pain in the arse.'

Adrienne simply sat on the end of her bed and waited.

Drue started checking the weapons she wished to bring, but couldn't stand the pressure of her friend's insistent gaze. 'Fine. His dark magic... It's affecting me more than I realised it would...'

'Oh?' Adrienne raised a single brow.

'That's all you need to know.'

Her friend laughed. 'So long as you're taking your contraceptive tonic.'

'Not that I'll need it, but yes. Always.'

'Good.'

'And you?'

'Every day,' Adrienne said seriously. 'I'd rather fucking die than risk a pregnancy in this shithole.'

Drue agreed. 'How did you get on with the other Warsword, Wilder?'

Adrienne offered a wicked grin. 'Well, let's just say that you might be dealing with the true beast of the two, but Wilder is by no means shy...' She winked. 'He's an animal in his own right.'

Drue snorted at that. 'Well, I'm glad you're having fun while I deal with... whatever it is I'm dealing with.'

'Just doing my duty.' Adrienne winked. 'So how many are we riding out with tomorrow?'

Drue shrugged. 'However many you recommend. I want to stop at the first watchtower to check on Gus. See if there's anything we can learn from there, then continue on to the steel source.'

'And you think it's wise? Showing a wraith where we mine the steel that kills them?'

'There's nothing to see. You'd have to be a miner to understand how it all works, and from what my father has told me, there's no mining at the moment and hasn't been any for some time. At least it should prove that I'm not meddling with their precious iron ore. Fucking Coltan was the one to report me, by the way...'

'What?' Adrienne stood, fists clenched. 'What a bastard. He's like a petulant child, Drue. He couldn't have what he wanted, so he decided to take you out of the picture?'

'It seems that way... I don't know what happened to him. He wasn't always like that.'

'Your brothers would have strung him up for this. I have half a mind to myself.'

'To what end?' Drue asked, suddenly weary.

'To teach the prick a lesson. He needs to leave you alone.'

'I've got it handled, Adri.'

Her friend shot her a disgruntled look, but let it lie.

'My brothers would be wetting themselves over the Warswords,' Drue said.

'So will Gus when he sees them,' Adrienne laughed. 'Did I tell you what he told me the other day?'

Drue nodded. 'I was there. *"When I grow up, I'm going to be a ranger like Dratos. And I'm going to eat as much cheese as I want."* Talk about setting goals.'

Adrienne snorted. 'That boy, I swear...'

With Dratos for an older cousin, and two other rangers as his adopted sisters, Gus had a tendency to hero-worship any sort of warrior. 'It's going to be hard to keep him away from Talemir,' Drue said.

'You truly think he's that dangerous?'

'He's a wraith, Adri. He can't be trusted.' Her hands trembled as she laced the ties of her now bulging pack. 'I've lost enough brothers. I won't risk Gus as well.'

Adrienne closed the gap between them and wrapped her arms around Drue. Drue sagged against her friend, exhaling a tight breath, her shoulders suddenly aching as she relaxed into Adrienne's embrace.

'We all miss them,' Adrienne whispered.

'I know.' Drue squeezed her back before pulling away. She never let herself sink too far into any comfort offered, for she was worried her grief might get the best of her. She gathered herself and nodded to the general. 'I told the Warsword we'll ride out at first light.'

Adrienne knew her well enough to recognise a dismissal when she heard one. 'I'll meet you at the stables before dawn, then.'

When Adrienne had left, Drue double-checked her bag and her weapons. She went through the list of things she needed to do before they set out to the watchtower. But when all the tasks were done, she still felt unsettled.

That damn Warsword had rattled her. Beyond rattled – he'd got under her skin, heated her blood in a way that she couldn't dismiss, couldn't forget. She paced the worn stone before the fire, allowing it to burn low because she was already too hot.

The image of the water sluicing down Talemir's sculpted, naked body sent a rush of need through her. She had seen her share of unclothed males throughout her life, but they were boys compared to the Warsword who had stood dripping and exposed before her, every inch of him honed by training and battle, every part of him corded with unforgiving muscle.

Drue swore under her breath, glancing up to find Terrence watching her, as though he knew exactly where her traitorous mind had taken her.

'It's not like I can help it,' she muttered in his direction.

But the hawk simply cawed and nestled his head in his chest feathers.

With another curse, Drue stripped off her clothes and climbed into bed, knowing full well that sleep would elude her for hours to come.

IT WAS STILL DARK when Drue reached the stables to prepare her mount for the ride. To her dismay, the Warswords were already there, waiting. Of course they were. Soldiers through and through.

'Morning, Wildfire,' Talemir said with a charming smile, as though it wasn't the crack of dawn. Their stallions stood saddled and ready beside them.

'My name is Drue,' she ground out, pushing past him into the stables, nodding in greeting to several rangers as she looked for her favourite mare. 'You can address me as such.'

'Where's the fun in that?' He followed her into the stall.

'You're not here to have fun.'

'No? You could clearly use some... Bit tightly wound there, aren't you?'

Drue's temper frayed completely, and she whirled around to face the infuriating Warsword, shoving him hard in the chest with all her strength.

He didn't move an inch.

Talemir laughed softly. 'You'll have to do better than that.'

Drue yanked her hands away from him, the heat of him like a brand, even through his leathers.

'What in the realms are you playing at?' she hissed at him, trying to shed her rage before she approached her blameless horse.

'Oh, we haven't even started playing yet.' Talemir winked at her.

Drue lifted her chin in defiance, letting the challenge gleam in her eyes. 'Is this some useless ploy to make me see you as a man rather than a monster?'

Something flickered across his expression then, something akin to hurt. 'No.'

She looked away, checking her mare's hooves and adjusting the bridle. But a quiet sense of unease filled the stall. Drue's hands stilled mid-task, but when she turned to face the Warsword, he was gone.

Good riddance, she thought, despite the discomfort churning in her gut.

There was no more time to dwell on the mind games of Talemir Starling. Drue mounted her mare and rode out of the stables to find Adrienne and the rangers waiting, the two Warswords sitting stoically atop their stallions.

To Drue's dismay, Coltan was among the rangers. Her irritation must have been obvious, because when Drue took her place beside Adrienne, the general leant across.

'Your father insisted,' she murmured in apology, thrusting her chin towards the gates, where the blacksmith stood reverently.

'Great,' Drue replied darkly. Her father held the misplaced belief that Coltan could protect her, that he'd grown up alongside her dead brothers and so would take her safety seriously. Drue hadn't had the heart to tell Fendran that Coltan's motives weren't so pure and that it was often this that saw any measure of safety go flying out the window. She was sorely tempted to divulge that information now, though. Coltan's actions on their last patrol had caused nearly catastrophic consequences.

Her father approached, holding something out to her. 'This is for you,' he said, pushing a scabbard into her hand.

Momentarily dazed, Drue took it. Using both hands, she half pulled the blade from its sheath, recognising it immediately. Her father had been working on this piece for over a week. She had assumed it was a request from Thezmarr, because if she wasn't mistaken – and she never was about weapons – it was Naarvian steel. The strongest steel in all the midrealms.

'Father,' she murmured in warning. It was against the law of all kingdoms for anyone other than a Warsword, let alone a woman, to wield a sword of such material.

'Hush,' he said, his voice low, reaching up to push the blade back into its scabbard. 'You have long needed such a weapon, Drue. And what sort of father would I be if I didn't provide you with the protection you needed? I've been collecting scraps of the stuff for years to make this.'

'But —'

'Were it up to me, you and your mother would still be planning balls, commissioning gowns and arguing over your needlework from the safety of our home. Alas, we found no safety there, and that is not the world we live in any longer. That is not who you are anymore. So let me give you this.'

Drue's heart seized. 'But Father, one look at this and people will know.'

'That is your smith's eye talking,' he replied with a satisfied smile.

Drue exposed a few inches of the blade again and saw what her father meant. The sword had been expertly and cleverly crafted to hide the distinct traits of Naarvian steel. He'd engraved embellishments, mixed two types of steel. Only a fellow blacksmith could discern such things. To the naked, untrained eye, it was simply a beautiful weapon.

Fendran Emmerson, the master of the Naarvian forge, was breaking the law for her, for his daughter.

'Thank you,' she murmured, strapping her new blade to her back. Did this mean she could kill a wraith now?

'Be safe, Drue...' her father said, suddenly hoarse. 'You're all I have left in these realms.'

'We'll be fine,' she replied, eyeing the company now waiting for her just beyond the gates.

An impatient cry sounded from above and Drue looked up to see Terrence circling the skies overhead.

'I have to go,' she told her father, her chest tightening at his worried expression. She knew it was hard for him to let her go each time, knowing the fate that the rest of their family had met at the hands of the shadow wraiths. But he let her go anyway, and for that, she loved him even more.

With a final squeeze of his hand, she urged her horse towards the others.

When she reached the party, Adrienne cleared her throat.

'It's a two-day ride to the nearest watchtower,' she said.

'And here in Naarva, we ride hard. Warswords, I hope you can keep up.'

The unit of rangers looked to the two warriors, who both grinned in the face of the challenge. There was no denying the awe that seemed to radiate from the Naarvians. It was a once-in-a-lifetime experience to ride side by side with one Warsword of Thezmarr, let alone two.

But Drue shifted, uneasy. For her fellow Naarvians didn't know who truly rode among them – didn't know that they had a monster in their midst, that the darkness they sought to fight was with them now.

Shaking off the feeling, Drue took up her place once more beside Adrienne. Both of them were eager to get to Gus at the watchtower, to check what sort of havoc he'd wreaked there, to chastise him for cursing and to whisk him safely back to the stronghold. Dratos had likely reached the end of his tether with the youngster, and no doubt had a report for them as well.

And so together, the two women led the company from the compound as the first rays of dawn bled into the sky.

THE PARTY of rangers and Warswords rode south, a journey that always reminded Drue of how much the shadow wraiths from beyond the Veil had taken from her and her people. Once the kingdom of gardens, thriving with life, Naarva was now a shell of its former glory. As they left Ciraun behind and the weak morning sun shone down over the lands before them, a hollow feeling spread in the pit of Drue's stomach. There was no escaping the evidence of her kingdom's fall. They rode through what had once been a wealthy district just beyond the walls of the citadel, the manors there now abandoned and covered in dark vines, their gates broken, their stores looted. She had once lived in such a place, tending to the gardens with her mother, their grounds vibrant with colour, pristine with rows and rows of blooms. Drue's chest hurt at the memory of it all, the memory of her mother, beautiful and resplendent whether she wore one of her glittering gowns or her apron and gardening gloves.

Drue pressed her mare onwards, keeping pace with Adrienne beside her. Her friend's expression mirrored her own – grief for all that they had lost here. Much of present-day Naarva was akin to an overgrown, unruly forest. Green vines so dark they looked black crept along many a surface. The roads were cracked and decaying, and what little life remained – a hare bounding in the distance, a raven flying overhead – seemed out of place.

Further south were the empty villages. Farmsteads had slipped into disrepair after their inhabitants had fled. There was no telling who had survived and who had fallen to the darkness. Drue knew that the underground compound, their safe haven, was just a fraction of the people who had faced the blight of the wraiths.

Drue must have lost herself in her thoughts, for when she next focused on the ride, she found herself beside Coltan.

He was watching her, his brow furrowed with concern. 'Are you alright?' he asked.

Drue sighed. 'I'm fine.'

'I know this part of the journey is hard for you. For all of us, really.'

'I don't want to talk about it, Coltan.'

'Me either.'

'Good.' For a brief moment, Drue thought they would be able to travel in companionable silence like she and Adrienne often did. She loosed a tense breath, spotting Terrence flying ahead, his great wings beating against the clouds.

But apparently, Coltan wasn't one for thoughtful quiet.

'I don't like how that Warsword looks at you,' he said.

Drue's skin prickled, but she ignored him.

'He looks at you like —'

'I didn't ask.'

'Ride with me,' Coltan continued, oblivious to her repulsion.

'No.'

'Why do you have to be like this? I'm only trying to protect you.'

Drue brought her horse to a sudden halt, her stomach hardening, her jaw aching from clenching her teeth so hard. 'When are you going to get it through your thick skull?' she snapped. 'I don't want or need your protection.'

'There's no need to be —'

'Be what?' she interjected. 'What exactly am I being by rejecting your advances, Coltan?'

'Your brothers —'

'Don't bring them into this.'

'They would have wanted us to stick together.'

'They would have wanted me to beat you senseless.'

'Drue!'

Her rage bubbled to the surface. She was so sick of Coltan using his friendship with her dead brothers to try to be close to her. It was nauseating. Especially knowing that he'd never pull this sort of shit were they alive. She wanted nothing more than to throttle him and leave him bleeding in the dust, but the hair stood up on the back of her neck and she knew that up ahead, the entire party had slowed, and could likely hear every word.

'Just leave me alone,' she muttered, squeezing her horse's sides to catch up.

When she rejoined the others, it was Wilder Hawthorne who shook his head in Coltan's direction. 'I can distract the others if you want to beat him senseless.'

So they *had* heard it all.

But to her surprise, Wilder's offer coaxed a laugh from her. 'I'll let you know.'

As THE DAY WORE ON, they passed more abandoned villages, more fields of crops left to perish. But Drue kept her grief at bay, instead studying the Warswords.

As the morning faded into afternoon, she longed to pass the time. She turned to Wilder on her left.

'What's Thezmarr like?' she asked, sensing the other rangers around her straightening in their saddles. It seemed that they too were curious about the formidable guild of warriors from across the seas.

Wilder shifted in his saddle and glanced at Talemir, as though seeking approval. The older Warsword simply shrugged, keeping his gaze ahead.

He's been unusually quiet so far, Drue noted, not sure why she cared.

'Thezmarr is a vast fortress,' Wilder explained. 'Hemmed in by jagged mountains and violent seas... It looks cold and dark from the outside, but within... within, it's home.' There was a note of longing in his voice. 'It has a Great Hall, where all the warriors and trainees of the guild take their meals, and at its heart lie the stone swords of the Furies.'

Drue sucked in a breath. She'd heard tales of those monuments, the ones that rose from the ground up into the rafters of the building, into the skies beyond. The stones upon which the names of dead Thezmarrians were carved. She wondered how many warriors the Warswords had known, whose names were honoured on those swords.

Her gaze flitted to Talemir, who rode straight-backed, jaw clenched.

A great many, judging from that expression.

'How long have you been a Warsword?' someone called from the back.

A look of pride crossed Wilder's face. 'I passed the Great Rite several months ago.'

'What was it like?' Adrienne chimed in.

Wilder shook his head. 'You know I can't tell you that.'

The Great Rite was one of Thezmarr's closest-kept secrets. No one knew what it entailed, what a would-be Warsword faced when he undertook it.

Drue found herself drawn to Talemir's side. 'What about you?' she asked.

'What about me?' His tone was a far cry from the flirtatious banter he'd attempted in the stables.

'How long have *you* been a Warsword?' Drue pressed.

'Long enough.'

'That's not an answer.'

'That's all the answer you'll get. Tell me, Wildfire... Why the interest?'

'I...'

'Aren't you worried I'm using my dark spells on you again?'

Drue baulked. 'No, I —'

'Forget it,' he muttered. He surveyed the territory before them, still overgrown and crawling with those ominous emerald vines. 'It feels like a lifetime since I was here. I didn't realise what it had become...'

Stiffening in her saddle, Drue faced him. 'Why would you, from your fortress?'

'We weren't told,' he said simply.

'Apparently not,' she replied, her voice cold. 'You came and fought, then you left. And we picked up the pieces.'

His knuckles bulged around his reins, but he spoke quietly, his words laced with anger. 'You know more than anyone how much that battle cost me. I'd appreciate it if you didn't remind me of it every two minutes.'

Rage simmered in his hazel eyes, and perhaps a flicker of darkness, too.

Drue said nothing more, for a monster was there, lying in wait.

AT LONG LAST, the sun began to set, and Adrienne instructed them to make camp. They took shelter by the edge of a forest and she deemed it safe enough to have a small fire.

Terrence flew in as Drue dismounted and tended to her mare, leading her to the nearby stream to drink her fill. The hawk landed on the ground beside the horse, tucking his wings in and dipping his beak into the cool water as well. Drue took her saddlebags and left both animals to their own devices as she found a spot for her tent. It wasn't long before she spotted Talemir across the clearing, rummaging through his own pack. She went to him immediately.

'What do you think you're doing?' she demanded, folding her arms over her chest.

'I thought I was setting up camp,' he replied. 'But

apparently you have other ideas?' There was a suggestive curve of his lip at that last comment.

Right, so he's back to being his infuriating self. Drue resented that her toes curled in her boots at his tone.

'I thought I made myself clear last night,' she said. 'You're to stay by my side at all times. I need to keep an eye on you.'

He blinked at her. 'You want to share a tent with me?'

'*Want* isn't the word I'd use. It's a necessity. I don't trust you.'

'So you keep saying. I didn't realise it meant you wanted to cuddle up with me.' That glimmer of amusement was back.

'There will be no "cuddling up". It's so I can watch you.'

'Whatever gets you off.'

Drue let out a noise of frustration. 'For fuck's sake. Just help me with the damn tent, would you?'

'When you ask so nicely, how could I refuse?'

Drue bit back another comment as the Warsword followed her to where she'd started setting up camp. Together, they arranged the tent wordlessly, and Drue didn't fail to notice just how small it now seemed at the foot of the mighty warrior beside her.

Talemir seemed to notice it at the same time and looked from the pitched canvas back to her. 'Aren't you concerned everyone will think we're...'

Sure enough, there were several curious glances shot their way.

'I don't care what everyone thinks, as long as they're safe. From you.'

'Even if that means trapping yourself in a tiny tent with me?'

'Even then.'

Talemir considered this before shrugging. 'Whatever you say, Wildfire.'

'Stop calling me that.'

He laughed at her then. 'Perhaps I will when you stop looking like you're about to burst into flame.'

It took all of Drue's willpower not to do exactly that.

Long after rations had been shared and the conversation around the fire had died down, Drue returned to her tent to find the Warsword already within. His huge frame took up much of the space, and there was no way they wouldn't touch when she lay down. The thought sent an unwelcome thrill through her. Talemir gave her an amused smile.

Damn him. She wriggled inside, lying flat on her back beside him, her blade of Naarvian steel tucked close.

In the blue-tinged light, from the corner of her eye, she saw him take a swig of something from a flask.

'I could use some of that myself,' she heard herself say.

'It's not liquor,' he told her. As he swallowed the liquid with a grimace, a web of white lines shimmered down the muscles of his neck before vanishing.

'No? What is it, then? Some special Warsword elixir?'

He hesitated. 'No... It's to help me.'

'What do you mean?'

He tucked the flask down his side of the tent. 'One of the alchemists back at Thezmarr – she's trying to help me by creating a tonic. This is batch number four.'

'And is it? Helping?'

Talemir lay down next to her, his shoulder brushing hers. 'Too soon to tell.'

. . .

IN THE DIM light of the tent, he peeled her clothes away, layer by layer, his hands trailing across her skin, lighting a blazing fire of need. His mouth was lush and warm and ravenous against hers, his tongue exploring, his teeth nipping at her bottom lip before he licked over the fading pain.

The Warsword was braced above her, his body radiating heat and desire, her legs parting around him as she cradled his lower half between her thighs, noting the bulge of his cock straining against his pants.

Drue's mouth went dry and her breathing became ragged as he discarded her chest band, exposing her swollen breasts to him, her nipples hard and aching for his touch. Talemir gazed upon her hungrily, as though memorising every curve, every inch of her skin before he kissed her again, rough and brutal, almost bruising. He trailed his lips down her neck, taking her nipple in his mouth.

She moaned, not caring who heard. Her blood was on fire and she needed desperately to feel him inside her, her body arching beneath his, craving more of him. In answer, he pressed his hard length against her, grinding into her, eliciting a soft cry from her lips.

A frenzy took hold of her, and she grabbed his belt, drawing him to her and fumbling with the buckle. She couldn't wait any longer. Heat swelled at her core as he gave her a dark, delicious smile, his hands moving to his pants, buttons coming undone beneath deft fingers —

DRUE SAT BOLT UPRIGHT, panting, her hand pressed to her chest, her blood thrumming in her veins. The pink-and-gold hues of dawn seeped through the canvas and a furious blush stained her cheeks as she realised what had happened, her desire still very much pulsing between her —

'Good dream?' Talemir said from the tent flap, a smile tugging at his lips. His gaze skimmed across her nipples, peaked beneath her nightshirt, and her parted legs.

Embarrassment surging, Drue snatched her blanket and covered herself, trying to catch her breath.

'Stay out of my head, Warsword,' she managed through gritted teeth.

6
TALEMIR

At first, Talemir had thought she was having a nightmare. She had been crying out softly in her sleep, writhing atop her bedroll. But when he'd gone to wake her, he'd noticed the way her breasts were rising and falling in a rhythm, her back arching and her legs parting, her hand drifting south...

He'd realised then and there that she wasn't having a bad time.

As much as the sight of her had ignited a roaring fire of need in his own veins, he'd never been one to spy upon a woman's private moments without permission, and so he'd left the tent, trying to think of anything except that taut body and those sinful curves, and what they might look like naked beneath him.

It wasn't easy, though. He'd lost count of how many times he'd paced the perimeter of the camp, couldn't recall what the rangers on watch had said to him. All he could think about was her, wondering what, or who, exactly, she'd been dreaming of.

He'd waited for what he thought was the appropriate time, all the while avoiding the insistent glare of that damn hawk of hers. At last, he returned to the tent with two steaming cups of tea.

As he'd lifted the flap, Drue had sat bolt upright, eyes wide, cheeks deliciously flushed. He hadn't been able to help himself.

'Good dream?'

Snatching the blanket to her chest, she'd looked away, embarrassed. 'Stay out of my head, Warsword.'

He bit back another suggestive comment. Instead, he offered her the steaming cup. 'Here.'

Still ruffled, she glanced across. 'What's that?'

'Tea...'

Her brow crinkled with suspicion.

'It's just tea, I promise.'

'You're bringing me tea now?'

He rolled his eyes. 'If it bothers you, I won't do it again.'

She seemed to consider this before at last reluctantly taking the cup from him and holding it between her palms. Apparently still mortified, she wouldn't look at him.

'I wasn't in your head, by the way,' he added quietly.

'I don't believe that for a second.'

'So it *was* me you were dreaming of, then...' He couldn't help but grin at that.

Her gaze shot to his, alarmed. 'I didn't say that.'

'You said plenty.'

Her hand flew to her mouth. 'I did *not* —'

'Not with words,' he teased. 'And don't worry... I certainly don't object to you dreaming of me. It's preferable to you trying to kill me in my sleep.'

Drue seemed to gather herself. 'I'm just waiting to see if you have your uses.' The movement caused her shirt to slip slightly, revealing the delicate tattoo he'd noticed before he'd left the tent. In dark blue ink was a series of simple flowers caught in a breeze, trailing across her shoulder blade. She hurried to cover it up.

'And what happens when I'm no longer useful?' he asked, dragging his eyes from her bare skin to her hard stare.

'Then I'll carve out your heart myself.'

'Figures.' Talemir sipped from his cup, allowing the hot liquid to warm him from within. He glanced at her, noting her fidgeting beneath the blanket. 'What is it?'

She met his gaze and seemed to mull over her words before speaking at last. 'Why haven't you told Wilder about... your condition? Surely he'd make a better confidant than me?'

Talemir rubbed the back of his neck, an ache of tension starting to build there. 'If you recall, I didn't exactly choose to confide in you, did I?' he said, words clipped. 'But Wilder... As I mentioned, he's been through a lot. And he's a much newer Warsword than I. His indoctrination to the guild, his loyalty to Thezmarr, they're all so heightened. He might try to kill me on sight.'

'Perhaps I should tell him about you after all.'

'Some days I'd agree with you,' Talemir admitted. 'But if he did that... I don't think he'd forgive himself, even knowing what I am.'

Drue was quiet at that.

'On that cheerful note,' Talemir said, making for the exit, 'I'll leave you to get ready... And to your dreams of me, of course.'

She threw her empty mug at him.

THE GENERAL, Adrienne, had given Talemir and Wilder permission to hunt before they started their ride. Though they answered to no one but the Guild Master of Thezmarr, Talemir had always found it decent to respect whoever was in command where they were stationed. Wilder didn't always agree with that sentiment, but luckily, there was no squabbling this morning because he was content with the outcome. Adrienne had tried to insist that they'd be disappointed, that the game within these woods was sparse and near impossible to catch, but Wilder had waved her off.

'Nothing is impossible for a Warsword,' he'd called, and Talemir had nearly snorted, recognising the comment as something he'd told the young man long ago.

In fact, he'd said those exact words to Wilder upon his passing of the Great Rite as he attempted to capture and tame his Tverrian stallion... Talemir and Malik had stood watching and drinking on the mountainside while the freshly initiated Warsword chased the majestic horse across the valley, lassoing his lead rope and cursing as the beast evaded him time and time again.

'Do you think we should tell him it works best to corral the poor thing uphill?' Talemir had asked his oldest friend.

'Nah.' Malik's enormous frame took up the entire rock he leant against, his grey eyes bright as he tracked his younger brother's movements. 'He'll figure it out. Eventually.'

'You're a mean bastard,' Talemir replied.

'Takes one to know one.' Malik offered him a flask. 'What d'you think he'll name it?'

Talemir took a long swig, wincing at the harsh burn down his throat. 'You mean if he ever catches the poor creature?'

Malik huffed a laugh, not taking his eyes off his younger brother as Wilder made another lunge for the horse. 'Yeah.'

'Oh, he'll go for something grand and heroic, no doubt.'

'I thought as much too,' Malik said with a roguish grin and a raised brow.

Talemir recognised that look. 'What do you have in mind?'

Malik gave an innocent shrug of those giant shoulders. 'Only that we get a say.'

Together, the friends sat, getting drunker and drunker as their young comrade fought to earn his Warsword mount. When at last Wilder captured the stallion and brought it to heel, he approached them proudly, face flushed.

'Got him,' he declared, leading the horse towards them. It was a beautiful black thoroughbred, with kind, golden eyes; a fitting match for the young warrior.

'Took you long enough,' Malik snorted.

'Please,' Wilder scoffed. 'Torj told me it took *you* two days.'

Malik nearly choked on his liquor. 'That pretty boy has barely wet his blade. What would he know?'

Wilder shrugged. 'Enough, apparently.'

Talemir observed this exchange with amusement. He loved watching the siblings of Thezmarr interact, for no matter how old they were, they always reverted to their childhood habits.

'Settled on a name?' Talemir prompted the youth.

Wilder looked relieved. 'I was thinking —'

'Biscuit,' Malik declared, his face deadly serious.

Wilder blinked at his brother. 'You're drunk.'

'We had to entertain ourselves somehow.' Malik grinned. 'But your stallion seems to like the name.'

'It makes no sense,' Wilder argued.

'Does too. His eyes are the colour of that gold shortbread Cook makes.'

Talemir's shoulders shook with laughter. 'Biscuit...'

To both the older warriors' delight, the horse seemed to warm to the name, whinnying softly.

Wilder ran a hand through his hair. 'Furies save me.'

Talemir and his protégé now stalked deeper into the forest, each holding an arrow nocked to their bow.

In the wake of Drue's questions, Talemir considered the young Warsword hunting beside him. He moved with predatory grace. His form was flawless, which was just as well, as Talemir had been the one to teach him. He was a few years off reaching the peak of his potential, though; he was still so raw. There was no doubt in Talemir's mind that Wilder was a good Warsword, an even better man, but the grief over what had happened to his brother had changed him, had ignited a near unquenchable thirst for vengeance. That was why Talemir hadn't confided in Wilder about what he was, what he'd become. He had spoken the truth to Drue in their tent: he truly feared that if Wilder discovered what he was, the young Warsword would try to kill him, and there would be no coming back from that.

Talemir loosed his arrow. It shot through the air with keen precision, spearing a hare beneath the brush clean through the eye.

'Couldn't let me have that one?' Wilder quipped, his own bow drawn.

'Let you?' Talemir scoffed. 'Beat me to it like a real man next time, apprentice.'

'I'm not your —'

Talemir nocked and loosed another arrow, adding a second hare to his tally. 'Perhaps if you weren't so busy complaining, you'd have more success.'

'Perhaps if you weren't scaring all the game away with your chattering...' Wilder released an arrow, missing his target by a hair's breadth.

'Unlucky, *apprentice*,' Talemir goaded.

Wilder's answering curse was enough to make Talemir chuckle, chasing his darker thoughts away. For the moment.

DESPITE THE GLOOM of the surrounding kingdom, the Naarvian company was in high spirits as the sun ascended, thanks to the roast hare they'd shared for breakfast. Perhaps Talemir had underestimated just how rare the fresh game was on the road in these parts. In the end, he and Wilder had brought several back to camp, skinning them expertly before roasting them atop the fire.

Spotting Drue strapping her saddlebags to her horse, her hawk braced on her shoulder, Talemir approached her cautiously. His hand still bore the laceration from the bird's cold welcome in the mess hall.

'Thought your feathered friend might want something to eat...' He offered her a slab of meat wrapped in a scrap of cloth. He had considered giving it to the bird directly, but didn't trust that he'd leave the encounter with all his fingers intact.

Drue took the offering from him slowly. 'Thank you,' she said, seeming unsure of herself.

He left her to it, but glanced across as he saddled his stallion, watching as she fed the giant winged creature the raw hare, stroking the plumage of his puffed-out chest. One day he'd ask her for the story of how she'd ended up with a hawk hatchling...

As they set out for their second day, Talemir rode beside Wilder, telling himself that the beautiful ranger he'd woken up next to that morning needed her space. He was drawn to her, that much was obvious, but if he could tame the darkness within, he could certainly control himself around her.

But that didn't stop him from picturing the delicate blush that had spread across her cheeks, or her lithe body tense and wanting, her curves arching towards an invisible touch. It was easy to let his mind drift to her as the steady rhythm of the ride took hold, but what he didn't expect was the shadows stirring within, a beast beneath the surface, opening an eye. Power thrummed through him, threatening to burst from his fingertips in talons and ribbons of onyx magic, and the muscles between his shoulder blades burned as his wings threatened to spear through his skin.

Talemir fumbled for the flask he kept tucked safely against his side. Hands trembling, he brought the tonic to his lips and took a long draught of the horribly bitter stuff.

'Bit early in the day, isn't it, Tal?' Wilder said, frowning as Talemir wiped his mouth on the back of his hand.

Talemir forced himself to grin. 'Never too early for a bit of Marise's fire extract,' he replied, saluting Wilder and naming the liquor he knew his protégé loathed.

Sure enough, Wilder grimaced. 'Marise is known for his wine for a reason.'

'Wine doesn't travel as easy.'

'Where there's a will, there's a way,' Wilder retorted, but thankfully, he dropped the subject, leaving Talemir to take stock of his faculties.

Truth be told, he had no idea what the tonic was doing for

his *condition*, as Drue had called it. Farissa, the Master Alchemist at Thezmarr, had warned him it was a dangerous experiment, that it might just as easily poison him as cure him.

'I don't care,' he'd told her. 'I can't live like this.'

But live he had. He'd suffered through the uncontrollable change several times since that final battle of Naarva, on those horrific nights where the moon refused to show itself, all the while keeping his shadow-self a secret from the rest of the midrealms, from Wilder and Malik. Not even to Farissa had he spoken his greatest fear aloud... The fear that this was only the beginning, that the darkness might spread, that there might come a day where he was a fully fledged shadow wraith, incapable of returning to his original form. He'd been upping Farissa's recommended dose ever since.

At first he hadn't wanted to accept the mission to Naarva to discover what was happening with the steel and the increasing strength of the wraiths, but then... then he'd wondered if there were answers here for him, or perhaps... others like him. For surely he couldn't be the only half-wraith? So he'd accepted under the guise of indulging Wilder's quest for vengeance, hoping his own future might not look so bleak.

Instead, all he'd found were more questions.

Talemir glanced across to find Wilder deep in conversation with Adrienne. For that, at least, Talemir was grateful. His former apprentice could use some good in his life.

As they rode, Talemir also noticed how close Coltan stuck to Drue's side, despite the obvious disdain she held for him. The stupid boy's persistence set Talemir's teeth on edge. However badly he wanted to knock the ranger off his horse, he knew it wasn't his business, knew enough about Drue to understand that she wouldn't appreciate that interference from him. He'd seen her fight her own battles already. Though it gave him a small thrill to see that the hawk, Terrence, had fixed his angry stare on Coltan now.

Talemir rode on in silence, thinking briefly of his own former lovers. There were many of them, but none with any meaning. They had all understood what it meant to lie with a Warsword: a night or two of passion, but duty would invariably come before all else. He never lingered for long, and that was always for the best.

Talemir watched Drue send the hawk ahead to alert the watchtower about their impending arrival, and he found himself drawn to her once more. He, Drue, Adrienne and Wilder took the lead, and as they travelled, he admired Naarva for the small ray of hope it offered. To the untrained eye, the fallen kingdom was a place of festering gloom, but there were pockets in which life still flourished. They passed a handful of hidden settlements, the inhabitants greeting them with quiet awe. They rode past a farm where, despite the emerald vines strangling much of the land, lilies bloomed in the cracks. Talemir had to believe that he might be afforded the same mercy, that there might yet be a part of him where light shone through the darkness.

Deep in his own thoughts, he reached into his saddlebag absentmindedly, pulling out his canteen of water and taking a long drink, grateful to be drinking anything other than that wretched tonic.

'What's that?' Drue's voice sounded beside him.

He followed her gaze to his open bag, where a book with a distinctly red cover peeked out from his belongings.

'What's it look like? It's a book.'

But to his surprise, a smug smile tugged on Drue's lips.

'It's not just a book... It's a romance book. You read love stories?'

'What did you expect? Military strategies and fire drakes?'

Drue was still smiling. 'Something like that... Perhaps war stories and heroics.'

Talemir met her gaze, letting his own amusement show. 'Alas,' he said, nudging his horse a little closer to hers. 'Don't we read to escape our own realities?'

She didn't miss a beat. 'So no great loves in your reality, then, Warsword?'

Talemir's eyes lingered on her, his blood heating. 'Not yet, Wildfire... Not yet.'

Wilder cleared his throat nearby. 'Tal's read them for as long as I can remember,' he interjected. 'Back when I was an apprentice —'

'You say it like it was so long ago,' Talemir cut in, teasing.

Wilder shot him a warning look. 'When I was an apprentice, Tal would sit reading his pink books while I ran laps around the entire fortress.'

'Likely because I'd already finished my laps.'

'Did I hear that right?' a deep voice boomed from behind them. 'We've got a Warsword in our midst who reads love stories?'

Talemir recognised the man as Baledor, the friend of Drue's father. He laughed good-naturedly, twisting in his saddle to address the older ranger. 'Don't underestimate the skills you can learn from a romance book.' He laced his words with innuendo. 'And no matter what I read, I could still kill all of you in my sleep.'

The company burst into a fit of laughter, and that was that.

. . .

THE GENERAL, the ranger and the two Warswords went on leading the party across the plains of Naarva, and Talemir continued to appreciate the beauty in its wildness. In the absence of structured society, the kingdom that had once been known for its gardens now teemed with untamed nature. With a glance at Drue, Talemir decided he liked it better this way. It was like her – fierce and unapologetic in what it was. He wished he could be more like that.

As if in answer, the cuff around Drue's wrist hummed, strong enough that he could sense it even on horseback. Her attention snapped to him, as though she thought he was making it happen deliberately. He longed to take it from her, to study it for himself, to know how she created it, this mysterious ranger, daughter of the Naarvian forge master... What had she imbued it with? And how? For only the royal households of the midrealms wielded magic nowadays. There was a lot she wasn't telling him, of that he was sure. And she was so protective of the thing. He hadn't so much as grazed it with his fingertips, but he could feel it... Feel *her*...

As desperately as he wanted to examine it for himself, he was above taking it by force, for now.

The afternoon slowly ebbed away, and soon, the first watchtower was within their sights. But something was wrong. Talemir could sense it crawling against his skin; he could taste the lingering evil in the air.

He brought his stallion to a halt and unsheathed his sword.

Instantly, the others drew their weapons as well.

'Shit,' Drue muttered, pointing to her hawk circling above the tower in distress. Without another word, she coaxed her horse into a gallop across the remaining plains. Talemir didn't think; he simply surged after her.

He could hear Adrienne calling their names into the wind behind him, but he didn't stop. The taste of darkness only increased as he closed in on the watchtower, stirring that monster within. He forced it down, ignored it, and when he reached the outpost, he leapt from his horse.

Drue was fast, already searching within, but Talemir's chest seized at what he saw.

Black scorches marred the stone, and the distinct shape of claw marks carved through the brick.

'Drue?' Talemir called out, entering the tower, poised to attack. Inside, tables and chairs were overturned, plates and mugs of spilt mead scattered across the floor. Shards of ceramic broke underfoot.

Footsteps sounded, and she emerged at the bottom of the stairs, panic-stricken. 'There's no one here,' she rasped, supporting herself against the wall. 'They've been taken. Gus has been taken.' Her face fell, devastated.

Outside, thunder clapped, so loud it shook the ground beneath their boots.

Drue surged for the door. 'They've come back —'

But Talemir gripped her arm, restraining her. 'No, they haven't,' he told her. 'I'd feel it,' he added quietly. '*You* would feel it.'

The rest of their party burst in.

'Where's Gus?' Adrienne demanded, looking around wildly. 'Where is he? Is he alright?'

'He's gone, Adri,' Drue said, letting her friend collapse in her arms. 'The wraiths have him.'

With a resounding roar, more thunder rolled onto the plains beyond the tower. There was nothing for it.

'Everyone inside,' Talemir ordered, his skin prickling. Ten rangers and two Warswords crammed into a tiny outpost that had just been attacked by shadow wraiths, the horses left to fend for themselves in the storm... It didn't look good.

When they had all taken shelter, Talemir stood at the entrance of the tower. With his hands resting on the grips of his blades and his whole body tense, he stared out towards the darkening horizon.

7
DRUE

Alone in the highest room, Drue braced herself on the windowsill and squeezed her eyes shut against the spots swimming in her vision. It took every ounce of willpower to hold it together, to stop herself from falling apart.

The wraiths had taken Gus and the others. *For what?*

She pictured the boy's face and her soul nearly fractured. What was the last thing she'd said to him? He'd been underfoot back at the stronghold and she'd been frustrated, delivering some hypocritical lecture on cursing and proper etiquette for young boys.

To which he'd replied, completely unfazed, '*Let's not talk about that anymore. Let's talk about mountain drakes and teerah panthers.*'

Now, the thought of him trapped and terrified, darkness lashing his body, was too much to bear. It was her brothers all over again. Her mother, too. People she loved carved apart by the talons of the shadow wraiths. The tightness in her chest

86

refused to loosen. If anything, it only clamped down harder around her heart.

Drue pressed her forehead against the cold stone, inhaling deeply through her nose, steeling herself against the onslaught of grief and panic that threatened to see her ride out senselessly into the violent storm that ravaged her homeland below.

But she had been trained better than that. *Adrienne* had trained her better than that.

Do not succumb to fear, her friend used to say during their earlier scouting missions. *Stop, think, assess.*

And so Drue pushed aside the terror for her young charge, and took comfort in the weight of the new blade at her back, one that could cleave through monsters. At least she had that. She cursed the raging tempest outside, knowing that it would wash away any sign of Gus, any trail she might follow. That was her first thought. The second was of the half-wraith in their midst. With no tracks to hunt down, Talemir Starling was her only chance of finding Gus and the lair.

'I shouldn't have sent him here.' Adrienne's voice broke through the chaos whirring in Drue's mind, hauling her back to the present.

'It's not your fault,' Drue told her, though she understood the agony on her friend's face. 'We couldn't have kept him tucked away in the stronghold forever.'

'Perhaps not forever, but a little longer,' Adrienne countered, following Drue's gaze to the plains outside, where the howling winds tore through the meagre remaining life of Naarva.

'At least Dratos is with him. He'll keep him safe until we find them.'

HELEN SCHEUERER

Reluctantly, Adrienne nodded. 'As unpredictable as he is, he loves that kid.'

'They're family. He won't let anything happen to Gus. The last of the Castemonts will stick together,' Drue said, whether for her benefit or Adrienne's, she didn't know.

'We all stick together,' her friend replied, eyeing the sword at her back. 'I take it that's no ordinary gift from your father?'

'My father doesn't make ordinary blades.'

Adrienne nodded. 'Good. We're going to need it.'

'You're not bothered that I'm going a step further with breaking the midrealms' laws?'

Scoffing, Adrienne shook her head. 'We're survivors, Drue. Have been for a long time. Did they just expect us women to sit back and do nothing? To leave our defence in the hands of others? Whether it's regular or Naarvian, when it comes to life and death, steel is steel and we'll use it as needed. Some stupid law created by a stupid man in a distant territory makes no difference in a fallen kingdom. There are no rules here.'

The truth of her words etched into Drue's heart. She was right. Laws and prophecies from over fourteen years ago had no place in Naarva. The fact that the Warswords themselves had only briefly mentioned their weaponry confirmed as much. 'So, what's the strategy?' she asked.

Adrienne rubbed her eyes, as though she were hoping to wake from a nightmare. 'Wait out the storm. Find Gus.'

'A solid plan of attack.'

'Great, because it's the only one I've got.'

For a time, the two women watched the lightning and thunder in silence, before Adrienne turned to Drue. 'I'd best rejoin the others. It's not good for morale when the general disappears.'

Drue nodded, but instead of returning to the group, she unsheathed her sword. She scoured the tower for clues, finding discarded weapons, smears of blood and those damn scorch and talon marks all over. The acrid scent of burnt hair hung in the air, the telltale smell of those monsters —

HER MOTHER HAD DECORATED *the formal dining room for the special occasion. The best plates and cutlery had been arranged perfectly, the finest linens and seat covers too. Flowers from all over the midrealms adorned the surfaces, in vases and draped from the sills and curtain rods – a spectacle of colour and grandeur amid elegant candlelight.*

'Galina,' Fendran's warm voice sounded from the door. 'You shouldn't have made such a fuss.'

'Nonsense. It's not every day you turn fifty,' her mother said, surveying the space with satisfaction. 'My husband deserves a fuss.'

'Then I gladly accept,' Fendran replied, beaming.

Soon, the regular chaos of family ensued and everyone was taking their seats – Drue's parents, side by side as usual, and her four brothers: Leif, Martan, Penn and Will, who were already fighting over which cuts of meat were best.

Smiling, Drue took her place facing the giant arched window that looked out onto the darkening grounds.

The candlelight danced as her mother got to her feet, raising her sparkling wine. 'To my husband. All my love and well wishes for your fiftieth name day. Here's to the next fifty together.'

Fendran's eyes shone with unshed tears as he lifted his glass in return.

Drue did the same, toasting her father gladly, and put her drink to her lips —

Darkness exploded.

Glass shattered.

High-pitched screams pierced the air and onyx power ripped through the entire Emmerson clan.

Everything Drue had ever feared came to life before her in wisps of shadow, sucking a terrified shriek from her mouth as her family suddenly lay dying around her.

'Galina!' Fendran cried.

'Ma!' Leif's voice broke through the dark.

In the pitch-black, Drue could hear rasping breaths and quiet sobbing, but she couldn't see, she couldn't see a thing, couldn't get to her family fast enough – talons carving through the night and shredding the skin of her calves.

She didn't remember fighting, but she must have, for her own fingernails were torn and bleeding. On her hands and knees now, she crawled through the shards of glass, towards where she thought her parents and brothers were.

Another wave of dark power swept through the room, sending whatever remained on the table hurtling through the air.

More screams sounded. Drue couldn't tell where one ended and the next began. She couldn't tell who they belonged to anymore, only that her family, her loved ones, were suffering.

'Pa...' she croaked, ignoring the slice of glass through her skin as she inched across the floor.

Silence fell.

Suddenly, there were no more screams.

No more chaos.

Nearby, someone lit a torch.

A ragged sob escaped Drue.

Her mother was sprawled on the bloody carpet, her torso brutalised, torn to shreds by talons, a cry of horror still frozen on her lips.

Penn lay beside her, holding her hand. Blood leaked from his nose, his eyes glassy.

A few feet away, Leif's body was sapped of colour, webs of black veins marring his skin. His lifeless gaze stared up at the chandelier, surprised.

Martan was face down, but when Drue turned him over with a trembling hand, she saw his throat had been sliced open with a talon. The carpet beneath her was spongy with his blood.

And then she found Will, whose chest had been torn wide, his heart ripped from his body.

Drue couldn't breathe. Couldn't get enough air into her lungs.

Sticky, blood-soaked fingers closed around her arm. 'They're gone,' her father told her, his voice cracking. 'They're gone.'

A VOICE CALLED SOMEWHERE in the distance. 'Drue? Drue, are you alright?'

Gentle hands gripped her by the shoulders, warm and solid, free of blood.

Blinking slowly, she came back to herself to find Talemir Starling crouched before her, concerned.

Rage surged at the sight of him, her heart hammering loud in her ears. He was *one of them*, kin to those monsters who'd laid ruin to her family, who'd crushed her and her father beyond repair.

Still gripping her sword, Drue made to scramble back from him, but her spine was already pressed against the cool stone wall. She was on the floor, she realised, huddled in a ball, facing the door of whatever room she was in. Always with a wall to her back, always facing the enemy.

'Wildfire?'

More than anything, the infuriating name yanked her from the aftermath of her episode. She glared up at him.

'What happened?' Talemir's hands were still on her, their warmth soaking through the arms of her damp shirt, highlighting how cold she was. Then he was pressing something into her palm.

A flask.

'I'll pass on the monster tonic, thanks,' she muttered, wondering if she'd be able to stand. She wasn't so sure. Her limbs felt frozen. But she didn't want to be trapped in the same place as *him*. He was a shadow wraith. She couldn't let herself forget it. Not after all his kind had done.

'It's not *monster tonic*,' the Warsword told her, insistently pushing the flask towards her. 'It's fire extract.'

'Sounds dangerous.'

'Only in large quantities. And when mixed with mead and wine. And other... substances.'

Still reeling, Drue accepted with a shaking hand, taking a long sip. She nearly choked. The liquor instantly burned as she swallowed. From the back of her throat all the way to her belly, it seared, warming her from within.

Coughing and spluttering, she flung the flask back to him. 'Furies save me, that's *awful*.'

Talemir grinned, taking a swig himself. 'Isn't it just?'

'Why in the realms would you give that to someone?'

The warrior shrugged. 'Looked like you needed it.'

Drue *did* feel warmer, less paralysed. The past and her fury still lingered at the frayed edges of her mind, but they were less insistent, less sharp. As she took in her surroundings, she realised she was back in the top room of the tower, with no recollection of how she'd got there.

They were still on the floor. Talemir knelt before her, his

great frame blocking her view of the door. Slowly, she stood, ignoring the large hand he offered to help her up.

'That's some sword,' he commented, eyeing the weapon she clutched. 'May I?'

She batted him away and sheathed the blade. 'No, you may not.' The last thing she needed was a Warsword inspecting a weapon she wasn't meant to have. 'What are you doing here, anyway?' she asked, trying to rub the warmth back into her arms.

'I came up here to take first watch.'

'Drew the short straw?'

'Volunteered. There's no way I'll sleep. My skin is crawling.'

Drue bit back a nasty comment about whether this particular sensation was in recognition of his own kind, but he seemed to follow her train of thought anyway.

'I never asked for this,' he told her, shaking his head and gesturing to himself. As though he were broken, as though she could see the monster within even now.

Try as she might, she couldn't. She could only see the man, the esteemed Warsword of Thezmarr, his handsome face lined with earnestness and grief.

But that did not mean the shadow wraith wasn't lurking beneath his skin.

'How did it happen?' she asked.

Talemir's whole body sagged. 'That's a long story.'

Drue motioned to the lightning carving through the sky beyond the tower's window. 'We have time.' What she didn't add was that knowing the enemy was half the battle, and that she'd learn whatever she could to defeat him.

Talemir considered her before putting his flask to his lips again, drinking deeply. 'I assume this is some ploy to study my weaknesses and destroy me?' He offered her the liquor again.

Drue took another swig, grimacing at the burn but grateful for the heat in her belly. 'Guess you'll have to wait and see.'

'Wonderful.'

Warsword and ranger stood side by side at the window, not touching, their elbows resting against the stone sill as they stared out into the darkness. But for the chaos of the storm, there was no sign of life in the inky black canvas of night.

Talemir sighed heavily before he spoke. 'It was during the last battle of Naarva, a little over six months ago,' he began, his deep voice laced with regret.

Heart quickening, Drue waited.

'As you know, Ciraun had fallen prior. I had been in the thick of the fighting there too, but was called back to Thezmarr to brief the Guild Master, to strategise on what else could be done to save Naarva. I was at the fortress there when we received the call for aid from the Warswords still stationed here... The wraiths came from both the north and the south, a far more unified and organised attack than we'd expected from them... I rallied the remaining forces at Thezmarr and we answered our brothers' call immediately. Within the hour, we set sail from the guild's port south of the Bloodwoods.'

Drue had heard of that forest: the sea of trees that bled the blood of warrior ancestors long dead. A rush of goosebumps raised the hair on her arms as the words washed over her, but she didn't interrupt, didn't ask questions.

Talemir pointed into the storm-ravaged night before them. 'The battle took place out there, beyond the falls, at the heart of the entire kingdom. They had already taken Ciraun to the north, and your university on the eastern island... They came at us from every direction. It was myself and Malik – Wilder's brother – leading the defence. But what we faced was less of an attack and more of an extermination. We lost more warriors and Warswords than I could count that day, and still we fought.'

Talemir drank more from his flask, as though the liquor gave him the strength to continue.

'Malik and I found ourselves caught in the fray – right at the centre of the battle, amid the ruins of an old temple. Your people call it Islaton.'

Drue knew the place. It was not so much a temple as a circular stone monument to the Furies. She had passed it several times in her travels en route to the University of Naarva, both as a noblewoman and, later, as the ranger she was now.

'Our men were being slaughtered around us. Malik and I fought back to back, carving out as many wraith hearts as we could, throwing the bleeding black masses on the ground and setting them alight for good measure. But they were relentless. All reports had underestimated the size of their swarm...' He trailed off then, gripping the sill, his knuckles paling. 'Malik fell first. I only knew because I heard Wilder's scream from across the battlefield. At the talons of two wraiths, darkness pummelled him against the ruins of the temple. I ran to him, but it was already too late. His head, his face... They were unrecognisable from the —'

Talemir sucked in a sharp breath, his words tumbling out, like they were breaking free. 'That's when it got me. The wraith. It was different to the others. It had horns; it was far bigger and its power far greater. Ribbons of shadow lifted me into the air and the rest of the world fell away. Every nightmare I'd ever had swirled before me, coated in darkness and pain... And then that thing... It reached inside my chest.'

His gaze slid to hers, and with that single look, Drue knew he had never told anyone this before.

'It held my heart,' he whispered. 'It held my heart, its talons piercing it and spreading its black curse. I felt every agonising second until Wilder speared it through the back. It was enough to distract the monster. It dropped me and I watched through a haze of shadow as Wilder fought it off. That was the last thing I saw... I woke up tied to my horse on the ride back to the ships, after darkness had claimed Naarva once and for all.'

'Gods...' Drue murmured, unable to look the Warsword in the eye.

'The moment I regained consciousness, I knew something was wrong. But it took weeks to understand what exactly plagued me. The wraith that had me in its clutches was no ordinary grunt of their kind. It was a *rheguld reaper*. A king of wraiths that has the ability to sire more. The fucking thing is still out there somewhere.' He shuddered.

'And no one knows?'

'Besides the Master Alchemist at Thezmarr, only you. Though I think Malik suspects.'

'Malik? He survived?'

'Barely. He is much changed since that day. He no longer speaks. He's completely nonverbal, among other things.'

Drue swallowed the lump in her throat, her warring feelings twisting within. There was real human grief there, and deep, unending trauma. 'I'm sorry. For what happened to you. And to your friend.'

'I don't need your pity.'

'There's a difference between pity and empathy, Warsword.'

He bowed his head. 'I suppose you're right. So now you know... how a monster is made.'

'Do you think that's why they've taken our people? To make more wraiths?'

Talemir rubbed the back of his neck. 'I couldn't say.'

Drue gazed outward, picturing Islaton and its white stone columns amid the once verdant grasses. She imagined the battle as Talemir had described, blood spattered upon those chalk-coloured ruins.

'I still smell it sometimes...' Talemir said, his voice distant. 'Even all this time later, when I'm back at Thezmarr. I smell that gods-awful burnt hair scent of them. I fucking hate it.'

'You don't smell like that,' Drue heard herself say, the words leaving her without a second thought.

Talemir turned to her, brows raised. 'No? What a relief.'

Drue nearly told him he smelt of rich cedar and dark florals, but she stopped herself. Instead, she started towards the door. 'Have you ever heard of the springs in Aveum?' she asked, pausing as she gripped the handle. 'I've read stories of the Pools of Purity. People from all over go on pilgrimages to find them, hoping the water there will cure all manner of diseases and ailments.'

'I know the springs you speak of. Upon passing the Great Rite, a Warsword is gifted a vial of such waters. But alas, not even the purest of springs can cleanse the darkness from me.'

'You used yours, then?'

'I tried. Perhaps I was already too far gone by that point.'

'Perhaps you needed more than a vial.'

'We'll never know.'

'If you say so...' Drue allowed. 'What else do they give you? When you pass the rite?'

'Steel from Naarva, as you know. A stallion from Tver, armour from Delmira, poison from Harenth...' He hesitated a moment, his eyes lingering on her wrist. 'Now that we've bonded over my harrowing past and you've wrangled some secrets from me, why don't you show me that cuff?'

Drue gave a dark laugh. 'Nice try, shadow monster.'

She left him to his watch.

THE NIGHT WAS LONG, punctuated only by the lashing of the storm and the trembling stone. Drue sat with the company, staying by Adrienne's side as the men talked of war and women. She had heard much of it before; many of the rangers were inclined to share the same stories over and over, for the fall of their kingdom had left them with little else but tales of supposed glory long past.

What seemed like hours later, Talemir descended the steps, Baledor taking his place at the post. The Warsword looked deep in thought as he lowered himself to the ground beside their small fire and accepted a hunk of bread from his protégé.

It was Wilder who sensed that the mood needed lifting. He clapped the older warrior on the shoulder and turned to the group. 'Have you ever heard about the dual sword wielding champion of Thezmarr?' he asked animatedly. In fact, it was the most animated Drue had seen him since they'd met.

'Furies spare us,' Talemir muttered around his bread.

That only spurred Wilder on. 'Here in your midst sits the

undefeated, record-holding hero of the Guild Master's Tournament!'

Talemir actually groaned as the rangers broke out in awed murmurs. 'You're going to pay for this, apprentice.'

Wilder smirked before turning back to his now captive audience. 'You've no doubt heard of the tournament... The annual sporting event that determines the very best of Thezmarr's warriors in a range of different categories. There's jousting, knife throwing, and our dear Talemir's specialty, dual sword wielding...'

Drue had witnessed the older Warsword brandishing both swords against the shadow wraiths upon their first meeting, and she couldn't deny his skill... So she listened to Wilder's tales of his former mentor's triumphs.

'For years, warriors and expert swordsmen from all over the midrealms have travelled to the fortress in the hopes that they'll take the title from Tal... To no avail. He's held the top place on all our record boards for six years now —'

'Seven,' Talemir muttered.

Wilder's face was bright with passion and delight. 'You've seen nothing like it,' he told the men. 'Tal wields those blades like they're part of him. They call him the Prince of Hearts back at Thezmarr for all the wraith hearts he's taken.'

Someone barked a laugh. 'Wraith hearts or women's hearts?'

'A Warsword never tells,' Talemir quipped.

Drue cleared her throat. 'And yet little old me nearly had him when we sparred at the northern perimeter.'

Wilder snorted. 'Hardly. And remind me, why *were* you trying to slay a Warsword?'

The group of rangers shifted in interest at that detail.

Drue threw Talemir a casual shrug. 'Just wanted to be sure

he was who he said he was.'

Talemir's hazel gaze brimmed with amusement. 'You lost that match.'

'As I said, I *nearly* had you.'

The Warsword gave her a lazy smile. 'I thought I made myself clear. You can have me anytime you like.'

Drue's cheeks flamed.

One of the older men laughed. 'Warsword or not, keep getting on her nerves and my coin's on Drue.'

'Hear, hear,' Adrienne added.

But Drue had stopped listening, for the steel around her wrist had heated against her skin, to the point of searing. Her gaze shot to Talemir, who was already on his feet.

A strange hiss filled the room, as did the pungent scent of burnt hair.

Drue heard Baledor shout from the top of the tower, but it was too late.

The monsters were upon them.

Steel sang as weapons were unsheathed from their scabbards and Adrienne barked orders about staying in formation.

Drue's eyes fell once more to the Warsword, the accusation on her lips. Had the half-wraith somehow alerted his brethren as to where they were? Had he sold them to the darkness?

The horror on his face said otherwise, but there was no time.

A gust of icy wind plunged through the tower and glass shattered, whips of shadow lashing.

Drue brandished the sword her father had given her. Now was not the time for questioning. Now was the time to fight for her life.

8
TALEMIR

Darkness coiled around their unit like a viper, timing the perfect strike.

Talemir held a sword in each hand, but the ground floor of the watchtower was too close-quarters to light them aflame.

Screams pierced the air as the shadows took the shape of nightmares incarnate and wrought their unique brand of horror upon the group of rangers.

Talemir didn't waste time thinking. He simply struck. He sliced through the black tendons behind one of the monsters' knees. Its answering screech told him to attack again while it was weak, and fast. He delivered swift and precise slashes, causing the creature to buckle before him.

From the corner of his eye, he saw Wilder pivoting against two wraiths, his blades gleaming with black and red blood.

Though Talemir longed for open space and the freedom to advance in a manner of his choosing, he knew it was strategically better to contain the skirmish within the walls of the tower.

'Draw them inside,' he shouted to whoever would listen, his heart thundering. 'We can bottleneck them here.'

Darkness battered him, but the pain didn't land as it once had. Instead, his own shadows yearned to answer the call. He had fought against wraiths several times since that fateful day and each time he'd experienced the primal longing to be one with the night. But those instincts clawed against those his Warsword training had instilled in him, the second nature that had been forged to slay the monsters, slay them all for what they'd done to the midrealms, to him, to Malik... To punish them for the stain they had left on his now black heart, and for the way they'd hardened Wilder, the boy, now man, who had once been so carefree.

A guttural roar escaped Talemir as he broke free from the whips of power threatening to take him. He shouted again as he advanced against his monstrous opponent. Then, he leapt upon the creature, digging his blades deep into the wrinkled sinewy flesh and carving out the first heart of the skirmish.

The shrieks were spine-chilling until the beast fell silent.

Talemir threw the pulsing black mass to the ground, dark blood spurting, that pungent scent singeing the inside of his nostrils. Wisps of obsidian blocked his view, but he vaulted into the path of another wraith, lunging expertly, delivering as much Thezmarrian punishment as he could muster.

From what he gathered of the blinding chaos, their unit of ten rangers and two Warswords faced at least five wraiths. All the while, their nightmares swarmed them, dragging them back into past trauma. Talemir scanned the crammed space madly, spotting Drue and Adrienne fighting back to back, Drue wielding a beautiful sword while Adrienne hacked at wraith limbs with a battleaxe. Both women held their ground impressively, while the other rangers tried to keep the lashings of dark magic at bay.

Drue moved as a dancer. Her rhythm and discipline were abundantly apparent as she ducked and weaved through the attack, but Talemir could also see the instincts of a killer honed by necessity. For a split second, he imagined what the midrealms would be like had she been afforded the opportunity to train at Thezmarr. Perhaps she would be a Warsword, wielding Naarvian steel, carving out the hearts of monsters alongside him.

Talemir and Wilder took the brunt of the force. They fought side by side as they had many times before, understanding each other's patterns and manoeuvres. But they found Drue and Adrienne at their sides as well, creating openings for them to drive their final attacks home.

'You're not at risk of joining them, are you?' Drue hissed in his ear as he delivered a vicious slice to their current opponent, severing its arm clean off.

Talemir whirled to the ranger, disbelief curdling in his gut. 'You can't be serious —'

'Your eyes,' she rasped, deflecting an incoming blow with a wince.

'What?' he half shouted over the pandemonium, dodging a swipe of barbarous talons, his own fury surging.

'Your eyes, Warsword. They've gone all dark and veiny, like you're —' She let out a cry as a cord of darkness struck her side, sending her flying.

Heart seizing, Talemir threw himself after her, but Drue was already dragging herself back to her feet, panting, her eyes bright with pain. 'Did you do this?' she croaked, gesturing around wildly. 'Did you lure them here?'

'Does it look like I'm on their side to you?' he yelled, beyond incredulous, beyond furious. He was not fighting tooth and nail to have something he couldn't control thrown back in his face.

Drue staggered towards them. 'Then rein the wraith side in,' she spat.

And suddenly he felt exactly what she referred to: the simmering of power beneath his skin, the tightness around his eyes, the burning between his shoulder blades where his wings threatened to burst through and the itch at his fingertips where talons longed to break free.

The darkness was trying to lure him, but Talemir Starling refused to let it take him. Not this time.

Taking a breath, he centred himself and then launched once more into the fray of battle. He became one not with the shadows, but with the blades that sang in his hands as they carved through the monsters before him.

Blood rained, shrieks cut through the roar of the howling storm, and still they fought on. Talemir thrust one sword through the side of another beast, twisting the blade roughly before dragging it across the creature's abdomen, its guts spilling from its withered flesh. Looping his other sword around, he hacked off an arm; the wraith lurched for him, snarling in his face, its breath sour and rancid.

A different scream pierced the night. A scream of inner agony from Drue. It was the same sound he'd heard ripped from Wilder's throat during the ultimate battle for Naarva, when Malik had been —

Talemir spun on his heels, nearly slipping in the blood coating the stone floor as he searched for her among the bedlam.

Drue was pinned to the wall by a wraith, and he surged for her.

'No!' she cried. 'To Adrienne!' She managed to free her hand, pointing frantically to the other side of the room.

A wraith stood looming over the half-conscious general, its talons poised above her breast.

'Save Adrienne!' Drue sobbed.

Talemir faltered, just for a second, as he sized up the wraith upon Drue first, and then the one at Adrienne's chest. Instinct roared at him to lunge for Drue, but that was not what she wanted. She wanted him to save Adrienne.

And so he did as the ranger bid, no matter how much it pained him.

He sprinted towards the general, launching himself at the wraith above her and tackling it bodily to the ground, the force of the impact vibrating up his bones as they hit the stone.

He unsheathed his dagger from his boot and dragged it viciously across the creature's throat, hot blood spraying, before plunging the blade into its chest, digging its heart out messily, flesh tearing apart at his hands. When the organ was cut from the body, Talemir leapt to his feet and flung himself towards Drue —

But she was upright and alive, her sword hanging loose at her side as she gasped for air, covered in black muck. She pointed to the broken windows.

'The last two,' she managed between ragged breaths. 'The last two fled.'

Slowly, in a daze, Talemir surveyed the surrounding carnage. It was as gory as any battlefield he'd seen, worse, even, because it was contained to such a small area. Coltan held

Baledor under the arms, keeping him in a sitting position, the older man bleeding profusely from the head. Raw red marks marred his exposed skin, likely where the darkness had lashed him. Several of the other rangers were also in various wounded states around the room, while Adrienne... She had recovered herself and was now crouched over Wilder by the door.

Talemir's throat constricted. He rushed towards them.

Adrienne had her hand beneath Wilder's head, trying to help him sit up from where he lay in a pool of blood on the stone floor.

'Wilder,' Talemir murmured, his voice raw.

His protégé wheezed. 'Just a scratch, Tal. It's this fucking armour.'

Wilder had passed the Great Rite after the fall of Delmira, where the Warsword armour had been made for centuries. His was a poor imitation of the previous craftsmanship and he had been complaining about its gaping fit for months. Talemir's gaze fell to the dark wet patch at Wilder's middle. Slowly, he lifted the soaked fabric from his friend's stomach.

His own stomach bottomed out at the horrific sight. The wound was deep, a single, ragged slice that spanned from Wilder's ribs through his abdomen, blood pulsing from it. A wraith's festering talon had carved through flesh, tissue and muscle, splitting Wilder apart.

Talemir swallowed the bile rising in his throat.

'Doesn't even hurt, Tal,' Wilder said through gritted teeth. 'But I could use some of that fire extract about now.'

Talemir tried to sound casual, but the words came out strained. 'Thought you hated the stuff.'

'Not really in a position to be fussy at the moment.'

Talemir forced a laugh and rummaged through his blood-soaked clothes, at last finding the flask and putting it to his friend's mouth. The amber liquid hit Wilder's lips, and he grimaced.

'Gods, drinking that hurts more than the damn wound,' he spluttered.

'Is he alright?' Drue's worried voice sounded over Talemir's shoulder.

Wilder groaned as he managed to sit up, more blood pouring from the injury as he did. 'Nothing I can't handle.' He glanced up at Talemir. 'What is that thing you're always on about? Something about Warswords and blood and steel?'

Talemir squeezed his shoulder. 'Warswords are not born. They're forged with blood and steel,' he said. 'But you earned that badge of honour long ago.'

Wilder closed his eyes against the pain. 'So I keep telling you, mentor.'

'Drink your vial from Aveum.' Talemir looked around for the young man's satchel, praying that the healing properties from the springs would cleanse the wound.

But Wilder shook his head. 'I'm saving that for something more important.'

'Stubborn bastard.' Talemir left his friend in Adrienne's care. The young general seemed to have the sutures in hand, and he knew Wilder well enough to know that he'd prefer not to be made a fuss of.

Outside, the storm had broken, and atop a crest in the terrain was Drue, staring out into the blood-red sky as dawn swallowed the night. After checking on the rangers, he snatched something from the ground and went to her.

There, he stood beside her, quiet for a time.

'Thank you,' Drue said, her voice cracking. Her whole body was rigid, like she was fighting to contain everything she felt within. She cleared her throat. 'Thank you for saving Adrienne.'

'You're welcome.'

A new silence hung between them, a truce of sorts. Until Drue glanced down and jumped at what she saw in his grasp.

Smiling, he offered it to her – the heart of a wraith. 'I considered flowers, but I thought you'd like this more...'

He half expected her to recoil, to cry out in disgust. She didn't. Instead, she reached for the bloody mass, the giant thing dwarfing her hand as she took it, her fingers brushing his, sending a thrill through his bones.

He watched her as she studied it. 'It's truly the only way to kill a wraith, isn't it?' she breathed in wonder.

'Yes,' he told her. 'Perhaps it'll be mine you hold one day...'

A smile tugged at her lips. 'Perhaps I'll carve it out for myself.'

9
DRUE

When at long last dawn spilt its golden rays upon the storm-ravaged lands, Drue stood at the watchtower well with Adrienne as they tried to wash the blood and grime from their skin. Together, they surveyed their company with resigned determination.

'You have to go back,' Drue declared, noting the numerous injuries, the worst of which belonged to Wilder Hawthorne. He could barely walk, his face pale, his brow covered in a sheen of sweat. It was no surprise. He and Talemir had taken the brunt of the wraiths' attack.

'He needs a healer,' Drue added before nodding to the rest of their group. 'Many of them do.'

'What exactly are you proposing?' Adrienne asked tersely.

'That Talemir and I go on. We have to find Gus, Dratos and the others. We have to find the lair and destroy it. Besides, I gave Talemir my word that I would show him the steel source.'

'You want to forge ahead with only a half-wraith for company?'

Drue's chest tightened. 'It's *Gus*...'

'It's not only Gus I'm thinking of,' Adrienne countered. 'What about you?'

'I can hold my own.'

'That wasn't in question.'

'Let me do this, Adri... Let me find him and bring him back. I'll send word with Terrence as soon as we've found them. We can wait for your arrival and show up in true force, not just an injured scouting party.'

Adrienne's brows furrowed as she weighed up the risks. The women were quiet as they watched Coltan round up the horses that had fled in the storm. Thankfully, they hadn't strayed far.

'You're sure about this?' Adrienne asked.

'As sure as I can be.'

Adrienne sighed. 'Wraith or not, I owe him a debt. I don't particularly like it.'

'Nor do I.' Despite her words, Drue looked to where Talemir was tending to his stallion, the mighty warrior sneaking glances at Wilder and monitoring his condition.

Drue rubbed her aching temples. He'd confided in her. She knew his deepest secret and the details of his darkest hour... Only her. Then she had seen him in the heat of the battle, his eyes dark with that night-flecked curse... The change upon him. But he'd controlled it. He'd fought at her side and saved her dearest friend...

The anger he had shown when she'd accused him of betraying them had been raw and genuine. But what did that mean, exactly? It surely didn't prove his innocence. It could have been a calculated reaction, part of a much bigger plan.

Something pulled her from that line of thought. His wings flashed in her mind. She'd only seen them the one time, in his chambers at the stronghold. But when he'd been on the precipice of change during the battle, and now, as she noted his gaze lifting to the skies, she wondered if he'd ever flown...

'Drue?' Adrienne elbowed her.

'Hmm?'

'I said alright. You and the Warsword go ahead, send word with Terrence. Do *not* engage with the wraiths until we arrive. Do you understand?'

Drue was nodding before Adrienne had even finished speaking. 'Yes, yes. I understand.'

The general flung her arms around her. 'Find him, Drue.'

'I will,' she promised.

'Luck be with you, sister.'

Drue gave her friend an extra squeeze. 'Not if he's been with you first.'

Their routine goodbye at least made Adrienne laugh.

Atop her mare, with the Warsword on his stallion at her side, Drue watched as the ranger company and Wilder departed for the stronghold at Ciraun. Many had been too wounded or exhausted to object, Coltan included, much to her surprise.

'Do you think Wilder will be alright on the journey back?' she asked Talemir.

The Warsword was straight-backed, his gaze lingering on his protégé as they disappeared over the hill. 'He's made of sturdy stuff. He always pulls through.'

Drue nodded. 'Good.' She turned her mare to face south. 'Shall we?'

Overhead, Terrence let out an impatient cry as he circled among the clouds.

Talemir actually flinched at the sound. 'I'd be a fool to deny you.'

'Glad we agree for once,' Drue quipped, squeezing her horse's sides.

They set out, urgency pulling at her. She had been right about the storm. It had washed away any trace of the wraiths and where they might have taken Gus and the others from the tower. But as she'd also suspected, the shadow-touched warrior by her side seemed to have an instinct as to which direction they should head.

'We always suspected that they had some sort of nest or lair in the lower parts of your kingdom,' he explained. 'Those southern lands are also some of the closest territories to the Veil... Malik was insistent that the wraiths were breaching those defences somehow. And now... now that I am what I am, I can feel it if I concentrate. I feel drawn to a certain place.'

Drue read the worry on his face. 'And that unnerves you?'

'Can you blame me? Drawn to the very thing that wrought such devastation on our realms? On the people I love?'

'No,' Drue said quietly. 'I can't blame you for that.' She shifted. 'If we continue south, we'll hit the steel source along the way.'

'So you'll stay true to your word? You'll show me what's being done there?'

Drue clenched her jaw. 'Have I done anything to suggest I'm not a woman who upholds my vows?'

'Not yet.'

'Then you have your answer.'

He gave her a nod. 'How long until we reach the steel source?'

'That depends.' Drue threw him a challenging grin. 'On how fast you can ride.' She didn't wait. She urged her mare into a surging gallop, the chilly morning air instantly whipping her face.

She didn't care; she wanted to cover as much distance as possible. She wanted to save Gus from whatever horrific fate awaited him and the rest of the rangers who'd been snatched from the watchtower. If that meant she also bested one of the most revered Warswords in the midrealms at riding, she'd gladly charge ahead. She'd been riding since she could walk.

Only she wasn't besting him.

Despite the sheer size of both him and his stallion, Talemir Starling was keeping pace beside her as they tore across the overgrown lands of Naarva.

She didn't miss the wide grin on his face as he directed his mount into an elegant jump over an obtrusive thicket of brush. There was joy there, unabashed joy. And for a moment, she let herself feel it too. There were few people left in Naarva who could keep up with her on a ride.

Above, Terrence dipped and soared, his great wings beating against the grey sky.

They rode alongside the river that ran from Ciraun to the southernmost point of the island, which opened up into a great lake. The air there was even crisper against Drue's exposed cheeks, but it made her feel alive, made her forget everything for the briefest of moments. At their pace, it wasn't long before they reached the great falls, the Furies' Grief, that plummeted into the lower half of the island, steep and unforgiving.

Drue brought them to a halt as they approached the cliff's edge. There would be no more galloping across the plains for the next little while, for the descent to the lower lands was sharp and perilous. They would have to take it very slowly indeed.

Drue dismounted, taking stock of the narrow, rocky path trailing down into the rock face.

'Do you know why these falls are named the Furies' Grief?' Talemir called over the roar of the water.

'No idea,' Drue half shouted back, still trying to spot the safest route to the top of the trail. With her reins in hand, she led her horse, as well as Talemir and his stallion, a few yards away from the full force of the falls. She'd made this descent a dozen times before and every time she struggled to locate the start of it amid the overgrown vines and crumbling façade.

'Why don't you tell me while I find this damn trail?' she said, still scanning the indiscernible mess of cliff and foliage before them.

'When the mother of the three Furies died, the goddesses of war cried so much that they carved a fissure in the land with their tears...'

Drue halted her search for the trail. She was captivated by Talemir's melodic voice. But the story itself stirred a longstanding rage within. The fact that the original Warswords, the Furies, were women had been conveniently ignored over the years. Monuments stood in honour of them all over the midrealms and yet Thezmarr, the home of the very warrior guild inspired by them, no longer allowed women to partake in training. Drue wondered had that rule not existed, if she might be there now...

Something caught her eye. 'There!' She pointed to where the trail began.

'Took you long enough,' Talemir said.

'You knew where it was this whole time?'

'Of course.' He mounted his stallion. 'Islaton is just beyond these falls and across the moors. I told you I've been here before.'

'You could have said something.'

'And here I was thinking you were enjoying my story.'

'And here *I* was thinking we were just about to get along.'

As infuriating as she found the Warsword, the trek down the steep decline was slow and laborious, and soon Drue sought a way to pass the time, to draw her focus away from the pain in her lower spine from leaning back in the saddle.

'These books you read,' she ventured, glancing over her shoulder at him.

A gleam of amusement already shone in those hazel eyes, and she almost didn't ask him.

'Yes?' he smirked.

She unclenched her jaw. 'What are they about?'

Talemir raised a teasing brow at her. 'What's got you curious, Wildfire?'

Drue clicked her tongue in frustration. 'Forget it.'

But Talemir urged his horse a little closer to hers. 'The one I'm reading at the moment is about the romantic adventures of the Valian Kindred.'

'The what?'

'The Valian Kindred. A race of warrior women from faraway lands beyond the Veil.'

'What do you know of things beyond the Veil?'

'Only the things I read in books.'

'Romance books.'

'Among others, yes.'

'Have you ever been?'

'Beyond the Veil?'

'Yes.'

'I can't say I have. Is that something you'd like to do?'

'I wasn't aware that was something the people of the midrealms *could* do,' Drue replied.

'As my apprentice would say, *where there's a will, there's a way.*'

'He's not your apprentice anymore.'

'So he would like to believe.'

Drue twisted in her saddle, glimpsing the Warsword, a fond expression lining his handsome face. 'Oh?' she asked. 'So when does an apprentice move beyond the rank?'

Talemir smiled. 'When he has an apprentice of his own.'

Drue turned back to the narrow trail before her. 'Do you think he'll ever take one on?'

'Of that I have no doubt,' Talemir replied.

Halfway down, the trail plateaued into a flat clearing and Drue insisted they rest the horses. Sweat gleamed on the poor beasts' coats. Once they were cared for, she turned to the falls, feeling the light spray on her face. The rushing water was a stark reminder of how filthy she was, despite her hurried attempts at washing at the well with Adrienne. Her skin was still speckled with blood, both human and wraith, not to mention all manner of other grime. She glanced at Talemir, who stood near the edge of the cliff, drinking from his canteen. Infuriatingly, the Warsword suited the dirty, rugged look.

But he was frowning.

A concerned expression spread across Talemir's face and Drue followed his gaze to where Terrence had just landed clumsily in the dirt.

Terrence didn't do clumsy.

Something was wrong.

But Talemir was faster than she was. He was already at the hawk's side, his previous fear for his fingers forgotten as he ever so gently spread Terrence's right wing out.

Amid the brown feathers there was matted blood.

Terrence gave a feeble cry.

'He's hurt.' The Warsword carefully fanned the feathers out, trying to locate the source of the bleeding.

Drue's chest grew tight. How had she not noticed? How had she allowed the poor creature to fly for miles? She made to shove Talemir aside, but Terrence wasn't fighting as he examined the bird's leg now.

'It's not his wing.' Talemir's brow furrowed. 'I don't think it's as bad as I first thought, but the wound needs to be cleaned.'

'I'll do it,' Drue said, at last pushing his hands away.

'That's probably for the best,' the warrior agreed. 'I'll leave you to it.'

Drue paid him barely any heed as she picked Terrence up. She hadn't held him like this since he'd been a hatchling.

Using water from her canteen, she cleaned the wound, ignoring the hawk's cries of pain. It was a jagged laceration to the upper part of his leg. She winced on his behalf as she bandaged it with a strip of fabric torn from her shirt. Drue didn't know if he'd got the injury in the storm, or if he'd tried to fend off the shadow wraiths in the dark. Either way, the guilt settled in the pit of her stomach like a stone. She should have checked on him, she should have —

'Here,' Talemir said, reappearing from the brush, holding out his hand. The Warsword offered a small, dead rodent. 'We don't know if he's eaten since that bit of hare yesterday morning. He'll need his strength —'

Drue stared at him. Even Terrence grew still with interest. *He caught that with his bare hands?*

'What?' Talemir asked.

Drue swallowed the lump in her throat. 'It's just...' She didn't know what to say. Instead, she settled for: 'Thank you.'

She watched, mouth slackening as Terrence, the hawk who hated everyone but her and Adrienne, drank the water Talemir now cupped in his palm. She stared for even longer as the bird hobbled on his good leg, gently taking the mouse the Warsword offered him.

Drue's chest tingled. Was she truly seeing *Terrence* eat out of the half-wraith's hand?

Talemir glanced up. '*What?*' he demanded.

'Nothing.' Drue looked away quickly.

'He's alright to fly,' Talemir told her, standing and instantly towering over her once more.

Drue went to her saddlebag for something to do and rummaged for her water. She drank deeply, training her focus on anything except the Warsword, who seemed to sense her confusion.

That was when she caught the scent in the breeze – jasmine. She'd recognise that scent anywhere. It was the aroma that had clung to her mother: her hair, her clothes, no matter the time of day.

Drue scanned their surroundings and spotted the flowers immediately. On the slope of the cliff was a patch of wild blue jasmine – her mother's favourite. The delicate cerulean petals flourished there among glossy, dark green leaves. Her mother had grown all sorts of jasmine in their greenhouse and the garden beds around their estate, but for whatever reason, wild jasmine, with blooms of this shade, had always eluded her, refusing to grow as easily as the rest. It had never fazed Drue's mother, though. Galina, the elegant noblewoman, simply tried and tried again.

'I will not let these flowers defeat me, Drue,' she had said once. 'Mark my words, there will be wild blue jasmine in my gardens before the next winter is upon us.'

But her mother hadn't seen the next winter, and Drue hadn't returned to their family home since. She had no idea if the blue blooms had flourished in their absence.

'We should keep moving,' she said, turning back to the horses.

Talemir was watching her, his mouth slightly parted as though he wanted to ask her something.

But Drue pushed past him and readied her mare once more. Terrence, who had made a quick recovery, spread his wings and flew ahead.

'How long have you been a ranger?' Talemir asked as they started the second half of their descent past the falls.

'Officially? A year or so.'

'Unofficially?'

'Adrienne began training me long before. When we sensed the unrest permeating the kingdom. She's the daughter of the captain of the royal guard.'

'And you?'

Drue hesitated for a moment, searching for a reason not to share the details with him. Finding none, she replied: 'I'm the only daughter of a noblewoman, and my father, Fendran – his family has manned the Naarvian forge for centuries.'

'An interesting match.'

'They were.'

'Your father taught you weaponry?'

'My father, my brothers, Adrienne... Everyone had a hand in it, I suppose.'

'And how did a noblewoman feel about her daughter wielding blades?'

Drue laughed. 'When my mother wasn't hosting balls or

flitting about the kingdom, she was elbows-deep in dirt in the garden, so she was hardly one for adhering to societal expectations. It's one reason why people loved her.'

'She sounds lovely.'

Drue struggled to swallow. 'She was.'

She waited for the pity, for the forced condolences, but to her great relief, none came. Talemir seemed to sense that she neither wanted nor needed those things.

'You've been on many missions, then?'

'Why all the questions, Warsword?'

'Just passing the time.'

'At least make it interesting.'

Talemir huffed a laugh. 'You want interesting? Alright. Most original way you've killed a man?'

'With a candlestick,' Drue replied without hesitation.

'A candlestick? Impressive. What happened?'

'Adrienne and I were tracking a missing family on the southern island, and we took shelter in an abandoned manor. We'd been travelling hard for days and we were both exhausted. She fell asleep while on watch and we were attacked by raiders. By the time I realised what was happening, I was pinned to the dining table by one of them... The only thing within reach was a candlestick. So I shoved it through his eye. Damn near hit the back of his skull.'

'Brutal.' There was no judgement in Talemir's voice. 'Served the bastard right.'

Drue nodded in agreement. She regretted nothing about that kill. 'What about you?'

'How much time do you have?'

'I think we'll manage.'

'Don't be so sure. There are *unlimited* creative ways to end a man.'

'Well, by all means, educate me. I might find your boasting instructive.' She gave him a pointed look.

Talemir grinned. 'A while back, I killed a man with a book.'

Drue snorted. 'You bored him to death, then?'

'No. One hit to the head with the hefty tome, and he was gone. Killed by a love story, no less.'

'Romantic.'

'There are worse ways to go,' the warrior quipped. 'My friend Malik laughed when I told him that story. It was worth it just for that. And before I became a Warsword, I killed a man with a fork.'

'A fork?'

Talemir shrugged. 'Nasty tavern brawl.'

'Oh? What started it?'

'The same things that start every tavern brawl. Missing coin, too much mead and a beautiful woman.'

'Who was this beautiful woman?' Drue heard herself ask.

'No idea,' Talemir said cheerfully.

'You killed a man over some woman whose name you don't even remember?'

'It was a long time ago, Wildfire.'

'I've told you to stop calling me that,' Drue ground out.

'You never know,' Talemir continued, like he hadn't heard her. 'She might not remember my name.' He paused, giving it some thought before offering an arrogant smirk. 'But I doubt it.'

Drue shook her head in disbelief.

'So just your candlestick kill, then? Looks like I have you beat, and I wasn't even trying.'

The thrill of the challenge surged within Drue. 'Fine. I see your fork and I raise you a ladies' glove.'

'Intriguing,' Talemir allowed. 'Do tell.'

'I happened upon a man trying to take advantage of a woman in the powder room. So I strangled him with my glove.' She raised a finger to the left side of her face, where a faint scar dragged down the centre of her cheek. 'He put up a fight. But not enough to save himself.'

'And the lady? I imagine killing someone at a society event doesn't go unnoticed.'

'She came to my defence, of course, told everyone what happened. She's actually the stronghold cook now. Gives me food whenever I want.'

'A good friend to have, indeed.'

'Next?' Drue said.

Talemir laughed. 'Wilder and I caught a wraith with a boat sail once. Of course, there's only one way to kill them, but a creative capture deserves a mention, no?'

'I'll give you that,' Drue allowed. 'How about this one... I gutted a man with the bill of a swordfish.'

Talemir stopped his horse. 'Good gods! Why didn't you *lead* with that?'

'I never show my cards all at once, Warsword.'

He let out a low whistle.

'Your turn,' Drue prompted, feeling smug.

Talemir was still shaking his head as he coaxed his horse onwards again. 'My friend Marise killed a fellow with a flying sparkling-wine cork.'

Drue burst out laughing. 'Was it on purpose?'

'Oh, absolutely. The man was trying to rob his cellar. Marise is very protective of his cellar.'

At long last, they emerged from the foot of the cliff, and Drue turned to face Talemir. 'That cork story doesn't count, by the way. Wasn't your kill.'

His answering smile sent a thrill through her. 'Don't worry about that. There's plenty more where those came from.'

Morning bled into afternoon as they followed the river, and an ease settled between ranger and Warsword. As reluctant as she was to admit it, Drue realised that laughter found her easily, and that she enjoyed listening to the melodic sound of Talemir's voice as story after story left his lips.

But a few hours before dusk, he grew unusually quiet, and she noticed him sagging in his saddle, his broad shoulders leaning a little too far to the right.

'What's wrong?' she asked, nudging her horse closer to his, peering into his face. He was pale, beads of perspiration lining his brow.

'Ah, it's nothing.' His smile was strained.

'It's not nothing.' She reached across and pulled his reins up short, stopping the horses. Talemir nearly slid from the saddle. By the looks of things, sheer willpower alone had kept him upright for the last few hours.

'What happened?' Drue demanded, helping him down from his horse. She sat him down on a nearby rock, the river rushing quietly beside them.

'No idea,' Talemir muttered with a wince.

'Where does it hurt?'

'I'm fine.'

'Oh, for the Furies' sake, don't be so stubborn,' Drue snapped. 'I mean to find Gus and the wraiths' lair, and I need you to do it.'

'Is that the only reason you're fussing, Wildfire?'

'Tell me where it hurts before I start prodding.'

'You can prod me any time – *fuck!*' Talemir barked as Drue

squeezed the muscle between his neck and his shoulder, where his leathers were ripped.

Blood oozed.

'You're wounded,' she told him, her hands already moving to his laces.

He didn't protest as she undid them, peeling the sodden material from his heated skin.

'You didn't think to clean this?' she said, staring down at the raw, angry claw mark that carved through his flesh.

'Wilder drank the rest of my fire extract. He needed it more than I did. And I didn't think it was too bad.'

'Well, it is now...' She gently touched the flesh around the wound. It was blazing hot. 'It's getting infected.' Her chest seized. 'You need a healer, or this will fester and you'll...'

'I don't need a healer.'

'*Yes you do —*'

'No.' Talemir gripped her hand and motioned towards the river. 'That's a freshwater source...'

'Water won't cut it at this point. The infection has already taken hold.'

'No, you misunderstand. Usually, alongside a river like that grows a particular weed – blackbore ivy, it's called. A ranger should know of such a plant. It's got star-shaped black leaves and grows in a messy sort of vine... If you can find some of that, I won't upend your quest.'

Drue had never heard of the weed, but she left the Warsword on the rock and went to the river's edge, scouring its banks for the foliage he'd described. She fought hard to keep her worries at bay, focusing on the task at hand. She got on her hands and knees, sifting through the messy underbrush, forcing her panic down, refusing to think of what might happen if she couldn't find —

'Got it!' she shouted, snatching a handful of the vines that matched his description perfectly. Clutching the black star-shaped leaves tightly, she darted back to Talemir and thrust them at him.

'What am I meant to do with those?' he said, voice strained against the pain. 'You have to crush them up. Here.' He moved aside on the rock. 'You need to grind them into a paste.'

Following his instructions, Drue used a smaller rock to pulverise the foliage into a thick, dark mixture.

'A ranger really should know this,' he managed through gritted teeth. 'What would you do if you were injured on the road?'

'Well, we don't usually drink the liquor we treat our wounds with,' Drue replied. 'How's this?'

Talemir surveyed her handiwork. 'Good. Now, if you'd be so kind as to put it on the wound...'

A bitter smell drifted from the paste as Drue scooped it up on her fingers. Gently, she applied it to the gash. She could feel Talemir trembling beneath her touch, and in that moment she realised she didn't actually wish to inflict pain upon him, half-wraith or not.

'Sorry,' she murmured as she added more.

'I'm fine,' he said quietly. 'The ivy should coax any infection from the wound. It acts as a cleaning agent against any toxins.'

'How long does it take to work?'

'I should be feeling better in an hour,' he told her, grimacing as the bitter aroma grew stronger. 'Just what I need. More filth added to this mess.' He gestured down at his blood-and-dirt-spattered clothes. 'Though I can't say I fancy freezing my bollocks off in the river.'

Sure enough, when Drue washed the remnants of the blackbore ivy from her hands, her fingers went instantly numb in the icy current. She returned to Talemir, surveying him critically. 'I'll make you a deal, Warsword...'

He looked up at her, brows raised. 'What sort of deal?'

'Recover quickly and I'll show you where you can wash off the blood and stench of wraith without freezing your precious balls off.'

Despite his eyes still being glazed with fever, Talemir smiled. 'Well, consider me intrigued. In fact, let's up the dose of this blackbore and we'll be on our way.'

DRUE HAD BEEN DEBATING with herself whether to mention the hot springs. As much as she longed to soak her aching muscles and scrub the grime from her own skin, it seemed an unnecessary waste of time to take the half-wraith there. But at this point, with Talemir injured and a cold night suddenly upon them, there was little reason not to set up camp by the steaming pools. They could rest and recover there before continuing on at dawn. Perhaps he'd let his guard down.

On horseback once more, she led them away from the river across several plains, to a rocky outcrop on the outskirts of the island where, beyond a series of enormous boulders, the hot springs lay.

Talemir whistled low as they neared the turquoise waters. 'I've never seen such a beautiful sight,' he said, dismounting with much more ease than he had before.

'How's the wound?' Drue asked.

'Never better,' he quipped, already pushing his boots off at the heel.

'You don't want to make camp first?' Drue led her mare to where it could graze.

When she turned back to the springs, Talemir already had his shirt off. 'Not a chance.'

Her mouth went dry at the sight of him. She was utterly transfixed at the view of that glorious torso once again. This time, his golden skin was spattered with blood and dirt and a smear of blackbore paste on his shoulder, but the mess took nothing away from his sculpted chest and broad shoulders... In fact, it suited him. He still wore that sapphire around his neck, the blue gem glinting in the last slivers of sunlight. Drue was tempted to ask who it had belonged to, for there was no denying that it was a woman's jewel. But she had no right to ask those sorts of questions and, to her dismay, she questioned whether she actually wanted to know the answer.

'What are you waiting for?' Talemir asked from the edge of the pool, hazel eyes bright.

A dare. A challenge.

One that Drue wouldn't lose.

'Nothing.' Calling his bluff, her fingers rose to undo the buttons of her own shirt. She felt his stare fixed upon her like a searing brand as her shirt came undone down the centre, the fabric slipping from her bare shoulders. She placed it over a nearby boulder, not yet daring to look at the Warsword.

Slowly, she untied the band of material around her breasts, the cold air kissing her skin, her nipples hardening.

Then she looked at him, her chin raised high, anticipation already throbbing between her legs. She had meant to unsettle him, provoke him even, but she'd underestimated her own body's response to the Warsword.

Talemir hadn't moved a muscle. His hooded gaze

devoured her, trailing across her exposed torso, drinking her in.

'Your turn,' she said in a low and sultry voice she hardly recognised.

'Considering you've already seen under these clothes, I'd say things are a tad unfair... but I'll play.' His hands went to his belt, sliding it from its buckle and tossing it aside. The buttons of his pants came undone beneath deft fingers and soon, the fabric was sliding down his muscular thighs, his thick, hard length springing free.

Drue's breath caught as he kicked away his leathers and stood before her, utterly naked.

A wave of longing swept through her heated blood. Drue searched herself for signs of dark magic, for some sign that the lustful haze was not of her own volition...

Nothing but natural desire coursed through her.

Much to her disdain, Drue knew she had found Talemir attractive from the moment she'd met him, but there was a beauty about him she hadn't acknowledged until now – something that went beyond the rippling muscles and the teasing smile on those full lips...

Her hands drifted to her own pants, and as the Warsword watched her, she stripped them away, then slid her undergarments down her bare legs. Last was the cuff. She slipped it from her wrist and placed it atop her clothes. Perhaps without it, she'd gain the upper hand. That's what this was about, after all.

Completely exposed, she closed the gap between them, joining him at the shoreline.

'Shall we?' she said, fighting to keep the tremor from her voice.

He stared after her, his lips slightly parted, as she walked into the steaming water, a sigh of pleasure escaping her as the delicious heat enveloped her.

'Suddenly shy?' she called back to him, wading deeper until the water kissed her collarbone.

The pool surged around the powerful frame of the Warsword as he followed her in, his hard cock bouncing with each step until his lower half disappeared below the surface.

'This was not how I expected this day to end,' Talemir murmured beside her. 'Not that I don't welcome the surprise...' His voice was deeper, laced with leashed longing.

Drue heaved a breath and ducked beneath the water in an effort to douse her own desire. She stayed under for as long as her lungs would allow, rubbing at the grit on her skin, wondering if this had been a terrible idea. What exactly had she been hoping to achieve? She couldn't for the life of her remember now.

When she emerged, pushing the wet hair from her brow, her gaze fell to Talemir, who was scrubbing the dirt away from his chest, his powerful back to her. Every part of her screamed to reach out and run her hands over those tapered muscles, across that golden skin flecked with faint scars.

It was impossible not to gravitate to him, his presence singing out to her like a cyren's song. When he turned around, she found herself before him, having moved through the water without even realising it.

'What do you want, Wildfire?' he asked quietly, his body tense beneath her stare. 'Is this a trap? A game?'

'You tell me.' What she was feeling – it more than unsettled her.

'I swear, I'm not plotting against you. I only want the truth.' His throat bobbed. 'It's you I don't know if I can trust... But I want to.'

Drue shoved aside every conflicting emotion warring within, the tiny voice screaming that she'd already crossed a line, that this was dangerous territory and went against everything she stood for... Heart hammering, she reached for him, her fingertips trailing up his rippling abdomen to his chest.

Drue wasn't sure he was breathing as she touched him.

'Drue...' he murmured, as if in warning, as if she might not be ready for what happened next.

But she was more than ready. She wanted him. There was no point in denying it any longer. She would allow herself this slip, this lapse in judgement. She would shove her past into a box and grant herself this one thing. And so she pressed her wet, naked body to his and, with her fingers tangling in his hair, brought his face to hers.

Her breathing hitched as their lips touched.

Featherlight at first, as though he was waiting for her to pull away.

She only hauled him closer, fire racing through her veins with the need for him.

He kissed her fiercely, his mouth warm and lush as it moved over hers, creating swells of desire in her. He tasted like juniper berries and temptation, which she was more than willing to surrender herself to.

As he kissed her, his hands slid down her back, gliding over her curves to the backs of her thighs, and he lifted her easily out of the water, groaning as her tongue brushed his.

Drue moaned as she felt the press of his cock against her, the sensation sending a ripple of pleasure to her core. She wrapped her legs around him, demanding more, white-hot need blazing through her.

He answered with another searing kiss, his hand closing

over her breast, rolling her hard nipple beneath his thumb, causing her to cry out, to arch into his touch.

'*Drue...*' he murmured, the sound vibrating down her whole body, pulsing between her thighs. He ground his cock against her and she rolled her hips against him, desperate to feel him —

He froze.

Abruptly, Talemir lowered her into the water and threw himself from her, as though burnt.

Heart pounding, Drue blinked at him, cheeks flushing as she covered herself below the waterline. Had she been too forward? What —

Then she understood.

Talemir stood a few feet away, his powerful body rigid and panting, as great membranous wings speared from his back.

10

TALEMIR

Talemir was fucking mortified. Completely and utterly *mortified* by his lack of control, by the mere thought of bringing this monstrous side of himself into what had just happened between him and Drue.

He'd felt the first ripple of power as she'd arched into him, her body melting so perfectly to his touch. When she'd rolled her hips, the tip of his cock almost sliding home, he'd lost all semblance of sanity and the shadows had ripped free of their restraints.

He had nearly shot into the skies with the force of it.

He'd practically thrown her from his shadow-ravaged body in terror.

Even now, as he turned from her, facing the shore, the weight of his wings hung heavy between his shoulder blades and ribbons of darkness unfurled from his very being. Internally, he raged, savagely trying to claw the beast back inside, trying to contain it.

Around him, his form flickered.

He didn't look at Drue as he left the spring, snatching his clothes from the shore and disappearing behind the outer boulders to salvage what little remained of his dignity. His heart thudded painfully, not just from the change, but from *her*, from what they'd almost just done. What she'd likely never offer again. Not after this. Or had it been another of her games? A ploy to undo him and prove once more that he was a monster among men? That he didn't belong with the Warswords, nor was he wraith enough to belong to the shadows... The thought carved a fracture within him as he shoved his wet legs into his pants and his wings disappeared completely. The weight was still there, though.

'Talemir?' her voice called.

He rubbed his neck and ran his trembling fingers through his hair. Gods, now he had to face her. After *that*. His body felt wound too tight. He was teetering on the edge of a mighty fall.

'Are you decent?' Drue asked.

That, more than anything, made Talemir relax. 'Bit late for that, isn't it?'

To his surprise, Drue laughed. 'I was being polite.' She appeared at the side of one of the giant boulders, fully clothed and wearing her cuff once more. A pang hit Talemir low in his gut. She peered at him cautiously. 'Are you alright?'

Heat bloomed in Talemir's cheeks. 'Yes.' He cleared his throat. 'Sorry, about... that.'

'It's fine.'

'I...' He could feel the blush deepening. 'I haven't been with anyone since... since the attack. I didn't know that would happen.'

Drue's brows shot up. 'How long ago was that again?'

'Long enough for a hot-blooded Warsword.'

Drue nodded. 'Let's just forget it happened, alright?'

Forget it happened. Only as the words left her mouth did Talemir realise just how much he didn't want to forget those moments with her in the hot springs, how she'd tasted, how she'd fitted perfectly to him. But if forgetting was what she wanted, he couldn't blame her.

'Consider it forgotten,' he said, forcing a smile to his lips.

'Good,' she replied. 'So you can help me with the camp.'

They returned to their belongings and picked a patch of grass sheltered by the rocks. 'You can use your own tent now,' she told him. 'I don't have to worry about watching you around the others anymore.'

Talemir's stomach bottomed out, his chest growing tight again. 'Glad to hear it.'

His insides churned as he set up his lone tent. He wanted nothing more than to crawl inside and sleep the rest of the wretched night away.

But as he was finishing hammering the pegs into place with a rock, Drue spoke his name.

He looked up, worried about what horrified expression he might meet. But it was curiosity lining Drue's features. 'Have you ever used them?' she asked carefully.

'Used what?' Talemir looked around the campsite.

She laughed softly. 'Your wings. Have you ever flown?'

'Oh.' Talemir looked away from her. He didn't want to talk about this. In fact, he'd rather face a dozen more shadow wraiths *and* a mountain drake than talk about this. 'No,' he said at last.

But Drue was insistent. 'Have you tried?'

Talemir busied himself with unnecessarily tightening the ropes of his tent. 'No.'

'Why not?'

'Because...' He trailed off.

'Because why?'

'What does it matter?' he bit out. Part of him wanted to tell her, to trust her with the sad and broken truth: that he was afraid. If he flew, it meant that he accepted what he was, that he was done with suppressing that side of himself and willing to embrace it fully. But the other part of him wanted to yank his shields up, to block out the very reality she brought surging to the surface.

He was a monster. That was all there was to it. He would never live a normal life again, would never be free of the shadows that prowled beneath his skin, would never fail to be lured by the song of the dark... Apparently he couldn't even be with a woman without the wraith tearing through his control and free will.

He rummaged through his pack and took a long drink of the bitter tonic Farissa had made for him. He could almost see the spiral of night before him, tempting him to shed his skin and join it... He drank more tonic, gulping it down, ignoring the terrible taste.

When he looked up, he found Drue was still watching him.

'Are you thinking of carving out my heart, Wildfire?' he asked, unable to keep the note of hurt from his voice.

She didn't look away. In fact, she looked into him, right to his soul. 'I hadn't decided...' she said, her eyes bright. 'On whether I should use a fork, or the bill of a swordfish.'

Talemir blinked at her, dazed. Then he loosed a tight breath, the tension leaving his shoulders. A laugh followed. 'The swordfish would probably be best.'

'My thoughts exactly,' Drue grinned.

He laughed again, a pleasant warmth spreading through him. Gratitude. Perhaps she wanted to forget what had happened between them, but her kindness, her empathy, shone through. And if that meant he got to laugh with her, pass the time with her, even in the most simple way, well... He had to be content with that.

Though they had erected both tents, neither one of them retired to the shelter of the canvas. Instead, they lay side by side, the campfire crackling nearby, and looked up at the inky black of the night sky.

A smattering of stars winked down at them, infinite.

Lying on the damp grass with their hands behind their heads, they didn't touch, but Talemir could feel her beside him, her energy, her presence. It was intoxicating. So much that it brought him back to those blissful minutes in the hot springs, before his embarrassment took hold again.

'Did I scare you?' he heard himself ask. 'Before...?'

She turned her head to him, her beautiful face illuminated by the moonlight. 'No.'

'Good.'

'They're...' She trailed off, a blush spreading across her cheeks before she tipped her chin back to the sky.

'What?' he pressed.

'They're beautiful, you know. The wings.'

For the first time in a long while, Talemir's eyes prickled. 'Oh.'

'Don't let it go to your head.'

He laughed, suddenly feeling lighter than he had all day. 'I absolutely will. Any more niceties to share this evening?'

'Is this the part where you want me to offer some platitude about how it's only in the dark of night that we can see the stars?'

'Poetic. Is that what I should tell myself when I need comfort against the shadows?'

'Tell yourself whatever you want.'

'Why? Because there's no saving me?'

'No,' Drue reprimanded. 'If you need words of comfort, perhaps remember this: there are all kinds of darkness in this world. Some good, some bad, and some with no agenda at all. It's what that darkness means to you and what you do with it yourself that matters most.'

Talemir's throat constricted, and he blinked rapidly up at the stars. He hadn't realised just how badly he'd needed to hear something like that.

'You're rather wise for a ranger,' he managed, choking back the emotion.

'So I've been told.'

THEY LEFT at dawn the next day. Whatever moment they had shared in the hot springs had passed and Talemir was still fighting the loss of it.

Am I the monster or the man to her? he wondered, stealing glances at Drue when she wasn't looking. He drank deeply from his tonic, deciding he would settle for her company, or so he told himself as they continued their ride south, Terrence flying overhead.

'There's no sign of Gus or the others this way,' she was saying, scanning the surrounding lands.

'Did you expect there to be?' he asked.

'Not really. I wondered if Dratos might have found a means to leave clues in their wake, but it was a fool's hope. What do you sense?'

The wraiths left no tracks in the earth, no trail of darkness in the sky. Not even the nauseating scent of burnt hair lingered in the air. A part of him was relieved, but he had promised Drue he would help her find her friends, find the lair... And that meant reaching into the part of himself that he tried so hard to bury deep.

Talemir straightened in his saddle and centred himself, breathing in, trying to discern the distinct scents and energies around them. When he concentrated, he could feel them – in the far distance, but they were there: the wraiths. They had a presence about them. They left a mark on the realm, a stain he could sense even from a great range. He hated it, hated that he knew that about them.

It made him undeniably one of them.

'We keep heading south,' he told Drue, gripping his reins tighter than he meant to.

'You're sure?'

He didn't want to admit it, but he did. 'Yes.'

'Do you think... Do you think they're alive? Gus and the others?' she asked.

He saw the terror in her eyes, and wished with all his heart that he could soothe her, reassure her. But it was not in his nature to lie, not after he had become living proof of the horrors the wraiths inflicted upon humankind. And he was a *Warsword*. What hope did a young boy have? Or even a grown ranger of Naarva? Though it had crossed his mind that there might be others like him, he knew the folk from the watchtower didn't fit the bill. But those thoughts wouldn't help Drue.

'I don't know,' he said instead. 'The wraiths I have dealt with in the past aren't known for taking prisoners.'

'You think they're lost to the darkness, then?'

'I couldn't say. I hope not. And I will help you find them, one way or another.'

Drue seemed to gather herself before giving him a stiff nod. 'Thank you.'

'Onwards, then?' he asked gently.

'Onwards,' she agreed.

DAYS PASSED. Both the conversation and the silence between Warsword and ranger were comfortable, companionable, but Talemir did not seek her touch, as much as he longed for it. Especially as the further south they travelled, the more Talemir's skin crawled. He didn't know if it was because they were drawing nearer to the supposed wraith lair, or because, slowly but surely, the darkest night of the month crept closer – and with it, his uncontrollable change. Judging by the position of the moon, it was only a short matter of time before it was upon him and he tore apart whatever fragile friendship and trust he'd built with Drue.

He made several attempts to tell her what would occur when the moon failed to show, but he couldn't get the words out, no matter how many times he reminded himself that she'd called his wings beautiful. She hadn't so much as touched him since, so despite her reassurances, he knew she was holding back, knew there was some lingering fear or horror that kept her at bay.

And yet, she made him laugh. She teased him and then got riled up when he teased her back, which often resulted in her spluttering some nonsensical insult before she burst out laughing. The sound was a melody to him, full of vibrant notes he wished he could take with him whenever the darkness truly claimed him.

Of course, he told her none of this.

· · ·

As the beginning of another dusk bloomed on the horizon, Talemir found himself in a sickeningly familiar setting. A circle of white stone columns cast long shadows across the withered grass, and a thousand memories rushed to the forefront of his mind.

Islaton.

Screams pierced the night. The scent of burnt hair and the metallic tang of blood as it spilt upon the stone filled his nostrils. Talemir rasped a breath and suddenly he was back amid the carnage, the wraiths closing in and Malik fighting at his side.

'Glory in death, immortality in legend,' Malik murmured in his ear as they charged towards the enemy. He had said those words on many occasions before, usually on the precipice of battle, but none as bleak as this. Never before had that phrase seemed so imminent, such a likely outcome.

All around them, wraiths shrieked and carved through their Warsword brothers, talons flashing, blood spurting.

A giant monster, perhaps ten feet tall, swept Malik from the ground as though he were a rag doll, not an enormous man in his own right. The wraith slammed him face-first into the stone, a horrific crack sounding upon impact.

Talemir cried out, lunging towards his friend.

Gone was that ruggedly handsome face, in its place, a bloody pulp —

But Talemir was suddenly kicking the air as he too was lifted. He flailed against the death grip, struggled still as the creature pinned him to a rock —

He strained against its hold, desperate to go to Malik, or at least stop Wilder from seeing him like this —

But what gripped him was no ordinary shadow wraith. It was bigger, horned, and worse in every way imaginable. He had never seen one in the flesh before. Only heard whispers of what they were...

Rheguld reapers.

The sires of the shadow wraiths.

Kings of darkness.

They thirsted for power.

And this one had found his.

Talons pierced his chest, tiny pricks of pain at first, then a blazing agony as those talons penetrated his flesh, reaching into his body as though he were nothing but mist and shadow himself.

Talemir screamed as terror and talons alike latched around his heart. The fear was not of death, never of death – Warswords knew better than to fear Enovius. But Talemir was afraid what might await him in its place: a life of darkness.

Wilder's nearby shout of fury drew the wraith's attention away.

Talemir fell to the ground on his hands and knees, blood trickling from a star-shaped pattern over his heart.

But it was too late.

He could feel the onyx power in his bones.

'Talemir?'

Talemir blinked rapidly, finding himself panting, his palms resting against rust-coloured stone.

'Talemir?' Drue said again, approaching him on foot, her hawk perched on her shoulder.

Struggling to swallow, his throat tightened painfully, as though his screams from the past were still lodged there. He couldn't remember dismounting and leaving his stallion on the outskirts of the circular monument. He couldn't remember anything but the horror.

Heart hammering, still dazed, he looked to where his hands rested now.

The rusted colour beneath his fingertips was old blood. There was no mistaking it. He and Malik and a dozen of their Warsword brothers had all bled at Islaton. All had lost someone or something that day.

'I get them too...' Drue said quietly at his side.

'What?' Talemir croaked.

'Flashbacks. Suddenly I'm not here, I'm back there, back where everything changed.' She pressed her own palm to the stone by Talemir's hand. 'This is where it happened to you.'

'Yes...' Talemir managed, not trusting himself to say anything more.

'You didn't deserve it,' Drue said.

'It happened anyway.'

'The worst things always do.' She inched her hand towards his until her fingertips brushed against his skin, until her warmth closed around him and offered comfort.

'How long have I been here?'

'A little while. I thought it best not to disturb you... Sometimes... sometimes that only makes it worse.'

'It does,' Talemir agreed. 'But I apologise, I didn't realise —'

Drue shook her head. 'It's not in your control. It's not your fault. Adrienne tells me the same thing every time it happens to me.'

Talemir stopped himself from reaching for her, his chest tightening at the thought of her suffering the same torment. 'Where do you go? When it happens to you?'

'To the night my brothers and mother were slain,' she replied without hesitation.

'By the wraiths.'

'Yes.'

Talemir bowed his head. He had seen her reaction back at the watchtower and had known then that she had suffered horrors of her own. His heart ached for her, wishing he could take that torment away.

'What's done is done.' She nudged him with her elbow. 'Now, shall we get the fuck out of this place? It's making my skin crawl.'

'Your best idea yet.'

Talemir's hands were still shaking as he mounted his stallion, but he let Drue lead, understanding that she was giving him the space to process what he'd just relived. He was grateful for that, for flashes of Malik's swollen and bloodied face swam in his vision and Wilder's shouts rang in his ears.

Briefly, his mind took him back to Thezmarr in the weeks that had followed that horrific event. When Malik's dimly lit quarters had smelt of potent potions and despair. When he'd been unable to feed himself, unable to walk. It had almost been too much to bear, to watch the mighty warrior struggle to lift his spoon, his spirit as broken as his skull. He hadn't uttered a single word since.

Sipping once more from his tonic, Talemir wondered if there would ever come a day where those memories didn't haunt him so deeply.

DRUE HALTED where dark water lapped the shore, a rickety pier jutting out from the black sand.

'The Strait of Enovius.' She motioned to the shimmer of land within sight beyond the sea.

'Named for the god of death?' Talemir said dryly.

'We've faced worse, Warsword,' Drue replied, a note of challenge in her voice. Terrence took that as his signal to launch from her shoulder and fly over the stretch of water.

'You're not wrong there.' He scanned the pier. 'So... how do we go about this?'

Drue watched the hawk disappear into the distance. 'There used to be a ferryman.'

'And now?'

'Now there's just a raft.' She gestured to the watercraft bumping against the wharf.

It was as basic as it got: a floating platform made of logs fastened with rope, a rudimentary rudder at the rear. There was a mast in the middle and a ragged scrap of canvas tied to it. The sides were barely a foot high, certainly not tall enough to keep out water from lapping waves...

Talemir was more than sceptical. 'You know how to direct such a... vessel?'

'What choice do we have?' Drue raised a brow. 'Unless you'd rather swim?'

'I've heard stories of the sharks that swarm these waters...' Talemir surveyed the dragging current for circling fins.

'Oh, yes,' Drue replied. 'Plenty of sharks in the strait. They're said to be servants of Enovius, escorting souls to his gates...'

'Wonderful.' Warsword or not, Talemir didn't overly fancy being ripped apart limb from limb by a bunch of giant fish with dagger-like teeth.

Drue laughed. 'I'll get you across in one piece...'

'Don't act so blasé,' he warned. 'If things go wrong, I

suppose I could always fly. It'd be you left for the feeding frenzy.'

'Charming.'

'Just stating the facts. It'd be in your best interests to —'

'Oh, shut up. It's not like I'm loving the idea either. But the steel source and, to my knowledge, the wraiths' lair are on the other side of the strait. So we only have one choice, unless you decide you can fly us both across.'

Talemir clenched and unclenched his jaw.

Drue surveyed the raft with a critical gaze. 'I've seen it packed to the brim with refugees. It should hold us and the horses with no trouble.'

'They're not going to like that.'

'That makes four of us, then. You going to help or what?' Drue was already making her way down the dunes towards the strip of black sand between land and sea.

Seeing the raft up close did little to bolster Talemir's confidence in the idea. Even so, he wouldn't be the one to baulk from the challenge, apparently even if it meant that he, Drue and their mounts sank to the bottom of the strait or were devoured by the gnashing jaws of ravenous sharks.

The pair untied the vessel from its ropes and dragged it to the sandbank, the horses watching them warily. The sun had almost disappeared below the horizon entirely, leaving them to work in the soft orange glow.

'We should make it across before dark,' Drue said, as though reading his thoughts.

'You've done this before?'

'Not alone, but yes. Prior to and after the fall of the kingdom, I've crossed the Strait of Enovius many times, and the strait to its east, to get to the University of Naarva.'

'You studied there?' Talemir asked, shifting the raft into the shallows.

'No, but my mother did. She loved returning to its halls, its gardens... It was a beautiful place once. Besides Ciraun, it was the pride and joy of the kingdom of gardens.'

'I wish I could have seen it.'

Drue gave him a small smile. 'Shall we?' she asked, nodding to the waiting raft and the uneasy horses pawing the sand nearby.

Talemir held the watercraft in place while Drue convinced the poor creatures to board. They whinnied and snorted in protest, but eventually, they were ready.

Together, Talemir and Drue pushed the contraption beyond the icy break, and only once they were up to their waists in the tugging current did they haul themselves up into the raft.

'So far, so good...' Drue ventured, shielding her eyes from the last of the sun's rays as she looked at their destination.

'It's early days.' Talemir followed her gaze and tried not to think of the flimsy thing rocking beneath them, making his stomach lurch uncomfortably. Travelling by sea had never been one of his favourite modes of transportation. The disquiet of the miserable horses told him they felt the same way.

But there was nothing for it now. He watched as Drue brought the small sail down from the mast and positioned herself at the stern, where the poor excuse for a rudder stuck out into the water.

He hadn't realised he'd been toying with his sapphire until Drue spoke next.

'Whose jewel is that?' she asked, cheeks reddening.

He glanced down at the gem, running the pad of his thumb over its faceted design. 'Why?'

'No reason,' she said quickly, averting her eyes.

Talemir suppressed a smile. 'It was my mother's.'

A flicker of relief crossed the ranger's face, and that only made it harder for Talemir to keep his smile under wraps. She had been jealous...?

The raft lurched over a particularly strong set of waves and Talemir had to grip the low side and swallow his nausea.

Drue turned to him again. 'Is your mother still alive?'

'Yes, actually. She survived the fall of Delmira. She got our family out of there before... before it all went to shit.'

'Where is she now?'

'The last I heard, she was on her way to Aveum. She had distant relatives there.'

'You don't stay in touch?'

'The life of a Warsword isn't one of regular visits and correspondence. The guild becomes your family. Thezmarr becomes your home. My mother always understood that, supported me.'

'Why the jewel?'

Talemir huffed a fond laugh at the memory, a conversation with his mother he had been too young to fully understand at the time...

'I wanted her to come to Thezmarr with me. I worried for her safety on the road. I worried about a hundred things when I thought of her on her own... She gave me a sad smile before handing me this —' Talemir wiggled the sapphire at Drue. 'The person who gave it to her was someone she had been very fond of long ago... For whatever reason, they too had needed to leave, and had told her... *Sometimes, to love someone, we have to let them go.* And that sometimes, *in order to go where we need to, we must turn away from one path, onto another...'*

'That's all very philosophical,' Drue said slowly.

'I suppose. But she told me that one day I would understand, and that when I did, I should pass the gem onto someone else who needed to learn the lesson for themselves.'

A chilly wind tore through the channel, the raft bobbing along the current, making Talemir queasy and desperate to distract himself. So he grinned at Drue. 'You thought it was a lover's jewel, didn't you? A gift declaring lifelong love or something like that...'

'I did not.'

Talemir's grin only widened. 'Liar.'

Drue scowled. 'So what if I did? It doesn't mean anything.'

'Doesn't it?' Talemir teased, tucking the sapphire back down the front of his shirt. 'I'd say that means you —'

'Don't even finish that sentence, Warsword. We've got a long journey ahead of us still and I won't have you —' Drue cut herself off, her gaze snapping to the waves just beyond their raft. 'Did you see that?' There was a tremor in her voice.

Talemir whirled around. There was nothing but black waves.

'Tell me you're messing with me?' he said quietly.

Her eyes were wide. 'I wish I was.'

Then he saw it: two fins emerging, breaking the surface. Sharks.

And he saw why. In the wake of their raft was a distinct trail of red. Drue's mare was bleeding from a cut on its back leg, the blood trickling slowly but steadily onto the floor of the raft and into the water behind them.

'Fuck,' he murmured. 'That's practically a beacon...'

Drue blanched as she spotted it. 'We're going as fast as the wind and current will take us, but the steering on this thing isn't overly sophisticated.'

'It's alright,' Talemir breathed, keeping calm. 'They can't —'

Something knocked against the underside of the raft.

'Shit,' Drue muttered, clutching the rudder. 'Stay in the centre.'

But Talemir wasn't looking at the centre. He was looking at the now countless pointed fins emerging from the sea's depths, scenting the blood in the water and circling the feeble raft, investigating the generous fare aboard. The hair on the back of Talemir's neck stood up as he judged the distances between their boat and the shore on either side. Both were too great.

He grabbed the horses' reins and attempted to soothe them. Both were on the verge of rearing up and capsizing the whole vessel. But with so many sharks circling them, the seas were even rougher than before and their raft rocked violently atop the waves.

'Fuck, Talemir...' Drue visibly swallowed her fear. 'Now's the time where you could fly away. I wouldn't blame you —'

Talemir went to her and clasped his hands over hers. 'I like the sound of my name on your lips too much for that, Wildfire.'

A flash of relief filled her eyes. 'So what then?'

Talemir raked his fingers through his hair, tension roiling off him as he ran through their options, each one more useless than the last. He suppressed the urge to pace, aware that with each second that passed, danger lurked closer and closer. Those countless razor-sharp teeth were near enough that he could see the bits of gore from previous kills between them.

There was only one option. And as loath as he was to try it, he wouldn't be the reason they perished in the strait.

'I need you to trust me,' he said to Drue, fighting to keep his voice even.

'What? What do you —'

'Drue.' Talemir held her chin between his fingers and lifted her face to his. 'I need you to trust me. I know I'm a monster, but at this moment... Can you do that? Can you trust me?'

The little colour remaining in Drue's cheeks drained, but she took a breath and nodded.

That was all Talemir needed to see before he closed his eyes and sought the darkness. He reached into himself, searching for that familiar tug, that cyren song.

But while it usually simmered close to the surface, now, it was nowhere in reach.

The boat rocked beneath him.

He heard the smack of a fin against its side.

For fuck's sake. He ground his teeth and cursed silently, digging deep for that tether of obsidian, for the whisper that so often tried to lure the beast from within.

Nothing.

Where the fuck was his magic when he needed it?

There was another loud thud, this time at the raft's other side. Water splashed aboard.

'Talemir...' Drue warned.

But Talemir didn't open his eyes. Furies damn him, he was going to get them out of this mess; he had to —

Focusing, he drew on every fucking moment where his curse had surged forth in a heartbeat out of his control, where he had been on the brink of bursting into night itself. He thought of

Drue in his chambers, baiting him into the shift. He thought of the hot springs, his wings spearing through his back. Each memory slammed into him, the impact powerful, tangible.

He may not have mastered his change, but in this moment, he would bend the darkness to his will.

This time, when he called, the shadows came.

And when Talemir opened his eyes, wisps of that onyx power surrounded them. Ribbons of it poured from his fingertips, lashing at any creatures that got too close to the raft, defending them. His magic didn't touch Drue, didn't touch the horses.

It bowed to his command. It shielded them all from danger.

With a flick of his wrists, the threads of power dipped into the bloody water behind and propelled them forward.

And suddenly, the frenzy of sharks was in the distance and the gap between their watercraft and the next shore was closing in fast.

Wind whipped through Talemir's hair, but he didn't break his focus until he felt the sand bank scrape along the bottom of the raft. There, he leapt into the shallows and began to drag the vessel onto shore, his magic flickering out like a candle in a breeze.

He could feel Drue's eyes on him, but he wasn't sure he was ready to face her. She'd given him her trust, given him permission, but that had been before she'd seen him use his power. He heard her jump into the sand. He heard the horses gratefully lurching from the raft onto sturdy ground, and still, he couldn't look, scared of what he might see staring back at him.

But as he fitted his boot to the stirrup and reached for the saddle horn to swing himself atop his stallion, a hand closed over his.

Slowly, he turned to Drue.

It was not fear on her face, but something else simmering behind those blue eyes.

'Thank you,' she said, her voice barely a whisper. 'How did you do it?'

Talemir ran his thumb over the back of her hand, her skin cold from the water, and met her gaze. 'Someone told me there are all kinds of darkness in this world. And that it's what you do with it yourself that matters most.'

A smile broke across that beautiful face. 'She sounds brilliant.'

'She's a pain in the arse, mostly.' Talemir answered her with a grin of his own as he dared to tuck a loose strand of hair behind her ear. 'But she has her moments.'

Drue laughed deeply, and to Talemir, there was no sound more exquisite.

II
DRUE

Drue couldn't stop stealing glances at the shadow-wielding warrior as they rode through the night. Talemir Starling had stayed with her when he could have left her to her death. His power had saved them from a terrible fate, had saved *her*. She could still feel the gentle imprint of his fingers gripping her chin as he stared into her eyes and asked her to trust him.

And gods, she had.

She had trusted a shadow wraith.

The truth of it had her reeling. As did that second touch between them, where he'd tucked her hair behind her ear, his fingertips brushing the side of her face ever so gently.

But he hadn't pulled her to him. He hadn't leant in to kiss her again. As much as she'd wanted him to, her heart hammering mercilessly. His kisses in the hot springs had been a searing brand upon her lips that she'd never forget, that she never wanted to. Only he hadn't touched her since.

The intensity of how much she wanted him scared her. For

it was no dark magic of his that toyed with her desires. It came purely from within – a force she needed to reckon with on her own.

THE NEXT MORNING, they reached the Naarvian steel source. After leaving their horses to graze nearby, she brought Talemir right to the edge, and together they stared into the layered crater in the earth. Drue had seen it many times before throughout her travels, but each time its vastness struck her anew. In the early sunlight, numerous colours sparkled from the tiers of rock within the pit that yawned deep into the ground. Though at first glance it looked like a site of destruction, the banded formation of earth appeared as a spectrum of hues – beautiful.

'Here it is,' she announced to the warrior at last. 'The source of your Warsword steel... It's said that the Furies themselves sent the star shower that caused it to open up in the ground...'

Looking at the crater now, she felt the weight of the sword strapped to her back, the sword she shouldn't have in her possession at all.

Talemir peered into the source. 'Where are the workers? The miners?'

'Have you not noticed the state of our kingdom?' she asked, frowning. 'They come when they have to, when your brothers back at Thezmarr need more weapons. Which is rarely, seeing as there are so few of them now.'

Talemir shot her a look of surprise.

Drue folded her arms over her chest, glancing up as Terrence flew overhead, scouting for any signs of danger. 'You think the forge master's daughter wouldn't know that fewer and fewer Warswords are surviving the Great Rite? I'm well aware that Wilder Hawthorne was the last to pass.'

Talemir made a noncommittal noise in his throat.

'In any case,' Drue said, 'the source is actually an iron quarry, where workers mine ore which is then smelted back at the forge and turned into steel for weapons. But as I mentioned, there's not much of that going on nowadays, even since before the fall of Ciraun. The royal family, before they disappeared, decreed that drawing attention to the source was dangerous, that the wraiths might discover that the work being done here could lead to their downfall. So the mining was officially shut down. Certain parts of it are only carried out every few seasons. If at all.'

Talemir stared at her.

She met his gaze. 'Do you believe me? That there is nothing untoward going on here? No one is sabotaging the source or its magical properties.'

He blinked.

'Surely this proves that I'm certainly not guilty of treason? Whatever lies you've been told, whatever additional strength the guild claims the wraiths have... I don't know anything about it.'

'Then what of your cuff? What is the magic or trickery there? You cannot tell me it's not Naarvian steel.'

'It is. But...' Drue's chest seized. She had trusted him amid shark-infested waters; she had trusted the ribbons of dark power pouring from him. Perhaps... perhaps she could trust him with this, too. Her hand went to her wrist, and she unclasped the cuff, offering it to him on her outstretched palm.

'It has nothing to do with the source. It's an experiment. One I carried out back in Ciraun. I forged it myself, treated it...

It senses when wraiths are near. Here,' she said at last, waiting for him to take it.

Tentatively, he did, only to drop it with a shout of pain, his skin scalded. 'What the fuck?'

The steel circlet rolled across the ground before Drue retrieved it, frowning. 'It burned you?'

Talemir showed her his blistered fingers. 'You tell me.'

'There is no magic or trickery. No *treason*.' She refastened it with a frown. 'Just flowers.'

'Flowers? You mean to tell me that the way to detect a wraith, to apparently *burn* one, is through... flowers?'

'In a way, yes. This was the kingdom of gardens, after all.'

Talemir stared at the cuff as though he didn't believe her.

'It's a particular type: a sun orchid,' Drue continued. 'My mother and my brother, Leif, told me about them, how rare they were. Then I discovered a patch of them, when I was fighting a wraith south of here. I saw it happen before my very eyes: a chemical reaction between these flowers that love the daylight, and the wraith's darkness... When the monster came into contact with the bloom, it reared back, like it had been burned... and the flower... Well, it moved, as much as it could, as though to veer away.'

Talemir looked up.

'When I'm in your presence, the cuff warms against my skin,' Drue told him. 'Not with the same force it does when true wraiths approach, like at the watchtower, like at the northern perimeter... That is far more intense. A dire warning.'

'And what did you do exactly? To the cuff?'

'I treated the steel with the essence of the sun orchids, just to see what would happen.'

'How?'

'I made an extract... and when I smelted the steel, I put the extract in the cooling tank.'

'So you *did* meddle.'

'Not with the source. Not in the way you accused me of.'

'No...' he replied quietly.

'The patch of flowers I used to treat this cuff is no longer there. I have been scouting for more of the same on my patrols ever since, to no avail.'

'What would you do if you found more?'

'Grow as many of them as possible. Coat every weapon possible. Spread as much of it around the midrealms as possible.'

'You think it's that powerful?'

'My cuff was the most successful of several experiments. Leif carried them out before me. I refined his work, but without a source of flowers, I can't continue.'

'Do you think the extract needs to be applied when forging weapons, or —?'

'No. I think it could be done to existing blades.'

'Interesting.'

'It would be, were there another field of sun orchids.' Drue tugged on his sleeve and led him down into one of the top levels of the mine. 'Come on.'

Together, they explored the crater and the layers of iron ore within. Drue showed him that there was no evidence of outside interference, that in fact, the quarry had been untouched for some time.

An hour passed, and Drue turned to Talemir as he rubbed the back of his neck with a grimace.

'What is it?' she asked.

Talemir sighed, shaking his head at the sight of the mine. 'Well, you've shown me that our troubles aren't related to the source of the steel. We assumed someone was poisoning it, sabotaging the mother source so all our blades were affected. But now I know that's not the case... it means one thing: that the wraiths are simply growing stronger... It's not our blades that have changed, it's the monsters.' He pinched the bridge of his nose. 'Our quests have become one and the same. I need to find out what's happening with the wraiths and how we can defeat them. Thezmarr and the midrealms depend on it.'

'So we continue on, then,' Drue replied. 'I promised Adrienne I would find Gus and the rest of our people. I mean to keep that promise.'

Talemir nodded, looking shaken.

As they made their way back to their horses, Drue nudged him. 'Can I ask you something?'

Talemir raised a suspicious brow, but inclined his head in permission.

'Why did you become a Warsword?'

The warrior huffed a dark laugh. 'To fight the monsters threatening the midrealms... The irony isn't lost on me, I assure you.'

'But why?'

'My family hailed from the outskirts of Delmira. I was there as a child when it fell. As I told you, my mother got us out, but I saw the devastation for myself. Told myself I'd do anything to keep the horror at bay. We failed, I know. When it mattered most, we failed.'

Drue swallowed a thick lump in her throat. She didn't try to correct him. She'd given her thoughts on the matter too passionately in the past to comfort him now.

'What did your family do? Before the fall?' she asked instead.

Talemir gave her a sad smile. 'They were farmers.'

'Farmers?'

He nodded. 'Does that surprise you? Can't you imagine me milking cows and rounding up sheep?'

'Was that what you did?'

'Not exactly, no. But it was a simple life. A quieter life than one of blood and steel and chaos.'

'Do you regret it?'

Talemir locked eyes with her. 'Never.'

'Even though it has led to so much heartache?' she pressed.

'It led me to you.'

Warmth suddenly radiated throughout Drue's body, flushing her chest, her cheeks. 'Oh.'

Talemir laughed softly. 'Does that sentiment surprise you?'

Drue stared at him for a heartbeat longer, her heart swelling, her pulse racing. She didn't know what to say, didn't know what to do besides suppress the urge to kiss him that roared within.

'There's an abandoned miner's village down there.' She forced a casual note into her tone. 'We can clean up and find some supplies.'

Talemir paused for a moment, as if he wanted to say something else, but instead, the Warsword mounted his stallion. 'Sounds good.'

IT DIDN'T TAKE LONG to reach the small town below the steel source. As with most places in Naarva, it was completely abandoned – no sign of recent life.

Feeling rattled by what the Warsword had said, Drue insisted she wished to wash in the nearby stream alone.

Shouldering her pack, she handed her reins to Talemir and left him outside an old apothecary.

'I won't be long,' she told him, and rushed off, craving the much-needed solitude to unpack everything that had come to pass since Talemir Starling had stepped foot into her kingdom.

Drue had been to this village before with Adrienne, so she knew there was freshwater close to the town square. She headed there in a daze, with Terrence flying low in front of her. Oddly, the hawk had kept his distance since his injury, but he seemed very much recovered.

Thankfully, the brook still flowed generously and Drue stripped off her outer layers when she reached its banks. Bathing in the hot springs felt like a lifetime ago now and she was sorely in need of a clean set of clothes and a decent wash.

The water was icy, but she braved it anyway, wading up to her knees in her undergarments. There, as she scrubbed away the grime of her journey, she tried to piece together what she felt for the Warsword, attempting to separate that from the memory of his hands on her body, his mouth on hers.

And then those great wings spearing from his muscular back.

How had things got so tangled between them? When she had met him, when her cuff had warmed against her skin and exposed what he truly was, all she had wanted was to carve out his black heart.

But now...

'*It led me to you*,' he had said, his rich-timbred voice full of sincerity.

Drue splashed water on her face, trying to find the voice of reason that usually sounded in her mind during times of peril. She had survived this long in a fallen kingdom full of shadow wraiths because of it... But it was silent now. The only thing she could hear was the thundering of her own heart at the thought of Talemir Starling —

A branch snapped.

And Drue paused before she turned around, gathering her courage to face the Warsword who had undone her so thoroughly.

'I think I was hoping you would join me...' she murmured.

But somewhere nearby, Terrence shrieked in warning.

Drue whirled on her heels to find a stranger leering at her, brandishing a rusted sword. 'Is that so, princess?' he taunted, taking a step towards her.

Drue's heart seized. She'd left her weapons on the stream bank.

Terrence made a nosedive for the man, who flung his blade at the hawk in a panic.

'Terrence, no!' Drue called. She couldn't bear the thought of her feathered friend getting injured again. Surprisingly, the bird obeyed, beating his wings furiously and flying off towards the town.

'Where were we, princess?' the prick jeered, advancing as his eyes roamed over her exposed skin and undergarments. 'I think you were asking me to join you...'

Drue's lip curled, and she clenched her fists, readying to fight as she scanned her surroundings for anything she could use against him —

There!

Long fronds of pond weed grew at the stream's edge. And that was more than weapon enough for her. Without a moment's hesitation, she lunged for it.

The man laughed as water sprayed.

But by the time the sound had left his lips, Drue had two pieces like ropes in her hands.

She used the first to disarm him, wrapping it in a blur around his sword arm and pulling the sorry excuse for a blade from his unsuspecting grasp.

'Bitch!' he shouted as the grass also lacerated his skin.

But Drue was already moving, the stream surging about her legs as she closed the gap between her and her opponent.

He'd expected her to be a cowering damsel.

But she was no such thing.

She wrapped the pond weed around his throat.

Once. Twice. Thrice.

And then she squeezed.

Ignoring his hands trying to claw at her face, Drue held her ground as the man thrashed beneath her hold, fighting for breath.

That little voice at the back of her mind came to life once more, told her she should at least question the bastard as to where he'd come from and how many others there were, but as Drue felt the life draining from him, she also felt justice being served. For there was no mistaking that look in his eyes, no mistaking what he'd intended for her, and for that alone, he deserved to die.

And so Drue strangled him in the shallows of the stream with a piece of pond weed.

12

TALEMIR

Talemir sensed the raiders almost as soon as Drue had left, and within seconds, a group of ten were upon him. For a moment he was almost insulted that they thought they were in with a chance against him, but then he'd seen one of them sneak off to follow Drue and he'd lost his shit.

He didn't need his wraith form to obliterate them.

But he used it anyway.

Their eyes bulged as they beheld the half-Warsword, half-wraith before them, his heavy wings appearing at his back and blocking out the sun behind him. Unsheathing his talons, he cleaved through the raiders without a second thought, their screams like a choir echoing through the village.

He wrought his shadow magic upon them, forcing them to their knees with leashes of dark power, compelling them to face their worst nightmares.

When they were quivering messes before him, some tried to run. He even let them get a few yards before he slayed them

163

with a single swing of his sword. The swirling mass of obsidian did the rest of his bidding, lashing and restraining each of the raiders until it was their turn to die.

Talemir cut them down, one by one.

When it was over, he sheathed his talons, his wings and shadows vanishing, and then he raced after Drue, Terrence leading the way from above.

He arrived just in time to see her drop a raider's body into the brook, his bug-eyed face purple, a frond of grass tight around his bleeding neck.

Standing in her undergarments, utterly soaked through, Drue looked up and gave him a wild grin. 'Add pond weed to the unusual kills list.'

Talemir didn't think; he simply moved, surging into the water and wrapping his arms around her tightly.

She was rigid with surprise at first, but then she relaxed into his embrace, resting her head against his chest, sagging against him.

'You're alright?' he asked in a whisper, glancing across at the body that now floated downstream.

'Never better. You?'

'Fine,' he murmured into her hair, quietly breathing in the lilac-and-heather scent of her, savouring every inch where their bodies touched.

The moment was over too soon when Drue broke away from him, trudging through the shallows to snatch up her clothes. It was only then that Talemir realised just how exposed she was... The thin white fabric of her undergarments clung to the curves and hollows of that glorious body, her nipples peaked beneath the transparent material. The delicate tattoo on her shoulder blade was bared once more, and Talemir felt himself stirring.

Gods, what he wouldn't give to peel those final layers away and taste her, to run his fingers across her soft skin.

Talemir averted his gaze. The last thing he wanted was for Drue to think he was a pervert as well as a monster.

He heard the rustling of her clothes and the quiet cursing as she shucked on her pants over wet legs. It took every ounce of willpower not to turn around, not to close the gap between them and take her in his arms again.

'Who were they?' he asked instead.

'Raiders, bandits... Naarvians who would turn against their own people. Scum.' Drue picked up her pack at the water's edge and started back towards the town square.

Their horses were waiting for them by an empty fountain and Talemir took up their reins as he followed Drue. 'You're familiar with their lot?'

'Not that man in particular —' She stopped in her tracks as she reached the heap of bodies outside the apothecary. 'Furies save us...' She turned to Talemir. 'You did this?'

'Yes.'

Drue nodded, crouching by the nearest corpse and rifling through his pockets. Ever the pragmatist.

'We took them by surprise,' she said, sifting through a handful of weathered parchment. 'But they usually plan their attacks. We've had reports that groups like these rally all over Naarva, preying on the weakened communities in hiding and offering them to the wraiths as sacrifices.'

Talemir set about sorting through the belongings of the rest, pocketing weapons and supplies along the way. The dead men were armed, but not with quality blades – many of them were rusted and ill cared for – and the rations in their packs were stale.

'Look at this,' Drue said, snatching his attention back.

From one body, she pulled a folded, battered piece of parchment – a map, covered in a messy scrawl of notes.

'What does it say?' Talemir asked.

Drue chewed her bottom lip as she considered it. 'It's directions to a stronghold... And...'

'And?'

'And plans to attack and kidnap inhabitants of a local shelter...'

'How far is it?' Talemir said at once. 'We can go there now, stop them before —'

But Drue was shaking her head. 'Not based on these numbers. We'll need a bigger force. As deadly as you are, Warsword, not even you can take out an entire stronghold.'

'Then what is it you suggest, Wildfire?'

The corner of Drue's mouth twitched, as though she may have been tempted to smile at the nickname. But she remained focused on the raider's plans. 'We send word with Terrence to the citadel, to Adrienne and my father... Our Naarvian units and your Warsword apprentice can join forces with us here, and we can attack the raiders' stronghold and rescue the people they've captured. It's even possible Gus and our watchtower guards are with them.'

'So you want to wait? Won't it take them too long?'

'Unlike us, Adrienne has the option to use the Ciraunian ships. They're in working order. If she travels by the seas and straits, and if the winds are kind, they'll be here in a matter of days.'

'Right.'

'In the meantime, you and I can scout the area.'

'Sounds like you've got it all figured out.'

Another half-smile. 'Perhaps I do.' She rummaged through her pack and, to Talemir's surprise, fished out a small pot of ink and a battered-looking quill. 'Turn around, will you?'

'What?'

She approached him and gripped his arms, physically turning him so he faced away from her.

'If you'd be so kind as to crouch a tad,' she added, pressing a piece of parchment across the breadth of his back.

Talemir almost laughed at the absurdity of it as Drue made quick work of penning a missive to Adrienne, using him as a desk.

'You couldn't have used one of the many walls?' he asked. 'Or found a table in one of these old workshops?'

'But you were right here,' she replied, the quill scratching against the surface of the parchment.

Talemir didn't know why, but it made him smile.

When Drue was done, she rolled up her message and whistled for Terrence. The hawk swooped down from where he had been perched on a rafter and patiently waited for his master to tie the scroll to his fully healed leg.

Talemir watched the bird, whose yellow-eyed stare didn't seem so angry anymore.

Drue stroked his feathers fondly. 'Take this to Adrienne at the citadel, no one else. Understand?'

Terrence gave her an affectionate peck on the finger before launching himself skyward.

'We should move the bodies,' Talemir said, nose wrinkling in distaste.

Drue nodded, and together they hauled the dead raiders out of plain sight, eventually pushing them into the mouth of the main river to be swept away.

Drue faced Talemir and the horses. 'I don't know about you, but after all this, I could use a stiff drink.'

'My apologies, but I'm all out of fire extract.'

Drue grinned. 'Luckily, I know a place.'

The beautiful Naarvian ranger was full of surprises, and as she led Talemir through the abandoned miners' town with such purpose, he appreciated her all the more.

First, they unsaddled the horses and cooled them down. 'Let them wander to graze and water themselves,' Talemir said. 'They won't go far.'

Drue murmured her agreement, and they watched as the Tverrian stallion and Naarvian mare made for the stream.

'You said something about a drink?' Talemir asked, turning back to the ranger.

'I did indeed, Warsword. This way.'

Drue brought them to a stop outside a large building, where white stones and wooden beams crafted the face of the tavern's structure. It was impossible to see through the boarded-up windows, but Talemir could imagine the raucous sounds and music that might have once sounded from within. He took in the sight with a pang of longing. The last time he'd been to such an establishment was with Malik to celebrate Wilder passing the Great Rite. There had been countless toasts to him becoming one of them, becoming a Warsword. Talemir's chest tightened. The three of them would never have such an evening again.

Regret surged, but upon seeing the rustic sign swinging in the breeze, Talemir stared in disbelief.

The Dancing Badger.

'What is it?' Drue asked, her brow furrowed.

Talemir pointed to the sign. 'If I couldn't see it with my own eyes, I don't think I'd believe it, but you've just brought me to the sister tavern of the one my warrior brothers and I used to frequent in Harenth...'

'What makes you say that?'

'The one in Harenth is called The Laughing Fox. And it's known for connecting a network of taverns all over the midrealms... I've never visited or known the name of the branch in Naarva. But here we are, it seems...'

'You're fond of the place in Harenth, then?' Drue asked, taking two steps at a time and reaching for the heavy wooden door.

'Very much so. I've shared some good memories with people there.'

'Beautiful women and brawls?' Drue quipped with a smirk.

'Wouldn't you like to know, Wildfire?'

The door creaked loudly as Drue pushed it open and let them inside.

Dirt and dust covered the stone floor, and a great cold hearth lay at the centre. In each corner was a generous booth, the sort of place Talemir imagined he, Malik and Wilder would pass hours and hours drinking and playing cards. Dark timber beams lined the ceilings, and iron chandeliers hung low over long tables below. Across the surfaces were discarded plates, cups and empty bottles, while the bar itself had clearly been ransacked.

'How do you expect there to be a drop left in this place with raiders scouring the town?' Talemir asked, his boots crunching atop broken ceramic pieces.

'Your friend Marise is not the only fierce protector of his supplies. My father told me long ago that the owner, Palmer, kept particular things under lock and key... In a secret cellar in addition to the trade one, to be precise. Wait here.'

Talemir stared after Drue as she ducked behind the bar and disappeared below ground. While she was gone, he sipped from his tonic and looked around, noticing that great barrels lined the outskirts of the room and the walls were packed with rows of painted portraits in mismatching frames.

Recognition flaring, Talemir approached one in the middle and shook his head once more in disbelief. For there was the familiar face of Albert, the barman and owner of The Laughing Fox in Harenth.

'What's your poison, Warsword?' Drue's voice sounded.

Talemir turned to find her holding several bottles. 'How in the realms did you manage to find those?'

Drue gave him a secretive grin. 'That's for me to know,' she said. 'So, what'll it be?'

Talemir took up a stool opposite her, unable to stop his own smile from spreading across his face. 'I'll take whatever you give me.'

A blush stained Drue's cheeks at those words and Talemir's chest swelled at the sight. Gods, she was beautiful. She didn't even realise it.

'Mead it is.' Drue placed the bottles down and rolled out a half-barrel from somewhere behind her.

'We're going to drink all that?' Talemir raised a brow.

'Don't be ridiculous.' Drue rolled out another. 'This too.'

Talemir laughed deeply, watching as she hauled one up onto the bench and located two tankards, wiping them with the hem of her shirt before positioning the first below the wooden spigot.

Mead flowed freely at the turn of the tap and Talemir's mouth watered at the familiar smell. When both tankards were nearly overflowing with foaming mead, Drue pushed one over the bar to Talemir.

He raised his towards hers. 'To strong pond weed and resourceful rangers.'

'I'll drink to that.' She smiled and clinked her tankard against his.

Talemir drank deeply, a deep hum of appreciation sounding from the back of his throat as the cool mead washed over his tongue. It was a welcome relief, a distraction from all that had occurred these past few days. The truth about the steel source was still fresh in his mind: that it hadn't been tampered with, and that the wraiths were getting stronger all on their own. Drue's former lover, Coltan, had lied. And the Guild Master hadn't cross-examined anything before he'd given the order to Talemir. One question bothered Talemir more than all the rest... What if he'd charged into Ciraun as intended and killed her upon that order alone? The concept terrified him.

'Where'd you go just now?' Drue asked, smacking the foam from her lips with a satisfied sigh.

Talemir blinked at her, a lie poised on his tongue. But he found he didn't want to lie to her, didn't want any dishonesty between them. He drained the rest of his tankard. 'I drifted into the past for a minute there...'

'Oh.'

'But let's make sure that doesn't happen to either of us for the next little while. What do you say?'

'I say, how do you propose we do that?'

Talemir scanned the tavern, searching for inspiration. He found it hanging from the wall in the form of a dartboard. Gods, it had been an age since he'd played.

'Darts,' he told her, nodding to the circular target by a handful of portraits.

'What are the stakes?' Drue asked, refilling their drinks before jumping up and swinging her legs over the bar. She sat there, dangling her feet over the side, waiting expectantly.

Talemir considered this, scratching the stubble on his chin. 'At the end of each round, the winner can demand a prize from the loser.'

Drue raised a sceptical brow. 'Oh? And what sort of prizes are we demanding of one another, Warsword?'

Talemir chuckled. 'It can be anything. A truth, a dare, a question. An item of clothing...'

'Is that so?'

'Only if you're willing,' he replied, with a note of challenge.

'I'm willing to see you lose.' Drue jumped down and dislodged the darts from the board.

Talemir folded his arms over his chest, joy sparking within. 'You can certainly try.'

'How many rounds?'

'Three.'

'Five,' Drue countered.

'As you wish. Shall we play the common midrealms game? The closer you get to the centre target, the more points you acquire?'

'Works for me. Three throws at a time?'

Nodding, Talemir accepted the trio of darts she handed him before he motioned to the board. 'Ladies first.'

He stood at the side of the bar, drinking his freshly poured mead and watching as she lined herself up in front of the target and held her first dart between her thumb and forefinger, rocking back and forth on her toes slightly. For someone downing mead and throwing darts in an abandoned tavern, she still held herself with an almost regal posture.

'Don't miss,' Talemir teased her.

'Oh, I don't intend to...' Drue threw her darts in quick succession, each one landing closer and closer to the bullseye.

She turned on her heel, facing him with a smug expression. 'Worried?'

'You wish,' Talemir replied, taking up his place.

He wasted no time throwing his darts, but they landed on the outside of the target, one even missing completely, embedding in the wall beside it.

Drue let out a gleeful chuckle, and Talemir bit back his smile.

'Let's have it, then. What is it you demand of me for your first win?'

Drue surveyed him brazenly before folding her arms, her chin jutting out. 'Take off your shirt,' she ordered boldly.

Talemir's answering laugh vibrated through his whole chest and into his bones. *So she's playing offensive. I can handle that.* He'd been curious to see what path she'd take them down, given the first victory. Keeping his eyes on her, he reached for the back of his shirt and pulled it over his head, revealing his bare torso beneath.

'Interesting choice of prize, Wildfire,' he said, his voice low as he watched her hooded gaze rake down his chest and abdomen, her lips parting slightly. 'Does it please you?'

Despite her initial bravado, Drue's cheeks were tipped with pink, and though it could have been the mead, Talemir suspected it was more than that. He tensed, waiting for her reply, his body tingling under her attention, but she ignored his question, yanking the small arrows from the board and taking up her stance.

She threw again, and this time, when Talemir had his turn, he actually tried.

Drue looked from his perfectly landed darts back to him, frowning. 'You let me win the first round.'

'A gentleman never tells,' he said with a wink.

She let out a noise of frustration and swigged her drink.

'Don't tell me you're a sore loser?'

Drue rolled her eyes and put a hand on her hip. 'Go on, then. What's your prize?'

Talemir was enjoying this far too much. He leant against a stool and took a long, deliberate draught from his tankard, as though he needed all the time in the world to consider what he wanted. He let his gaze rove across her lazily, noting the colouring of her cheeks, the hitched breath caught in her chest. It wasn't just the mead she was responding to, that was for certain.

But instead of asking for a piece of clothing, he opted for something else, something that had been gnawing away at him ever since their first night in the tent together on the road from Ciraun.

'What does your tattoo mean?' he asked quietly.

Drue visibly baulked, clearly not expecting such a personal question amid their flirtation. But Talemir had realised that he wanted more than flirting. He wanted to know the fierce ranger who'd withstood so many storms...

For a moment it looked like Drue might object, but after she'd opened and closed her mouth several times, her hand drifted to her shoulder. 'It's my mother's favourite flower.' Her fingers slowly pulled the neck of her shirt aside to reveal the inked skin. 'Blue jasmine. There is a bloom for her, and one for each of my dead brothers...'

At her silent invitation, Talemir took a step towards her and bowed his head to get a closer look at her tattoo. The jasmine, complete with delicate petals and intricate leaves, had been inked in expert fine lines, creating a graceful artwork across Drue's shoulder blade.

Without thinking, Talemir traced it with his fingertips, finding Drue hot beneath his touch.

'It's beautiful,' he murmured.

Time slowed as they stood close enough that Talemir could see the goosebumps rushing over Drue's skin.

'I got it just after they died,' she said, tugging her shirt back over her shoulder.

'Would your mother have liked it?'

Drue laughed at that. 'Gods, no. She thought tattoos were for soldiers and sailors. But I think that's partly why I got it. Whenever I can't remember the finer details of her face, or the exact way she'd move through the gardens, I can always recall how she might scold me for getting such a permanent mark on my body.' Silver lined the ranger's eyes, but she blinked away her tears and squared her shoulders once more. 'Right, you've had your answer now, Warsword. Prepare for defeat.'

'Do your worst, Wildfire.'

She did, beating him fairly and with no sense of modesty whatsoever.

'Well?' he asked.

Drue's gaze scanned his bare chest again. 'I could make you play the rest of the game nude...'

'You could,' Talemir challenged, gracing her with the lazy smile he knew she found infuriating.

'But I won't.'

'No?'

'Not this time...' Drue caught her bottom lip between her teeth. 'Tell me about the best book you've read. Your favourite of all time.'

It was Talemir's turn to be surprised. He hadn't been expecting that one. He went to his pack by the door and produced a midnight-blue tome from the innermost pocket. It was different to the volume he'd allowed the others to tease him about on the way to the watchtower. This book was special. He handed it to Drue, suddenly feeling vulnerable.

She turned it over in her hands, running her fingers across the embossed title. 'What's it about?'

He met her gaze. 'It's about a maiden who falls in love with a beast.'

Her throat bobbed as she carefully thumbed its pages. 'Wishful thinking?'

Talemir didn't move. 'You tell me.'

'I'm no maiden,' she said quietly. 'But I'll wager there have been plenty who have fallen in love with you.'

'I'm not concerned with others.'

Her gaze shot up to his.

Talemir didn't flinch, didn't look away. He let her see him, and everything he desired. 'I don't want to play anymore...'

'Rules are rules,' Drue murmured. 'But perhaps... perhaps a sudden death?'

His whole body taut, Talemir threw each of his remaining darts, closing around the outer ring of the middle target. 'Your turn,' he managed.

Drue didn't break eye contact. Instead, she flung all three of her darts at once without so much as a glance at the board.

The soft thud of impact sounded, and Talemir stared in disbelief.

All of Drue's darts had hit the inner ring.

She'd won.

Talemir was hardly breathing. 'Well, victor... What is it that you want?'

Drue rested a callused palm against his bare chest. His heart thundered mercilessly beneath her touch as she looked up at him. 'Kiss me,' she said.

13
DRUE

The moment those words left Drue's lips, Talemir's mouth was on hers. He surged forward, his hand cupping the back of her head, his fingers toying with her hair as his huge frame enveloped her.

Her breathing hitched as his tongue swept against hers, eliciting a moan from deep within her.

That sound rumbling between them seemed to be Talemir's undoing, for any notion of restraint was destroyed as he lifted her bodily from the ground, her legs parting around him, his hands roaming to her backside before he slid her onto the bar. There, he pushed her back, settling between her thighs, his hard length straining against his pants, pushing against her.

He was ravenous, as though he had bottled every ounce of pent-up energy since the hot springs and was unleashing it upon her now. Drue felt the same way, and she answered his demanding kisses with fierce ones of her own, her lips crushing against his, her tongue exploring his mouth in a desperate frenzy.

More – she wanted *more* of this. She wanted more of *him*.

Her hands trailed down his muscular chest, tracing the scars around his heart, his skin blazing beneath her touch. His nipples hardened at the brush of her fingertips, a moan escaping him as she palmed his bulging cock through his pants.

'Wildfire,' he murmured, the name vibrating against her lips and skittering along her bones, sending a pulse of longing straight down her centre. He seized her hair, his grip tightening, a deliciously sharp pain blooming amid the pleasure.

His kiss was searing, an imprint that would never fade now. With her trembling hands she continued to explore the strength of his powerful torso, revelling in the muscle that corded his whole body and the shift of those muscles as he leant in and ground himself against her.

She gasped at the contact, meeting each of his movements with her own, a white-hot need blazing through her, demanding more friction, more touch. She arched into him with a frustrated cry, her breasts aching, her undergarments wet as she trembled with longing.

'Talemir,' she murmured against his lips, grinding against him insistently. Apart from the Warsword's shirt, they were both still fully clothed. That wouldn't do. Drue reached for his belt, but he caught her by the wrist.

'Not yet,' he said.

Drue pulled back, panting. 'What? Why?'

'I want to see you, touch you, taste you...'

Drue leant on her palms, legs spread around him, the tops

of her breasts flushed and heaving. 'What are you waiting for, then, Warsword?'

He gave her a dark, wicked smile as his hands reached for the laces of her shirt. One by one, he tugged them apart, his warm breath tickling the dip where her neck met her shoulder. Drue's body tightened as the fabric fell open, revealing her round, full breasts and her hard nipples begging to be touched. She felt herself growing wetter by the second as he ran his thumb across her bottom lip and then trailed his fingers down her throat, down between her collarbones to circle one breast and then the other, teasing her nipples with featherlight touches.

Panting, she arched her back, trying to guide him to a firmer approach, but he continued his teasing, so much so that she bucked off the bar's surface, wriggling in frustration. It took every bit of willpower she had not to launch herself at him. But he wanted to see her, to touch her, to taste her – that was his request, and who was she to deny him? She could be patient —

He closed his mouth over her nipple, sucking hard, teeth scraping, dragging a moan from her throat, her head falling back as she writhed.

His fingers found the buttons of her pants, each one springing free. She lifted her hips, allowing her pants to be dragged down her legs. Her undergarments quickly followed, leaving her completely exposed atop the surface of the bar, her thighs spread, revealing the wetness he'd coaxed from her.

Drue's cheeks heated, but Talemir devoured her with those hazel eyes, a man on the verge of starvation, his body taut, holding his breath at the sight of her.

'Furies save me, Drue...' he muttered, grasping her thighs and spreading her wider. 'You're perfect.'

Drue nearly whimpered as cool air caressed her wet, sensitive skin. Talemir knelt before her and brought his mouth to her.

The first lick of his tongue nearly ended her.

He dragged it up her centre, molten and intoxicating.

Drue fell back against the bar, her moan echoing through the tavern. She didn't care. Only Talemir and his tongue existed as he circled the sensitive spot, dragging unabashed cries of pleasure from her.

She gripped his hair, finding it soft as silk.

He groaned against her, a finger tracing her soaked entrance before sliding home, pumping in and out of her.

Her trembling legs clamped around Talemir as he worked her, his tongue and fingers now moving in unison, coaxing ripples of desire from her.

'Fuck...' she cried, every thought evaporating as that ultimate crest of ecstasy began to build in earnest.

She rocked against him as he fucked her with his fingers and teased her with his tongue, sending gentle, taunting flicks across her clit.

The rhythm intensified, and at last, Drue let go, shuddering, crying out as she rode the wave of her climax to breaking point. She arched off the bar, sending the tankards flying with the force of her orgasm, and Talemir wrung every last ounce of pleasure from her before he removed his mouth and fingers.

Naked, limp and panting, Drue didn't move.

She trembled in the aftermath of what Talemir had done to her, of what he'd created within her. And all for her – he hadn't sought or found his own release.

Slowly, Drue sat up, her skin flushed, her inner thighs slick.

Talemir's muscular arms were braced either side of her, his hair hanging loose over his lust-glazed eyes. Drue looked down to find the evidence of his own arousal bulging in his pants.

She reached for him, desperate to learn the feel of him in her hand before guiding him into her body.

Warm fingers closed around her wrist, stopping her. 'That was about you,' he said, his voice hoarse, his breathing uneven.

'I want to feel you, all of you, inside me,' Drue told him, not taking her eyes off that impressive length straining beneath the fabric, an ache already building back up within her.

'Not yet, Wildfire.' He brought her face to his and kissed her deeply. 'Not yet.'

Talemir retrieved a blanket from his pack and wrapped it gently around her before scooping her up in his strong arms, carrying her over to one of the corner booths. Her eyes were suddenly heavy.

There, he cradled her to him as he eased himself onto the old cushions and made room for her to lie down, her head resting in his lap.

'Are you alright?' he asked, his deep voice rumbling against her, sending a thrill through her bones even now.

'I'm more than alright.' She felt more relaxed than she ever had, weightless from the mind-altering experience of him.

'Good,' he murmured, stroking her hair gently.

Part of her wanted to argue, wanted to straddle him then and there and have her way with him, to wring the pleasure from him as he had from her, to hear his cries of passion and be *his* undoing.

But the soft, rhythmic caress of his hand through her locks had her sighing with a different form of contentment.

And that little voice of reason only whispered once:

How can this man be a monster?

14

TALEMIR

For as long as the Furies bade him live, Talemir Starling would forever remember the taste of her. Until his dying breath he would recall the sounds she made when she climaxed and the way her mouth had parted in a cry of ecstasy.

She was fierce and beautiful.

She was everything.

The meddling ranger he'd been ordered to slay.

The Naarvian woman who'd clawed her way out from the darkness of a fallen kingdom.

The flicker of wildfire in the deep night.

And now, she slept soundly in his lap, nestled against him with all the trust in the realms, despite what he was, despite what she'd seen him become.

How did this happen? Talemir ran his thumb over his lips, the memory of her mouth on his etched into his mind, strong enough to last a thousand lifetimes. No matter what came to pass between them now, he was tethered to her, and her mark upon him would remain.

Carefully, he slipped out from underneath her, tucking the blanket firmly around her and covering up her bare leg. He knew she hadn't slept well on the road, full of worry for her friend Gus and plagued by nightmares when the sun went down. For a moment he just watched her, noting the way her eyelashes brushed the tops of her flushed cheeks and how she curled up into herself. He could stare at her for hours, he realised. But that was not why he'd peeled himself away from her. No. It was about time someone looked after Drue, and he was more than happy to pick up the mantle.

As his Wildfire slept, Talemir collected her discarded clothes and stripped off his own. Wearing just his last clean pair of undershorts, he explored the rest of the tavern. He drew water from a well out the back and found a tub and a washboard. There, he scrubbed their filthy clothes with soap until the water turned grey. Deeming it safe enough to start a fire in the long-cold hearth, he did so, coaxing the flames to life over the kindling he gathered before hanging their clothes over an array of chairs to dry. The Dancing Badger's food stores had been raided, but it mattered not. Talemir took up his bow and quiver and went hunting.

He knew he must look ridiculous in his boots and undershorts, his arrows strapped to his bare back like some sort of caveman, but there was no one to see him and twilight was the best time to hunt game. The grasslands around the stream were littered with hares and it took him no time at all to shoot a few through the eye. For a brief moment he wished Wilder was there to tease, his young protégé always a touch too impatient with archery. But he would learn in time. Talemir scanned the skies for Terrence, before remembering the hawk was on his way to Ciraun to bring them aid against the raiders. Time had passed so strangely these past few weeks. In the blink of an eye, Talemir had found himself on a ship to Naarva, at the pointy end of a ranger's blade, and now... now he was somewhere else entirely.

He trudged back to The Dancing Badger, realising how much he'd needed the fresh dusk air to settle the raging fire within. The fire that Drue Emmerson had ignited in him and fanned into a blazing inferno ever since. He entered the tavern quietly, careful not to wake her. He wasn't sure he was ready to face her yet; he didn't trust himself to meet her gaze and not spill forth every emotion that roiled in him now.

Talemir Starling had never been a common man. He had been a legendary Warsword of Thezmarr, and then a shadow monster living a half-life, but now... those were not the most powerful things about him.

He shook the thought from his head and took the hares to the kitchen, where he skinned them expertly with his blade. A lifetime ago, his father had taught him the best way to remove the hide and gut the animal, a lesson that had been ingrained so deeply he could practically do it with his eyes closed now. Talemir had taught the same to Wilder, who'd been hilariously squeamish at first. Smiling to himself, he set about making a meal – a rich hare stew, a recipe Malik had taught him on one of their many adventures. Luckily, raiders apparently had no use for dried herbs and spices, and so Talemir used these generously in the heavy pot he hung over the hearth, creating a decadent broth for the meat, the aromas making his mouth water. All the while, he thought of Drue, wondering how she would be when she woke and if she would regret what had happened between them...

Talemir's chest seized painfully at the prospect, for he

longed to do what he'd done again and again. His cock stirred beneath the loose fabric of his shorts at the idea of seating himself between her legs and —

'Keep your shit together, Starling,' he muttered to himself, shaking his head and pinching the bridge of his nose. He forced down some more of Farissa's tonic, hoping it would help keep his baser instincts at bay. But it was as though he suddenly had the resolve of a teenager – or lack thereof, his mind spearing towards sex every few seconds. That image of her laid bare on the bar, writhing beneath his touch, was intoxicating. How could he not think of it? How could he not imagine burying himself deep inside her?

'For fuck's sake.' He busied himself with the stew, with turning their clothes on the makeshift line so that they would dry quicker.

He went to the well to refill their canteens. When he returned, Drue was awake, sitting up in the booth, her hair mussed and her face flushed from sleep.

'Something smells incredible,' she said by way of greeting.

'I thought we deserved a decent meal,' Talemir replied, offering her one of the canteens.

She stared up at him, wide-eyed, as though seeing him for the first time. 'Thank you.'

Talemir wanted to ask her how she was feeling, and he desperately wanted to pick up right where they'd left off, but he did no such thing. Instead, he returned to his place by the fire and stirred the stew. He would not be the one to overwhelm her. He would give her whatever space and time she needed...

Drue padded towards him, still wrapped in the blanket, still utterly naked beneath. 'You washed our clothes, too?'

'Mm-hmm.'

Drue's eyes were lined with silver and she chewed her lower lip. 'No one has washed my clothes in a very long time,' she said quietly.

Talemir waved her off. 'It's nothing.'

'No, it's not.'

'I suppose I don't wash just anyone's undergarments.'

A slow smile spread across Drue's face, and she raised a brow. 'Not even Wilder's?'

'Furies, no.'

She moved closer to the fire, the blanket slipping from her shoulder, revealing that delicately inked tattoo once again. Talemir had to stop himself from closing the gap between them and delivering a series of soft kisses along the blooms there. He would take his cues from her.

'The clothes aren't quite dry yet,' he said instead. 'But I've got a spare shirt if you want?'

Drue bit her bottom lip again and nodded.

Talemir retrieved the shirt, handing it to her with a stupidly prideful sense of satisfaction that she'd be wrapped in something of his. Feeling like a foolish youngster again, he turned around to give her privacy, but it didn't stop the pulse of arousal shooting through him as he heard the blanket drop to the floor.

His shirt was enormous on her, reaching the top of her knees. Drue laughed as she looked down at herself. 'How do I look?'

'Perfect,' Talemir said without thinking, his cheeks heating. She had him under her spell, there was no doubt about that now.

Smiling, Drue set about spreading the blanket across the stone floor and retrieving a handful of cushions from the booth they'd vacated. 'We should eat in front of the fire.'

'And dip into Palmer's wine collection,' Talemir added, going to the kitchen to find bowls and cutlery.

'Agreed,' Drue called out. He heard the clinking of glasses soon after.

When he emerged with their utensils, he found that Drue had set up a picnic-style spread: the last of their flatbread, along with two long-stemmed glasses and a bottle of something that looked incredibly old and expensive. And there she sat, legs bare beneath his shirt, smiling up at him. It was the perfect combination of everything.

He filled their bowls with steaming stew from the pot and handed them to her before hesitating, considering how he might sit down without his undershorts bunching up and exposing —

'Not that I mind the view, but here.' Drue passed him a second blanket.

Laughing, he wrapped it around his waist before joining her on the floor. 'So, you don't mind the view, eh?'

'Oh, shut up,' she replied, handing him a bowl.

Grinning to himself, Talemir tucked into the food. The moans of satisfaction coming from Drue told him she thought it was just as good as he did, not to mention making him grateful for the blanket. Her noises did vulgar things to him.

'This is amazing,' she said between mouthfuls. 'Thank you.'

'You're welcome.' He took a sip of his wine. 'This isn't half bad either...'

'Half bad? It's amazing. I think the label says it's from beyond the Veil?'

Talemir reached for the bottle, tilting it to the fire so he could read the script across the square of parchment. He let out a low whistle. 'I'll be damned,' he murmured. 'It's from Valia...'

'Where?'

'Valia, in the Upper Realm. Remember that first book I told you about? The one about the society of women warriors?'

'Mmm?'

'They're the Valian kindred. Famous for their fearless warriors and their wine.'

Drue laughed. 'A territory known for love stories, warriors and wine sounds like your kind of place.'

'Can you think of a better combination?'

Drue's eyes met his. 'No, I don't think I can.'

Talemir clinked his drink against hers, winking. 'Glad we're in agreement, Wildfire.'

He heard her breathing hitch at the use of the nickname, and as their glasses chimed between them, her perfect body seemed to go taut.

'Everything alright?' he asked, trying to keep the wicked smile from his lips.

'No,' she said.

Talemir froze. Had he misread the situation so badly?

But Drue placed her glass on the floor and shifted to her knees, eyeing him with a hooded gaze. 'There is some unfinished business between us, Warsword.'

'Oh?' The sight of her on her parted knees, wearing his shirt over her naked body, was more than enough to fuel the desire that was already simmering below the surface.

'I want to see you come undone.' Her throat bobbed as she inched towards him. 'As you undid me...'

At those words, Talemir went molten. 'You can have whatever you want from me,' he said, suddenly hoarse, his breath catching.

When she reached him, she set aside his drink and bowl and pulled him to his knees, tugging the blanket at his waist, the heavy fabric falling away to reveal his tented undershorts, his cock throbbing almost painfully beneath.

Gods, he wanted her. Had wanted her from the moment she'd threatened to carve out his heart on the northern perimeter. There was no need for that now – she already held it in her hands. It belonged to her.

Drue stared at him, her blue eyes brimming with lust as they roamed over his chest and rippled abdomen. Her tongue swept across her lower lip as her gaze dropped to the V-shaped dip of sinew and beyond...

'See what you do to me?' he murmured, watching her as she took in the sight of his straining erection.

He bucked as she palmed the hard length of him through the material, swearing under his breath at the bolt of pleasure that shot through him at the basic contact. With her hand still on him, Drue tilted her face to his and kissed him.

Talemir groaned against the lush curve of her lips, his blood heating as her mouth opened for him and her tongue brushed his. He cupped the sides of her face, holding her in place as he kissed her, savouring the taste of her and the way her body answered to him.

He could feel the fabric of his undershorts growing damp at the tip of his cock as she gripped him through the material, pumping once, twice, drawing a moan from the back of his throat.

Then the waistband was being drawn away from his blazing skin and he sprang free, heady and heavy, the need for her like a raging current, sweeping up everything in its path. She dragged the undershorts down his muscular thighs, leaving them bunched at his knees. He didn't care; he'd rip through them if he had to.

Talemir dropped his hands to the buttons of her shirt, nearly moaning again at each inch of her as it was revealed. She was the most glorious thing he'd ever seen. The fabric parted down her middle, revealing a column of golden skin before falling from her shoulders and gathering at her arms.

Her breasts were perfect. Round and full, with tight pink nipples that hardened under his gaze. As he cupped her in both his hands, his calluses scraping against her soft skin, Drue gasped, and he leant in to kiss the hollow of her neck, feeling her pulse flutter beneath his lips.

She was staring at his cock and the bead of moisture gathered at the tip as her grip tightened around him and she stroked him up and down in a way that made his whole body tense with pleasure. Gods, he had to touch her, had to —

Drue pushed him back, her palm flat against his sternum. 'This is about you.' She echoed his previous words, her voice husky.

'Drue, I —'

But he let her guide him to the floor. Furies knew he was hers to command. He'd do whatever she asked. Lying on his back, he looked up at her as she braced herself above him, her breasts pressed against him.

He dragged her down, crushing her body to his, and kissed her fiercely, wanting to feel every inch of them touching, wanting to slide deep inside her. She deepened the kiss, meeting every stroke of his tongue with hers as her hands explored the plane of his chest, teasing his nipples before lightly dragging her fingernails down across his abdomen.

He twitched beneath her, could feel his cock leaking for her.

Then she was kissing the column of his throat, trailing her lips down his body. He was torn between the exquisite, taunting pleasure of it and wanting to flip them over so he could seat himself between her thighs and —

'Fuck!'

Drue closed her mouth over the head of his cock and every thought emptied from his mind as his shaft slid in deeper until it bumped against the back of her throat, the sensation warm, lush and deliciously torturous. She withdrew from him, her teeth lightly scraping, only to lick the broad crown of him before swallowing him down again.

'Gods, Drue... If you keep doing that...'

Drue worked him with her mouth and her hand, moaning around him, the sound vibrating down his cock and into his tightening balls until Talemir saw stars on the ceiling.

A dark frenzy threatened to take hold, but he had to be sure.

'Drue... Drue?'

She looked up, blue eyes meeting his as her lips were still closed over him. The sight alone nearly had him spilling into her mouth.

'This is what you want?' he panted. 'You don't want to —'

His pulsating cock disappeared down her throat and that was answer enough. His fingers curled in her hair and his head dropped back as she devoured him, spirals of warmth building at the base of his spine, spreading through his whole body.

Talemir let go. The surge of pleasure was unlike anything he'd ever felt before. His heart pounded mercilessly. Nothing existed but Drue and the ecstasy she now wrought upon him with her wicked mouth. Engorged and straining, his cock begged for release, and with every stroke of her tongue, the sensitivity increased, the crescendo rising from his balls as Drue cupped them, squeezing gently.

'Drue...' he warned, her name like a prayer.

Every muscle contracted. Every burst of pleasure exploded in a tidal wave.

Talemir's whole body shuddered with the intensity of his climax.

He erupted.

Release tore through him and he came with a shout, spilling and spilling himself down Drue's throat.

She swallowed every bit he gave her.

Talemir couldn't catch his breath as Drue eased off him and crawled to his side, a smug smile playing on her lips.

'I think that makes us even?' she said coyly.

Talemir didn't have a response at the ready. Words refused to come to him, his shock at what she'd wrung from him still utterly raw. All he could do was watch her as she lay beside him, propped up on her elbow, settling her head in her hand as she looked at him.

What had just passed between them was beyond anything he understood of these realms. It was a magic to make the sanest man go mad, not forged of shadow and darkness, but of what he felt for this woman.

'No witty retorts for me, Warsword?' Drue asked quietly, resting her free palm against his chest. His heart hammered wildly beneath her touch.

He closed his hand over hers and, not trusting himself to speak, turned to her and kissed her soundly.

15
DRUE

Golden rays of dawn light filtered through the gaps in the boarded-up windows, spilling across Talemir's sun-kissed skin beneath Drue's fingers. She blinked slowly, finding herself curled up against the Warsword's chest that rose and fell steadily with each slumbering breath. Her bare legs were draped over his and she was still naked but for his now crumpled shirt that remained open at the front.

She didn't move, not wanting to break the spell just yet. Instead, she surveyed the man beside her, noting the long, black lashes kissing the tops of his high cheekbones, the subtle parting of his soft lips as he slept, and further south, the dark hair trailing down his navel and below the blanket draped across his lower half. Her toes curled at the memory of what lay beneath... She hardly recognised the sultry vixen she'd become the night before. Talemir had coaxed out that part of her, had her claiming her wants and desires with utter abandon. And she had liked it. A lot.

But as much as Drue longed to spend the day locked away in the abandoned tavern exploring every inch of Talemir Starling, there was work to be done. Reluctantly, she withdrew from the warrior, pulling his shirt around her as she tip-toed to where he'd hung their clean clothes to dry the night before.

Her chest seized at the thought of him letting her sleep and using the time to scrub her garments. She pulled them on with a quiet sigh of gratitude, relishing the feel of the fresh fabric on her skin rather than the perpetually damp clothes of life on the road.

As quietly as she could, she made porridge and tea for them, the earthy aroma wafting around the tavern and at last causing Talemir to stir. He sat up, blearily rubbing his eyes and reaching beside him – for her, she realised.

'Morning,' she said from her place by the hearth, where she'd cooked over the hot embers.

Clutching the blanket slung low around his waist, Talemir stood, running his other hand through his hair. Drue did her best not to stare, for he was just as impressive in the morning light as he had ever been.

'There's porridge,' she said unnecessarily. 'And tea. I thought we should eat our fill before —'

His mouth tugging into a smirk, Talemir's gaze shot back to her, and he wiggled his brows suggestively.

'Don't even say it,' she quipped.

'I didn't say a word,' he replied, accepting the mug from her, his powerful muscles shifting as he did.

Finishing up her breakfast and downing the rest of her tea, Drue went to ready the horses, leaving Talemir to dress in private. She wasn't sure she trusted herself not to jump on him if he dropped that blanket in front of her.

Everything that had passed between them yesterday... It had set her alight from within. The things he'd done to her, the things he'd made her feel... No lover had ever offered her pleasure like that before. No lover had ever stirred that thing inside her that made her want to give it back. But Talemir... Talemir was different.

Drue retrieved the horses from a clearing by the stream and tried to push those thoughts from her mind. With the raiders' map in hand, she waited for Talemir outside the tavern, glancing up at the sign that swung in the morning breeze.

The Dancing Badger... She wondered what its sister venues were like and who had founded such a network. It had been a long time since Drue had seen any formal establishment in full swing. She hoped that elsewhere in the midrealms, where things were less bleak, such places were teeming with fiddlers and dancers, with life and laughter, and that perhaps one day, she might see them for herself.

'Ready?' Talemir asked from the door.

Drue nodded, fitting her boot to the stirrup and mounting her mare.

'Just to be clear,' she said as Talemir swung himself up into his own saddle. 'We are not attacking today, no matter what we see... Today we scout, and glean as much information as possible to present to our forces when they arrive. Understood?'

Talemir smiled, taking a swig from the flask she knew to be his *monster tonic*. That web of white lines appeared on his neck, remaining a beat longer than she remembered before fading again.

'Out of the two of us, you're the hothead, Wildfire. I should be asking you that question.'

'Understood?' she pressed anyway.

'Understood.'

'Good. Then let's learn what we can about these bastards.'

Together, ranger and Warsword rode out of the abandoned miners' village, following the raiders' map further south.

THEY TRAVELLED for half a day before they saw any sign of the bandits. Boot prints in the dirt, discarded ration sacks, the cold remains of campfires.

'They don't have horses,' Drue observed as they came upon a forest.

'That's an advantage to us, then.'

Drue nodded her agreement. 'If the map's correct, then their stronghold should be just beyond these woodlands.'

'It hasn't led us astray yet. Shall we?'

'We should go on foot from here,' Drue told him.

They left the horses in a deep, sheltered part of the woods and together, they crept through the trees.

Talemir moved as silently as any predator of the night, a dagger unsheathed in his hand at the ready. Drue followed suit. There was no way of knowing what they were walking into, or if they'd be set upon at any moment. But they met no such obstacles, and they covered the woodlands quickly, finding themselves at the crest of a ridge, looking down into the former town below. There, they lay on their bellies, watching the raider activity unfold.

'Depending on where that unit came from, they might have realised that their men are missing by now,' Talemir said, surveying the handful of buildings sprawled in a dying field.

'I should have questioned the one in the stream,' Drue ground out. 'I let my anger get the better of me.'

Talemir scoffed. 'You had a single body at your feet. I think out of the pair of us, it was me who could have shown more restraint and interrogated one of them.'

'Why didn't you?'

A muscle twitched in Talemir's jaw. 'I... I saw that bastard go after you, and after that... Well, I killed them without a second thought. All I could think of was if he got his hands on you —'

'I had it under control.'

'So I discovered.'

'If I can nearly fell a Warsword of Thezmarr, a meagre bandit is surely easy pickings?'

That muscle twitched again. 'It's not that I doubted your abilities.'

'Good.'

'Thanks to you, we have their plans and maps. They'll do nicely, by the looks of things,' Talemir said, pointing. 'They're using the village as a fortress. The main hub of movement is coming from that old warehouse to the east.'

Drue followed his line of sight and immediately saw what he was talking about. There were many comings and goings in the larger building.

'How organised do you think they are?' she wondered aloud.

'Hard to say from here. It doesn't look like there are guards stationed anywhere. If these are just former citizens of Naarva, they might not be so disciplined.'

'Let's stay here for a while, see if we can discern any sort of pattern, and then I want to get closer. We might be able to get a look inside, to get a better layout to report back to Adrienne. What do you think?'

'I think you could have been a general yourself. You have a keen mind for strategy, for weighing up the risks...'

'If only Thezmarr allowed women to wield blades,' she said quietly, suddenly aware of the press of her sword at her spine.

'Perhaps one day it will again.'

As they spied upon the village of raiders, Drue noticed Talemir toying with the sapphire around his neck. It seemed strange, for until now he had not been one for fidgeting. What was it that his mother had said upon gifting him the jewel? Drue sifted through her memory.

'Sometimes, to love someone, we have to let them go... In order to go where we need to, we must turn away from one path, onto another...'

Is that what Talemir is thinking about now? she wondered, the idea making her shift uncomfortably. Was it unease she sensed within him? Was it regret?

He noticed her looking, catching her gaze. But when his eyes met hers, there was something so earnest there, something that clamped around her heart.

They had watched the raiders long enough, she decided.

Talemir had been right in his suspicions that the bandits were not overly organised. It was easy enough to sneak into the village, easy enough to scale the walls and navigate the rooftops. They found the perfect vantage point to peer into the warehouse from the roof of a nearby building and took stock of the layout inside.

It was immediately clear that it was the hub for all their activity. She could see that it held all their supplies, both weapons and rations, with several men moving about within.

But what Drue hadn't been expecting was the cage.

Her body went cold as she spotted it through the window.

In the centre of the warehouse was a metal crate, complete with thick bars.

A cage of people.

Her people.

Innocent Naarvians captured and trapped by *scum*.

Her hand flew to her sword.

Talemir's arm flung out in front of her. 'Stop.' His voice was pure command. 'You said no attacking.'

'You felled ten raiders yesterday. We can take them.'

'How many men have you counted in the last hour alone?' he demanded.

'I...'

'Exactly. Fifty. And that's just the ones we've seen.'

'They're in a *fucking cage*, Talemir.'

'And we'll be no use to them trapped alongside them,' he said firmly. 'We do what we came here to do. We map out the warehouse, note the guard changes, and now we try to discern the number of hostages. Every single piece of information will help us create a refined strategy that will get those people out alive.'

Drue's hands itched to unsheathe her blades and launch herself at the monsters inside that warehouse, at the bastards who would sacrifice their own people to the shadow wraiths.

'Drue.' Her name on Talemir's lips brought her back from the brink of a violent fury. 'Do I have your word that you won't go charging in there?'

She clenched and unclenched her jaw, rage still simmering just below the surface. She squinted, trying to make out the faces behind the bars.

'Drue?' Talemir demanded.

'Yes,' she ground out. 'You have my word.'

He gave a stiff nod. 'We should get back to the horses.'

Drue froze. 'We can't leave them…'

Talemir's warm hand closed around her arm. 'There is nothing we can do for them right now. We need to take this information back to the tavern.'

'What if they move? What if they take them —'

Talemir pointed to a group of men who were feeding logs onto a fire and passing jugs of liquor between themselves. 'They're not going anywhere tonight, Drue.'

'We could stay here, keep watch —'

Talemir shook his head. 'We need to get back to our own base. Eat, rest… Ready ourselves for when Adrienne and the others arrive.'

Drue knew he was right. They needed to be at their best for when they burned those fuckers to the ground. Reluctantly, she let Talemir lead her away from the stronghold as she silently vowed to wreak havoc on the raiders when she and Adrienne led the attack against them.

As they sat atop their horses once more, the sky darkening around them, Talemir became quiet. Drue noticed his gaze kept flicking towards the waning yellow crescent against the inky night.

'We'll have a new moon soon,' she said, thinking of how much time had passed since the Warsword first stepped foot on her shores.

But Talemir didn't reply. Instead, he rummaged in his saddlebag and retrieved his tonic, bringing it to his lips and drinking deeply.

The action sent a little ball of unease rolling through her.

He doesn't even know what it is, she thought. *And he doesn't take it in measured doses as medications ought to be administered...* But whenever he caught her looking, she turned away, making no comment. Nor did she mention those strange white lines appearing on his skin with each dose, which seemed to be hanging on for longer each time.

The thing between them was too fresh, too raw and untried for such conversations.

She didn't speak again. But he kept glancing to that sliver of moon, and for a split second, Drue thought she saw a glimmer of darkness flash across his face.

When at long last they returned to the tavern and set the horses loose, Drue couldn't take the silence any longer. 'Is something wrong?' she asked as he pushed open the heavy door to The Dancing Badger. She had never been one to tip-toe around things and she damn well wasn't going to start now.

Talemir took another swig from his flask and busied himself with lighting the fire in the hearth. 'Nothing's wrong,' he told her.

Frowning, Drue followed him inside and marvelled as the steel cuff warmed against her skin, not sensing a monster, but a lie.

16
TALEMIR

Talemir hated lying to her, but he also couldn't bring himself to tell her the truth. He was a coward. Instead, he forced down his tonic, ignoring the wave of nausea it now brought with it. He knew full well that when the new moon graced the skies and the night was at its darkest, the change would be upon him.

He had faced it several times since the final battle of Naarva, each time as painful and heart-wrenching as the last. Wings spearing through his back, talons unsheathing from his fingertips and that song of shadow that made him want to unleash himself upon the midrealms.

How could he tell her that? After everything they'd shared, he couldn't bear the shame of her witnessing that. Of proving her right – that he was every bit the monster she had claimed he was from the start.

And so he feigned fatigue from the ride, though they both knew he could ride for days, and set up his bedroll separate from hers.

Talemir knew his actions made little sense, knew he should confide in her, that in spite of their beginning together, she might yet understand. But that shame, a burning ball of it within, stopped him every time he went to open his mouth.

The fire burned low, and he lay on his side, his body humming with the awareness that Drue was only mere feet away, that the night before he'd fallen asleep holding her. But with her so close, he felt even less in control over his shadow-self than usual, and the last thing he wanted was a humiliating repeat of what had happened at the hot springs, or worse.

Judging from the sliver of crescent moon left, he had five days, probably less, before the darkest night was upon him. He could leave, but that would mean leaving her without his protection, and he couldn't stand the thought of that. All he could do was hope that Adrienne and her Naarvian forces arrived before the new moon did, and then he could slip away.

THE NEXT DAY was a repeat of the one before, though things between him and Drue were noticeably stilted as they rode to the raider headquarters. They scouted the surrounding areas of the village and checked on the captives in the warehouse from afar. He could tell Drue was itching to burst in and rescue them, but again, he reminded her they needed to wait for the general.

Talemir could feel her watching him, assessing him, so much so that he'd taken to hiding when he drank his tonic. She had clearly noticed he was taking more than usual. Furies save him, she was as sharp-eyed as that hawk of hers.

They spent hours retracing their steps from the day before, double-checking the numbers they'd noted down and any patterns that emerged this time around. Drue sketched a map and a more detailed drawing of the warehouse layout, including all its exits and windows that could be seen from various hidden vantage points across the stronghold.

He watched her as she rolled up the parchment, her blue eyes fierce and determined, her movements purposeful. She never stopped assessing, never hesitated as they ducked between buildings and scaled the walls. She would have made a fine warrior of Thezmarr, perhaps even a Warsword, had she been given the opportunity.

'You can tell me, you know,' she blurted, as they trudged back to their horses a few hours later, the information they'd gathered safely tucked away.

Talemir glanced across at her, meaning to claim ignorance, but Drue saw right through him.

Her answering stare brimmed with challenge. 'Whatever it is that's bothering you, I want you to know that you can tell me. That you can tell me anything.'

Talemir's heart knotted at that. Gods, she was strong – far stronger than him, a force to be reckoned with all on her own. And he knew that what had come between them, the strained tension that had wound its way around him, had never been her fear of him, but his own.

'And if you're not ready,' Drue continued, peering right into his soul, 'then you're not ready. But I'll be here when you are.'

Her words caused a lump to form in his throat, his chest tightening. Her graciousness, her bravery – it humbled him. And so he decided not to deny his fears, not to her. Never again to her. 'Thank you,' he managed, voice cracking.

Drue smiled as they reached their horses. 'What do you say to round two of darts when we get back?'

'Are you going to insist I take my clothes off again?' Talemir quipped, suddenly feeling lighter than he had all day.

Drue returned his grin. 'Among other things.'

Those words alone sent a thrill through him. 'I hope you don't expect me not to retaliate this time.'

'Oh, I'm counting on it.'

It wasn't long before they were riding back towards the miners' village, and all Talemir could think of was everything he was going to do to her, how he was going to worship her until she screamed his name.

'Should I even ask what's on your mind now, Warsword?' she asked from beside him as the afternoon wore on.

'Why do you say that?'

She straightened in her saddle. 'It's a rather different silence to the one between us this morning...' she ventured.

'I'm not sure you can handle it,' he teased.

'Try me.'

'I want to pick up where we left off on our first night in the tavern...' he said slowly.

'And?'

Talemir wet his lips. He might not have been ready to tell her about the shadows that called to him upon the new moon, but when it came to this, he was not ashamed of what he wanted and how badly he wanted it. He met her gaze and didn't hesitate. 'I want to make you come so hard you see stars.'

Drue blinked at him.

'I want to make you come so hard you forget your own name.'

Her lips parted slightly.

'I want to bury my cock so deep inside you that all you remember is mine.'

A blush stained Drue's cheeks and spread down her neck.

Talemir nudged his horse closer to hers and leant across the gap between them. 'And that's just the first hour, Wildfire... We have all night ahead of us...'

Biting her bottom lip, Drue nodded slowly, adjusting her grip on her reins. 'Then we'd best pick up the pace, Warsword.'

Talemir barked a laugh. 'I'll race you.' And he didn't wait. He urged his stallion into a gallop, for the sooner they returned to the tavern, the better.

Warsword and ranger raced across the Naarvian plains as the sun dipped behind the hills and the abandoned miners' settlement appeared in the near distance.

Only it wasn't abandoned anymore.

A wide shadow cast across the dirt road in grand, sweeping rotations.

Talemir's gaze shot up to the sky. Where a hawk circled among the clouds.

Terrence.

Talemir heard Drue's intake of breath.

And on the horizon, he saw them too: Wilder and Adrienne, and the Naarvian forces at their backs.

WHILE TALEMIR WAS RELIEVED to see his protégé, fully healed and chomping at the bit to deliver justice to the raiders, he couldn't help but curse the young Warsword's timing. At their approach, the night Talemir had envisioned for himself and Drue vanished before his eyes. But as Drue dismounted and flung herself into Adrienne's arms in front of the tavern, Talemir smiled. There would be time for him and his ranger soon enough.

He tore his gaze away to find Wilder grinning before him. 'You came all the way to Naarva only to make camp at *The Dancing Badger?*'

Talemir clasped his protégé's shoulder and embraced him. 'It would seem that way, apprentice.'

'Reunited for less than two minutes and you're already dishing out that shit?' Wilder quipped, clapping him on the back and returning the embrace.

Breaking away, Talemir smirked. 'You'd think I was ill otherwise.'

'True, I'd likely go into shock.'

'We couldn't have that, now, could we? Only just got you back in one piece.'

Wilder shook his head. 'At least tell me there's some mead inside.'

'I can do you one better.'

'I doubt it.'

'There's wine.'

Wilder's eyes bulged. 'Don't toy with me, Tal. I've just crossed shark-infested waters for you.'

Talemir laughed, unable to stop himself from glancing at Drue, who was laughing with Adrienne on the tavern porch. 'Wouldn't dream of it.'

'I sent word back to Thezmarr,' Wilder said quietly.

'You did?'

'Things here are more dire than we were led to believe, Tal. These people need help.'

Talemir was suddenly cold. 'And who do you think will answer the call?'

'Torj Elderbrock,' Wilder replied. 'Maybe even Vernich, if Torj applies enough pressure. If they each bring a unit of their own, perhaps we could get things more under control.'

'I see.'

'You don't agree?'

Talemir braced himself. 'I don't know what to think. All I know is that missives have been lost. Messages mislaid. And the wrong information passed along.'

'What are you saying, Tal?'

'I'm saying we need to keep our eyes open. Even with the guild.'

Soon, Talemir found himself sitting between Drue and Wilder before a fire blazing in the hearth, along with Adrienne, Drue's father, Fendran, and his friend, Baledor, as they discussed the situation with the raiders. He and Drue relayed the information they'd gleaned from their surveillance and the bad news about the prisoners held captive inside the warehouse.

'Bastards,' Adrienne spat when he was done.

Drue murmured her agreement.

'We'll get them out,' Talemir told them. 'With the forces you've brought, and Wilder as well, we can launch an attack swiftly.'

Wilder was nodding beside him. 'We can run through some basic drills tomorrow, decide on our formations. We'll have your people freed in no time.'

'And then we continue on to the wraiths' lair together,' Drue added. 'We may yet be able to save Gus, Dratos and the others from the watchtower.'

'From what Adrienne's told me of Gus, he's a survivor,' Wilder added. 'Dratos, too. He sounds like enough of a pain in the arse that even the wraiths might get sick of him.'

Both women gave him a grateful look.

Wilder seemed right at home with the Naarvians, and for that, Talemir was glad. Though the young Warsword had verbalised nothing of the sort, Talemir suspected he'd been lonely since his brother's injury.

'And what of our mission, Tal?' Wilder asked more quietly, sensing his gaze.

'I visited the steel source,' Talemir said. 'But found nothing untoward there.'

'What about Drue?' Wilder murmured under his breath. 'Wasn't the initial report about her? Was she not the one accused of meddling with —'

'She has nothing to do with it.'

'Since when?'

'Since I inspected the steel source with her. Since I asked her myself.'

'And you trust her?'

'Without question.'

At this, Wilder paused, glancing across at Drue.

Talemir followed his gaze. In Adrienne's presence, Drue came more alive than ever. The women were trading stories of their journeys, laughter bubbling at their lips. The sly, knowing looks they exchanged told Talemir they were saving the best details until they were alone.

It felt surreal to have them all here, when only two nights earlier, Talemir had had Drue spread before him on the bar as he'd feasted upon her... And where they all sat in their chairs now, he'd spilt himself into her wicked mouth on the floor —

A gust of wind swept through the tavern.

And something wet landed in Talemir's lap.

He sprung back to find a bloodied dead weasel draped across his thighs.

Disgusted, he looked up to see Terrence landing on the arm of Drue's chair, puffing his feathered chest out proudly.

Drue herself was biting her fist to keep from laughing. 'I think it's a gift...' she managed.

Talemir glanced from the mangled creature in his lap to the hawk, who was preening, looking incredibly pleased with himself.

'Uh... Thanks...?' he said, grimacing as he picked the dead animal up by the tail.

Terrence gave a contented squawk.

And the crew burst out laughing.

Except for Fendran, who watched Talemir thoughtfully. 'Strange, that...' he said. 'That bird usually hates everyone.'

When the laughter had died down and Talemir had rid himself of the weasel, Wilder leant in, looking serious.

'Something has changed between you two...' He gave a subtle nod towards Drue. 'You look to her constantly. Not just for her beauty, but... something else.'

'Don't be ridiculous, Wilder.'

'I'm not blind, old master... I've never seen you like this with a woman before.'

Heat bloomed in Talemir's chest, and he stared across at Drue once more, unable to deny it. 'She's no ordinary woman,' he told his apprentice.

17

DRUE

After hours of talking, Drue stretched as she stood, her muscles stiff both from the days of riding and from sitting still for too long. The night had grown late and soon everyone around her was settling their sleeping arrangements. Many from their forces had spread out across the village, taking shelter in the abandoned buildings throughout. Thankfully, Drue's father and Coltan, who'd insisted on accompanying him, were also allocated elsewhere.

The tavern became Adrienne's domain, with her inner circle of rangers and soldiers claiming the cushioned booths and unceremoniously unravelling their bedrolls on the floor. Wilder had pushed all their chairs back and reserved spots by the fire, but there was no sign of Talemir.

She was still in shock over Terrence's *gift* to the Warsword. Her father had been right. The hawk usually hated everyone. In fact, he hated men specifically, and she had seen his initial disdain for Talemir. And yet...

As Drue looked around, she felt a pang of regret for the

evening of passion that had been stolen from her, her toes curling in her boots at the thought. She had just brought him out of whatever despair he'd clearly fallen into when the others had arrived. Though she'd been incredibly relieved to see Adrienne, and to find that Wilder and the other injured parties had recovered, she selfishly wished she'd had one more night alone with the Warsword.

'Are you going to the well, Drue?' Adrienne asked, interrupting Drue's thoughts and waving her canteen hopefully.

Drue's brow furrowed. 'I wasn't, but I can...'

'Much obliged,' Adrienne said, tossing her the vessel. 'I'm parched.'

Slightly baffled, Drue chuckled at her friend's assertive nature and threw her bedroll down. Taking Adrienne's canteen as well as her own, she exited through the rear of the tavern. Outside, night had truly fallen. Only a sliver of moon remained, leaving the rest of the sky a dark blanket punctuated with stars. Drue realised with a start that she'd had no grasp on the hour as she tucked the canteens under her arm and struggled to remove a torch from its outer wall sconce. Everything had happened so quickly – the conversation with Talemir on the way back from the raider stronghold, Adrienne's arrival and all the planning afterward.

The Warswords and Adrienne worked nicely together: both efficient and brutal with their strategies. Which was just as well, because the image of those poor people trapped in that cage flashed before her eyes and Drue's stomach squirmed with guilt. She had hated leaving them there both times. But she'd known Talemir was right. To attack would have meant risking their lives. Instead, she clung to the fact that the surveillance they had done was going to pay off. She was confident about their raid tomorrow. With Adrienne and the Warswords leading the Naarvian forces against inexperienced rebels, what could go wrong?

At last she dislodged the torch and held it before her, illuminating the narrow path to the well. Like the rest of Naarva, the land behind the tavern was overgrown with wild vines, and Drue batted away stray branches and webs of spider silk as she made for the water source.

But when she reached it, she was not alone.

With a torch of his own stuck in the earth at his feet, Talemir stood at the well's edge, hauling the bucket from its depths, his mother's sapphire glimmering as it knocked against his chest.

In the soft glow of the torchlight, Drue was reminded again of not just his sharp handsomeness, but his true beauty. Some of his hair had escaped its knot and hung down around his face, brushing the tops of his stubble-covered cheeks, his large hands reeling up the rope from down below.

'What are you doing out here?' he asked by way of greeting.

'Adrienne asked me to fetch some water for her...'

Talemir huffed a laugh. 'Did she now?'

'Why?'

He gestured to the handful of flasks at the foot of the well. 'She told me to do the same.'

'Meddlesome woman,' Drue muttered.

'I can always leave if you'd prefer...'

'No.' The word flew from Drue's lips too quickly.

Talemir smiled and took the canteens from her hands, his fingers brushing hers, sending a bolt of anticipation through her, bringing their last private conversation to the forefront of her mind once more.

I want to make you come so hard you forget your own name.

Drue held her breath as she watched Talemir fill the flasks. Every movement was confident, precise, his battle-honed body almost looking out of place doing something so mundane as fetching water from a well. He was born for wielding a blade, for slaying monsters and making women

—

Drue stopped herself from finishing the thought. It was not for a ranger to say what a Warsword, or a half-wraith, had been born for.

But even so, the energy between them grew taut – unbearable.

When Talemir offered the vessels back to her, Drue couldn't stand it any longer. With her whole body suddenly on edge, she set them down and closed the gap between herself and the warrior, wetting her lips as she gazed upon him.

And gods, that face... His chiselled jaw, his hazel eyes, his slightly crooked nose and the way his expression softened at the sight of her... It made her want to grab hold of him and not let go.

Instead, Drue rested her palm on his sculpted chest, feeling the staccato beat of his heart beneath. 'I've been thinking about what you said...' she ventured.

Another slow smile spread across Talemir's lips. 'Have you now?'

'Yes.'

'And?'

Drue stood on her tip-toes, leaning in so that her breath mingled with his. 'And I want you to do those things. I want you.'

Talemir went incredibly still. She wasn't sure he was

breathing, but his eyes were ablaze with desire. 'Are you sure? Even with everything you know? Everything you've seen?'

'I like what I've seen,' she told him, her voice low and sultry, her hand reaching for what she knew strained against his pants —

He gripped her wrist gently, stopping her. 'You know that wasn't what I meant.'

Drue hesitated, frowning and trying to read his now unreadable expression. 'Has something happened? What changed since our ride?'

Talemir rubbed his neck. 'The night got darker,' he said cryptically.

'What does that mean?' Drue demanded.

Talemir closed his eyes, exhaling deeply. 'Nothing.'

Drue clenched her jaw. 'I have told you that you need not tell me things you're not ready to tell me, but don't disrespect me by lying.'

His gaze snapped to hers. 'You're right.' He took her hands in his. 'I promise, I won't ever lie to you.' Talemir pulled her closer to him once more, her body melting into his.

Every part of her responded instantly, crying out for him – his fingers, his mouth, his —

'I have grand plans for the next time we're alone, Wildfire,' he told her. 'I will not waste them out here on a damp patch of dirt in the dark.'

Drue went molten, her breath catching in her throat, her skin ablaze with the yearning to be touched. She pressed herself against him, her breasts heaving against his chest, her lower half grinding against the hardness of him.

A soft groan escaped him. 'For all those plans... you'll need your strength.' He brushed his lips against hers, a quiet vow of what was to come.

'I could say the same to you,' she said at last, using every ounce of willpower left to keep from throwing herself at him.

'I have no doubt.' He traced her lips with his once more before pulling away.

A tight breath escaped Drue, and she nearly whimpered as the cold swept in between them.

But he looked at her, his hazel eyes as intense as before. 'Stolen snatches of time won't do when it comes to you.' He collected the flasks he'd brought and started back towards the tavern.

Dazed, Drue stood there. Her whole body had come alive in his presence, at his words, at the brush of his lips. Gods, she had never wanted someone like this before. Never imagined the need could be so great that she would consider throwing all caution to the wind.

And yet he'd remained stoic. He'd managed to keep his desires under control... Did he not feel as she felt? Cursing herself, Drue snatched up the remaining canteens. This was not who she was, some simpering fool who worried about such things. Swearing under her breath, she grabbed the torch and made her way back.

Inside, Adrienne was stretched out on her bedroll several feet away from Wilder and Talemir. Both Warswords were making a show of sleeping, though Drue knew Talemir better than that, at least. Like her, the warrior took a long while to drift off.

'Nice night-time stroll?' Adrienne smirked as Drue approached.

Drue tossed her the canteen and elbowed her as soon as she was in range. 'You're a gods-damned menace,' she hissed.

'You're welcome,' Adrienne replied sweetly.

'Welcome?' Drue huffed. 'If I had balls, they'd be bluer than —'

Adrienne snorted loudly and Drue glanced around to see if anyone had heard.

'You make it too easy,' Adrienne quipped. 'It's an interesting development since I saw you last... You've failed to mention —'

'I have no idea what you're talking about.'

'Your red face says otherwise, my friend...'

Drue's cheeks burned hotter in answer. 'Now's hardly the time for an interrogation.'

'And what if I die tomorrow not knowing what's happened between you and —'

'Shhh. For fuck's sake, Adri. I'll kill you myself if you don't shut up.'

Adrienne laughed softly. 'A likely story. Who'd give you all the decent watch shifts? Who'd correct your swordplay form? Who'd serve up a dashing warrior on a platter for you —'

'Furies save me.' Could Talemir and Wilder hear all this? The possibility was mortifying, and Adrienne was having far too good a time revelling in her discomfort. 'What of you?' she shot back.

'What about me?'

'You seem mighty familiar with a certain —'

But Adrienne only laughed quietly. 'Nice try. But it's clearly you we need to discuss. Last I heard, your Warsword was a shadow wraith.'

The words cleaved through Drue, cold and precise.

Adrienne's face softened. 'I don't say it with malice...'

'I know,' Drue breathed, suppressing the urge to glance at Talemir.

'Well?' Adrienne pressed. 'Does it matter?'

The question made Drue's stomach harden. If her friend had asked her that weeks ago, as the two of them tracked a party of wraiths across the plains, the need for vengeance ruling her every thought, her every move, as it had for months, Drue would have laughed. Of course it mattered.

But Talemir was different. She *knew him*, didn't she? He was not some monster who wrought his shadows upon the midrealms like poisoned whips lashing the innocent...

'I don't know,' she said.

Adrienne raised a brow. 'I think you do.'

Drue clicked her tongue in frustration. 'Since when do you know everything about everything?'

'Since always. Now will you shut up? Some of us are trying to sleep.'

Drue kicked off her boots and lay down, shaking her head in disbelief at her friend, who grinned at her. But even when she settled onto her bedroll and closed her eyes, blankets warm around her, sleep did not come easily.

EARLY THE NEXT MORNING, Drue and Adrienne pushed several tables together in the tavern and spread out their maps and notes on the raiders' headquarters. Between Adrienne's leadership, Drue's ranger knowledge of Naarva and the Warswords' battle experience, they left no stone unturned when it came to finalising their attack on the stronghold. Drue had to admit, she'd never seen such a refined strategy.

As discussed the night before, Adrienne called all the fighting men and women of their forces to the town square for a training session with Talemir and Wilder. With Terrence perched on her shoulder, Drue watched from the outskirts as the two warriors shucked off their jackets and their shirts to spar before the crowd. Both men were leagues above those she'd known in Naarva, both in terms of their ridiculously muscular builds and even the way they held their blades – as though the weapons were an extension of them.

'Apparently they breed them differently at Thezmarr...' Adrienne commented from beside her.

Clearly great minds thought alike.

'We're going to run through three basic drills with you,' Talemir told the crowd gathered before them, his rich voice projecting to the far reaches. 'We'll start with defence, then move on to angles of attack and then deception. My apprentice and I will demonstrate.'

Drue laughed at the glare Wilder shot his former master. But that soon vanished as both men took up their stances.

'Did you ever think us lowly Naarvians would receive personal training from Warswords?' Adrienne asked quietly, her arms folded over her chest, her eyes fixed on the fighting forms before them.

'Definitely not,' Drue replied, equally mesmerised as Talemir assumed what she recognised to be a defensive stance.

Talemir twirled his sword, drawing the weapon up and to the outside by his temple, the point aimed at Wilder's throat. 'You see here, how I have created distance between myself and my opponent?' he called to the onlookers.

Wilder gave him a roguish grin and took a step towards him, brandishing his blade.

'As the opponent advances, I need to structure my cover. I need to place my weapon between my vital organs and my enemy's sword. Like so.' Talemir brought his blade down in a single, swift motion, the steel singing as it collided with Wilder's, blocking it from his path. 'There's also enough space to absorb the incoming blow and to counterattack. Always think about distance and cover when defending yourself. Create space between yourself and your opponent, and avoid exposing your delicate parts —' He blocked Wilder again, sidestepping and parting his feet into a lunge position, his sword poised between them once more. 'From a stance like this,' he continued. 'I can protect myself well, while also creating a direct threat to my opponent. From here, I can deliver a straight thrust, or turn to cut diagonally...' He demonstrated with slow, deliberate movements that were easy to follow.

'Why don't you show them in real time?' Wilder said, looking bored.

Talemir smirked. 'Are you so eager to lose to me in public?'

'You're not as young as you once were, *master.*'

'I'm still a champion of Thezmarr. Are you sure you want to be embarrassed?'

Drue tensed as Wilder didn't reply with words, but launched into a flurry of strikes and lunges. Talemir met every blow with a confident block, a smile playing on his lips as his protégé advanced, slashing and slicing, a blur of silver steel.

'You still leave that left side open, apprentice,' he teased, tapping Wilder's ribs with the flat of his blade.

Wilder swore.

'Never retaliate with anger.' Talemir spoke to the crowd again, blocking another jab from Wilder. 'Always keep a cool head, and remember: distance and cover.'

The older Warsword stepped to the right, forcing Wilder to change the angle of his attack, forcing him to strike off-centre so that his balance wasn't even —

'I thought I taught you better than this, apprentice,'

Talemir said, parrying and bringing his blade down across Wilder's, blocking another blow before withdrawing.

The two Warswords continued the dance, their blades clashing as they attacked, broke away, parried and sliced.

Not a bead of sweat appeared on either man's brow, but the muscle twitching in Wilder's jaw told Drue that his former master's taunts were finding their mark, despite the prior warning.

Talemir grinned widely as he surveyed his frustrated opponent and then the mesmerised Naarvians. 'Warriors are taught that it's better to seize the offensive than wait for the right time to counterattack. That is the mindset we want you to have against these raiders when we reach their stronghold tonight. They are not trained soldiers. They will hesitate; they will lose their formations quickly. We need to take advantage of that.' He turned back to Wilder. 'Let's look at some angles of attack.'

Wilder was all too eager to oblige. 'There are eight essential angles of attack when it comes to swordplay and cutting your opponent to the ground: straight down, straight up, diagonally down to the left and to the right, diagonally up to the left and right, as well as left and right strikes horizontally.' As he named each of these, he demonstrated against Talemir in slow movements. 'Of course, there are other variations, but for simplicity's sake, let's stick with these.'

Watching the Warswords spar showed Drue just how little she knew about the world of combat. Since Adrienne had trained her and she had fought among the Naarvian rangers, she had thought herself competent, perhaps even superiorly skilled, but now... Talemir and Wilder's bodies moved as though they'd learnt an entirely different language: cutthroat

222

and brutal, but also full of grace – each action fluid like water, every swing of their blade without hesitation. Their prowess was unparalleled and both she and Adrienne watched in awe.

'The last thing we'll show you is deception,' Talemir's voice rang out again.

Everyone seemed to shift on their feet in anticipation. It wasn't every day that common Naarvians saw inside the training ring of the legendary Thezmarrian Warswords.

Wilder spoke next. 'Some of you may have learnt the basics of swordplay long ago, where rules of honour were engaged and expected... But against evil, fair fighting is a sure way to get yourself killed. Learn the rules so you know how your opponent might break them, and how you yourself can turn those expectations on their heads.'

'First,' Talemir continued, lifting his sword, 'close the distance with your weapon raised, preparing for what should look to be a mighty overhead blow... Then, shift your weight and kick.' He showed them with his left leg. 'Aim for your opponent's liver, their groin or their midsection. Keep your sword up, ready to block a strike if the kick is unsuccessful.'

The men ran through several more examples of deception. Each one had Drue's hands itching to hold a sword and try it out for herself.

Finally, Talemir turned to the crowd. 'We have a few hours before we're due to ride out to the raiders' compound. Pair up. Let's see what you can do.'

18

TALEMIR

Talemir hadn't been able to stop himself from glancing across the crowd at Drue throughout the demonstration. In the early morning sun, the red streaks in her hair caught the light and her blue stare was more determined than ever. When the assembly broke apart, all he could think of was how he wanted to spar with her, how he wanted to share his knowledge with her – knowledge that, in her hands, would be deadly against any attacker.

But as the Naarvians surged through the town square, pairing up and finding the space to run through the drills themselves, Talemir lost sight of Drue. *She must have found a better spot to spar with Adrienne somewhere*, he figured.

And so he walked among the sparring Naarvians with Wilder, correcting their forms where he could, running through the examples again when someone wasn't sure. The rangers were of good fighting stock, though they lacked the finesse and the discipline of those who'd trained at Thezmarr. Even so, they were determined, like Drue, to defend their people against those who would do them harm. They were keen to deliver justice to the raiders.

Now and then, he glimpsed Wilder nearby, teaching the Naarvians the lessons Talemir himself had taught the young man. The sight made his chest swell, along with the thought that someday, it would be Wilder's turn to take on an apprentice, to guide another warrior to the Great Rite.

'Sir?' One of the young Naarvians yanked him from his reverie. 'Is the distraction technique like this?'

Shaking himself from his daze, Talemir patiently watched the lad before correcting his clumsy form.

'You were never that nice to me,' Wilder said dryly, as the boy scampered off to show the others what he'd learnt.

'You were never that polite.'

'Horseshit. I was a saint.'

Talemir scoffed. 'And I bedded all three Furies.'

Wilder snorted at that. 'You and Malik were ten times worse when you were apprentices. I've heard the stories.'

'Malik was the worst of us,' Talemir told him. 'I merely followed the leader.'

'Typical. Blame the poor bastard who's not here.'

'Malik would admit it proudly.'

'Probably,' Wilder allowed, looking out across the sparring pairs. 'They're not bad, are they?'

'I've seen worse.'

'When you look in the mirror, you mean?'

'When I look at you,' Talemir retorted.

Wilder grinned. 'I don't believe you.'

But Talemir's gaze snapped to the sky. Terrence came soaring towards them, dipping low.

Talemir's skin prickled, and as if in answer, the hawk circled him in close proximity, demanding his attention.

'What's this about?' Wilder frowned.

'Something's wrong.' Talemir was already moving, following Terrence as he beat his wings, moving away from the square. 'Stay with the rest,' he called back, before taking off at a run after the hawk.

The bird led him down a series of small alleyways, soaring between buildings, twisting and turning elegantly before ducking through an open door to what might have once been a butcher's shop.

Inside was empty. But Talemir instantly heard raised voices from the next room. Terrence landed soundlessly on a workbench and waited as Talemir crept towards the second door, listening.

'— give it a chance, Drue. You're just upset about Gus, about —'

'Don't you dare attempt to explain my own feelings to me, Coltan.'

'Please, don't take it like that. I just... I know we're good together. We've always been good together. Even your brothers thought so.'

'What a ridiculous line of argument. Why in the realms would my brothers give a shit about who I was fucking?'

'You don't need to curse. I only —'

'Don't touch me.'

Talemir's blood went cold.

'Drue, just remember how it used to be. How good —'

Talemir had heard enough. Sword unsheathed, he stormed through the door to find Coltan crowding Drue in the corner of the dank room, his hands clutching at her waist, Drue's forearm braced against his torso to hold him at arm's length.

'Release her,' Talemir said, his voice cold as ice.

'Are you following her now?' Coltan sneered. 'I see the way you look at her.'

'I won't tell you again,' Talemir growled, stalking towards the scrawny bastard.

Coltan had the good sense to pale, but not sense enough to shut his trap. 'This is between Drue and me. You have no business here —'

Talemir's hand shot out and wrapped around the Naarvian's throat, lifting him bodily from the floor like he weighed nothing. Coltan's face reddened instantly.

'You made it my business.'

'Talemir,' Drue said, touching his sword arm. 'I can defend myself.'

'That's not the point,' Talemir ground out, squeezing Coltan's throat. The ranger's eyes bulged in his head. 'You shouldn't have to.'

Coltan clawed at his hand, his feet kicking out at Talemir in panic.

'You're killing him,' Drue pointed out.

'Good.'

Coltan rasped, his eyes going bloodshot, his face turning purple now. Talemir relished every moment of the bastard's suffering. He'd seen how the pathetic lout harassed Drue, how he guilt-tripped her, how he tried to use her family's tragedy against her to get what he wanted. No, he deserved to have the life squeezed out of him; he deserved to —

'Talemir,' Drue warned.

Coltan's eyes pierced his, silently pleading.

Talemir gave his throat a final brutal squeeze for good measure, absentmindedly wondering if he'd mangled the bastard's vocal cords yet.

'Touch her again,' he said, leaning in, crushing Coltan to

the wall behind him, ensuring the punishing grip mirrored his words. 'And you die.'

Talemir dropped him and Coltan collapsed to the floor like a sack of potatoes, gasping and wheezing and clutching his throat.

To his surprise, Drue crouched beside him and, for a split second, Talemir questioned if he'd gone too far.

But Drue pulled a dagger from her boot and poised the tip under Coltan's chin. Spittle foamed at the corners of his mouth as he looked up at her in panic.

'I know it was you who sent that accusation to Thezmarr... I've known from the moment they arrived here and you nearly pissed your pants. What were you trying to do?'

Coltan panted, pulling back to avoid the tip of her blade.

But Drue kept it pressed close to his skin. 'Why did you do it?' she demanded.

'I...' the bastard coughed. 'I thought they'd just tell you to stop, to go back to being a lady. I didn't think... I didn't think they'd send *them* here. I —'

'You wanted me to go back to being a *lady?*' Drue spat out each word in disbelief.

Talemir watched as the truth of it all dawned on her. She had clearly known that the boy was infatuated with her, that he felt entitled to her. But this...?

As he panicked, more stupidity tumbled from Coltan's mouth. 'You were Adrienne's top ranger. She was sending you everywhere. Without me. You cared more about your duties to her than you did about me and —'

'I've heard enough,' Drue cut him off. 'Get out of my sight. And don't ever speak to me again,' she commanded.

Bruises already forming around his neck, his eyes still

wide and bloodshot, Coltan scrambled from the room, half falling over himself as he ran.

The shop door slammed behind him, echoing through the silence that now hung between Talemir and Drue.

She sighed heavily, sheathing her dagger at her ankle and standing. 'I had it under control.'

'I know you did.'

'Then why interfere?'

'Because you did not pick that battle, and sometimes, it's nice to be fought for.'

Drue seemed to consider this.

'Do you want to talk about it?' he asked. 'Did he hurt you?'

Drue shook her head. 'He manipulated the situation so that Adrienne ended up paired with someone else for sparring. I should have just outright refused partnering with him, but...' She shook her head again. 'It's exhausting constantly being on the defensive, constantly having to disagree. Sometimes it's just easier —'

'That,' Talemir stated, reining in his rage with all the strength he could muster.

'That what?'

'That is exactly why I interfered.' He peered into her face so she could see that he meant every word. 'You should never have to carry that burden alone.'

Drue froze. She looked distant for a moment, as though she were toiling through every instance like this from her past. Slowly, she nodded. 'Thank you.'

Talemir inclined his head.

'You would have killed him,' she commented.

'Without hesitation.'

'But you didn't... Why?'

'You didn't want me to.'

'It's that simple?' She raised a brow at him. 'Just like that, a mighty Warsword is mine to command?'

Gods, he wanted to kiss her, wanted to tell her that his shadow-infested heart was hers and hers alone to command, to do with as she willed.

Instead, he forced a laugh. 'Don't let it go to your head.'

Drue eyed him, her face grave. 'Teach me. I will not be the only Naarvian who missed out on training because of some prick.'

'You saw our demonstrations.'

'It's not enough. Show me. Show me how to best you.'

And so Talemir did.

OUTSIDE, Wilder had overseen the rest of the sparring session and assembled a weapons checkpoint with Drue's father, Fendran. The master forger sat at a makeshift table in the town square and the Naarvians lined up before him to present their blades for assessment.

As Talemir and Drue approached, Talemir noticed the older man's hands shaking as he took each blade and held it out before him. Drue's intake of breath beside him told him she'd caught it as well, and she didn't hesitate to go to her father's side. There, she whispered to him, and Talemir saw the telltale signs of a child trying to reassure their parent, but Fendran's furrowed brow did not abate.

'He's worried for her.' Adrienne's voice sounded from Talemir's left and he turned to find the general leaning against a nearby post, her gaze on the Emmersons. 'Fendran's already lost a wife and four sons to this damn conflict...'

'He won't lose Drue,' Talemir replied. 'Not on my watch.'

'Nor mine,' Adrienne vowed. 'But it's easy to forget that

he's old. He always looks so strong and powerful in the forge, surrounded by his hammers and fires. Out here... he looks frailer than I remember. I think Drue sees that too.'

'He's not to take part in the battle,' Talemir said.

To his surprise, Adrienne didn't recoil at the command. Instead, she nodded. 'I've already given the order.'

BEFORE LONG, noon was upon them and Adrienne had the Naarvian forces assembled on horseback. Talemir found himself once more next to Wilder, their stallions eager to ride out beneath them.

Talemir was relieved to see that Drue rode beside Adrienne, and that the bastard Coltan was nowhere in sight. Talemir wasn't sure he trusted himself not to obliterate the lout again if he laid eyes on him so soon after what had transpired earlier.

His gaze found Drue again —

'You wear your heart on your sleeve alongside that totem,' Wilder said, nodding to the emblem of three blades that graced the band around Talemir's bicep.

Talemir looked from his Warsword totem back to Drue across the way. 'What does it matter?'

'It tells the world your weakness, Tal.'

Talemir steeled himself against the truth of those words. 'I have no weakness,' he told his protégé.

At Adrienne's command, they rode out.

The half-day's ride to the compound passed quickly, and as evening fell, they moved into smaller groups and surrounded the stronghold as planned. Night settled around them, and without thinking, Talemir positioned himself at

Drue's side, where together, they waited for the general's signal.

Atop the crest in the land, overlooking the raiders' base, the Naarvian units were stationed half a league apart. In the dark, the signal finally came: three steady waves of a torch.

Twisting in her saddle, Drue faced him. 'Ready?' she asked.

'When you are,' he replied.

Together, they led the charge down the ridge, attacking the raiders' stronghold at last.

19
DRUE

D rue's heart hammered mercilessly, her blood roaring in her ears as they charged the stronghold from all angles. The swing of her sword made hope sing from within her, for there was nothing more she wanted than to bring the traitors to justice. To her, the raiders were worse than the wraiths that had plagued their lands and felled their kingdom; they had turned on their own people.

Along with the rest of her small cavalry unit, Drue burst onto the exterior perimeter of the village. Shouts rang out as armed men surged from the buildings.

They had expected this. They had planned for this. The surveillance she and Talemir had conducted had rewarded them tenfold.

On horseback, Drue and the others fought through the meagre outer defences, bringing down one opponent after the next, cursing each and every one of them for betraying their fellow Naarvians.

As they closed in on the heart of the stronghold and the buildings drew closer, Drue leapt from her horse and into the fray of the skirmish, more eager than ever to wet her blade with the enemy's blood and deliver swift vengeance for all those captured and caged within the warehouse.

We're coming for you, she chanted silently. *We're coming for you.*

She fought in close quarters with Adrienne, Talemir and Wilder, the four of them making a formidable unit, leading the attack with great success. All around them, Adrienne's forces were winning, infiltrating the stronghold just as they had all planned.

Drue engaged with a raider who tried to flee. No way in the midrealms was she letting one of those bastards get away. With Talemir and Wilder's demonstrations fresh in her mind, she attacked. Gripping her sword in both hands, she prepared to deliver a full-force overhead strike to her opponent before sidestepping him and delivering a brutal kick to his liver. As the man staggered back, winded, she advanced, utilising every moment of advantage, and without hesitation, she lunged, thrusting her blade into his gut.

Blood sprayed and a cry of agony escaped the raider's lips, but Drue was already moving on to her next opponent. She'd slay them all for what they'd done to her people, for how thoroughly they'd betrayed their fellow Naarvians.

In her peripheral vision, she spotted Talemir. He fought with his back to her, dual wielding his great swords against several opponents. His whole being hummed with power and she didn't know if it was the Warsword side of him or the wraith.

Drue didn't care.

She leapt to his aid and together, they battled side by side

234

and back to back, working as one to drive the raiders into the ground. Somehow, they fell utterly in sync, their timing and their distance complementing each other. Their rhythm and awareness of one another was a kind of magic foreign to Drue. Not even she and Adrienne fought this well together.

She ducked and parried, blocked and struck blow after blow, her strength, her energy barely wavering. A strange calmness had taken hold within as she wielded her sword, her movements answering the attacks raining down on instinct —

'We're nearly at the warehouse!' Adrienne called out. 'You two take the furthest doors. Wilder and I will take the north. I've already sent Baledor and four of his men to cover the other exits. We'll have them surrounded!'

With their victory in sight, Drue's spirit surged, and she gutted her final opponent, sprinting for the southern exit. Talemir was right at her side, the pair of them grinning almost manically at the sheer chaos of battle.

Drue kicked in the door and burst into the warehouse, her sword raised and ready to attack. The overpowering scent of oil filled her nostrils and her gaze shot to the cage where the people were being held.

Sure enough, thick liquid dripped from its corners.

Adrienne and Wilder rushed inside from the northern doors, only to freeze at what they saw.

Moments later, Baledor and his men did the same.

Drue's heart seized, her breath catching in her throat.

Unlike all the previous times she and Talemir had spied on the warehouse, there wasn't a patrol of raiders guarding their prize, but a single man, who held a blazing torch mere inches away from the oil-soaked cage.

'Drop your weapons,' he rasped. 'Or they're dead.'

20

TALEMIR

'Talemir...'

His name on Drue's lips was a plea.

She had frozen beside him, dozens of her fellow Naarvians facing a horrific death before them. But one wrong move from him, from any of them, could set the whole cage alight.

'Weapons down,' the man barked, brandishing the torch menacingly.

Talemir assessed the warehouse and every viable option, the darkness crackling inside him at the feeling of being cornered, outmanoeuvred.

How had this man known where to be and what to do? Rage blinded him for a second, rage at what the raiders had intended to do to these innocent people – offer them to the wraiths, potentially so they could be turned into monsters like him.

Shadows writhed inside Talemir, clawing at his insides, begging to be freed, to be unleashed —

Although the man at the cage had the advantage, he flinched when he looked upon Talemir, as though he could see the monster behind the face.

'Talemir...' Drue lowered her weapon.

Adrienne, Wilder, and their forces were doing the same.

Every fibre of Talemir's being objected to surrender, but he too dropped his sword beside Drue's.

'Use it,' she whispered. 'Use your power to save them...'

For a moment, Talemir froze. But as though it heard her, the darkness called again, and this time Talemir didn't hesitate to answer it.

Shadows swept in like whipping coils of night, extinguishing every candle, every light source, one by one. The entire warehouse went pitch-black, but for the torch the raider held; then it too was snuffed out.

People screamed.

But Talemir became one with the night. Invisible to the rest, he surged with the wisps of onyx magic, moving through time and space differently, becoming a part of the shadows he felt swirling around him.

Shouts and terrified shrieks continued, the cage rattling, the sound of swords being seized and brandished echoing through the building, its inhabitants suddenly sightless but for Talemir.

One moment he had knelt at the northern exit; the next, he stood before the raider, black power thrumming through every part of him, the song of darkness calling his name.

'I don't respond well to threats,' he murmured, tendrils of shadow writhing at his command, squeezing the raider's wrists, knocking the useless torch from his hand.

Talemir shed just enough power that the man and the man alone could peer upon his face, knowing that the veins around his eyes had gone black, that his stare mirrored that of the darkest evil. He didn't need his swords for what came next. He could end this man with the lashings of shadow —

'You're one of them,' the raider gasped, and the scent of urine filled the air. 'You're —'

A strangled, gurgling sound followed and the hot slap of blood hit Talemir's chest.

And at the smell of iron, suddenly, Talemir came back to himself, finding Drue by his side, her dagger dripping with the raider's blood, his throat slit from ear to ear.

Somewhere, light flared as a torch was lit.

And all Talemir could do was stare at the ranger. His kill on her blade.

'You...' he managed, dropping the raider's corpse to the ground. 'How did you... Could you see?'

Drue crouched, wiping her messy dagger on the raider's shirt before sheathing it at her ankle. 'No, I couldn't see. But I could sense you... Could feel you, somehow...'

'And you killed him. Why?'

Drue looked around carefully. 'He was about to spill your secret.'

'But...'

Drue waved him away. 'Let's get these poor people out of that damn cage.' She was already storming towards the bundle of chains and the heavy lock hanging around the door. 'Someone find the key to this! And someone fetch Fendran. He might have something to prise it open!' she yelled, sizing up the contraption. Then, more gently to the people within, she said: 'Don't worry, you're safe now. We'll have you out of there as soon as we can.'

The rangers surged to do her bidding and Talemir was

reminded yet again of how respected Drue was; the noblewoman turned wraith tracker...

While they waited for whatever came first – Fendran or the key – Drue assessed those captured.

'Gus isn't here,' she said quietly when Adrienne approached.

'Then we'll find him.'

A woman inside the cage pushed her way to the bars. 'This isn't all of us,' she croaked.

Talemir handed her a flask of water and motioned for the other rangers to do the same.

She took several grateful gulps before speaking again. 'They took some of us elsewhere, outside this village.'

'Who? Why?' Adrienne asked.

'They argued about it,' she replied weakly. 'Who to take. They said they wanted the strongest among us, the most skilled. At what, they didn't say. They just interrogated us, and every day took another away.'

'Did they say where?' Drue pressed.

'The lair,' someone from the back chimed in. 'At least, that's what I heard.'

Talemir gripped the bars of the cage. 'Did they say what for?'

The woman only shook her head.

Drue patted her hand through the crate. 'Thank you.'

Another voice from within sounded. 'What happened before?' a boy asked. 'How did it go all dark? How —'

'You say the raiders have been working with the wraiths for a long time, yes?' Drue cut in. 'It makes sense that the monsters have shared some of their magic with the traitors... It would appear the raider in question meddled with what he couldn't control.'

There was a murmur of agreement from within the cage, but the hair on the back of Talemir's neck stood up. Drue had not only killed for him to keep his secret, but now she was lying to her own people... It was more than he deserved. Unease shifted in his gut, but he remained silent.

Fendran arrived and managed to prise open the cage. The captives spilt free, crying out in gratitude and relief, some collapsing into one another's arms, some simply collapsing.

The night was far from over. Talemir and Wilder helped tend to the wounded and those in shock, having been trained in basic battlefield healing, while Drue and Adrienne took stock of what the raiders had left behind.

What seemed like hours later, Adrienne called everyone to the stronghold for an address. The cage had been removed and the raiders' supplies pilfered and spread across several tables.

'Victory is ours,' she announced.

A thunderous cheer echoed back at her.

'While the war is not over, the battle is won, and tonight, we feast and celebrate like kings!'

More vigorous applause broke out, and somewhere in the corner, the first notes of a melody sounded. The raiders, it seemed, had been living well. They had supplies from all over Naarva and a range of luxurious goods, including a harp, which Baledor, to Talemir's surprise, took up to play.

Apparently, the Naarvians were desperate for something good, because soon, music filled the blood-soaked warehouse and casks of wine and mead were cracked open.

Talemir met Drue's gaze across the unlikely celebrations and she smiled. She had no idea how beautiful she was, and at the sight of her, no victory had ever tasted sweeter. Despite all that plagued him, Talemir let himself appreciate the moment, let himself savour the fact that for once, the two of them fought a common enemy and not the monsters who were a part of him. He knew that battle was to come, but for now...

Drue approached him, handing him a cup of wine. Together, they surveyed the festivities. Wilder danced with Adrienne in the middle of the warehouse, looking a little more like himself than he had since Malik had been injured.

Talemir's chest swelled. He was happy for his friend, for his brother in arms.

Feeling Drue's gaze upon him, he turned to her.

She was luminous.

And it was her brightness that tugged something deep inside him. A wave of dread washed over him. He dropped his wine and lurched for the exit.

Talemir burst from the warehouse to find the sky moonless.

Gods – he hadn't realised. He'd been too wrapped up in everything.

It was the darkest night of the month.

The shadows within him writhed once more, screaming to be released.

Spotting a set of stairs on the side of the building, Talemir lunged for them, his heart hammering painfully as he hauled himself up to the rooftop, out of sight. When he reached the top, he doubled over, agony lancing through his back and fingertips.

He gasped, eyes watering, only to look up and find that Drue had followed. She stood there, staring at him, her eyes wide.

All this time, he'd been trying to convince her – convince *himself* – that he wasn't this creature, this monster.

But he was.

When the curse called, he answered.

And he hated himself for it.

He gasped for air, unable to look away from her, unable to hide his shame, his shadow-self.

'I'm sorry,' he breathed, right as the darkness claimed him.

21

DRUE

Drue yielded a step, her hand covering her mouth as she watched Talemir transform in the torchlight's glow. She had seen the change in glimpses before, but nothing like this, nothing like the uncontrollable shift that occurred right before her eyes. Talemir's eyes darkened, becoming almost black, like the veins fracturing around his temples. His handsome face twisted in pain as those giant, membranous wings speared from his muscular back, tearing through his shirt, leaving it in tatters hanging from his heaving frame.

Sharp talons unsheathed from his fingertips, shadows dancing at their points, wisps of power unfurling from the Warsword —

Beneath the starless night, Drue didn't take her eyes off him. She was rooted to the spot as hero became monster, his wings opening between his shoulder blades, spanning an impressive distance either side of him, ribbons of obsidian coiling around him, and reaching for her...

The curse pouring from Talemir compounded. It fought to cloak him in its darkness completely, a swirling mass that warred against him, seeking acceptance, seeking freedom. It sang to her too, though no nightmares, no visions of the past came.

Drue could see his talons cutting into his palms as he resisted the power's embrace, the tendons bulging in his neck at the sheer force of will.

And still she didn't move.

For what she saw in those eyes was not Warsword, not wraith, but intimately human... It was *fear*. Bright, unadulterated terror as Talemir battled with his inner nature.

The man was still there.

The man she'd come to know, the man she...

As though recognising something in her gaze, Talemir's form flickered, but in the dark of the new moon, he couldn't control it, no matter how hard he seemed to fight.

A pained groan escaped him, perspiration beading at his brow while the shadows punished him, while the darkness demanded payment.

Drue's heart ached for him, understanding that it wasn't just the physical agony of the shift that tortured the Warsword, but something far deeper, far darker: the hatred of himself and what he now was.

It was that realisation that had Drue reaching for him, closing the gap between them, her hand wrapping gently around his black-veined forearm, his skin cold to the touch.

But at that contact, his form flickered again between warrior and wraith.

'Drue...' he murmured, fighting for breath, staring at her as though seeing her for the first time.

'It's alright,' she told him.

He shook his head in disbelief. 'How is it that in a world leached of colour, I see you brighter than the sun?'

'What do you mean?'

Talemir's whole body heaved, flickering between the two forms again. 'When I am... this,' he said slowly. 'I see the world around me in black and grey... There is no colour, only shades of darkness. But you...'

Drue closed the little remaining space between them. 'Tell me.'

Talemir reached for her, but recoiled at the sight of the black talons protruding from his fingertips.

Drue took a breath, covering those claws with her hand. 'Tell me,' she said again.

Talemir's dark gaze met hers. 'You are a spectrum of colour in the shadows. You pull me back towards the light...'

Words failed her.

For a second, Drue's heart seized, stopping mid-beat before it started to pound without mercy. Her skin tingled all over and her knees threatened to buckle as she realised she had been living in darkness too, and that Talemir had —

Slowly, his wraith form faded.

The talons beneath her grasp dematerialised, her hand now meeting ordinary, smooth, clipped fingernails. A cool gust of wind kissed her face as the great wings at his back vanished, causing him to keel forward, the sudden lack of weight interfering with his balance.

Drue caught him, steadied him.

The strips of his ruined shirt fell from his shoulders, leaving his golden torso bare beneath the stars.

Hazel eyes met hers, intense and piercing.

Last, the ribbons of shadow departed, vanishing into the night like wisps of smoke in the breeze.

As they did, the world around them roared to life once more. The music from the warehouse below drifted up to them, the laughter and the revelry too.

Talemir looked down at where they clung to each other.

'We could be dancing,' he whispered.

Drue followed his gaze, unwilling to let him go. 'I thought you didn't dance...'

The Warsword placed his hand on her waist and clasped his fingers around hers, drawing her to him, his body flush with hers as he guided her into a slow waltz. 'There are many things I don't do that I would gladly do for you,' he murmured.

He steered her into a turn and they fell in time with the melody that flowed from the warehouse windows below. Even so large, Talemir was graceful and sturdy, finding the rhythm easily and holding her close.

As much as Drue missed the ballroom melodies and the sweep of her feet across a dancefloor, there was something she wanted more. For the first time since Talemir's transformation, she looked around the rooftop. There were several stacks of pallets scattered all over, and barrels – of what she didn't know. In one of the far corners, a guard had clearly been stationed, for a torch burned low and a pile of furs told her they'd abandoned their post in a hurry.

'I can think of better things to do than dance right now,' she whispered.

He paused, his whole body tensing around her.

'Talemir,' she said. 'There will be no moment more perfect than this one.'

The warrior loosed a tight breath. 'You're sure?'

'Yes.'

As soon as she uttered the word, he pressed his lips to hers in a searing kiss.

Every wall, every barrier between them fell away as Talemir held her and kissed her deeply, his mouth warm and lush and teasing. He tasted like juniper berries and Drue's blood heated in response. Desperate to touch him, she traced his bare chest, his tapered back and the breadth of his shoulders, wanting to memorise every inch of him with her hands.

Drue opened her mouth to him, allowing his tongue to brush against hers, sending a bolt of pleasure through her whole body and down to her centre. She pressed herself to him, feeling the hard pressure of his cock grazing her abdomen, making her heart stutter.

Heat swelled between her legs in answer.

'I want you,' she murmured against his lips.

Her words seemed to ignite something in the Warsword, for he pulled back, just for a moment, his gaze intense. 'I'm yours.'

A dark frenzy took hold of them both and Talemir's hands were tearing at her shirt, letting it fall to the ground behind her. He freed her breasts from the band she wore and swore quietly at the sight of them, of her nipples peaked against the cool night, before scraping his teeth down the side of her neck as he palmed her breast, eliciting a moan from her. She arched into him, white-hot need blazing within, her undergarments growing damper by the second.

'Fuck...' Talemir hissed as Drue explored the thick, hard length of him through the fabric. Her mouth went dry and her heart pounded wildly at the thought of him between her legs at last. Damn the layers between them. She needed him naked, now.

Unable to take her eyes off his erection straining beneath the material, she fumbled with his buttons, her hands trembling.

'Here.' Talemir took over.

Drue's toes curled at the rumble of his deep voice, as each button popped open and Talemir slid his pants down over his muscular thighs, his impressive cock springing free. He removed his boots and clothes completely, standing before her, running his hands over her.

'Gods,' she murmured, blinking slowly as she took in the sight of him.

Every inch of him was remarkable and perfectly indecent. No one had any right to look like that... Sun-kissed skin, a powerful, towering frame and muscles carved by the Furies themselves. And his face – gods, his face undid her. Those hard angles, that square jaw so beautiful in the torchlight. He watched her, seeming to sense every thought that flickered through her mind, and he smiled, eyes bright.

It didn't matter that they stood in the middle of a rooftop under the sky; it didn't matter that he'd just transformed from Warsword to wraith, from wraith to Warsword. None of it mattered except him, and the roaring need to feel him inside her.

She wrapped her hand around his cock, stroking him longingly —

'Tell me how you want me, Wildfire,' he said, caressing her breast like he had all the time in the world, pinching her nipple and slipping his other hand down the front of her pants.

But the words wouldn't form on her tongue, not as he kissed her fiercely, not as his fingers slid right down her centre, cupping the heat there, his thumb circling her clit.

Drue cried out, ripples of pleasure building instantly, rolling through her body, destroying any ounce of control she might have been holding onto. She bucked beneath his touch, a quiet plea for more.

Talemir stripped her pants and her undergarments down her legs, leaving them caught around one of her ankles.

'On second thought,' he growled, 'I know exactly how you want me.'

Words were still lost to Drue as his hands enveloped her, gripping her bare backside and lifting her, carrying her to one of the nearby barrels by the glowing torch. He set her down atop it, the timber cool and rough beneath her skin.

Talemir paused, taking a moment to survey her hungrily, as though he wanted to learn every inch of her by heart.

She did the same, her focus dropping past his rippling abdomen to the V-shaped sinew pointing to his hard cock, the tip glistening.

Drue licked her lips. Her body was alive with pleasure, so unlike anything she had ever felt before. She didn't know what came over her, didn't recognise the sultry woman panting before the Warsword, but with her mind foggy with the haze of lust, she spread her legs for him and touched herself, circling the wetness there, in invitation.

Talemir's mouth fell open at the sight of her, his cock twitching. 'Gods, you're beautiful.'

And with those words, the last thread of restraint between them grew taut and snapped. He enveloped her with his powerful frame, his fingers threading through her hair and bringing her face back to his.

The kiss was a brand, a claim.

I'm yours, he had said, and now he was showing her, unleashing himself upon her. He pulled her to him, crushing her breasts to his chest, drawing a gasp from her and sending another thrill of longing from her sensitive nipples down between her legs.

His teeth caught her lower lip, creating a pulse of delicious pain that mingled with her pleasure.

Drue wrapped her quaking legs around his waist and arched her hips towards him, demanding contact, demanding all of him. She would settle for nothing less now.

'Fuck me, Talemir,' she murmured between breathless kisses.

'I feel like I've waited a hundred lifetimes to hear you say that...' He fitted the crown of his cock to her wet entrance.

At the press of him against her, Drue whimpered, desperate to feel that hard length filling her, imagining him buried deep inside her. She scraped her teeth against the strong column of his throat and ground against him, desperate with need.

Making a frustrated noise, she reached down between them, cupping his balls and squeezing gently, drawing him to her.

He eased into her, only an inch or so, allowing her time to adjust to the size of him.

Drue's breath hitched at that first hint of the sensation to come. His cock was large, large enough that she could feel herself stretching around him.

The feeling was intoxicating. She rocked against him and Talemir groaned, the sound rumbling against Drue, skittering along her bones, her legs parting even more.

Still, he only pushed another inch into her.

'Talemir...' she panted into the crook of his neck, a plea, her fingers digging into his back.

At last, Talemir slid into her in one glorious stroke.

Drue's moan echoed in the night as the force of him dawned on her.

He stretched her wide, filled her completely, a slick, heated joining of which she could never have enough.

He pulled out, almost fully, only to slam back into her with a moan of his own.

Drue's head tipped, a cry of pleasure upon her lips as Talemir fucked her, slow and deep, driving her back onto the surface of the barrel, the roughness of the wood only adding to the delicious sensations.

Every thrust was more heady than the last, answering her arched hips, building that addictive pressure within.

Warmth spread in Drue's chest, flushed her face and the tops of her breasts as she moved with Talemir, as he coaxed every ripple of pleasure from her, driving his length into her over and over again, plunging deep inside her.

Soft cries of need escaped her as she lost herself to the sensation of him, as she felt the first bursts of a climax building at the base of her spine, at her core.

Talemir fused his mouth to hers, muffling her sounds, deepening the kiss as he reached between them and circled the most sensitive part of her once more with his thumb.

'Come for me, Drue,' he murmured against her lips.

Heart hammering, Drue tensed, his words and his touch causing that wave within her to crest. Furies save her, she had had lovers before, but none of them like this, like him. Like the gods themselves had crafted him for her and her alone, and her for him. He fitted her so perfectly, and only Talemir stirred those deepest, darkest desires, pulling her over the edge —

'Tal —'

He pounded into her, his pace increasing, ravaging her, drawing every wicked sensation from her body, setting her alight so completely that the world around her fell away. Drue gave herself to the pleasure, to the crescendo that he wrung from her with every thrust, every circle of his thumb. Drue couldn't breathe fast enough, couldn't catch enough air to keep up with what was happening inside her.

A half-sob escaped her. 'Talemir.' Utterly molten, her body quaked as she fractured, riding her climax into oblivion, pulling him closer, wanting him deeper, her inner walls clenching around him.

'Fuck, Drue —'

Seconds later, Talemir erupted, sinking even deeper as he came, completely uninhibited and wild.

His whole body collapsed over her, shuddering, his moan vibrating through her as he spilt into her.

Drue clung to him, rolling against him, wanting to wring as much pleasure from him as he had from her, wanting him undone before her as she now felt before him.

'Gods,' he panted, leaning against her.

Drue still couldn't catch her breath, the aftermath of her climax still coursing through her, Talemir's cock still seated inside her. 'That was...'

'Like nothing else,' Talemir finished for her, staring down at their sweat-slicked bodies, to where they were still joined. He rested his brow against hers. 'How did I find you?' he murmured. 'How did this happen...?' He trailed off, words failing him this time.

Drue traced the curve of his shoulders lightly. 'I believe I tried to kill you.'

Talemir huffed a laugh. 'A woman after my own heart.'

'Something like that,' she whispered. The weight of what they'd done fell over her like a heavy blanket. Whatever it was between them had amplified, morphed into something beyond recognition, beyond sanity.

Talemir carefully withdrew from her, the evidence of his pleasure now dripping down Drue's thighs.

She didn't care. Instead, she watched his face, those hard lines and strong jaw working through an array of emotions she couldn't pinpoint. She gripped his chin with her fingers, as he had done to her, and kissed him again.

22

TALEMIR

There had always existed a magic to make the sanest man go mad, and it was not shadows and darkness, but love: deep, unending love.

As Drue kissed Talemir, slowly and thoroughly, he realised that.

He loved her and all that she was.

And what she was... was everything.

She was the glowing beacon in the harbour of obsidian.

She was the flicker of flame that met his shadows.

And he loved her. He'd suspected it before. He'd danced around the edge of the feeling, but now... now he knew.

As her tongue brushed his, as her hands gently trailed along his skin, the words bubbled at his lips, demanding to be spoken.

Instead, he kissed her back, his cock already stirring again as he lifted her carefully from the barrel, taking her to the pile of furs that some watchman had left behind and laying her down.

Talemir lay beside her, unable to let her go, and slowly, the world came back to him. Melodies and the revelry from the warehouse still drifted up to them. He had no notion of the hour, no concept of how long they'd been away from the others, and he didn't care. All he cared about was the woman in his arms, the woman who hadn't feared his darkness, but embraced it.

'Are you alright?' he asked her, unable to stop himself from noting her flushed cheeks and the staccato rise and fall of those glorious breasts, as though she hadn't yet recovered from him. He hoped she never would.

A slow smile spread across that beautiful face. 'I am. Are you?'

Talemir felt fragile, as though she had shattered him into a million shards and pieced him back together anew. He felt raw and alive, terrified and euphoric all at once.

'I am,' he said.

I'm yours, he'd told her. He'd practically offered her his dark heart on a silver platter.

Looking at her now, still naked among the furs, he'd do so again in a heartbeat. He'd do many things again in a heartbeat.

He propped himself up on his elbow, his leaking cock already hard, throbbing for her.

Her eyes dipped there, and a smirk tugged at her lips. 'Ready again so soon?'

'You've clearly never fucked a Warsword,' he told her.

'I'm happy to be educated.'

'Thank the Furies.' He hooked her leg over his hips and fitted himself to her again, their breaths mingling in the crisp night.

Drue's gaze went wide, and she cried out as Talemir slid

home, as his hands dug into her backside and pulled her down over his length.

He drank in the sight of her lips parted in pleasure as he moved inside her, the sensation of her utterly intoxicating. Bringing his mouth to her nipple, he bit down, causing her to gasp and grab a fistful of his hair.

Pain pricked at his scalp, but it only amplified the silken heat of her around him.

Talemir moaned, increasing his pace, thrusting into her again and again.

She was panting and clenching, clawing at his back.

A desperate cry of pleasure escaped her, and she shuddered uncontrollably, her release clearly barrelling through her, wave after wave. And Talemir gave her everything he had.

THE WATERY RAYS of dawn woke Talemir first, and he gazed down at the woman curled against him, wrapped in his arms. Gods, he would have traded anything to have the luxury of waking her slowly, with his fingers, his tongue, his cock... But the pair of them had been gone long enough. Talemir was surprised that Wilder hadn't sent out a search party for him – that was, unless Adrienne had spent the night entertaining him.

Talemir took a deep breath, inhaling the scent of Drue, savouring the moment for a second more, before gently extracting himself from her.

Groaning, she reached for him drowsily. 'It's not morning,' she mumbled.

Warmth blooming in his chest, he leant down to press a

soft kiss to her temple. 'As much as it pains me, it's definitely morning.'

Drue pulled the furs over her head.

In the bruised light of dawn, Talemir collected their clothes and shoes from across the expanse of the rooftop. His shirt was in strips from where his wings had speared through flesh and fabric alike. That was going to be an interesting explanation to manage.

As Drue rose from the blankets, her naked body gilded by the soft rays breaking through the clouds, Talemir tugged his pants on hastily, lest his cock —

Too late. He was already hardening for her.

Cursing quietly, he tossed Drue's clothes to her, and she dressed.

When they were done, they looked at one another and Talemir shook his head. Drue's hair was mussed, her outfit in disarray, her expression sheepish, and from the way she moved, he could tell that her skin was still sticky with him.

'How do I look?' she asked, eyebrows raised.

Talemir bit back a laugh. 'Beautiful, as always.'

Drue folded her arms over her chest. 'But?'

A chuckle tumbled from him. 'But you also look like you've been fucked sideways.'

Drue burst out laughing. 'Great.' She dragged her fingers through her hair. 'I'll never hear the end of this.'

'Likely not.'

Her gaze raked across his bare torso, full of suggestion, making his cock twitch again.

'Right,' he said firmly, clutching his ruined shirt, needing to move before he stripped her naked again and bent her over the stack of pallets. 'I'll find the others and see what the plan is. You go and...'

'Make myself presentable?'

'Precisely.'

'You're not exactly debrief-ready...' she ventured.

'I'll make do.'

With a smirk and a final, teasing brush of her fingertips across his chest, Drue crossed the rooftop and disappeared down the steps.

Talemir waited several moments, breathing in the crisp morning, hoping to quell the surging inferno within.

He had no such luck. Only one thing would sate him now.

'Fuck,' he muttered, rearranging himself in his pants and tugging on his tattered shirt before descending the stairs.

TALEMIR WASN'T PREPARED for the shit-eating grin on Wilder's face when he entered the warehouse, his shirt in ribbons around his torso.

'Rough night, Tal?' Wilder clapped a hand on his shoulder, all too smug.

'None of your —'

'The sounds I heard from the roof made it my business...'

Talemir cringed inwardly, accepting the spare shirt that Wilder pulled from his pack somewhere and shedding his tattered one, drawing a few stares from onlookers.

When he'd finished buttoning the shirt – which was clearly one of Wilder's and a little tight – Wilder gave his shoulder a squeeze. 'I'm glad you found some comfort before we return to Thezmarr,' he said more seriously. 'Furies know we've needed it.'

It was one of the first times that Wilder had ever alluded to his struggles since the final battle of Naarva, and Talemir almost tried to coax more from him, until the words hit a note inside him.

Comfort? It was so much more than that with Drue. Talemir's gut hardened as the rest of Wilder's words washed over him – the innocent comment was like a cold bucket of water being dumped over his head. Suddenly, the pocket of bliss he'd experienced fractured, reality crashing down around his ears.

Return to Thezmarr... Of course. He was a Warsword of the guild. He had duties, responsibilities... All he had thought of was Drue. Everything else had seemed so miniscule in the face of what they had shared.

Only decades of training kept his face neutral. 'What are the plans moving forward?' he asked.

Wilder's brow furrowed slightly, as though he wanted to say something more on the subject, but he didn't. Instead, he surveyed the room, and Talemir followed his gaze to where tables had been set up at the far end and Adrienne was poring over a bunch of maps.

'Adrienne's been waiting for Drue...' Wilder gave a knowing smirk.

Drue herself strode into the warehouse, her shoulders back, her chin held high. Somehow she looked completely unruffled, as though she'd had a decent night's sleep and was ready for the day... He clearly hadn't done his job properly —

'Easy, brother...' Wilder grinned beside him. 'I'll wager she only just managed to —'

'Don't even finish that sentence,' Talemir cut him off.

From afar, they watched as Drue met a sly-faced Adrienne at the table. The glare Drue shot her friend told Talemir she was being subjected to the same grief.

'What did I miss last night, anyway?' Talemir asked his protégé as they started towards the women.

'A lot,' Wilder replied. 'Someone discovered a case of fire extract, so the rangers dug into that something fierce. Adrienne beat the shit out of that prick, Coltan —'

'What? Adrienne beat Coltan?'

Wilder nodded enthusiastically. 'Pummelled him to the ground, more like.'

'Why?'

'He talked shit about Drue. Adrienne just lost it. Beat him up and kicked him out of the forces.'

'About time.'

'Adrienne said as much. Apparently, he's been on her nerves for years.'

'Wish I could have seen it.'

'She knows how to land a punch. Let's just say that.'

The Warswords reached the women and Talemir schooled his features into a neutral expression once more. 'Is the plan still to locate the lair?' he asked.

Drue answered without hesitation. 'Yes. Adrienne has told me that some of the captives have opened up a little more since their liberation. They've spoken at length now about what the raiders discussed in front of them. The gist is that it's known there are more cages in the lair, and that they hold live captives. Gus might be there – there might still be hope...'

Beside her, Adrienne was nodding. 'We give our forces another half hour to recover from last night's antics, and for any injured parties to be assessed for the journey. Then we head south.' She looked to Talemir. 'Drue told me you might be able to track the wraiths?'

Wilder shot him a confused expression, but Talemir nodded. 'I have a rough idea of what to look for.'

'Good. We move out shortly.' Then, Adrienne made a point of looking between him and Drue and said with a straight face: 'I suggest you two eat something. You must be famished.'

Drue's answering glare could have given even the sturdiest warrior pause, but Adrienne merely laughed.

Talemir, however, looked at the food left over from the night before, his stomach growling. Adrienne was right; he was ravenous.

23
DRUE

Once more, Drue found herself astride her mare, riding out across the dying plains of Naarva, leaving the former raiders' base behind. Terrence soared overhead, his usually calming presence offering her little comfort.

For the first time in a long while, the travel and movement did not soothe her restlessness, but inflamed it. The lair of the shadow wraiths had always eluded her, but now, Talemir Starling rode at their sides.

With him, what happened next could change Naarva, change her, forever.

Drue glanced across at him, riding a few feet away. He looked fearsome atop his stallion in his Warsword armour, his expression hard and determined, such a far cry from the man who'd coaxed laughter and cries of pleasure from her lips the night before.

She couldn't fault his stoicism now. They were both invested in this journey, in what it meant for the future of the midrealms, and had been since the very beginning... But what came after? What happened when it was all said and done?

Drue shook her head, chastising herself. They still had to locate the lair and deal with whatever they found... There was no *after* until then. *After* could wait.

'You look like you're a million leagues away from here,' Adrienne commented quietly, nudging her horse up alongside Drue's.

Drue started, her friend's voice wrenching her from her reverie. 'I suppose I was.'

'Worried for Gus?' Adrienne asked.

Drue's shoulders sagged. 'Worried for everything.'

Her friend nodded. 'I know the feeling.'

'Do you think we're doing the right thing, Adri? Coming this way? Seeking them out?' Drue hadn't realised that was a concern of hers until it left her tongue.

'It's been a long time coming... Those monsters have concealed themselves for too long, cloaking themselves in their shadows. Now,' she said, with a glance at Talemir, 'we might actually have a chance against them.'

'I hope you're right.'

'Drue, I wouldn't have brought our forces here if I didn't think there was hope. You know that.'

Drue swallowed the lump in her throat. She did know that. Steeling herself against that which she could not control, she forced a grin. 'Heard you dealt Coltan some Naarvian justice...?'

Adrienne's answering smirk was wicked. 'I couldn't have him talking shit about my right-hand woman.'

'Finally.'

'He's gone,' Adrienne told her. 'I packed him off with some of the poor sods who'd been captured. Told him if he had a shred of decency left in him, he'd escort them safely to where they needed to go.'

'Good.'

Adrienne gave her a mock bow from her saddle. 'At your service, Lady Emmerson. So, is now the time when you tell me all the gory details about last night?'

Drue snorted. 'How long have you been waiting to ask?'

'Since the crack of dawn.'

'I...'

'Don't deny it. Wilder and I heard you.'

'You what?'

Adrienne laughed. 'Don't worry, it was just us. We sought some privacy of our own, only to find the rooftop well and truly occupied. Like the good friend I am, I got the fuck out of there and made sure your father was far from earshot, too.'

Drue's cheeks grew hot, despite the chill to the air. 'Gods,' she muttered.

'So?' Adrienne pressed, grinning.

'If you're so keen for details, why don't you spill them yourself?'

Adrienne chuckled. 'Ahh... The younger Warsword is... intense. Best lover I've ever had by a long shot. Insatiable almost...' She gave Drue a conspirator's smile. 'But we agreed we're not right for each other in the grander sense.'

'No?' Drue heard herself ask. 'How do you know?'

Adrienne shrugged, unbothered. 'He's been through a lot, got a lot of healing to do. And when he's through with all that...' She huffed another laugh, shaking her head. 'It'll take a woman who's more warrior than me to match the force of him.'

'You're a warrior, Adri,' Drue said, brow furrowed.

'Of a very different kind.'

'But —'

Adrienne waved her off. 'It's no bad thing, Drue. It's empowering to know such things and enjoy the pleasures life offers you anyway.' She cast another knowing look at Drue. 'Speaking of which... You're not ready to talk about him, are you?'

Drue glanced across at Talemir once more. His gaze was locked ahead, his broad frame straight in his saddle as he rode next to Wilder.

His words and actions of the previous night swelled in Drue's chest. If she focused, she could still feel the imprint of him on her, not just on her lips and her skin, but on her soul. Much had been left unsaid between them.

She found herself shaking her head.

'I had a feeling.' Adrienne smiled. 'I'm here when you are. In the meantime, perhaps a talk with your worried father wouldn't go astray? He's riding at the back.'

A pang of guilt hit Drue low and deep in her gut. She hadn't checked in with Fendran since the end of the skirmish. 'Is he alright?'

'He's fine, just scared for his only daughter. It's no secret to where we ride,' Adrienne told her. 'Go.' She motioned to the rear of the company. 'I need to get these fools back in formation anyway. One night on the drink and they forget everything I've ever taught them...' And with that, she rode off, shouting orders to her rangers, leaving Drue to find her father.

Fendran was indeed at the tail of the party, talking to Baledor, but his eyes lit up at the sight of his daughter.

'Pa,' she greeted him, urging her mare beside his horse as Baledor gave her a wave and made himself scarce.

'Drue,' Fendran said, smiling sadly. 'How are you?'

'Well enough. You?'

'Well enough.'

It was how it always was with them, or how it always had been since that fateful day in the manor. They had never learnt to share their grief, share their feelings with one another. Instead, they had spoken of wraiths and weapons and warfare. But now, it was clear that something plagued her father, and that he wanted to say more than a handful of words to her.

'What is it?' she asked.

He seemed to consider this carefully before glancing across at her, peering into her face, trying to read her.

Drue was shocked to realise how old he suddenly appeared without the glow of the forge fire.

'I know this quest of yours has spanned each day since your mother and your brothers' passing...' he said quietly.

Drue stiffened in her saddle. They never spoke of them, never uttered their names aloud, and now her father was broaching the subject of his own free will? She was so sure he would hammer out his grief in the forge forever.

'I know I have done nothing to quell your notions of vengeance and justice. The opposite, in fact.' He eyed the blade at her back. 'But there is life outside of these monsters, Drue... And I worry... I worry you will let their evil consume you too.'

'Where is this coming from?'

'In the brief moments since I have joined this quest, I have seen a glimmer of light in you... And as we ride towards the home of darkness, I do not want to see it dimmed, or snuffed out.'

'Pa...' Drue's throat constricted.

'Is he a good man, Drue?' Fendran asked. 'This Warsword of yours?'

Drue's cheeks flamed, but her father's question remained, stark and honest. He waited, and the moment stretched between them.

'Yes,' she said at last. 'He is a good man.'

As they travelled further south, the air grew colder. Drue rejoined the front of the company and rode between Talemir and Adrienne, with Talemir subtly guiding them across the darkening, overgrown lands.

Drue could feel it in him now: when he sensed the wisps of darkness she couldn't see.

Thankfully, no one questioned how exactly they were navigating towards the lair, though from the watchful expression on Wilder's face, the younger Warsword was suspicious, his brow etched into a scowl as Talemir finally brought them to a stop at the edge of an eerie forest.

'It's beyond here,' Talemir told them, eyeing the outer line of trees with trepidation.

Drue realised with a start just how warm her cuff was against her wrist.

'How do you know?' Wilder asked instantly.

'Call it a hunch.'

'You've never been one for hunches, Tal. What's going on?'

Drue watched the exchange with an inward grimace. She didn't know how long Talemir could keep his secret, or if he even should, when it came to his protégé. Wilder had clearly realised something was amiss, and he was clearly unhappy to be out of the loop.

But Talemir didn't respond. Instead, he turned to

Adrienne and Drue. 'We should go ahead of the forces, figure out what we're dealing with.'

Drue agreed. 'When we know, we can send Terrence back with a message and further instruction.'

Upon hearing his name, the hawk flew to her, landing deftly on her shoulder and remaining there.

Adrienne seemed to weigh up her options, fiddling with her reins as she did. 'Alright,' she said at last. 'We go ahead.'

The general left her orders with Baledor and took the lead into the woods.

The forest was colossal and gloomy. Climbing vines hung from every tree, strangling the trunks and blocking out the light from the canopy. A collection of thorny bushes dominated the ground, as though they had been planted there to deter anyone from entering. Even in Naarva, wildlife still thrived in the pockets of flora, but here... there were no sounds of rummaging critters, no birds calling in the distance. A forest that would naturally hum with the chaotic orchestra of nature was silent, deathly so.

Drue and her companions were quiet as they urged their horses into the dense thicket, the beasts uneasy beneath them. Drue could hardly blame them; her skin crawled with every passing moment, the sensation intensifying as they travelled deeper into the woods.

Talemir was tense beside her, his jaw clenched.

What could he feel? What could he sense beyond the strangling vines?

Time slowed and warped in the suffocating density of the forest. Drue had no idea how long they rode between the trees – it could have been an hour; it could have been five – but all the while she felt unsettled, the hair on her nape standing up.

She heard Talemir's intake of breath before she actually

saw it herself, bringing her mare to an abrupt halt: the end of the forest and the edge of a jagged cliff. They had reached the southernmost point of Naarva. Past the mainland was a brief stretch of dark water, and then... the midrealms island that housed the Scarlet Tower. It belonged to no single kingdom, but the worst of all of them inhabited it. She could see the peak of its turret amid the heavy clouds.

Drue sucked in a breath of her own.

For beyond that lay the Veil. A towering, impenetrable wall of mist, the very defence that the shadow wraiths were rumoured to have broken through.

But there was no sign of the monsters themselves. Nothing.

'I don't understand,' she breathed. 'I expected a camp, a lair...'

Wordlessly, Talemir pointed down.

Terrence dug his claws into Drue's shoulder as she peered over the edge of the cliff, only to have the air stolen from her lungs again.

The rock plateaued below into the ledge of a second bluff, and what Drue saw made her heart seize. Her steel cuff blazed against her skin.

There was only darkness.

Only doom.

24
TALEMIR

At the edge of the midrealms was a cesspit of evil incarnate.

Across the plateau of jagged rock, the band of wraiths lingered, tendrils of onyx power leaking from their talons, coiling around each other like serpents of the night. Their membranous wings folded behind their backs, mirroring those that had speared from Talemir's flesh. Not beautiful, as Drue had told him, but horrific – monstrous.

As though in recognition, his shadows writhed within him, begging to be released, begging to join his brethren below. It took all his might to contain them, to speak in an even, steady voice.

'We need to get closer. We need to find out how many there are, and if Gus and your people are there...'

Talemir and the others dismounted, urging their horses to run back to safety before wriggling on their stomachs to peer over the ledge at the horrors that festered below. The wraiths stalked the cliff, their elongated, sinewy frames and slow, predatory movements making them the stuff of nightmares. Talemir couldn't look away... They were a part of him.

From here, he was able to study them in more detail than the close quarters of battle had ever allowed him before. Their builds, although warped, told him they had been men once, like him, and that darkness had corrupted them from the inside out, twisted their bodies and their minds until they were the slaves of the shadows.

Is that the fate that awaits me? Talemir felt suddenly nauseous.

Drue was moving along the cliff's edge, searching for a way down.

She can't be serious... But the determined set of her jaw, the fire in her eyes, told him otherwise.

'There's two dozen...' Wilder murmured beside him. 'With the right strategy, we could take them.'

But Talemir shook his head. What they saw was not the complete picture. He could feel the obsidian magic whispering against his bones. The power he felt thrumming here was far greater than twenty-four wraiths, far more ancient, too. Something didn't add up.

'There's a narrow path,' Drue called quietly, nudging Terrence from her shoulder onto a lone branch. 'We can get closer this way.'

'Only to scout,' Talemir said, filling his voice with command as he approached her, the same tone he used with the shieldbearers at Thezmarr.

Drue's gaze gleamed with defiance as she gave Terrence a reassuring stroke. 'Wait here. We'll be back.'

'And I go first,' he added, gently pushing her aside and unsheathing one of his swords. He reached the top of the rocky track, so narrow he couldn't stand with his two feet side by side.

Both Drue and Adrienne wordlessly allowed him to lead.

Wilder frowned. 'Since when do either of you ladies allow us to take the lead with anything?'

'Leave it, Wilder,' Talemir growled, starting down the path in a half-climb, half-scramble.

Frustration rolled off his protégé in waves. He could feel it, tangling with the power that thrummed below. But there was no time to deal with him now. In single file, the four of them made their way down the cliff face at a snail's pace. With a weapon in one hand and the other held out for balance, there was no room for error.

The sickening scent of burnt hair drifted towards them on a sharp, icy breeze, lodging in Talemir's nostrils. He almost gagged.

When they reached the foot of the first bluff, they took cover behind a series of giant boulders and peered out at the wraiths still stalking the ledge.

Twenty-four of them. Wilder was delusional if he thought they had a chance at defeating them. But that was his grief talking.

And yet, even with two dozen monsters before them, what Talemir felt in his bones didn't match the sight before them. 'This doesn't feel right...'

A scrape of rocks beneath boots sounded and his heart froze as Drue disappeared behind more jagged stones —

Talemir lurched after her in a panic, but someone grabbed the collar of his shirt, dragging him back.

'Let her go,' Adrienne hissed. 'She's the best ranger in all of Naarva. She knows how to track, how to not be seen... She doesn't need your hulking mass lumbering after her and blowing her cover. Trust her.'

Shadows prickled at his skin and the song of darkness grew louder as panic seized him. He felt it unfurling inside him, creeping along his veins. The tips of his fingers tingled, talons threatening to shoot out at any moment. The centre of his back burned —

Is this where I lose control? Even the thought itself was tinged with a darkening haze.

But Talemir heeded Adrienne's warning, as much as his instincts screamed against it. The image of Drue in their hands, the notion of those talons piercing through her chest —

'Psst,' came her voice from a mass of rubble. Then the top of her head appeared, those red streaks in her hair glinting in the weak sunlight. She gestured to the band of wraiths pacing before them. 'They're in front of the entrance,' she whispered. 'There's a cave... Their true lair...'

Adrienne blanched. 'Right. *Now* we should go back. We have no idea what we're walking into. It was impossible odds before, but now...'

'We should burn it to the ground.' The words left Talemir's lips laced with hatred.

Drue gaped at him. 'Not a chance,' she said. 'Gus and the others, our people, must be in there.'

'Then it's too late for them,' Talemir replied.

'It might not be.'

'How long have they been in the wraiths' clutches, Drue?' Talemir's voice was hard, cold, even cruel. But he had to make her understand. 'If they are alive, they are no longer who they once were. It would be a mercy to end them.'

'A mercy?' Drue's nostrils flared, her eyes filling with fire.

'You can't mean that. Not after everything you've been through, after everything you've —'

'What's she fucking talking about, Talemir?' Wilder interjected.

Talemir ignored him, training his gaze on Drue and Drue alone, letting the darkness cloud his gaze, just for a moment. 'That's *exactly* how I know it would be a mercy.'

'Over my dead body,' Drue ground out, her grip tightening around her sword.

The threat hung between them, as vicious and dangerous as the power that stalked beneath his skin.

Adrienne cleared her throat, and Wilder stepped between them.

'So we get closer,' he said. 'Get the wraiths' numbers, find your friends and assess. One battle at a time. Agreed?'

Gods, Talemir could have clobbered him. Wilder's guilt and grief made him more reckless by the minute, but if he knew what awaited them in that cave... If he could feel the force of power that Talemir could feel, not even he would throw himself so willingly into that danger.

'Agreed,' Drue replied instantly, already turning on her heel.

A stream of protests on his lips, Talemir's hand shot out, gripping her arm. 'I go first,' he told her, forcing her to look at him.

She glared at him. That soft, vulnerable side of her from their night together was gone. She jerked out of his hold. But after considering for a second, she let him pass.

Talemir took the lead once more. If anything were to happen, he could buy her and the others some time. Inside him, the darkness vibrated as though in answer, as though it would relish the opportunity to be free of its shackles. Talemir fought it back down and moved behind the rocks, following Drue's clipped directions.

He now had her *and* Wilder's rage to contend with, but it didn't matter – not if he could keep them safe, not if he could save them from a horrific fate. Though Talemir didn't fancy their chances as he spotted the access to the true lair up ahead.

The stench of burnt hair was overpowering.

He heard Adrienne dry-retch from the rear of the group. He didn't blame her; the smell was repulsive. It coated the back of his throat and stung his nasal cavity with every inhalation.

Talemir led them up a slight incline to the mouth of the cave, careful to stay hidden from the wraiths below. His skin hadn't ceased crawling, his shadows singing as he grew closer, singing in recognition.

Brethren.

Home.

Talemir struggled to swallow, struggled to fight that inner nature clawing at his insides. It had never been this bad, this close to the surface...

He forced one foot in front of the other towards the lair, knowing that if he didn't keep going, Drue would. But when he reached the corner of the entrance, he froze, wrangling with the urge to recoil, to sweep Drue up in his arms and run as far away from this gods-forsaken place as possible.

'We need to leave,' he stammered, blocking Drue's view.

It was Wilder who pushed to the front, scowling. 'What's got into you?' he hissed. 'You never back down from a fight, sure as fuck not from *wraiths.*' He spat the last word with venom. 'What are you not telling —'

Drue's gasp of horror cut him off as she peered around

him into the cave and saw what he'd been trying to shield her from.

His blood went cold as he too looked upon them.

It was not a swarm of monsters as expected.

There was organisation to this evil, planning and scheming and discipline.

And at the heart of it all was the thing that stalked Talemir's nightmares, the thing that had pierced his heart and poisoned it with darkness.

A king of wraiths.

One of several.

'Furies save us,' Adrienne murmured, her mouth agape. 'What the fuck are those things?'

Talemir took a shallow breath, his throat burning with the pungent stench of the cave. '*Rheguld reapers*,' he said, not taking his eyes off the largest one, the centre of everything. Like the wraiths, it had perhaps once been human, but now, infected with shadow power, its elongated, leathery body towered above all else, perhaps reaching ten feet tall. Atop its head were a pair of curling horns that nearly brushed the stalactites on the ceiling, and the claws at its fingers leaked darkness.

'The reapers are the leaders, the kings of all wraiths,' he whispered to the others. 'They're smarter, stronger, bigger than their lessers. They can infect a person, reach into their chest and curse them with the same shadow magic.'

'How do you know all of this?' Wilder interrupted sharply. 'Why —'

Talemir silenced him with a shake of his head and stared into the cavern. It was the first time he'd seen a reaper since he himself had been cursed. Half choking on the thick, rotten air around him, he wondered if the monster who had sired him was in this lair, if the creature would recognise him. The strange stirring in his chest answered yes to both questions.

It was also the first time he'd been in the presence of wraiths without the bedlam of a battle. Here, he could sense their power, feel it permeating the cave and all the connections that came with it. The monsters below were linked, threads of dark magic tethering them to one another in ways he couldn't yet understand. But there was something here, something he needed to know; he could feel it leaching into his bones.

He loosed a tight breath. 'Every one of those foul things was a human once...' He reached out and gripped Drue's hand, squeezing it. 'See what they become? There is no hope for your friend, Drue... I'm so sorry.'

'Tal! Seriously. How do you know?' Wilder snapped. 'What aren't you telling —'

Adrienne raised a fist in warning. They fell silent as she pointed below.

The reaper at the centre of the cave paused... It lifted its head, sniffing.

Talemir's blood went cold. Could it sense him? Was he connected to —

Drue elbowed him, nodding to the right of the monster. 'That's an antechamber over there... That's where they'd be holding prisoners.'

Talemir's heart was breaking. He couldn't allow this, couldn't stand it. He grabbed her chin firmly, forcing her gaze to his. 'Enough, Wildfire. They are lost to you.'

Drue's breaths came fast and shallow, her stare intensifying before she hit his hand away from her as though his touch had burned.

A silent scream left his lips as she twisted from his grip entirely and darted deep into the cave.

Leaving Wilder and Adrienne crying out soundlessly in his wake, Talemir didn't think.

He lunged after Drue, calling upon his own shadows as he had only a few times before. He threw them out towards Drue first, the wisps of obsidian obscuring her lithe frame as she sprinted around the edge, ducking behind cover where she could, running straight for the antechamber she'd pointed out.

Hidden in his own darkness, Talemir moved like tendrils of smoke across the cavern, unnoticed by the monsters, heart hammering wildly to the drumbeat of his own power.

The cave was swarming with wraiths and reapers and he wove between them, his magic kissing theirs in a terrifying dance.

But Drue made it to the antechamber.

And he followed.

When he entered, he wished he hadn't.

Torches lined the walls, but they did nothing to quell the swelling dark. For the space was full. Full of Naarvians: some of them already wraiths, some of them mid-change, all of them chained to the wall like animals. There were those crying out in agony, those snarling, swiping their talons in a manic frenzy, those who hadn't made it.

Drue gave a strangled cry, skidding to her knees on the damp ground before a smaller creature, the remains of a knitted jumper hanging off him in strips.

'Gus?' she sobbed. 'Gus, I'm here. We came for you —'

Talemir's instincts kicked in and he coiled his shadows to his will, blocking the entrance to the antechamber for their protection just as Wilder and Adrienne burst in, horror etched on their faces.

For a moment, they were hidden from the monsters beyond, but it didn't matter, for there were plenty of monsters within. Some, like him, had taken on wraith traits still in their human form – wings, talons, black veins webbing their skin... Others had shifted fully, complete with elongated bodies and leathery, sinewy flesh. But the anatomy didn't matter. The blank, black stares and the stench told Talemir that they were lost. And those who weren't would be soon enough.

'It's too late,' Adrienne gasped, scanning the state of her once fellow Naarvians, now creatures of the night.

Drue was clutching the limp half-wraith, rocking him in her arms. He looked younger than Talemir had expected, still very much a child, with an unruly mop of dark curls framing the pallid complexion of his face. With a broken cry, Drue peeled the tattered knit away from his too-thin body, revealing the wings that drooped from his bony back and the talons that darkened his unmoving fingertips. His onyx gaze was vacant and unblinking. Gone.

'Darkness has claimed them all,' Wilder murmured in shock, before his eyes found Talemir and widened. He had seen what Talemir had done, what he truly was...

A monster, just like the rest.

Just like the creature who had felled his brother.

Sorrow closed a fist around Talemir's heart, but he couldn't fall apart now. He had to be strong for Drue, for all of them. He had to do what was right for the midrealms, for the poor souls whose free will had been taken from them, whose bodies and minds had been cursed with such poison.

With acid on his tongue and daggers in his chest, he sought the nearest vessel of shadow and lifted his blade.

'What the fuck are you doing?' Drue's voice carved through all else.

Talemir couldn't look at her, couldn't bear what he would see written on her face. He looked only to the poor bastard and the uncontrollable onyx ribbons unfurling from him. 'Ending this.'

'No.'

But Drue didn't understand the torture. Drue couldn't see that there was no hope for these creatures. He had been a Warsword when he was turned, and he was a Warsword now. Through the powers of the Great Rite, he possessed strength and endurance that these poor people did not. He had been trained to fight evil for as long as he could remember, and that had saved him. But there was no saving the Naarvians. They were succumbing to the curse; many already had. The most merciful thing he could do was put them out of their misery, and eliminate them before they were added to the army of darkness outside.

'It is the right thing to do, Drue...' He raised his sword.

There was a blur of movement.

Steel sang as swords met.

Drue blocked his blow, placing herself between the Naarvian–wraiths and him. 'I've come all this way,' she spat, her beautiful, tear-streaked face contorted with rage. 'And I did not do so only for you to kill them now.'

'Drue,' he pleaded. 'Don't do this.'

'You will have to go through me, Talemir.'

Talemir's grip on his sword did not slacken. 'I don't want to hurt you.'

'You already have.' Drue's silver-lined eyes hardened.

But Talemir couldn't leave things here, couldn't allow the wraiths to strengthen their army with people who had once been innocent Naarvians. He would have to disarm Drue and then do what needed to be done.

She would never forgive him for it.

But if he didn't, he would never forgive himself.

He hit her blade aside, but she stepped to the left, answering with a strike of her own, delivering a precise slice to his bicep.

He felt the sting as blood welled.

But she did not yield. Her stance shifted into offence. And then, Drue attacked.

She was a blur of steel and fire, a dancer on her feet, quick as lightning.

'Talemir —' Wilder called from somewhere, but Talemir focused on Drue, her blade swinging for him.

He blocked it, the impact singing up his arm.

She was not holding back.

She meant to hurt him.

Meant to kill him.

Their blades clashed, rattling the stalactites above. Talemir prayed to the Furies that his barrier of shadow blocked out the ringing and that the reapers beyond the antechamber were oblivious to the chaos unfolding in their midst.

Drue thrust her blade upward, just as he and Wilder had taught her.

Talemir blocked, his heart aching fiercely.

This could only end one way —

Drue took a long step to the outside, adding momentum to the twist of her hips as she brought her blade back around on him —

'You will not have them,' she snarled, bracing her sword against his, her breath kissing his face.

Talemir threw her off, sending her sprawling across the ground and lunging for one of the wraiths.

Adrienne's voice echoed over their battlefield. 'Please, we have to work together —' she was saying.

But Drue scrambled to her feet and lunged for him again. There was no fear in her eyes, only fury as she carved her sword through the air in a deadly slash.

Talemir stared at her, his muscle memory kicking in through the shock as he realised Drue was using his own moves against him, the manoeuvres he had taught her.

In a furious frenzy, they parried back and forth across the antechamber. Each time he tried to deliver a merciful blow against one of the wraiths, Drue blocked him, only to break away and attack him anew.

Their blades clashed again, each of them leaning close in a battle of strength.

Gods, he didn't want to hurt her. She was everything, the reason why, above duty and honour, he had to see this through. There had to exist a world in which darkness did not prevail, a world where she could live free from the shadows.

'I have told you since the beginning,' he pleaded, his heart fracturing as their swords pulled them close. 'I am not your enemy.'

Drue's lip curled as she forced his blade back. 'You are now.'

She whirled on her toes, looping her weapon around and bringing it down in a powerful, two-handed blow.

He deflected it, just. Withdrawing, he took a few steps back, but Drue only advanced, her eyes savage with rage.

'Stop this madness,' Adrienne called.

Wilder jumped in between them, but Talemir threw him aside, his strength somehow amplified.

'Drue.' He tried to reason with her again, defending himself against a series of slices, jabs and thrusts that rained down upon him.

'I trusted you,' she spat, feinting right and delivering a solid kick to his liver.

He grunted in surprise. Another move he'd taught her.

'And you would betray me?' It came out a half-sob this time, but her attack was none the weaker. 'After I have accepted every part of you? *Loved* every part of you? After all that, you would kill my people —'

The word she emphasised cut deeper than any blade.

Everything around them faded.

'They are not your people anymore.' He blocked a vicious slash to his leg.

'They will always be my people.'

Steel met steel again, and this time, Talemir forced them closer, locked her weapon to his.

Her breath brushed his face, and he peered into her eyes, so full of pain and confusion, so beautiful.

That blue gaze dropped to his mouth. She was going to kiss him, and amid all the violence and rage, he would let her, he would close his mouth over hers and tell her he loved her too —

The cold press of steel kissed his skin instead, digging into his chest.

Talemir looked down to see her blade poised at his heart.

'If you try to kill a single one of them, I will end you,' Drue whispered, her lower lip trembling.

Talemir didn't take his eyes off that sword. Throughout their travels he had sensed something about it was different, but the strange colour of the alloy had tricked him.

But as the metal pressed against his flesh, he recognised it for what it was.

Naarvian steel.

A weapon forbidden to all those except Warswords.

A blade that could very well kill the warrior and the wraith within.

His eyes went wide as she applied more pressure. 'You are breaking the laws of Thezmarr, the laws of all the kingdoms, by wielding that blade.'

'Haven't you seen? Naarva is no kingdom. Naarva has no laws.'

Talemir's grasp on his own sword weakened, his limbs going numb.

'Did you hear me?' Drue hissed, before repeating her words. 'If you kill a single one of them again, I will end you.'

'Do it,' Talemir told her. 'There is no hope for me, just as there is no hope for these creatures...' A single tear tracked down his cheek. 'I told you when we first met that you could carve out my heart before the end.'

His skin broke beneath the pressure and a trickle of blood ran down his chest, down Drue's blade.

She flinched at the sight, the violence in her eyes guttering.

Drue hesitated.

For a second, the truth lay stark between them.

She couldn't kill him, and he couldn't force that upon her.

There was only one thing he could do.

And so Talemir did what he had to.

He gave in to the darkness.

25
DRUE

Darkness erupted, and Drue was free-falling. Cold wind whipped her exposed skin as she tumbled through the air, arms and legs flailing, a scream caught in her throat. She could see nothing but inky black, could feel nothing but the kiss of the air as she plummeted through it.

It seemed to last an age, as though time and space warped around her.

The scent of cedar and dark florals tangled with shadow, a featherlight touch to each of her senses.

Then, she hit the ground, soft grass cushioning her.

For a moment, all she did was breathe. In and out, in and out, trying to quell the panic and grief and sorrow that threatened to bubble up from inside her.

A cloak of shadow was pulled from her body, bathing her in the golden light of dusk.

Squinting, Drue looked around. 'How...?' But the rest of the words wouldn't form, her skin still buzzing with the magic that had swept them from one place to the next. She had never known wraiths to do such a thing. But with the Warsword, they had done just that. They had travelled a considerable distance without moving a foot on the ground.

Talemir had shadow-walked them from the monsters' lair to safety...

'What the fuck?' Adrienne managed before dry-heaving.

She and Wilder were nearby, looking equally shocked and shaken. They had been returned to the outskirts of the forest, where the Naarvian forces had been ordered to wait. Around them, rangers were screaming in terror at what they'd just witnessed. Some were outraged, cries of vengeance on their lips.

And Talemir was gone.

A strangled noise escaped Drue, and she doubled over on the grass, her spine curling, pain hitting her deep in her chest. Her hand splayed wide across her breast as though that could somehow contain all that raged within, but it would not stop. She felt herself caving in. Everything coursing through her was suddenly too much.

She tipped her head to the sky and screamed. She couldn't save them. She couldn't kill him. She had failed in every sense. There was nothing left —

A firm hand gripped her shoulder. 'Drue?' Adrienne's voice sounded distant, far away from this gods-forsaken place, from this nightmare.

The antechamber flashed before her eyes, the memory of its stench filling her nose until she gagged. The sight of her people with leathered skin and talons, the sight of Gus, his jumper in ruins, his stare black and vacant.

Adrienne shook her. 'Drue, I'm here.'

'But Gus isn't,' Drue croaked. 'Neither is Talemir. He's gone.'

'What do you mean, he's gone?' Wilder stormed towards them. He looked dishevelled and unhinged, that same rage he'd carried with him since the moment they'd met still simmering below the surface.

That, more than anything else, grounded Drue.

She couldn't recall crying, but her face was wet with tears and she palmed them away with her sleeve. Talemir Starling did not get her tears. Not after what he'd done. Not after betraying her, leaving her.

Drue turned to the younger Warsword, letting her own fury shine through. 'He's left us. Abandoned us.'

'I don't believe you,' Wilder bit out.

It was then that Drue realised everyone was staring at them. The rangers had been waiting for word from Terrence and instead had seen their leaders fall from the sky in a cloak of shadow before their very eyes.

Now, the hawk circled overhead, cawing in distress.

Drue was on her feet in an instant. She had had her moment of weakness, and now it was time for strength.

She lifted her chin in defiance, eyeing Wilder critically. 'Don't you?'

The Warsword opened his mouth as though he meant to argue, ready for a fight. Drue didn't back down; she was just as ready. The duel with Talemir had barely scratched the surface of her fury.

But to her surprise, Wilder took a step back.

She watched as he moved about the camp, snatching up his pack and shouldering it before taking his stallion from an intimidated stable hand.

Talemir's horse was gone too, she realised.

It was another blow.

In fact, there was no trace of him, like he had never been here at all. If only the ache in her chest allowed her to believe it.

Wilder mounted and Drue gaped up at him, shaking her head. 'You're just like all the Warswords. Once again you abandon the people of Naarva when we need you most.'

The warrior's nostrils flared, and he pierced her with a furious glare. 'I would never.'

'Then where the fuck are you going?' Adrienne chimed in, her knuckles white around the grip of her sword.

'I'm going to get him back,' Wilder ground out. 'We can't win this without him.'

'Watch us,' Drue spat.

But Wilder's horse reared, towering above them all, before launching into a gallop across the plains.

The rangers watched him go.

'Fucking Warswords,' Adrienne muttered.

But Drue didn't have the heart to echo the sentiment. Hers lay bruised and broken at the pit of her stomach.

THE NAARVIAN FORCES camped on the edge of the eerie forest while Drue and Adrienne tried to regroup.

In the privacy of Adrienne's tent, Drue put her head in her hands, her body heavy with grief and exhaustion.

'What the fuck happened back there?' Adrienne asked her quietly.

'You saw what happened, Adri.'

'What I saw didn't resemble the whole truth of the matter...'

Drue loosed a breath. 'He wanted to kill them all.'

Adrienne waited.

Drue heaved a sob. 'And he was right, wasn't he? It *would have* been a mercy.'

Adrienne slid an arm around her, drawing her close. 'That is not for a mere ranger to decide. But I understood where he was coming from.'

'So I robbed them of mercy? Of relief?'

'I can't answer that,' Adrienne replied.

Hot tears burned Drue's eyes and she could no longer keep them back. For so long she had clamped down on that side of herself, the side that could break down and be remade anew. Now, the tears fell, and she sobbed against her friend.

'So they're all truly lost? After everything we have done to get here... Gus and the others are gone?'

Adrienne's tears dripped onto her shoulder. 'I think so...' she whispered.

They stayed like that for a time, quietly crying together. Another brother lost to the shadows.

At last, Drue wiped her puffy eyes and broke away from Adrienne to blow her nose. Exhaustion latched onto every bone. 'What now?' she heard herself ask, her voice small.

'I don't know.' Adrienne was still hunched over, resting her elbows on her thighs, her head bowed. It was always to her that everyone looked, always her that everyone expected answers from, even when she herself was in the throes of grief.

'Perhaps a strategic retreat?' Drue offered. 'We live to fight another day? We save our strength and our numbers for then?'

'Perhaps.' Silence lingered for a moment. 'Did you know Talemir could do... whatever it is he did back there?'

Drue's gaze was unfocused, the sound of his name like a

lance to her heart. She carved her fingers through her hair, holding it up before releasing it. 'No.'

'What even was that?' Adrienne shook her head.

'Shadow magic.'

'But... He hid us from all of them. He cloaked *us* in darkness and *flew us* out of there... All three of us. I mean, *is that what happened?*'

'I don't know. It felt like falling to me...' Drue murmured. 'Not that it matters.'

Adrienne read the dismissal in her last comment. She did not want to talk about Talemir. Not for a long time. If ever

—

The flap of the tent fluttered and suddenly, Terrence was flapping his wings before her, darting about the canvas wildly, distraught.

'What is it?' Drue asked, trying to gauge what was wrong.

He delivered a sharp peck to her shoulder – he never did that. Drue leapt to her feet and as soon as she did, the hawk shot out of the tent.

'I'm going after him,' she said to Adrienne, following.

Adrienne was close behind, and as they left, the commotion of the camp became clear. There was shouting nearby, a fight —

Drue and Adrienne launched themselves towards it. Their forces had been warned to keep noise and fires to a minimum so close to the wraiths' lair, but when the women came upon them, the Naarvians were so incensed with whatever was going on that they paid the pair no heed.

'What the —' Drue's words died on her lips as she saw what lay at the heart of their mob.

They had captured a wraith.

The small thing writhed against the ropes that bound it,

the men hitting it with spears, archers with arrows nocked to their bows taking aim —

Drue blinked rapidly, trying to focus on the winged creature restrained with lengths of rope. But there was no leathery flesh or horns, no claws tearing at the binds. Beneath the mud and tattered clothing, beyond the weak ribbons of shadow drifting outward, was a familiar form.

Her heart surged, and Drue threw herself into the chaos, leaping in front of the wraith.

'Stop!' she yelled. 'Stop! It's Gus!'

'Have you lost your mind?' someone called. 'That's not Gus!'

There was a roar of agreement.

'That's not the boy who was taken from us —'

'That's a damn shadow wraith, it's one of them —'

But Drue didn't move. She faced down the arrows, the spears and the angry rangers.

Soon, Adrienne was at her side, her eyes wide as she took in the creature Drue's body shielded.

'It *is* him, you fucking idiots!' she told the others.

The crowd surged around them, anger and violence blazing in their eyes.

'That's not Angus Castemont, I tell you,' another deep voice boomed.

A heavy silence followed before —

'Yes I fucking am,' a youthful voice shouted over the rest.

There was a moment's pause.

'Sorry for cursing,' came a mutter from behind them.

Drue's gaze met Adrienne's first, her chest swelling, then she turned on her heel, and threw her arms around Gus.

'You're...' Tears streamed down her face as she squeezed the boy tightly. 'You're alright.'

'Well... I mean... I have fucking *wings*, Drue,' he told her, frowning.

Adrienne snatched him from Drue's grasp into a bruising grip of her own. 'What'd we tell you about cursing, you little shit?'

'That it's only needed for certain occasions...' he repeated back to them, as though no time had passed.

A deep laugh sounded and Fendran appeared, clapping the boy on the shoulder, careful of his wings. 'If ever there was an occasion... This is it, eh?'

Drue was still shaking her head in disbelief, but in the presence of her father, as his words rang out across the forces, several others chuckled.

Spears and arrows were lowered.

Drue and Adrienne hurried to remove the ropes from their young charge.

Drue scanned him critically for signs of the dark power she'd seen in that cave, for the thing that had haunted Talemir so thoroughly that he'd fled.

His beloved knitted jumper was gone, and across his thin, bare torso were faint webs of black, but his eyes, which had been an unnerving onyx before, were back to their usual blue.

By her assessment, Gus was bruised and battered but —

'Drue, is there any food?' he blurted.

But very much himself.

The tension around the camp dissipated at once, and those who'd been uneasy before laughed nervously with the rest.

Both women had to bite back their questions until the boy had been fed and watered, his cuts and scrapes tended to. At long last, he sat in Adrienne's tent, wrapped in a blanket, a steaming cup of tea before him, looking at them expectantly.

'How?' Drue blurted at him. 'How are you here? I thought you were dead, or —'

'I wasn't,' he said happily.

'Clearly. So what happened?'

Gus looked from Drue to Adrienne and back again. 'I think I was asleep for ages,' he told them.

'Do you remember the attack on the watchtower?' Adrienne asked.

The youngster shook his head. 'Nope. Just went all dark.'

'Do you remember the journey to the lair?'

'Nope.'

Drue exhaled through her nose. 'What *do* you remember?'

Gus shuddered. 'Waking up in that place...' he said slowly, grimacing. 'It smelt so bad in there. And then I was chained up and one of those... horned things was reaching into my chest. I was screaming lots —'

Drue's own chest tightened, her hand seeking his.

But the boy was strong. 'I think I slept again after. Then... these happened.' He gestured to his wings. They were much smaller than Talemir's, more pink than red and black...

'Do they hurt?' Drue asked.

'No. But they make me walk funny. But I only realised that *after* I escaped and tried to find you.'

She almost laughed at that, recalling how Talemir's balance had been thrown off between forms. 'How did you escape?'

Gus' brow furrowed, and he scratched his head. 'I heard you in there, but I wasn't... awake yet. But then the room went black. And it wasn't the same dark as when those things are near. It was warmer. I thought I should follow it. Dratos helped me.'

'Dratos helped?' Drue exchanged a look with Adrienne. *One thing at a time,* she reminded herself. 'Did you fly?'

'Fly?' Gus blinked at her as though she were the town fool. 'How can I fly when I can barely walk?'

Drue had no answer for that. Instead, she asked: 'Gus, are there others like you down there? Others who, say... might have wings, or claws, or shadows, but are still... Well, themselves? You said Dratos helped?'

Gus nodded enthusiastically. 'There are loads!' he exclaimed. 'Well, some are dead. And some are... bad now. But there are others like me! And yeah, Dratos is still there! He said he's ready to slay some fucking wraiths —'

'Angus!'

'Well, he is.'

'He's conscious? He's in fighting form?'

'Uh-huh.'

Drue couldn't process the information fast enough, but when she looked up to Adrienne, her friend was beaming.

Despite the ache still pulling at her chest, Drue felt her own exhausted face split into a wide grin.

'There's hope yet...'

26
TALEMIR

Talemir Starling had lost all hope.

Shadows coiled around him, a sickness he would never be rid of, a plague that evil had wrought upon the midrealms.

Far to the east, he sat on the edge of a cliff, looking out to the black waves, the towering wall of mist that was the Veil and the peak of the Scarlet Tower among the clouds. Perhaps that was where he belonged, along with all the other monsters of humanity.

His shadows jerked in response.

He'd become the very thing he hated. He'd embraced the night so completely that he'd *shadow-walked*. That knowledge, that *instinct* had been lying in wait within, standing by to be unleashed. And though he'd used it to get those he cared about to safety, it still left a bitter taste on his tongue. He was a monster. He knew the darkness so intimately it had allowed him to bend time and space and distance to his will.

And now everyone, including Wilder, knew it.

His curse was no longer a secret. His wraith-self could no longer be hidden.

Talemir heaved a trembling breath and knocked back more of the bitter tonic Farissa had prepared for him. There was little point, and it made his stomach lurch terribly, but he did it anyway – for what purpose beyond punishment, he couldn't say.

All he could hear was Drue. All he could feel was the kiss of her blade against his heart.

He'd done the right thing, leaving her, of that he was certain. She was better off without him. Perhaps before he'd become a monster, they could have been something, but now all he would bring her was pain and grief and suffering.

Like the poor souls in the wraiths' lair. Doomed for darkness.

The only comfort he took from his leaving was that he'd never have to hear her words fraught with agony caused by him ever again. Until his final breath he would remember the ranger forged with fury and strength, beautiful and chaotic, even if she wished him dead. It was with images of Drue swimming in his vision that Talemir at last let darkness claim him. It dragged him under, recognising itself in him.

A SHARP KICK to his side woke him.

'Get up.'

Talemir rolled over with a moan, to find Wilder glaring down at him.

'I taught you better than to wake a sleeping warrior,' Talemir muttered, realising too late that his shadows were still drifting around him.

He snatched them in.

'You taught me a lot of things I'm not sure I believe in anymore,' Wilder bit back, his rage palpable.

Talemir's chest tightened. 'How did you find me?'

'Followed your horse's tracks. I knew he'd seek you out.'

Talemir looked around, confused to find his stallion grazing nearby. The beast had always had a blind sense of loyalty.

But his horse was not the pressing issue at hand. Talemir stood, brushing the grass from his clothes, and surveyed Wilder, his horse wary only a few feet behind him.

Unimaginable tension was taut between the Warswords, corded with Wilder's simmering fury. He was deathly still, but for his fists clenching and unclenching by his sides. A muscle pulsed in his neck.

'I'm sorry,' Talemir said, his throat thick. He found he couldn't look at his protégé, not now that Wilder knew what he was —

'Sorry? For what, *exactly?*' The words were loaded, venomous.

Talemir flinched. 'Everything.'

'That's not good enough.'

'I know.'

Wilder shoved him.

Talemir staggered back, keenly aware of the cliff's edge.

Would it matter if I went tumbling over it? The thought was sharp in his mind, a question, a dare...

'How could you keep that from me?' Wilder demanded, advancing, his nostrils flaring. 'We're family, you and I. How could you?'

'Wilder —'

'Don't fucking *Wilder* me,' he snapped. 'You're fucking *one of them.* You're a fucking *shadow wraith*, Talemir —'

'I'm still me.'

'Are you? Because the Talemir Starling I know wouldn't have abandoned an army, or the woman he clearly loves, to a doomed fate.'

The words hung heavy between them, raw and true.

'They were better off,' Talemir said weakly. 'Better off without me. All I do is poison everything. I'm a monster.'

Wilder shoved him again, hard. 'Yes, you are,' he growled savagely. 'And you didn't trust me with that. You trusted Drue, even *Adrienne* with that information – strangers, but not me?'

'You're different —'

'Damn right I'm different. I'm your fucking brother, Tal.'

'I'm also now the thing that robbed you of your real brother.'

Wilder's face fell. 'You're not. I saw —'

Talemir drew himself up to full height and let the shadows ripple from his whole body. He called upon his wings, snarling as they speared through the muscles of his back and flared before his protégé. His claws shot from his fingertips, black and sharp, ready to cleave through flesh and bone. He felt the crackle of the dark magic beneath his skin, shooting through his veins, and from Wilder's slack-mouthed expression, he knew he now appeared every bit the wraith he was.

'See?' he growled, every part of him writhing with power. 'This is what I have become.'

Wilder's chest heaved and he bared his teeth, a furious shout breaking from him before he lunged at Talemir, tackling him to the ground.

Talemir saw stars as both his and Wilder's full weight landed on his wings, the agony blinding. But before his vision had focused, a fist collided with his jaw.

Teeth singing, Talemir's eyes streamed instantly, pain blooming up the right side of his face. He turned his head and spat blood into a patch of flowers.

For a moment, he thought his eyesight was compromised. The blooms *shifted* as his blood hit the petals. He blinked hard. No, he wasn't seeing things. The flowers had *physically shied away* from the deep red splatters, away from his half-wraith blood.

The Furies were well and truly laughing at him now. For these were the very same blooms that Drue had been searching for: sun orchids.

But Wilder's assault had only just begun. Lost in a rage, he pinned Talemir in the dirt and was already drawing his fist back for another blow —

Talemir blocked on instinct, twisting his legs around Wilder and kicking him off. 'That was a shit punch,' he goaded, fire igniting in his chest.

'No doubt a reflection of my shit teacher,' Wilder sneered, unstrapping his sword from his belt and tossing it aside.

Fading back into his Warsword form, Talemir did the same. Suddenly, it didn't matter that Wilder's rage was founded and his was not; it coursed through him all the same, a fiery current demanding to be unleashed. If Wilder wanted a fight, he'd get a fight.

His protégé's nostrils flared, recognising the challenge, and he raised his fists, setting his stance wide.

Blood roared in Talemir's ears, his jaw already throbbing. Talemir raised his own fists, and shifted on his feet, itching to exchange blows.

'You really think you can take me, apprentice?' he taunted. 'You're not nearly ready, Warsword or not.'

'Fuck you.' Wilder attacked.

There was no slow build-up, no testing the waters, for they knew one another's strengths and weaknesses inside out. They launched themselves at each other, a flurry of fists and pain.

Wilder pummelled him, his knuckles colliding with Talemir's gut, his temple, his kidney. And Talemir let him come, tasting blood in his mouth, a cut on the inside of his cheek.

Gods, one day, the midrealms wouldn't stand a chance against Wilder Hawthorne.

Talemir took blow after blow, letting his protégé lose himself in his attack.

Then, Talemir struck. He delivered a jab, a cross, a hook and an uppercut all in brutally quick succession, circling like an enraged teerah panther.

Wilder's teeth were lined with blood, but that rage hadn't even begun to dissipate.

Nor had Talemir's.

They fought another round, vicious and gruelling.

'You happy now?' Talemir shouted, shifting his weight and dodging a strike to his eye.

'Not even close.'

Talemir blocked a hook to his face and delivered a hard and fast jab to Wilder's ribs, eliciting a grunt of surprise.

'You always leave that side open,' Talemir ground out. When would the boy learn?

'And you always talk too much —' Wilder swung, his fist colliding with Talemir's aching jaw.

Talemir saw stars again, stumbling.

He'd had enough.

Darkness roared around them, swallowing them both in a swirl of obsidian power.

When it faded, Wilder was on the ground, bound and restrained by shadows.

Panting, Wilder looked up at him, shocked. 'You cheated.'

'Did I?' Talemir wheezed, bracing his hands on his thighs to catch his breath. 'What do we always tell shieldbearers about fair play? What did we *just* teach the Naarvians?'

Anger still simmered in the younger warrior's gaze, but it was not the raw, uncontained rage from before. He scowled up at Talemir. 'Against evil, fair fighting is a sure way to get yourself killed.'

Wiping the sweat from his brow, Talemir released his shadows, the black wisps drifting off into the air. 'Exactly.'

Wilder sat up, spitting more blood onto the grass, his bottom lip split.

His own fury ebbing away, Talemir offered his hand. 'I am sorry, you know.'

Wilder looked at the outstretched palm, conflicting feelings warring in his expression before he reached up. 'I know.'

Talemir helped him up, both of them grimacing in pain.

'Your left hook needs work,' Talemir said quietly.

The look Wilder gave him was incredulous. 'You truly don't know when to shut up, do you?'

Talemir gave him a sad smile.

Wilder ignored it and gestured to the horses. 'We can make it back to camp in time to help if we hurry.'

Talemir froze. 'I thought I made myself clear. I'm not going back.'

Wilder turned to him, fists already clenching again. 'I don't believe you.'

Talemir stood firmly.

'You'd truly do this? You'd leave her defenceless against your kind? You care that little for her?'

Talemir surged forward, clutching a fistful of Wilder's shirt, nearly lifting him bodily from the ground. 'You know nothing of how deeply I care for her.'

'Then fucking show it.'

'You said so yourself: I'm *one of them*, Wilder. How can I —'

'Use it against them, you stupid bastard,' Wilder roared. 'You saved us in the lair. You beat me just now. We fucking *need you*. And not just the Warsword Talemir, but the *wraith* in you too.'

Talemir hesitated.

'Tal,' Wilder said. This time, his voice was gentle. 'There's hope —'

'Were you in the same cavern as I was?'

'Yes. But I was also there *after* you left. I found the boy – Gus – the one Adrienne and Drue have been looking for.'

'What?'

'He escaped and was wandering the outskirts of the woods. He had wings, but he was himself – a pain in the arse, really, but human... In control... He said there were others like him.'

Talemir wasn't breathing.

'I sent him back to camp as I came to find you. Drue and Adrienne will know by now. And if there's one thing you know about those two, it's that they won't leave their people to that fate. They will fight.'

'They need us...' Talemir murmured, his eyes falling back to the orchids he'd been tackled into.

'Yes, brother. They do.'

And Talemir realised, heart soaring, that it had not been a random patch of those flowers, but an entire field. Tugging on his riding gloves, he snatched up a handful, tearing them by their roots. Suddenly, nothing else existed for him. He whistled and his stallion came cantering towards him; it had barely stopped when he swung himself up into the saddle.

Wilder was grinning almost manically, his teeth still bloody. 'Let's go slay some monsters.'

But as they started back to the camp, an icy sweat broke out over Talemir's skin. He let out a moan of pain as he doubled over, spots blurring his vision.

'Tal?' Wilder's voice was distant. 'Tal?'

Talemir wanted to reply, wanted to tell him he would fight until his last breath against the wraiths, to save Drue, to save them all. But sharp agony, low and deep in his gut, robbed him of speech, of all senses.

He slid from the saddle.

Suddenly, he was back at Islaton, surrounded by a circle of white stones and a swarm of monsters.

The *rheguld reaper* was reaching into his chest all over again, piercing his heart —

'**D**rue!' The voice carved through the night, forcing her upright on her bedroll. 'Drue!'

Her name was laced with desperation, urgency.

She shot out of her tent in time to see Wilder Hawthorne riding into camp, the dying campfires illuminating a body hanging over his horse in front of him, a riderless stallion in tow.

Talemir.

Drue broke into a run.

Heart hammering, she skidded to a stop as Wilder swung down from his saddle, and she helped him pull Talemir's unconscious body from the horse.

'What happened?' she managed, taking in the sight of his sweat-slicked brow and his ashen complexion. His handsome face sported a range of bruises and cuts.

Together, they lay him down on the damp grass. He was shaking beneath their touch.

'I don't know...' Wilder said, his breaths coming short and fast. 'One minute he was talking to me. We were on our way back to you, to help, but then he collapsed.' Wilder ran a panicked hand through his hair. 'We fought. Hard. It could be an internal injury. I could have done this.'

Drue was patting down Talemir's body for any sign, any clue as to what was going on. He wasn't bleeding anywhere; no bones seemed broken.

She removed his riding gloves. Nothing but split knuckles.

But she froze as she spotted the skin beneath the collar of his shirt. There, his beautiful olive complexion was marred with a network of fine white lines.

Feeling nauseous, she skimmed a hand over his breast pocket, and pulled the familiar flask from his jerkin. It was far lighter than she expected. She shook it. Nothing.

Yanking off the cork, she sniffed its contents.

'Monster tonic,' she muttered, tipping it upside down, only to see a single drop leave the vessel.

'What?' Wilder asked, bewildered.

'He was taking this – a tonic prepared by one of your alchemists at Thezmarr,' she explained, not taking her eyes off her fallen Warsword. 'I don't know how much he was meant to be taking, but leading up to the skirmish with the raiders, I noticed him drinking a lot more. A lot more than seemed right.' She pointed to the strange marks on Talemir's neck. 'It was causing this.'

Wilder put his face in his hands. 'How could I not have known? How —'

'It's not your fault,' Drue said, pulling Talemir up into a sitting position, resting against her. 'He hated what he was so much that he poisoned himself with the damn tonic.'

Wilder scrambled to his feet. 'I'll find a healer.'

Drue shook her head and pointed to Adrienne's tent. 'Get Gus.'

'Gus? The boy?'

'Yes.'

Thankfully, Wilder asked no more questions, and darted away.

Drue pressed her brow to Talemir's, finding him clammy. 'You damn fool.' She placed the flat of her hand on his chest, noting that his heartbeat was terrifyingly slow. 'You already left me once. Gods, I'll kill you myself if you do it again...'

But Talemir showed no sign of hearing her.

His eyes moved rapidly under the lids, his mouth parting in a cry of pain.

Whatever he faced now were his own monsters.

Gus came running towards her clumsily, his wings flapping almost comically. Wilder and Adrienne followed close behind.

'Is this him? Is this the Warsword–wraith?' Gus asked, full of awe.

'Yes.' Drue clutched Talemir to her chest. 'And we called for your help.'

'How?'

'You have to tell me, Gus... How is it that you are you? And the others fell to the darkness? How —'

Gus panicked. 'I don't know!'

'Think,' she commanded. 'What was different about them? About you?'

'I don't —'

'Try,' she begged.

'I was younger than most of them...?'

'What else?'

306

The tips of Gus' ears turned pink. 'I... I didn't fight,' he said, embarrassed.

'Why not?'

'I... I liked them.'

'Liked who?'

'Not who. What! My wings. I liked them. I know they're like a monster's, but... but they're strong! I might be able to fly. Is that so bad?' he asked, his gaze imploring her to understand.

'No...' she breathed, a small piece of the puzzle falling into place.

'I'll get the healer,' Adrienne interjected, her voice hoarse.

'We are past that.' Drue leant in, so her nose brushed Talemir's cheek. 'You have to change forms, Warsword,' she whispered. 'I think the only way to beat this... The only way to survive, to fight the poison... Is in your strongest form —'

A soft moan of pain escaped the Warsword's lips.

She clutched him tighter. 'Talemir,' she murmured into his ear. 'You need to accept what you are if you want to live. It might be the strongest part of you, but it's not the only part —'

Breath catching in her throat, Drue looked down, finding tendrils of shadow rippling from Talemir's skin.

As light as a whisper at first, and then intensifying, blooming like flowers around her, thrumming with power.

'Drue...' Adrienne warned from nearby.

'It's alright,' she said, cradling the Warsword in her arms. 'You're alright.'

Darkness poured from Talemir, from his talon-tipped fingers, from his chest in pinpoints where the reaper had pierced his heart.

But Drue was not afraid. Not of the Warsword, not of the

wraith, and not of the darkness as it swept in around her, a billowing black mist.

The shadows fluttered against her skin, as soft as a sigh before a kiss.

They danced along her bones, hummed gently in her chest and toyed with her hair, playful and tender, graceful and warm.

And when the ribbons of darkness abated, a winged Warsword knelt before her.

28
TALEMIR

Talemir Starling had cut down more enemies than he could count. He had faced nightmares incarnate and become the darkness itself, and yet when it came to facing Drue after what he'd done... His heart stuttered.

Talemir Starling's heart *stuttered*.

Drue's beautiful face hardened.

And Talemir, despite all that had occurred between them just now, braced himself for a different battle.

Drue folded her arms over her chest, a vision of anger, regardless of the tears that streaked her cheeks. 'So you came back.'

Talemir winced at the sharpness of her words, but couldn't blame her for them.

He had left.

He had left her to face the horrors of the world alone.

'I'm sorry,' he said, still on his knees.

By now, the entirety of the Naarvian forces had emerged from their tents and were staring. Staring at the wings that were folded in at his back, staring at a winged Warsword kneeling before a ranger. They gathered around at a safe distance, murmuring between themselves, but seeming to understand that this was Drue's fight.

'I made a mistake,' he said.

'Several,' Drue bit back.

'Several,' he agreed. He wanted to reach out and touch her, to wrap her in his arms and reassure her he would never do something like that again. But those were actions, and his actions had burned her. Now, he realised, it was time for words.

'Why?' Drue demanded. 'Why have you come back?'

'Because there's no one else I want fighting at my side, whose home I'd wish to defend. If you're going into the depths of darkness, I'm going with you.'

'You did that, and you left. When things got hard, you *left*. Why should I believe you now? Why —'

'Because I'm in love with you.' The words flowed from him easily, the most natural response in the world, the starkest truth he could offer her.

Drue blinked, and Talemir heard her breath catch. 'What...?'

Hadn't she known? He'd practically told her before. *I'm yours*, he'd said. But the shock on her face told him otherwise, told him he should have told her he loved her the second the all-consuming feeling had bloomed in his broken chest.

Ignoring the others, he grasped her hands in his. 'Since the moment I met you, I have felt like I was soaring. With you there is no ground beneath my boots, no rail to hold on to, and for a time there, I fought it with all my might... But no more. I've let go. And Wildfire, it's more than I could have ever imagined. With you, I didn't fall in love. I rose amid it, stronger than ever before.' Talemir took a trembling breath, baring his soul like he never had. 'I love you against all reason.'

Drue stared at him, her fingers loose in his.

'If it's not enough,' he managed, bowing to unsheathe the dagger in his boot and, on one knee, pressing it into her hands, 'then carve out my heart, Wildfire. It's yours.'

29
DRUE

A winged Warsword was on his knees for her, offering her his heart.

In front of everyone.

Illuminated by the glowing embers of the campfire, his handsome face was ravaged by devastation, his hazel eyes lined with silver.

As though sensing that what was unfolding before them was less of a threat and more of a private moment, the crowd dispersed, leaving her alone with Talemir.

Drue wanted to rage at him for abandoning her, for breaking her into a million pieces, but he was here now, and there was no question – he had made it clear: his shadow-infested heart was hers.

She exhaled slowly, the realisation dawning on her.

Her own heart, with its own darkness, was his as well.

Drue pulled Talemir to his feet. The warrior towered once more above her, his head bowed to her.

'You'll take no more of that tonic,' she told him, searching his face.

'No, not a drop more,' he vowed.

'You need to accept every part of yourself.'

'I do,' he murmured.

The same thing that had once terrified her now liberated her – this thing between them was real, and it was as vast and unfathomable as the sea. And just as formidable.

With Talemir by her side, she could take on the world.

Drue brought his face to hers and kissed him, his bruised lips hot and swollen against hers, his eager mouth opening to her, allowing her tongue to sweep in and brush his, sending a current of longing through her.

But she pulled back, peering at his handsome, battered features. 'I love you, too,' she whispered to him and him alone.

Talemir loosed a tight breath, and then he moved. Suddenly, his hands were in her hair and he was kissing her fiercely, crushing his body to hers.

Tears pricked Drue's eyes. Her chest was swelling, teeming with everything she felt for this man. Love didn't happen once, she realised. It happened every day, in little moments, in the quiet gaps between grand words, in the lingering touches, in the hope it promised in the dark. Love was something that breathed and expanded, that was made and remade, again and again, reforged only to become stronger.

Drue melted into Talemir, her palms running up his chest, around his shoulders, where they grazed the soft membrane of his wings.

Talemir answered her with another kiss, hot and heady, full of desperate need, his hands sliding to her waist, to the curve of her —

'Do you mind?' Adrienne's sharp voice splintered the moment.

Reluctantly, they broke apart.

Adrienne and Wilder stood a few feet away, looking unimpressed, both with their arms crossed over their chests.

'In case you've forgotten,' Adrienne quipped, 'we've got a rescue to plan and a lair to destroy...'

'Yeah, the make-up sex will have to wait,' Wilder added gruffly, his cheeks tipped pink.

A low laugh rumbled from Talemir, and he pressed a kiss to Drue's temple. 'Later, then,' he murmured.

'Later,' she agreed.

It wasn't long before Drue found herself in familiar territory: crowded around a table, strategies and plans laid out before her with Talemir, Adrienne and Wilder at her side. Her father and Baledor were there too, and Gus, who had rather sweetly appointed himself the unofficial spokesperson for the half-wraiths still trapped in the lair.

Drue and Adrienne watched him, unable to stifle their amusement. The poor boy wasn't much of a spokesperson, for he was speechless most of the time, staring at Talemir in awe.

Warmth bloomed in Drue's chest as she spotted the pink tinge to Talemir's cheeks. He was clearly embarrassed by the attention.

'We only have a handful of options, as I see it,' Wilder was saying. 'Two, if I'm completely honest.'

'And they are?' Drue asked, turning back to the matters at hand.

'We could attack the lair directly,' the younger Warsword said slowly. 'Or we could create a diversion, draw them out, and when they vacate the lair, send a team in to rescue your people.'

'Attacking the lair directly puts those inside at risk,' Talemir countered.

'Agreed,' Drue chimed in.

Adrienne splayed her hands across the map of the island. 'So we create a diversion. How can we draw them out?'

'Use me,' Talemir said without hesitating.

Drue's heart seized. She only just had him back; she couldn't stand the thought of losing him again.

But Talemir continued. 'They seek power. I have theirs and that of a Warsword... I'll be a beacon to them.'

'And then what? We're free to be slaughtered out in the open while a bunch of half-wraiths may or may not be rescued?' Baledor demanded, before shooting a belated grimace of apology in Gus' direction.

Gus scowled, his wings twitching behind him.

'No,' Talemir replied. 'When we first entered the lair, I felt all the connections among them...' He said it slowly, as though he himself were only just putting the pieces together. 'It's taken until now for me to fully understand... All wraiths are sired to a reaper. It's how they were created. From the network of tethers I felt inside that lair, I suspect if you kill the reaper, you kill the wraiths it sired.'

Drue's blood ran cold. 'How do we know doing something like that wouldn't kill you? Kill our own people?'

Baledor spoke again, brushing aside Fendran's hand as it moved to stop him. 'Does it matter? It's for the greater good.' The older man turned to Gus. 'I'm sorry, lad, but if you were older, you'd understand.'

'I don't need to be older.' Gus' dislike was written all over his young face. But tucking his trembling hands behind his back, he turned to Talemir, eyes widening at the warrior's breadth and wings. 'Do what you must,' he said grimly.

Talemir gave him a kind smile. 'That's very brave of you, Gus. However, I believe those people like you and me won't be affected when the sire is killed.'

'Why's that?' Wilder demanded.

'Because though we accept the darkness, we half-wraiths cling to our humanity with all the strength we have. We are more human than shadow monster —'

'So you believe,' Adrienne cut in.

Talemir nodded. 'So I believe.'

'But it's a gamble,' Drue argued, panic wringing her heart.

'One we have to take.' Talemir's fingers slipped into hers, squeezing gently before he released them to cross the tent to where he'd left his saddlebag.

'There's something else on our side.' He donned a riding glove and produced a crumpled bunch of flowers. He dropped them on the table before her. 'I know you'd prefer a wraith heart, but I thought these might be more useful in our current situation...'

Dazed, Drue picked up the blooms. They seemed to sing beneath her touch. Her cuff hummed in response as well.

'But I'll bring you a reaper's heart before long, Wildfire,' Talemir murmured in her ear.

'Can someone explain to me what the fuck flowers have to do with anything?' Wilder demanded, his patience clearly wearing thin.

Drue suppressed a smile as she removed her cuff and handed it to the younger Warsword. 'They're a very rare species. They love the sun so much that darkness is their very opposite... I treated that steel with their essence and it recognises when they're near —'

'That's how you knew about him,' Wilder murmured in disbelief, looking between her and Talemir.

She nodded. 'Yes. And when I finally told him about it, we discovered that he couldn't touch it...'

'I'd rather not demonstrate that unpleasant experience again,' Talemir added. 'But it burns to the touch... A weapon against them. There's an entire field of these flowers.'

'How far is this field?' Fendran asked.

'A few hours' ride east.'

Adrienne scoffed. 'You didn't get very far when you fled.'

'Far enough for someone who has never shadow-walked three people to safety before,' Talemir retorted, turning to Drue. 'Could we put the essence of these orchids into our blades? To weaken the wraiths? To defeat the reapers?'

Drue studied the blooms in her hands before handing them to her father. 'What do you think?' she asked the forge master.

He was quiet for a long moment. 'I'll need a fire,' he said at last.

Drue saw Talemir and Wilder exchange looks. 'What?'

It was Wilder who spoke. 'Only Naarvian steel can actually kill a wraith or a reaper...'

'Which means that we treat as many ordinary blades and arrows as possible with the supply of flowers Talemir brought and we gather more before we initiate the attack,' Adrienne said. 'Our forces will aim to beat back the wraiths, occupy them so the two of you —'

'And me,' Drue cut in, unsheathing her sword.

Everyone stared at her and her blade of Naarvian steel – Wilder looked like he was about to start another row, but Adrienne held up a hand.

'And Drue,' she said. 'The Warswords and Drue will target the reapers. If Talemir's theory is right, it'll be enough.'

'And if he's not right?' Baledor asked, pinning Talemir with a critical stare.

'Then Naarva falls a little sooner to the impending darkness,' Drue replied coldly.

DRUE SAID her goodbyes to Adrienne in the privacy of her tent. Her friend would lead the rescue mission with a small force she'd handpicked, while Drue would lead the diversion with Talemir.

Adrienne hugged her tightly. 'Have I told you I'm happy for you, my friend?'

Drue squeezed her back and laughed. 'Even amid all this?'

'We take our happiness when and where we can. I'm glad you found yours, even if it's in the middle of a storm of darkness.'

Drue fought to swallow the lump in her throat. 'Luck be with you, sister...' she murmured.

Adrienne answered with a grin. 'Not if he's been with you first.'

EVEN WITH THE plan set in motion, Drue had to defend Talemir and his intentions more than once. The Naarvians were wary of him, more so than Gus, who was still clearly a child. But Talemir... Talemir had displayed true darkness, had unleashed it upon their camp. They were scared of him, and she didn't blame them. He was the very thing they had spent their whole lives fearing. To them, he represented the evil that had stolen their lands and taken their loved ones.

As they made their way through camp, Drue met their gazes with a hard challenge in her stare. *He is no monster,* she wanted to scream at them.

Talemir weathered the attention and wariness stoically, but she could see that it cut him deeply, that it confirmed the fears he'd carried inside himself for so long.

'You don't have to defend me,' he told her quietly as they saddled their horses. 'I understand their reservations.'

'I'll always defend you,' Drue said stubbornly.

'And I love you for that.'

The words sent a thrill through her.

'But it highlights some issues we might face, if we live through this...' he pointed out.

Drue closed the gap between them and kissed him soundly. 'One battle at a time, Warsword.'

He smiled against her lips. 'I'm yours to command, Wildfire.'

Together, they rode out of the camp at the head of the army.

And when dawn came, they would be ready.

30

TALEMIR

They rode through the night, preparing pyres along the coast as they went, ready to be lit upon the signal, ready to guide the wraiths right to them.

Talemir and Drue led the company, the mood taut with anticipation, fear and uncertainty. Talemir knew the forces would follow Drue and Adrienne to whatever end, but the fact that he, the half-wraith, had claimed a role of leadership, didn't sit well with them. Still, they tolerated him, knowing their chances were slim to none without him.

The lack of acceptance from the Naarvians niggled at the back of Talemir's mind, and he knew that there would be no place for him among them, or at Thezmarr, when the conflict was over. But he had Drue by his side, and as she had said: *one battle at a time.*

Drue and Wilder strategised as they rode, devising traps they could lay for the wraiths to incapacitate them while the Warswords dealt with the reapers. Wilder remained surprisingly quiet about the fact that she had a Naarvian steel blade sheathed at her back.

Talemir listened to them, realising just how much the Naarvians had adapted since the fall of their kingdom, how resourceful they'd become. It was little wonder when Drue was one of the people in charge. Pride swelled in his chest at the thought.

The hours passed quickly, and soon they came upon the field of sun orchids. The first rays of dawn bled into the sky, illuminating the sea of golden blooms before them.

Drue brought her horse to a stop alongside Talemir's and he heard a quiet gasp escape her.

'Fendran!' she called to her father.

The forge master came forward, his expression similarly pained as he looked upon the flowers.

Drue's mouth was set in a hard line and Talemir recognised her determination. As much as she would have loved to admire the flowers that reminded her of her mother and brother, there was important work to be done.

She turned to her father. 'Harvest a hundred or so blooms and grind them down into a paste as best you can. You'll find the rest of the ingredients and instructions on this list.' She held out a piece of parchment and a small jar from her pocket. 'This is what's left of my own supplies.'

Fendran took them both, nodding.

'Heat the blades and douse them in the extract,' she explained. 'We have no forge, but fire will do. That's how I've re-treated my cuff these past few months. Coat as many weapons as you can.'

The blacksmith asked no questions. He set off to do his daughter's bidding, and Talemir had to admire his faith.

'What else?' Talemir asked her, stomach fluttering in anticipation.

'Wilder and I will make sure the traps are coated with it as well.'

Nearby, Wilder shot into action, leaving Talemir feeling useless.

'Your part will come soon enough,' Drue told him, reaching across to pat his arm before leaping down from her mare.

He gave a stiff nod and went to find Gus and Baledor.

When he returned from briefing them about lighting the signal fires, Talemir found that a path had been carved into the sea of orchids, and a clearing created in the centre of the field, designed to draw the monsters right into the heart of that which weakened them. He just needed to make sure he didn't touch the flowers as well.

Several traps similar to those he'd seen laid out for bears lay camouflaged by bracken amid the blooms, creating false pockets of safety where wraiths might land in an attempt to escape the burning sensation of the sun orchids around them.

Clever, brutal and strategic, just like Drue.

The Naarvian forces worked quickly and efficiently under her orders, looking to her for reassurance. She gave it to them, never faltering, never showing weakness, and Talemir loved her even more for it. She was a beacon of hope, not only for him, but for her people as well.

As though feeling him, she looked up from where she conferred with her father and Wilder. Her gaze locked to his, and she nodded.

They were ready.

Talemir swallowed the lump in his throat. It was time for him to do his part.

He raised a hand to where Gus was waiting by an unlit pyre. The young boy saluted him before touching his torch to the kindling, the fire roaring to life. A moment later, another fire was lit, and another, and another, setting off a chain of signal blazes all down the coast, right to the cliff of the lair.

Then Talemir let darkness reign.

His talons unsheathed, his wings flared and Talemir tipped his head to the blood-red sky and opened himself to the onyx power within. Tendrils of magic poured from his claws, from his chest. He summoned it into being from the depths of his cursed heart and sent it wide, back west, to where the wraiths waited.

In an instant, he felt otherworldly attention tug towards him and he knew it had worked.

They were coming.

'Ready yourselves, Naarvians,' he called, his voice echoing across the plains.

Drue and Wilder fell into place at Talemir's side.

Darkness still shimmered all around him, but he turned to face the forces, the people of Naarva whom Thezmarr had failed before, the people he was determined not to fail again.

'I know I am not who you would choose to have fighting at your side,' he called to them, projecting his words to the far reaches of their formation. 'I know you have lived in the shadows of the wraiths for far too long, that you have fought the darkness valiantly, tirelessly. I cannot promise you songs of victory, but I can vow that we will meet darkness with darkness, that my shadows are your shield and I will wield them upon the enemy with the same wrath you feel in your veins, for I feel it too.'

There was a beat of silence, a beat of hesitation, before steel sang as it was unsheathed from scabbards.

Talemir's heart seized as Drue unsheathed her own sword and raised it above her head. 'Today,' she called, 'we rise as one against the darkness. Today, we drive those monsters back to the festering hole from which they came. Who's with me?'

A thunderous cheer echoed across the field of blooms.

The people of Naarva united once and for all as darkness blotted out the sky.

31
DRUE

The wraiths came first.

'Wilder! The archers!' Drue shouted, not tearing her gaze away from the incoming swarm, her heart racing.

'Nock!' Wilder commanded. 'Draw. Loose!'

A volley of arrows treated with the orchids' essence shot through the air as the throng of monsters swept in.

Ear-piercing shrieks rang out across the field and leather-skinned creatures fell from the sky, hitting the earth hard, screaming upon contact with the blooms. Arrows shredded their wings, pierced their sinewy flesh, bringing them crashing down —

'Loose!' Wilder yelled again.

Drue sprang into action, her flaming blade already swinging. She moved from one fallen wraith to the next, following Talemir's lead as he carved out their black hearts in quick succession. Wilder delegated command of the archers elsewhere and did the same as the swarm multiplied on the horizon, cold sweeping in around them, along with the putrid scent of burnt hair.

Whips of shadow lashed through their formations, sending their forces scattering, screams of agony piercing the air.

'Reform the lines!' Drue roared into the madness. 'Reform the damn lines!'

Those who were able regrouped, looking to her for further instructions.

Pushing aside the fleeting thought that this was Adrienne's job, Drue squared her shoulders and brandished her sword. 'Hold the formations!' she barked. 'Hold!'

Above, arrows and wraiths still blocked out the light, and a fresh wave of shadowed assault came for them.

'Attack!' Drue screamed.

All around her, the Naarvians fought hard, doing everything they could to incapacitate the monsters – arrows, spears, swords, all cleaving into the distracted and weakened creatures.

Drue scanned the chaos wildly as power lashed out like a nest of vicious vipers.

'Tal, to your right!' she cried, fear spiking amid the blur of battle.

The mighty Warsword blocked without hesitation and the wraith screamed as he cleaved its arm from its body and pinned it to the ground with his other blade. Drue sprang forward, gutting the monster without hesitation, slicing through its chest and ripping its heart from the cavity. She panted, not expecting the heavy seeping mass to trigger her gag reflex.

Choking down bile, she kept fighting, blood roaring in her ears as she moved through the fray. It was unlike any battle she'd been in before; more fraught and chaotic than those of the past. Drue swung her blade in a near-mania, carving into the enemy with an unleashed ferocity. Each slice into sinewy flesh was for her mother, every thrust of her sword for her brothers. She lost herself in the song of war, in the rhythm of vengeance.

The assault was a blur of movement, shadows swirling around them, the sounds of people shouting, some screaming in pain, echoing over the field. The clash of steel rang out, as did the metallic snap of the traps releasing as they caught monsters in their spiked jaws. The iron scent of blood mixed with that of burnt hair, searing Drue's nostrils as she whirled her blade again and again.

Wraiths and Naarvians alike wreaked havoc, and the sensory overload of the battle had her gasping for air, momentarily searching for a way out of the pandemonium. It was crushing, the violence and gore unending and pressing in from all sides.

But she would not succumb to panic. That was not what Adrienne had taught her. *Stop, think, assess.*

Despite the stench, Drue took a deep breath and kept moving. She fought by muscle memory alone as she searched the skies for the reapers. Both she and Talemir had speculated that the wraith kings would wait until the forces were at their weakest to attack, but they hadn't expected it to last this long...

She parried and blocked, sliced and carved, dodged and attacked, but it wasn't enough.

The wraiths kept coming.

And there was no sign of the reapers.

Blood dripped down Drue's arm. She didn't know when she'd been cut. She felt nothing.

Shock.

All around her Naarvians were fighting, were dying.

Talemir and Wilder duelled against several wraiths at once.

Her heart seized with regret as she met Talemir's gaze across the bloodbath, not for the end, but for the time she'd wasted denying what she knew in her heart.

Drue cleaved into another monster and charged deeper into the battle.

If this was it, then so be it.

She would defend her kingdom to the death.

32
TALEMIR

Drue was a vision of blood-soaked glory and Talemir's heart hammered with longing at the sight of her amid the war of shadows.

He moved along the paths the Naarvians had created through the orchids, hissing in pain when a bloom brushed against his bare skin. He fought with the strength of a Warsword and a wraith combined, while he let his onyx power strike the weaker creatures down.

A few feet away, Wilder was attacking two monsters at once, his steel a blur of silver and fire as he dual wielded, just as Talemir had taught him, and taught him well. The younger warrior felled two wraiths at the same time, slitting their throats and pinning each of them to the ground with a blade through their wings. He unsheathed the dagger at his boot to cut out their hearts.

On Talemir's other side, Drue whirled her own blade like a Warsword in her own right, a force to be reckoned with, a force honed by necessity and rage. She slayed a wraith then and there.

She spun on her heel, facing Talemir. 'Where are the reapers?' she shouted, her face flecked with black and red gore. 'We need them if this is going to work!'

'They'll come,' Talemir called back, slicing across more leathery flesh and leaving Wilder to hack out its heart.

'We can't keep this up much longer,' Drue warned, felling another creature.

She was right. The Naarvian forces were weakening.

Talemir took a breath and gave in to that second instinct, the one that he had fought with for so long, now an inextricable part of him. He sent another beam of obsidian power up into the sky. It pulsed above them, a dark calling card.

Everything about the battlefield intensified: the screams, the bloodshed, the terror, and suddenly, Talemir saw why...

The first *rheguld reaper* appeared in the near distance, morphing from one pocket of sky to the next, obscuring itself in a black fog. The ground vibrated as it landed in the clearing of the blooms, hissing viciously, its shadows lashing out, whipping the Naarvian forces and devouring their cries of agony.

Talemir and Wilder both lunged for it, brandishing their blades, ducking and dodging its savage attacks. It swiped at them with its talons, meeting their steel with a clash of violence and despair.

Talemir's shadows battled those of the reaper, a furious lashing of power. With each strike, Talemir knew that this wasn't the one who had sired him, wasn't a king of dark kings. That monster hadn't graced them with its presence yet.

Wilder shouted as he delivered a fierce blow to the

creature's torso, black blood spurting, the creature stumbling back with a wicked hiss. Talemir raised his sword in defence, but Wilder advanced, forcing the monster into the sea of blooms, smoke rising from its leathered skin as the golden petals seared it.

The thing shrieked in agony, and Talemir noticed the almost manic grin on Wilder's face as he plunged his sword into the monster's chest. He knew his protégé wasn't simply fighting wraiths, but the wraiths who'd hurt his brother so badly.

As Wilder's blade carved out the first reaper's heart, an outbreak of blood-curdling shrieks sounded. Wilder cast the heart aside and a dozen wraiths dropped dead, their flesh flaking from their bones, drifting into the air.

'It's working!' Wilder yelled. 'Killing the reaper brought down its kin!'

A cheer from the Naarvians exploded, their resolve renewed in the face of such hope.

Similarly heartened, Talemir released another pulse of power outwards, onyx magic thrumming from his very being, demanding to be seen, to be heard, to be felt —

Suddenly, he smelt smoke.

And in seconds, the field of sun orchids was up in flames.

A group of wraiths had turned their own burning arrows against them.

Fire roared all around. Unimaginable heat singed them all, the blaze so hot, so furious that it rushed over the land in a great wave.

'No!' Drue shouted as the inferno raged, swallowing their advantage, devouring their hope of survival. 'No!'

But fire knew no master, and it ravaged the crop, the sun

orchids blackening and wilting, the earth scorched beneath them.

Something rippled in the world just beyond Talemir's reach.

A chorus of terrified shouts sounded from the burning field around him.

Three reapers crested the horizon, almost blocking out the sun entirely.

'Talemir!' Drue called out, her face panic-stricken.

The reapers were upon them in mere seconds, coils of darkness whipping their forces, beating them back from where they had pinned and trapped wraiths. Amid the smouldering earth, they shrieked in recognition, struggled to free themselves and go to their masters.

Cruel magic lashed at the Naarvians from above, the reapers circling.

The one at the heart of the attack... Talemir recognised it. His sire. The monster who had inflicted the curse upon him, the reaper who had made him what he was today. And now, Talemir would show it just what it had created.

Fighting back the fear, choking down his inner protests, Talemir drew himself up and spread his wings. If he wanted to meet the reapers in a fight, he had to fly. He had to face them in the clouds.

A determined caw sounded by his ear, and Terrence swept in out of nowhere, beating his wings.

That was all Talemir needed to see.

He surrendered himself to his inner nature, to that dark power that lashed within. He felt it surge through his entire being, and when it demanded to be recognised, to be unleashed, he obliged.

The Warsword braced himself and followed instinct,

launching himself into the sky. Air whipped his skin, tangling his hair, making his eyes stream as he soared, Terrence flying right alongside him. His own wings beat powerfully at his back.

The dark power did not consume him; instead, it set him free.

He was born to have the wind beneath him and the shadows bending to his will. There was nothing more natural than this, nothing more right. He took a dive, relishing the kiss of the clouds against his skin and the vastness of the sky. His wings were as much a part of him as his limbs, as his mind, as his heart, and with them, he would bring down the monsters that sought to break the midrealms.

With the world burning beneath him, Talemir shot straight for the reapers, brandishing his flaming swords mid-flight.

Terrence gave another cry and aimed for the eyes of the largest one —

Arrows soared from below, piercing the wings of the two lesser reapers, sending them spiralling to the burnt field, while Talemir dived for his sire.

He swung his swords, finding that without the ground beneath his feet, the motion sent him reeling. High above the Naarvian forces, he needed to embrace the wraith side of himself completely if he wanted to survive, to win.

If he wanted to claim the reaper as his.

Talemir leant into his new form, allowing his wings to beat without so much as a thought, allowing himself to bow to instinct, to veer when his body demanded it, to give in to each fall.

He had far from mastered the skill of flight, but he was and always would be a Warsword through and through. Decades of training had hammered the fear from him, had left him with a discipline so refined he could swing a blade almost anywhere. And with that thought echoing in his mind, Talemir Starling attacked.

He struck with his right blade first, then his left, swiping at the reaper's deadly talons and slashing at its vulnerable wings.

The creature hissed, sending shadows shooting towards him, striking like vipers. Talemir let his own darkness swallow them, commanded his own shadows to cleave them in two. He lunged with his blades, jabbing at the monster's exposed middle, eliciting a rasp of pain.

There was a unified cry below, and Talemir chanced a glimpse down to see Drue and Wilder slay one of the fallen reapers, a dozen wraiths dying alongside it, their skin turning to ash in the wind —

Pain tore at Talemir's arm and he jolted back, cursing himself for his break in focus.

Blood poured from a gash in his bicep and forearm – *red blood, not black,* he thought distantly before he lunged.

In a whirl of wings and steel, he struck, his blades carving through flesh and bone, the following shrieks telling him he'd caused significant damage. He didn't let up. Instead he threw a high strike from his left side to the reaper's right, where its wing was exposed.

Blood sprayed.

Panting with the effort, his own wings still beating hard, Talemir cut upward with his other sword, cleaving into that sinewy flesh, that grotesque withered skin.

An arrow from below caught it in the shoulder, another through its thigh.

The creature's clouded blue eyes widened in shock, its magic bursting uncontrolled from its body now.

Talemir's power forced it back, lashed out in sharp, unrelenting blows.

A spear carved through the sky, narrowly missing the reaper's head.

Talemir didn't stop. His shadows unfurled from him, wrapping around the reaper's throat, tightening and tightening.

The monster's wings faltered as it thrashed, clawing at Talemir's shadows, desperate for air.

The creature's mouth opened. Words escaped its poisoned lips, words Talemir knew to be a long-lost ancient language, and yet he somehow understood... They came out in a hiss, coated with venom.

'There are more of us than you know,' it wheezed. *'More come through the Veil every day. The* rheguld reapers *and our army of wraiths will continue to spread. Darkness will prevail. You will all die —'*

It made a horrific gurgling sound.

For Talemir had shoved his sword up under its chin and through its head.

Talemir choked on a gasp as he felt a cord within him sever, the sensation sudden and icy. Only instinct kept him airborne through the shock.

Black blood showered Talemir and those below.

He yanked his blade from the creature and let it fall. The reaper plummeted to the scorched ground below.

And as it did, countless wraiths began to fade, their skin peeling away in flakes, caught in the breeze.

Still reeling from the ripped connection, Talemir sucked in a deep breath of crisp air, searching himself for any consequences of what he'd done. But besides the initial jolt, there was nothing. He was whole.

He landed deftly by the reaper's body and, with his dagger, slashed out its poisoned heart. His wraith sire was dead. Panting and clutching the hot mass in his hand, he looked around, dazed and disorientated, watching as the remaining wraiths fled back across the seas to the Veil.

Then, Drue was there, bruised and bloodied, soot staining her cheek, more beautiful than he'd ever seen her before.

Talemir dropped the reaper's heart on the burnt ground and pulled the fierce ranger into his arms.

Forgetting everything else, he kissed her.

It was a kiss that started the world anew.

33

DRUE

Talemir Starling, the winged Warsword, kissed her amid the ashes. Drue clung to him desperately, pressing her body to his as though to memorise every dip and curve that fitted so perfectly together.

They had done it.

Together, they had defeated the wraiths and the reapers.

She kissed him back fiercely as the surrounding darkness abated, fading away, drifting into the wind.

When they broke apart at last, Drue looked up at Talemir, his hazel eyes bright despite the blood coating his skin. The midday sun passed through the clouds, illuminating the red in his wings.

He brushed his lips over hers again. 'You're alright?' he breathed.

She craved more contact, but understood he needed reassurance first. 'I am. Are you?'

The Warsword nodded, pressing his brow to hers, seeming to breathe her in for a moment.

Squeezing his hand, Drue stepped back at last to survey the aftermath of the battle. The earth was scorched beneath their boots, not a single bloom left in the cinders. Drue's throat seized at that.

But the fire had been a cleansing too, for there was no sign of any wraith but the one by her side, and the boy-wraith in the near distance.

Wilder joined them at the heart of the charred field.

'Eight dead,' he told them, his voice sombre. 'Two dozen or more injured...'

Drue's chest tightened and Talemir's thumb stroked the back of her hand. 'Any word from Adrienne?'

The younger Warsword nodded. 'Blue smoke to the west not long ago. They made it.'

Drue felt her whole body sag with relief. Adrienne had rescued the others and set the horrific lair ablaze.

Thank the Furies, she thought.

But there was more to do. 'Do we know how many wraiths escaped?' she asked.

Wilder sighed. 'Hard to say when a horde of them just evaporated...'

'What about the reapers?' Talemir demanded, his speech rough.

'At least one reaper fled back to the Veil,' Wilder allowed. 'We did all we could, but —'

Drue lifted a hand to silence him, realising that some of the Naarvians had stopped what they were doing to listen. 'We emerged victorious,' she said, projecting her voice so all could hear. 'We took terrible odds and turned them in our favour. We persevered, we fought bravely, and now that foul lair is nothing but dust and its inhabitants no longer curse our lands.'

A cheer sounded.

Talemir leant in, his words only audible to her and Wilder. 'I fear this is not the end of all darkness,' he said quietly.

Drue let his warning wash over her, but it didn't dampen her spirit. For she knew that although what he said was true, what they had achieved here today was an unprecedented victory, and she would carry that with her forevermore.

Exhausted but alive, Drue and the others helped tend to the wounded and wrap the bodies of the fallen in shrouds. Her heart bled for their families, for those they had left behind. Baledor was one of the dead. Her father sat by his body, drinking from a small flask.

'Father.' Her eyes stung upon approaching, her chest seizing as she looked upon Baledor, a man she'd known her whole life. 'I'm so sorry,' she said to her father.

'Don't shed tears on behalf of Bal, Drue,' he replied sadly. 'He would be pleased, you know... To know that he helped leave the realm a little brighter.'

She nodded, not trusting herself to speak.

'You should be proud, daughter.' Fendran's voice cracked as he stood and enveloped her in his arms. 'You led our people to victory. You saw your mother and brothers avenged.'

Drue couldn't remember the last time her father had held her, but she accepted his embrace without hesitation. 'Thank you,' she murmured.

A familiar cry had her gaze snapping up to where Terrence circled close above.

Breaking away from her father, Drue held out her arm, bracing for Terrence's weight. Sure enough, soon his claws wrapped gently around her forearm and he tucked his wings in, offering her his leg.

There, a scroll was tied.

Drue recognised Adrienne's messy handwriting at once and unravelled the parchment with trembling hands.

We're all safe. Mission was successful.

Regroup halfway between camp and field.

Luck be with you. (Though he had a grand old time with me first.)

Drue breathed another sigh of relief and sent Adrienne's orders down the chain of command. Everyone was tired, but no one wanted to stay amid the ruins any longer.

An hour later, with their wounded cared for and their dead wrapped in shrouds, they rode out to meet their general.

THERE WAS a reason Adrienne had chosen the halfway meeting point. In her eagerness for battle, Drue hadn't noticed the cottages on the way to the field, but now she spotted several dotted around a patch of woodlands. It wasn't exactly a village, but a tiny hamlet, perhaps once occupied by a few families, now empty.

Drue swung down from her horse and was nearly bowled over by Adrienne a moment later.

'You did it,' her friend exclaimed, almost squeezing the life out of her. 'You fucking *did it.*'

'We all did,' Drue replied, unable to help the grin splitting her face as she glanced across at Talemir, who dismounted in one swift motion. He smiled, the sight making her knees weak.

But she turned back to Adrienne. 'And you? All is well?'

Adrienne clasped her shoulder, beaming as she pushed Drue towards a small group gathered around a fire. 'Better than well.'

There were about a dozen people, maybe more, some of

whom Drue recognised from the stronghold at Ciraun. Some of them sported wings like Talemir and Gus, while weak shadows rippled off others. They looked tired, but whole —

'Nice of you to join us at last, Drue Emmerson,' said a familiar voice.

'Dratos,' Drue sighed, stepping forward and shaking the ranger's hand. 'It's good to see you.'

Black wings were tucked in at the man's back, but he wore a wolfish grin as he kissed her knuckles. 'Thank you for what you did in the lair, for fighting for us.' His words were ones of unexpected reverence. 'We owe you a great debt.'

Warmth flooded Drue's side as Talemir approached.

Dratos looked up, his eyes narrowing at the sight of the Warsword. 'You...' he said, his voice a growl. 'You're the one they call the Prince of Hearts... You would have killed my little cousin. You would have killed us all.'

Talemir didn't blanch, but he bowed his head in regret. 'I would have, and for that, I'm sorry.'

The winged ranger raised a brow and took a swig of something from a flask. 'Maybe next time, do a more thorough check...?'

'I thought you were lost to the darkness.'

'A fugue state, Warsword. Couldn't do shit for a while there. Didn't you experience the same when you —'

Talemir stiffened beside Drue. 'I... I'm sorry.'

Dratos seemed to consider whether he wanted to continue berating the man who had just helped defeat the shadow wraiths.

In the end, he gave Talemir a mock salute before draining the rest of his flask and surveying him critically. 'You know... I do believe my wings are bigger than yours...'

Talemir barked a laugh. 'Un-fucking-likely.'

But Drue was already pulling him away.

With their forces reunited, the celebrations started and went on well into the night. After managing a quick wash in the nearby stream, Drue toasted to the Furies with her people. She sang and danced with them around the campfires and ate her fill from the deer Wilder had killed for them in the forest. But as the hours passed, she knew she couldn't deny herself any longer. Throughout the festivities, something else called to her, a playful darkness, a ribbon of power tethering her to the Warsword who stood patiently on the outskirts of the camp.

Talemir was waiting.

Drue slid her hand into his and pulled him after her, to the garden she'd discovered earlier by one of the cottages.

'I want to show you something.' Her heart was already swelling.

She led him down an overgrown path, into the fenced yard, the Warsword wordless at her side.

Before a rose bush, she stopped and pointed to a flower that bloomed there amid the thorns.

A rose as black as night.

'My mother always preferred blue jasmine and the sun orchids,' she said quietly.

Talemir stared.

'But these were always my favourite. They're called midnight roses. They have the darkest petals in all of the midrealms.'

'Is that so...?' Talemir breathed.

Drue pressed her body to his, at last asking the question that had plagued her. 'Will you return to Thezmarr now that this battle is won?' The fear lingered in her chest, for she knew he was a man of honour, a man of duty, a Warsword of the guild through and through, no matter the wings or the dark magic in his veins.

But Talemir shook his head. 'No,' he whispered against her lips. 'My place is by your side. Now and always.'

Tears pricked Drue's eyes, and she kissed him deeply. 'Then love me,' she commanded him. 'Love me in your shadow form.'

Talemir blinked at her, as though just realising what she was asking of him. 'You're sure? I can make the wings disapp—'

'No.' Drue had never been more sure of anything. She let her hands span the breadth of his chest, his skin warm beneath her touch. 'I want to know and love every side of you, the light and the dark.'

Talemir's chest rose as he took a breath. 'Then you'd best hold on, Wildfire.'

He swept her up into his arms and kicked the door of the cottage in.

As they entered, the first thing she realised was that he'd been here earlier. She noted the lack of dust and the tidiness of the small space. It was not the looted chaos she had expected. Drue turned to him, the question on her lips.

A rare blush tipped Talemir's cheeks. 'I figured we deserved more than some rundown old hut... And that the noblewoman in you might appreciate the fresh sheets...'

Moved beyond words, Drue kissed him.

Kissing her back, Talemir kicked the door closed behind them and pinned her to the nearest wall, her legs wrapping around his waist, careful of his wings.

'You don't want to use the bed, after taking such care with it?' she murmured against his lips.

'All in good time,' he said, withdrawing to leave a trail of kisses down her neck.

Desire already coursed through her, but when Talemir unsheathed a talon and cleaved through the front of her shirt and her bandeau, she was set alight.

That talon traced a line from the hollow of her throat, down between her breasts, to her navel. Drue's nipples hardened, her breath quickening as the winged Warsword drank in the sight of her, his gaze heady and hooded.

The words on Drue's lips failed her as Talemir bent his head and took one of her nipples in his mouth, sucking hard, biting just enough to blend pleasure and pain.

Her head tipped back and hit the wall. She was already wet, already wanting him so badly. She needed to get her pants off; she needed to get *his* pants off. Wriggling, she tried to get down, but Talemir held her there firmly, not finished exploring her torso with his teeth and tongue and hands. She arched into every point of contact, every ounce of friction between them, the anticipation, the longing building and building within.

Her shirt hanging in strips from her shoulders, Drue plunged her fingers through Talemir's soft hair as he squeezed her breasts and pinched her aching nipples.

She panted. It was both too much and not enough.

At last he let her down, but still he didn't take her to the bed. He turned her so that her back hit his chest. He stripped away the remains of her shirt and roughly tore down her pants, gleaning a cry of surprise from her.

'Gods, you're beautiful,' he muttered, holding her by the throat with one hand and tracing her curves with the other. From behind her, he spread her legs, the crisp air teasing exactly where she wanted him.

Drue let out a whimper of frustration. Her hands blindly went to work on his pants, brushing over the thick bulge pressing against her backside.

She managed to get the buttons undone, managed to slip her hand —

A deep moan escaped her, and she forgot what she was doing as Talemir's fingers trailed up her centre from behind, sliding through the wetness there.

His grip on her throat tightened, and he teased her clit with light circles.

Drue bucked her hips, demanding more.

Slowly, his fingers dipped inside her.

'Fuck,' she cried, spreading herself wider for him, already desperate for release.

'We will...' he murmured into the damp crook of her neck, leisurely drawing his fingers from her before sliding them back in, his pace infuriatingly slow, each stroke long and savouring.

'Tal...' she panted, reaching behind her to free his cock from his pants. His heated length pressed into the curve of her backside. She struggled against him, attempting to bend over, to line him up —

'Someone's impatient tonight.' He gave a wicked laugh, curling his fingers, eliciting a desperate moan from her, his teeth grazing the column of her throat. 'I was going to take my time... Learn every inch of you slowly... But I see you're having none of that —'

She bucked her hips again, wanting – no, *needing* to feel him inside her.

Talemir kicked off his pants that had bunched at his ankles and pushed her towards the bed at last.

She twisted to face him, studying the bright ring of green

around the hazel of his eyes, the way his hair stuck to his damp nape... As the backs of her thighs hit the mattress, her gaze trailed down his carved body, taking in the glorious view of his cock, thick and long and ready for her.

Talemir gave her a dark, delicious smile before pushing her onto the bed.

The mattress sank around her as he climbed between her legs, his wings flaring powerfully behind him at the view: her, exposed and wet.

He paused for a moment, as though he enjoyed torturing her, as though he would leave her panting and wanting. But then he gripped her thighs and spread her even wider, only to blow a cool stream of air on her aching core. There, he teased her mercilessly, applying pressure, but not quite sliding home with his fingers.

'Talemir,' she cried, a pulse of longing rippling through her.

'I don't know what I prefer more,' he murmured, kneeling before her and lowering his mouth to her. 'When you say my name like a curse...' He closed his lips over her, sucking gently on her clit, teasing, only to pull back. 'Or when you say it like a prayer...'

'Talemir...' Her voice was low and husky, full of warning.

With a wicked grin, the Warsword surveyed her in a haze of lust, before at last gripping his cock and fitting it to her.

White-hot need blazed inside Drue, homing in on that spot that ached for him.

'I love you,' she told him, almost senseless.

Shadows rippled from Talemir, ribbons of onyx wrapping around her wrists and pinning them above her head. Her back arched, her breasts swollen and begging for contact.

'I love you, too.' He lifted her hips and sheathed himself inside her in one dominating thrust.

Her hands still trapped beneath his shadows, Drue arched as pleasure exploded through her, her entire body suddenly molten.

Talemir plunged into her, and she lost all sense of restraint and decency. He freed her wrists, and she moaned his name, squeezing her breasts almost to the point of pain before digging her nails into his muscular backside.

Warmth bloomed between her legs as Talemir fucked her long and hard and deep, each movement coaxing desperate cries from her. Each stroke of him inside her built more and more intoxicating pressure, a rush of emotion cresting alongside it.

Gods, this man...

Shadows danced across her writhing body as he fucked her, as she felt every inch of him.

Drue rocked against him, demanding more and more until their bodies were slick with sweat and Talemir braced himself over her, devouring her mouth in a savage kiss.

'Come for me, Wildfire,' he commanded, his voice thick with desire.

Talons appeared at his fingertips and he raked them over her sensitive breasts, his movements becoming harder, rougher —

Drue's climax suddenly crested, rushing through her, an onslaught of almost unbearable pleasure. She cried out loudly, gripping a fistful of sheets, arching into Talemir, clenching around him —

Talemir swore, collapsing on top of her as he shuddered with his own orgasm, spilling inside her.

For a moment, they stayed like that, panting.

'Gods,' Talemir murmured, kissing her bruised lips and pulling out of her.

Drue didn't let him go far, twining her legs with his, the need to be close still so raw and primal.

He rolled to the side of her, closing his wings around them. She marvelled at them, the red-and-black membrane so soft yet so strong.

Talemir laughed as she traced it lightly. 'Who would have thought this curse would have such benefits?'

'You're not cursed,' Drue told him, her voice quiet and serious. She had been thinking about it for some time now. 'You're shadow-touched...'

Talemir stilled beside her.

'The darkness took a lot from me...' Drue kissed him soundly, desire already reawakening within. 'But it also gave me you.'

34
TALEMIR

Talemir couldn't get enough of her. He took Drue twice more in the night and once again in the morning, his need for her insatiable, his love for her beyond words. In bed with her, with the early sunlight filtering through the broken windows, he felt weightless. The only thing he was tethered to was her.

They'd marked each other with teeth and nails, and in his case, talons. But the true markings went much deeper than that. Drue had marked his very soul.

With her pressed to his chest, his wing curled around her, he didn't want to move, didn't want to acknowledge the world outside. But in the distance, he could hear the camp coming to life after the celebrations, and he knew it wouldn't be long before someone came to find them.

Talemir kissed the top of Drue's head, breathing in her lilac-and-heather scent. It was then that he realised she smelt like the fields of Delmira, like home. She only wriggled closer, her hand already drifting south —

He caught her gently by the wrist. 'As much as I'd love to fuck you again, Wildfire, I fear time is no longer on our side.'

'We can be quick,' she whispered against his heated skin, the words stirring his cock to attention.

'I'm insulted you think so,' Talemir quipped, gripping her chin and lifting her face to his.

Drue laughed, kissing him, her hand twisting from his grasp and wrapping around his erection.

Unsure that he'd ever be able to refuse her, Talemir happily relented, propping a hand behind his head and giving her a lazy grin. 'Do your worst, then.'

Drue obliged, pumping him in her palm and eliciting a moan from him.

How was it possible she had so much control over him? How could he want her so badly again so soon?

But the naked vixen simply smiled and shifted her weight until she was straddling him. She lowered herself onto him in one torturously slow glide.

'Fuck,' he groaned. The slick heat of her was intoxicating.

She pulled up, hovering over the crown of his cock so that he nearly slipped from her entirely, only to slam back down on him, riding him hard and fast.

Pleasure shot through his whole body, building from his balls and rippling into his shaft.

'Furies save me,' he murmured, watching her move, her breasts bouncing. Every single stroke sent a heady pulse of desire down his cock, every movement clouding his entire body with lust for her.

Drue looked wickedly smug as he tried to thrust into her and she pinned him down, grinding slowly against him.

Two can play at that game. Talemir twisted from her grip easily and pressed his thumb to that sensitive spot, circling her clit with just the right pressure he knew she loved, drawing a moan from deep inside her.

She bucked against him, her inner walls clenching around him in answer, and he swore, vaguely wondering which of them would cave first.

Her. It had to be her.

In one swift, powerful motion, he flipped them over so he was on top, then rolled her onto her stomach, kissing along her spine and tracing the contour of her backside with his fingertips.

'On your hands and knees,' he told her.

Panting, Drue did as he bid. On all fours before him, she presented herself to him: flushed, wet and glorious. He had never seen a more beautiful sight.

And when he slid inside her, he saw stars.

A man unleashed, he pounded into her and reached around to pinch her hardened nipples, still sensitive from the night before. Drue pushed against him, arching her back, allowing him deeper.

Talemir nearly came then and there.

But he pulled himself back from the brink. He wasn't finished with her yet. He hauled her up against him so her spine was flush with his chest and his fingers found her clit again, circling it until her breathing was ragged and she flung her arm out, gripping the back of his neck, demanding more.

'Tal,' she cried out.

Her whole body trembled around him and she moaned again, this time letting go of all control, meeting every one of his thrusts with a backward push.

And only when he had wrung every last drop of desire from her, only when she was half sobbing with pleasure in his arms, did he allow his own climax to rush through him.

He came with a broken shout, clutching Drue to him tightly, emptying himself into her with a ragged gasp.

'Fuck,' he murmured against her sweat-slicked back, spots swimming in his vision.

They collapsed onto the bed, a tangle of limbs.

'Were you saying something about there not being enough time?' Drue muttered.

'I'm glad you proved me wrong,' Talemir panted.

They lay there for a while, catching their breath, Drue gently stroking the outside part of one of his wings. Eventually, when his heart rate was relatively even, Talemir propped himself up on his elbow and looked at her.

Her skin was still flushed, her peaked breasts rising and falling, her gaze hooded in the aftermath of pleasure. 'Yes, Warsword?'

Talemir smiled. 'Before you pounced on me, I was going to ask what our plans are now. The others are packing up as we speak... What do you intend for us to do?'

A serious look passed over Drue's face and with a groan, she hauled herself from the bed, scanning the cottage for her ruined garments.

'I brought your pack.' Talemir pointed to the corner of the room. 'I made sure you had spare clothes in there.'

Drue scooped up the bag, rummaging through it. 'Thank you.' Locating a shirt, she pulled it over her head, though it did nothing to hide her nipples or the beautiful bare legs beneath.

'The field was completely destroyed yesterday...' she said slowly, running a hand through her hair. 'The one weapon we have against the wraiths...'

Talemir nodded. 'I know.'

'So we need to replant. Salvage whatever remnants we can

of roots and seeds from the site, from the orchids you brought us as well, and replant them in multiple locations across Naarva, send them to trusted places all over the kingdoms. While the wraiths may be gone for now, they'll be back. And when they are, we and the rest of the midrealms will need to be ready.'

'I agree.'

He watched as Drue pulled on her clothes and braided her messy hair. 'There are also twenty shadow-touched people who will need protection and help...'

'Gus and the others...' Talemir said quietly. 'They won't be accepted back at the stronghold in Ciraun, will they?'

Drue shook her head sadly. 'No.'

'So where do we take them?' He had made it clear that he would follow her anywhere.

'I'll have to check with Adrienne, but... On the eastern island of Naarva, there's an old university. It might make a suitable spot for us, while we get to know the other shadow-touched people, while we regroup for whatever lies ahead.'

Finally, Talemir swung his legs from the bed and stood.

Drue eyed him appreciatively.

'Don't look at me like that, or we'll never leave this cottage.'

'Noted,' she said with a grin, and tossed him his clothes.

Talemir tugged on his pants and, hiding his wings, pulled on his shirt as well, doing his best to make himself presentable. As much as he didn't want to go, there were a few conversations he needed to have before they departed.

On the threshold of the cottage, he pulled Drue into his arms for a firm kiss that promised more debauchery between them later, before heading off to find Wilder.

. . .

His protégé was tending to the horses, looking restless and ready to leave.

'There you are!' he said, spotting Talemir. 'We're just about to head out —'

He cut himself off, clearly reading Talemir's expression.

Wilder's shoulders heaved. 'You're not coming back, are you?'

'No,' Talemir replied, guilt squeezing at his heart.

'Why?'

'You know why...' Talemir ventured.

'Because of Drue?'

'Because of many things, Wilder.'

A muscle in Wilder's jaw twitched. 'First you keep secrets from me, and now this?'

'One day you'll understand.'

'Understand that you're breaking your Warsword vows? That you're abandoning Thezmarr?'

'Thezmarr wouldn't have me, not as I am now. You know this.'

'Farissa did,' Wilder bit back.

'Farissa is one of a kind. I no longer belong with the guild, but among the shadow-touched.'

'No. You can hide it. The guild need never know. You can't tell what you are, looking at you now —'

'I don't want to hide who I am, Wilder,' Talemir said gently. 'Not anymore. This is my choice and my choice alone. I'm leaving the guild for a greater cause – the shadow-touched people need a leader, need help. Perhaps the day will come where you need us too.'

Wilder clenched his fists, one of his hands drifting to the hilt of his sword.

'Are you going to fight me again?' Talemir asked, keeping

his voice light. 'I proved to you earlier that you're not ready, not nearly ready to best me.'

Wilder's lip curled in anger, but he didn't reach for his blade. 'You expect me to keep this – you and the other half-wraiths – a secret from Thezmarr?'

'Yes,' Talemir said simply. 'The guild will call for our deaths without understanding us. You're lying if you say otherwise.'

'So it's that simple, is it? What the fuck do I tell them happened to you?'

Talemir sighed, glimpsing Drue across the camp. 'Tell them I found a wife.'

Wilder swore. 'And what about me? You'd abandon your apprentice?'

Talemir smiled sadly. 'You haven't been my apprentice for a long time, my brother.' He reached for the jewel around his neck and pulled it free, closing the gap between himself and his protégé and pressing it into Wilder's palm. 'I promise you will understand one day. And when you do, you'll know who to give this to.'

'I'll never forgive you for this,' Wilder ground out.

'But you will,' Talemir told him gently. 'For now, your purpose is clear.'

Wilder laughed darkly. 'Fuck you.'

But Talemir gripped his shoulder. 'Not all is as it seems at Thezmarr. You know this in your bones. You know this after talking to the Naarvians. You have noticed your call for aid went unanswered? There has been no sign of our brotherhood. Keep the current state of this kingdom a secret,' he said. 'To the outside world, Naarva should appear as it has for the last year or so: an overgrown ghost kingdom but for its forge.'

'I take no orders from you,' Wilder spat. 'You're no longer a Warsword, no longer a brother of mine.'

'Your anger with me will fade in time, Wilder,' Talemir assured him. 'But for now, you need to go on. You need to hunt the reapers. Here —' He pressed a small vial of extract into Wilder's hands. 'This is the last of it. Treat your swords with it. We'll endeavour to make more.'

Pocketing the bottle, Wilder shook his head and mounted his horse. 'Fuck you, Tal,' he said again, before riding off towards the horizon.

Someone let out a low whistle nearby and Talemir turned to find Gus' cousin Dratos, the half-wraith ranger, watching, a bemused expression on his face. 'That went well...'

But there was nothing malicious in his words, only pity.

'Let's hope my next conversation goes better,' Talemir replied, running his fingers through his hair.

To his surprise, Dratos fell into step beside him.

'So, no hard feelings between us?' Talemir asked tentatively.

'If you're good enough for Drue and Adrienne, you're good enough for me. I hear even the damn bird likes you.'

Talemir huffed a laugh. 'Well, he's supposed to be a decent judge of character, I'm told.'

But Dratos was still staring after Wilder. 'If it matters... I think you did the right thing.'

Talemir gave him a grateful look. 'I hope so.'

A SHORT TIME LATER, Talemir stood face to face with Fendran Emmerson, doing his utmost to stop himself shifting nervously from foot to foot. It was an outdated notion as far as he was concerned, but the Naarvians he had spoken to still respected the tradition.

But before Talemir could open his mouth, Fendran gripped his hand firmly. 'My daughter hasn't needed my permission or blessing for anything in a long time, nor would I be fool enough to try to impose either upon her,' he declared, his voice gravelly. 'But for what it's worth, Warsword – shadow-touched or not, you make her happy, and that's all a father can ask for.'

Talemir's heart felt tender, both from Wilder's outburst and Fendran's kindness, but even more so from the sheer hope that now swelled there. The shadows upon Naarva were gone for the moment, and he and the people like him had a future ahead of them.

He watched Drue say tearful goodbyes to Adrienne and her father, while Gus took an inelegant tumble from his horse, his wings still interfering with his balance. Luckily, he was joining their party on the journey to the old university, and there would be time enough to teach the boy how to move with them, not against them.

When at last the company separated, Drue came to his side, her eyes bright with tears, but happiness too.

Talemir took her reins from her and passed them and his own to Dratos with a grateful smile.

'What are you doing?' Drue asked. 'We're about to ride out...?'

Talemir grinned, tugging his shirt over his head and looping it through his belt.

Drue blushed. 'Uh... As much as I enjoy the view, is now the —'

'I thought you might like to go ahead of the company,' he

said, calling his wings forth. They speared through the muscles of his back, only this time, there was no pain.

They flared proudly behind him.

Slowly, Drue smiled at him in realisation. 'You want to fly...?' She stared in wonder.

Talemir took her up in his arms, pressing a kiss to her lips. 'With you? Always.'

He braced his knees and launched them skyward, eliciting a shriek of delight from Drue as she clung to him, grinning from ear to ear. The crisp air kissed their skin and tangled in their hair, the white clouds close enough to touch.

'Hold tight, Wildfire,' Talemir murmured.

And together, they soared east, towards a new home, a new future, a new hope.

EPILOGUE
TALEMIR

Six months later...

Amid the fallen kingdom of Naarva, on the island to the northeast, blue jasmine, sun orchids and midnight roses bloomed. Hidden among the vines, the university, which had slipped into disrepair, was in the slow process of being restored, but as evening settled, work ceased and made way for something else.

Talemir Starling gazed out onto the quadrangle, the sandstone pillars wrapped in flowers, candlelight illuminating the small podium at the far end where he was expected in just a few brief moments. His chest swelled as he took in the aisle, soft shadows drifting along it like gentle wisps of smoke.

'Nervous?' Dratos asked with a grin. The shadow-touched ranger sat on a nearby window ledge, wings tucked behind him as he chewed on his pipe. Over the last six months, he'd been instrumental to the progress of their little colony and the restoration of the university. He had helped Talemir with the others, with those who weren't as accepting of their darkness. Dratos was perfect for that, because he'd embraced his own with all his heart and was rarely seen without his wings or shadows dancing around him. But however helpful he was, he was also a pain in the arse. He'd taken to calling Talemir the 'Shadow Prince', rather than the Prince of Hearts, and had grandly dubbed himself Dratos the Dawnless.

'No,' Talemir replied, accepting a swig from the former ranger's flask. It was the truth. He had been waiting for this day since the moment he'd clapped eyes on Drue Emmerson.

But that didn't mean there wasn't a subtle, bittersweet note to the occasion. Only because Talemir wished Wilder were there with him. He hadn't seen or heard from his protégé since the battle, and though he'd never admit it to the younger warrior, it felt like a little piece of him was missing.

Neither of them, upon taking their Warsword vows, had ever envisioned a day where they might make new vows, deeper and longer-lasting than those of the Great Rite. It felt wrong that Wilder wasn't here to witness such a feat.

All Talemir could do was take comfort in knowing that his former apprentice, his brother in arms, was on his own path now, and that they would no doubt one day meet again. He knew in his bones that Wilder Hawthorne had a much bigger part to play in the destiny awaiting the midrealms.

'It's time,' Dratos drawled, tossing his pipe aside and jumping down from the ledge, happily clapping Talemir on the shoulder.

Talemir mirrored his grin. 'Finally,' he said.

Standing upon the small platform, warmth spreading through his chest and tears prickling his eyes, Talemir looked at the faces before him. Fendran and Adrienne stood right at the front, beaming back at him, while Gus, sporting a brand-new knitted jumper, was grinning at Adrienne's side.

But standing a little further away was someone else. Someone Talemir did not expect.

Towering over everyone else was Malik the Shieldbreaker.

Talemir clapped a hand to his mouth at the sight. How in the realms had he got here? After everything Malik had been through, travelling across the realms was the last thing Talemir would have expected from him.

Tears streamed down the giant Warsword's scarred face. Smiling broadly through them, he nodded to Talemir from across the way, an enormous dog sitting at his feet, wagging its tail.

But the first notes of a harp soon drifted down the aisle, and Talemir stared at the most beautiful woman he'd ever seen.

All the air left his lungs.

Drue walked towards him, delicate wisps of shadow swirling at her ankles courtesy of their people, in a dress not of traditional white, but black and red, the same hues as his wings.

And she looked every bit the Queen of Night.

The gown was made of dark lace and sheer, shimmering fabric that kissed Drue's collarbone and clung to her arms in elegant sleeves. The plunging neckline accentuated her breasts, the material cinching in at the waist only to flow out freely from her hips and drape elegantly around her legs, a daring slit up one thigh, the train trailing behind her.

As usual, Drue's blue eyes were lined with kohl, but she had painted her lips a deep red to match her dress, while her hair had been braided and swept up into a regal bun at the back of her head, flowers threaded throughout.

Only when she reached him at the podium did Talemir breathe.

Drue smiled. 'Hello, Warsword.'

'Hello, Wildfire,' he murmured, his throat thick with emotion as he grasped her hands in his.

Before their friends and family, amid the blooms and gentle tendrils of shadow, Talemir Starling and Drue Emmerson exchanged vows.

Love was a language of few words, older than humanity, older than the ancient power that thrummed in Talemir's veins, but a language he understood intimately thanks to the woman before him – his wife.

A single tear tracked down Talemir's cheek and Drue kissed it away, her eyes bright with tears as well.

The ceremony was short and simple, the promises between them expressed in the silver rings they exchanged, and the first kiss they shared as husband and wife.

Wife... The word chimed through Talemir like a bell as the small crowd gathered around them, embracing them, kissing their tear-streaked cheeks and shaking their hands.

Drue Emmerson was his *wife*...

THE CELEBRATIONS WENT on late into the night. They danced and drank and laughed with their people, their family. When Talemir embraced Malik and tried to introduce his oldest friend to Drue, words failed him and fresh tears tracked down his face. The giant former Warsword simply grinned at Drue and pulled her into a bear hug. If only Wilder had been there to see it.

It felt like an age before Talemir had the opportunity to pull Drue aside. Her face was flushed, her eyes alight with joy.

'There you are, husband,' she said, pressing a kiss to his mouth.

'There you are, *wife*,' he said, smiling against the lush curve of her lips. 'Can I whisk you away somewhere?'

'Please,' she murmured.

Talemir swept her up in his arms, the fabric of her gown billowing as he freed his wings and launched them into the night sky, the stars winking all around them.

He took her to a secluded spot in the nearby mountains, one he'd spent hours preparing earlier that day. He had scattered midnight rose petals, arranged dozens of candles and readied a basket with wine and food. He had also prepared a makeshift bed of blankets and cushions, knowing that they would want a private moment just between the two of them after all the festivities.

'This is beautiful, Tal,' Drue whispered as he landed deftly and set her down.

'As are you,' he said, holding her at arm's length to survey her properly. She was beyond stunning. 'I've never seen you in a dress before,' he managed.

Drue gave a wicked smile. 'No, you haven't... What do you think?'

Slowly, he grinned back at her, recognising the glint in her eyes. 'You look... incredible. You always look incredible. But this...'

'Yes?'

He fisted a layer of her skirts. 'I like this for its accessibility.'

Drue laughed. 'Adrienne scoured all the ruined manors of Naarva to find this gown. She hunted down a seamstress and sent Terrence back and forth a dozen times to get my measurements – all for you to appreciate its "accessibility"?'

'I'm a simple man.'

'That's not the word I'd use,' she quipped, running her fingertips across the width of his chest.

Fire roared to life in his veins. 'Then what words do you deem appropriate, wife?' he half growled.

Drue's touch trailed down, down the ridges of his abdomen, to the bulge in his pants.

Perhaps they didn't need words.

Talemir groaned as she palmed him through the fabric, rubbing the length of him hard enough that pleasure rippled through him. But he snatched her hand away. His wife wouldn't be getting her way tonight, at least not at first.

His body enveloped hers as he kissed her deeply, and her mouth opened for him, allowing his tongue to brush against hers. She tasted like his favourite wine.

Talemir led her backward until she was against a ridge of rock.

'Lift your dress and spread your legs.'

Drue whimpered against his lips, the sound sending a thrill of power through him. This was one of his favourite games between them, commanding her until she was a pleading mess of desire before him.

She did as he asked, drawing her skirts up around her hips, swathes of fabric billowing in her arms.

Longing surged as he found her bare beneath. He hummed appreciatively. 'Accessible indeed...'

Talemir lowered himself to his knees and pressed a kiss to each of her thighs.

Drue shuddered above him in anticipation. 'Nice to know those books in the library have been educational...'

Talemir laughed against her skin. Amid the university's

dusty shelves, they'd discovered a treasure trove of romance novels that now lay in piles by their bed.

'I'm all for credit where credit's due, Wildfire. But you know well enough that this is all me.' Talemir licked right up the centre of her, eliciting a heady moan. Good – that was just how he wanted his wife: writhing in pleasure at his touch.

He flicked his tongue across her clit, and Drue's hands plunged into his hair. That was all the encouragement he needed. Talemir feasted on her. Teasing and licking, circling that sensitive part of her, he worked her until her thighs clamped around his head, until her scream echoed into the night.

When she was soaking, he slid a finger, then two inside her, marvelling at how such a tight spot could accommodate his cock, hard and straining against his pants. He moved his fingers in the rhythm he knew she liked, in the way she'd told him made her see stars.

Talemir looked up, finding his wife's head tipped back to the night sky, one hand clutching her skirts around her waist, the other pinching her own nipple, her breasts spilling from the top of her dress.

He nearly came at the sight of her.

He worked her harder, pumping his fingers, licking at her.

'Yes...' she murmured. 'Yes, Tal.'

When she said his name like that, a gentler part of him caved in pure joy, for it was love and lust entwined in the most beautiful way.

Talemir fucked her with his tongue and fingers, finally bringing her over that sweet edge, revelling in the force of her climax, her thighs trembling by his ears.

Panting, Drue gazed down at him with hooded eyes. Her lips parted. 'I love you,' she said, her voice thick.

Talemir smiled and scooped her up, setting her down on the blankets. His Wildfire vixen made no move to pull her skirts down, but lay on her back, spreading her knees for him. An invitation.

'Fuck,' he moaned at the view, his cock throbbing almost painfully. 'I love you, too.'

Talemir stripped away his pants and seated himself between her legs, hooking them over his shoulders so that her feet tickled his wings.

Drue arched her hips towards him, ready for him.

The candlelight gilded her, illuminating her lustful gaze, her peaked nipples and full breasts, the wedding dress pooled at her waist and her gorgeous legs bent between them.

Wife, he thought, emotion welling.

And then all thoughts emptied from his head as Drue guided him into her. She clenched around him, moaning deeply. The noise vibrated down his cock and into his balls.

His eyes widened at the sensation, and a low, rumbling sound of need escaped him.

Drue held her legs beneath her thighs and Talemir sank even deeper into her, the ecstasy building as he thrust over and over again. He had learnt the feel and shape of her over the past few months, had learnt what made her sob from pleasure, learnt every part of her intimately, but gods... She was everything, and he was addicted to her.

Talemir's wife writhed beneath him and he kissed her, capturing her lower lip between his teeth, as he pounded into her hard and deep.

Her breath caught, and he knew she was on the edge. This time, he wanted to go with her.

At the very thought, his balls tightened, begging to empty into her.

And at his final thrust, Drue cried out, her whole body flushed and trembling.

Talemir erupted at the sight of his wife's pleasure as she came around his cock. His climax was uninhibited, unapologetic, shadow magic dancing around them as he moaned.

When he had caught his breath, he captured her mouth with his, hard enough to bruise. 'This will never end,' he told her, voice raw. 'This wanting, this needing of you.'

'Good,' she panted, grinning.

Talemir held his wife close beneath the stars, the joy in his chest utterly uncontained despite all there was yet to face in the midrealms. But this night and all the nights that followed were theirs, together.

Drue seemed to sense his thoughts. 'We're married,' she whispered, smiling in awe at the term. 'You're officially mine, Talemir Starling.'

Talemir laughed, the sound like a light melody on his lips before he kissed Drue gently. 'I was yours from the moment you vowed to carve out my heart, Wildfire.'

THE END

Read on for a note from the author plus a preview of *Slaying the Vampire Conqueror* by Carissa Broadbent—the first book in **Mortal Enemies to Monster Lovers**!

AUTHOR'S NOTE

Thank you so much for taking a chance on Talemir, Drue and *Slaying the Shadow Prince*. It truly means the world to me and I hope you loved reading it as much as I loved writing it.

For those who enjoyed the deliciously steamy epilogue, I've got a little something for you... You can read the scorching wedding night scene from Drue's point of view for free. Download your spicy bonus scene here:

https://helenscheuerer.com/ssp-bonus-epilogue/

While Talemir and Drue may have got their happily ever after, a certain brooding protégé Warsword still has a massive adventure ahead of him. Wilder Hawthorne's love-swept story kicks off in *Blood & Steel*, where he becomes the unwilling warrior chaperone to Althea Zoltaire. He doesn't know what he wants more: to kill her, or kiss her...

Blood & Steel is the first book in the epic romantic fantasy series, *The Legends of Thezmarr*. And just between us... Talemir and Drue are expected to join the series a little later.

In the meantime, if you enjoyed *Slaying the Shadow Prince*,

I would love it if you let your friends know so they can experience Talemir and Drue for themselves. If you leave a review for *Slaying the Shadow Prince* on the site from which you purchased the book, Goodreads, or your own blog, I would love to read it! Email me the link at <u>hello@</u> <u>helenscheuerer.com</u>

In fact, I always love hearing from readers. Drop me a line if you've got a question or simply want to gush about fantasy romance books!

Once again, thank you for joining me on this wild ride.

Happy reading,

Helen

SLAYING THE
VAMPIRE CONQUEROR
PREVIEW

CARISSA BROADBENT

I

I didn't miss sight anymore. Sight was an inefficient way to perceive the world around you. It was a crutch. What I was given instead was far more useful.

Take this moment, for example—this moment when my back was pressed to the wall, dagger in my hand, as I waited to kill the man on the other side.

If I was relying on sight alone, I would have to crane my neck around the doorframe. I would have to risk being seen. I'd have to go by whatever I could make out in the darkness of him and his lover, squint into that writhing mass of flesh, and figure out the best way to make my move.

Inefficient. Room for error. A terrible way to work.

Instead, I *felt*. I *sensed*. Through the magic of the threads, I could still perceive the boundaries of the physical world—the color and shape of the scenery, the planes of a face, the absence or existence of light—but I had so much more than that, too. Crucial, in my work.

My target was a young nobleman. Six months ago, his

father died. Within weeks of him receiving the keys to his father's significant cityscape, he began using all that newfound wealth and power to steal from his people and build more wealth for the Pythora King.

His essence now was slick with desire. The Arachessen could not read minds, not truly, but I didn't need to see his thoughts. What use were his thoughts when I saw his heart?

"More," a female voice moaned. "Please, more."

He mumbled something in response, the words buried in her hair. Her desire was genuine. Her soul shivered and throbbed with it—her pleasure spiking as he shifted angles, pushing her down to the bed. For the briefest of moments, I couldn't help being jealous that this snake had better sex than I did.

But I drove that thought away quickly. Arachessen were not supposed to mourn the things we gave up in the name of our goddess—Acaeja, the Weaver of Fates, the Keeper of the Unknown, the Mother of Sorcery. We could not mourn the eyesight, the autonomy, the pieces of our flesh carved away in sacrifice. And no, we could not mourn the sex, either.

I wished they'd hurry up.

I pressed my back to the wall and let out a frustrated breath through my teeth. I blinked, my lashes tickling the fabric of my blindfold.

{*Now?*}

Raeth's voice was very quiet in the back of my head—she was nearly out of Threadwhisper range, all the way downstairs, near the entrance of the beach house. When she spoke into my mind, I could sense a faint echo of the ocean wind as it caressed her face.

{*Not yet,*} I answered.

I felt Raeth's irritation.

{*I don't know how much longer we have. He's distracted, isn't he? Take him and go before he starts to pay attention.*}

Oh, he was distracted, alright. His woman wasn't the only vocal one now, his grunts echoing against the wall behind me.

I didn't answer right away.

{*Sylina—*} Raeth started.

{*I want to wait until the girl is gone.*}

As I knew she would, Raeth scoffed at this. {*Wait until the girl is gone? If you wait that long, someone will notice that something is off.*}

I clenched my jaw and did not answer, letting her Threadwhispers fade beneath the sounds of our target's enthusiastic climax.

Threadwhispers were very useful. Communication that couldn't be overheard, that could transcend sound the same way we transcended sight. It was a gift from the Weaver, one for which I was very grateful.

...But I hated that it meant I could never pretend I hadn't heard something.

{*Sylina!*}

{*She might not know,*} I told her.

What he is. Who he is. What he's doing, and who he's doing it for.

I had no qualms about killing the nobleman. I would take more joy than I should in feeling his presence wither and die beneath me—and that would be my little secret, a guilty pleasure. But the girl...

Again, Raeth's scoff reverberated between us.

{*She knows.*}

{*She—*}

{*If she's fucking him, then she knows. And if not, she has terrible taste in men. What difference does it make?*}

And then I felt it.

A sudden crack through the air. Sound, yes, a distant *BANG*—but the sound was nothing compared to the sensation that ripped through the threads of life beneath the physical world, a force powerful enough to set them vibrating.

I froze.

My target and his paramour stopped.

"What was that?" the woman whispered.

But I was no longer focused on them. Not with the force of the vibrations, and Raeth's wordless panic spreading slowly across them, rolling toward me like a pool of blood.

{*Raeth?*}

Nothing.

{*Raeth? What was that?*}

Confusion. Fear. I felt it, though it was dimming, because she must have been walking away from the door—then running, out into the city streets.

{*Raeth!*}

But she was out of range now. All I could feel from her were faint reverberations.

That is, until I heard her scream.

An Arachessen was not supposed to abandon a mission for anything, not even for the sake of saving a Sister's life. But every thought of my dutiful teachings drained from me the moment I felt her terror, visceral and human and too familiar in ways I'd never admit aloud.

I ran.

Down marble steps, across tile floors, newly slick with I didn't-even-know-what, through the door where my Sister had been moments ago, standing watch. The air hit me, salty and ocean-sweet.

And with it came the sensation of *them*.

The vampire invaders.

Decades later, I would not forget this moment. Exactly how it felt when they made landfall. Their magic sickened me, tainted and cursed, making the air taste so thickly of blood I nearly gagged on it.

Sisters of the Arachessen are trained extensively in the magic of every god. From the time we were children, we were exposed to all magics, even when our bodies protested, even when it burned us or broke us.

This, I recognized immediately, was Nyaxia's magic. The heretic goddess. The Mother of Vampires.

Hundreds, perhaps thousands, of them crashed upon our shores that night.

Sound was useless, all the bangs and screams and groans of crumbling stone running together like the rush of a waterfall. For a moment, I was blinded, too, because the sensations were so much—every essence, every soul, screaming at once.

In that moment, I didn't know what was happening. I wouldn't understand until later exactly what I was witnessing. But I did know that this wasn't the work of the Pythora King. These were foreigners.

{*Raeth!*}

I threw the call as far down the threads as I could, flinging it toward her like a net. And there, near where the land met the sea, I felt her. Felt her running—not away from the explosions at the shore, but toward them.

No.

Idiot girl. Stupid girl. Impulsive. Impatient.

I ran for her.

{*Raeth! Fall back!*}

But Raeth didn't listen.

I was getting closer, dodging slabs of broken rock, dodging clusters of the strangest fire I'd ever felt—not hot, but cold, devouring trees, devouring buildings. My head pounded, my magic wailing with overexertion at having to constantly reorient myself, over and over.

But I didn't miss a single step.

Raeth was at the shore. At the docks. Many, many presences surrounded her—so many I struggled to separate them from each other. Human. Vampire. I couldn't count them. Too many. More coming. Pouring onto the shore in a wave of sea froth and magic and explosives and bloodthirsty rage that I could feel throbbing in my veins.

{Sylina!}

Asha's voice was sharp as she called to me. Even a little afraid.

I'd never felt my commander's fear before.

I'd never disobeyed her before, either.

Because in that moment, Raeth screamed. Another explosion of dark magic roared through the air, so powerful that when it faded, I was on my knees, splinters of the pier digging into my flesh.

And Raeth was simply gone.

It is difficult to describe what it feels like to sense the death of a Sister. I could not see her. I could not hear her voice. But when you're near another of the Arachessen, you can simply feel them the way that one feels the body warmth of another, all their threads connected to yours.

All that, all at once, severed.

The dead did not have threads.

Raeth's color was purple. Sometimes it was a little warmer when she was happy or excited, a pinky-glow hue of delight.

Sometimes it was colder when she was moody, like storm clouds at sunset.

Now it was nothing, a hole in all of us where Raeth should have been. It was strange how viscerally it reminded me of another distant memory, a memory I was no longer supposed to have, of how it felt to witness life snatched away in the unforgiving jaws of war.

Asha felt it, too. Of course she did. We would feel it everywhere.

{Let her go,} Asha said again. *{Come back. We need to leave now. We'll complete our task another time.}*

Task? Who cared about that limp-dicked little nobleman now?

I had bigger game.

Because there *he* was.

Even in the sea of vampires and magic, he stood out. His presence was bigger than all of theirs, a gravitational force. All the rest of it—the countless souls, the grey of the sea foam, the cold of the night—framed him like a throne, as if the universe simply oriented itself around him as he rose from the surf.

Even then, through the chaos, with the lack of information I had, I knew I was witnessing something deadly and incredible and horrible. I knew, from that first moment, that he was the leader.

I'd burn his presence into my soul after that. Every angle of him. Every scent that war carried across the sea breeze. Even from this distance, I could sense his appearance through the threads—that he wore fine clothes, and even finer armor over them. His hair was long and reflected the moonlight, soaked in salty tendrils around his shoulders.

And of course, there were the horns. Black as night,

protruding from his upper forehead and curling back. They were like nothing I'd ever witnessed before. The product, surely, of some dark, unknown magic.

He was cursed. He was tainted. I could feel that even from here. And as he stepped right over Raeth's body, I didn't even think as I reached to my back and withdrew my bow.

I was a fantastic shot. Human eyes are fallible. But the threads are never fooled.

I had a perfect opening. A single thread stretching from me to him, straight to his heart.

{Get back here, Sylina!} Asha commanded.

{I have the shot.}

{You're too far.}

I was not too far.

I drew.

{We can't sacrifice another Sister here!} Asha roared—so strong her words made me lurch, my head splitting.

He stepped onto the shore. The thread between us stretched tight. I felt his head turn. Felt his gaze fall to me. Felt his toxic magic shiver down the connection.

{Sylina, the Sightmother commands *that you come back.}*

I could make it.

I could make it.

My hands shook. Every shred of my focus went toward cutting through all these sensations, falling only on him. Nothing else existed.

But the Sightmother's stare was on me, too. A Sister did not disobey the Sightmother.

I lowered my bow and backed away, fleeing into the chaotic night. By the time I reached Asha, I had so overexerted my magic and my senses that I was stumbling over rocks in the road. I knew I had a punishment waiting for me at the Keep, but I didn't care.

It was punishment enough. That moment.

The moment I let him go.

I'd think about that moment for a long, long time.

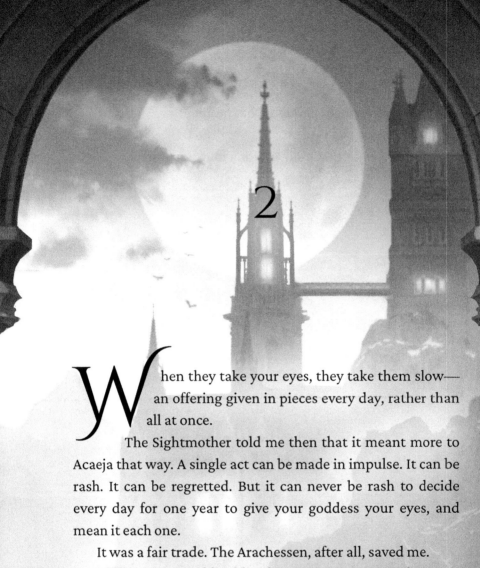

2

When they take your eyes, they take them slow—an offering given in pieces every day, rather than all at once.

The Sightmother told me then that it meant more to Acaeja that way. A single act can be made in impulse. It can be rash. It can be regretted. But it can never be rash to decide every day for one year to give your goddess your eyes, and mean it each one.

It was a fair trade. The Arachessen, after all, saved me.

I was ten years old. Older than most. I was acutely aware of that then and would remain aware of it forever after—those ten years of life that separated me from my Sisters. Most of them barely recalled the process of their initiation, nor did they remember the life they had before coming here. The Arachessen and the Salt Keep were all they knew. Sometimes I pitied them, because they would love this place even more if they understood what it had been like to live beyond it.

I did. I remembered it all.

I was old enough to remember the way each drop of Marathine extract burned going into my eyes. I was old enough to remember the visions that came after, visions that would leave me jerking awake at night with tears crusted to my face. And above all, I was old enough to remember that even that pain was an embrace compared to the outside world.

People thought that we were so isolated, that we did not hear the things they said about us. Foolish. We heard everything. I knew that people talked about us like we're insane—as if we'd made some unimaginable sacrifice. It was not a sacrifice. It was an exchange: *Close your eyes, child, and you will see an entire world.*

Contrary to what people thought, we were not blind. The threads of life than ran through our world, and our mastery over them, told us everything we needed to know. Everything and more.

The first time, it was the Sightmother herself who leaned over me, pinning my arms to the stone table. I was frightened, then, though I was smart enough to know that I shouldn't be. I hadn't yet gotten used to the sight of the Arachessen and their covered eyes. As the Sightmother leaned over me, I didn't know where to look, so I stared into the deep crimson silk of her blindfold. She was the kind of woman who defied markers of time. The faint lines around her mouth and nose did little to dull the uncanny appearance of her youth.

"You must be very still, child," she said. "Even in the face of great pain. Do you remember how?"

I liked the Sightmother's voice. It was smooth and gentle. She spoke to me like she respected both my vulnerability and my intelligence, which was very rare among adults. The moment I met her, I knew I would do anything for her. Secretly, I imagined the goddess Acaeja with her face.

"Do you understand, Sylina?" she said, when I did not answer.

It was the first time she'd called me by that new name. It felt good to hear it, like I'd just been let into an open door.

I nodded, my mouth dry. "Yes. I understand."

I knew, even then, that this was another test. I'd been tested before they allowed me into the Salt Keep. The ability to withstand pain was a non-negotiable skill. I was good at withstanding pain. I showed the Sisters so, and I had the broken fingers to prove it. Decades later, I would still feel a bit of pride when I touched my left hand.

The Sightmother had smiled at me, and then nodded to the Sister at my side.

When it was done, tears streamed down my face, and blood pooled in the back of my throat—from my tongue, which I had bitten so hard I couldn't eat solids for a week.

It was worth it, though. They told me later I was the only recruit that didn't make a sound.

I NO LONGER NOTICED THE Sightmother's blindfold, because I, like all my Sisters, had my own. Tonight, I wore my red one, the same shade that the Sightmother had donned when she leaned over me that day, seventeen years ago. An accidental coincidence, and I only thought of it now, as I sat at the gathering table with my Sisters, my fingertips in the gritty pile of salt that had been spread along the large, circular table. Forty of us gathered here, each pressing our hands to the salt

—our grounding connection to each other, and to the Weaver, the Lady of Fate, the goddess Acaeja, to whom we had all sworn our unending loyalty.

But I was acutely aware of the empty chairs. More empty still since our last meeting, when Asha and I returned from the south the day the invasion began.

It was impossible not to feel their absence. The breaks in the chain, the expanses of salt left untouched.

Raeth was lost in their initial landfall. And then, later, Vima was lost in Breles. Another city conquered by our invaders, another lost Sister.

The vampires moved quickly. They didn't waste time. It was clear that their goal was to take over all of Glaea—why else would they start at the southernmost shores and then move slowly north?

So, it was not a surprise to me when the Sightmother cleared her throat and said, "The vampires have taken Vaprus."

Utter silence. But we all felt the ripple of fear, of grief, through the threads.

I tilted my head to the third empty chair. I didn't need to ask to know the truth. But a young Sister, Yylene, said weakly, "Amara?"

The Sightmother let out a long exhale. We all sensed her sadness before her words came. "She has been lost."

Yylene bit her lip, sagging a little over the table. She was only seventeen. Loss still hit her deep. But then, I supposed it hit us all deep. We just learned how to cover the wounds with other things. Stitch it up with the threads of our next task.

My jaw tightened, and I tried to exhale my frustration before anyone else could sense it. My whole life, I had never felt more seen, more accepted, than I was here at this table—

connected to all my Sisters, to my Sightmother, to the goddess Acaeja herself.

But these last few weeks, what had once felt like connection had started to feel stifling, as it grew harder and harder for me to strangle the shameful thoughts I was not supposed to feel.

"Do we have any further insight into what they want, Sightmother?" Asha asked. I found it slightly satisfying that I could hear, could feel, the tinge of anger in her words, too.

"I assume," the Sightmother said mildly, "they want to conquer."

"The Obitraens have never conquered a human nation before."

Obitraens—those of the continent of Obitraes, the home of vampires and the domain of Nyaxia, the heretic goddess. Obitraes consisted of three kingdoms: the House of Shadow, the House of Night, and the House of Blood. They squabbled among themselves, but had never been known to venture forth into human nations—at least, certainly not as a coordinated act. And this? This was nothing if not coordinated. This was an army.

"We know that the House of Blood is the most unpredictable of the vampire nations," the Sightmother said. "It's impossible now to say why they have moved."

"Has there not been a formal declaration?" Asha asked.

"No. The king of the House of Blood has offered no declaration of war."

"Then this man... this commander... could he be acting independently?"

"We can't say."

There was a certain weakness in the Sightmother's voice

at that—a helplessness from a woman who was never helpless. I hated hearing it.

Everyone was silent for a long moment.

"Perhaps it's all a mercy," Asha said softly, at last. "Let them destroy each other. Maybe it will thin the herds."

My head snapped toward Asha. I couldn't choke down the sudden wave of indignation at that statement.

I bit my tongue, right over the raised ridge of scar tissue from when I was ten years old, until the pain supplanted the anger.

Too late, though. I could feel the Sightmother's gaze on me.

"What do you wish to say, Sylina?"

"Nothing, Sightmother."

"No lies are spoken here."

The refrain was uttered frequently around this table, as we pressed our fingertips to the salt—and maybe it was true, because we were never more exposed to each other than we were around this table, but it didn't mean that there weren't thoughts that were unacceptable to express. To even feel.

I shouldn't have answered at all.

But before I could stop myself, I said, "There could be a high human cost to letting that happen."

"I would think that you, of all people, Sylina, would know this," Asha said, in a pitying tone that made me want to leap across the table and slap her. "We act on the will of Acaeja alone. Not our personal feelings."

Yes. True. The Pythora King had ravaged our country, leaving Glaea in a state of perpetual war since his own ruthless conquering path, two decades ago. But even that would not be enough to make the Arachessen act. The Arachessen didn't make decisions based on morality—some made-up measure of right and wrong, though of course, by any measure, the Pythora King was wrong. Worse, the Weaver had shown us that the Pythora King disrupted the natural order. His actions moved our world away from its course.

That is the measure of an enemy of the Arachessen. Acaeja's will. Balance. Not evil or righteousness.

But this... it felt...

"Acaeja has no hatred for Nyaxia's children," Asha reminded me. "She may support this. Sometimes, gods deem a purge necessary."

I choked out, too angry to stop myself, "A *purge?*"

"No progress comes without a cost."

My temper had been short lately. Too short. Especially with Asha. Sometimes, when I heard her voice, I could only hear how it had sounded as she commanded me to stand down.

I could have taken the shot. These seats would not be empty.

And yet, I knew that she was right. Nyaxia, the mother of vampires, was an enemy of the White Pantheon of human gods. Two thousand years ago, when she was just a young, lesser god, she had fallen in love with and married Alarus, the God of Death. But their relationship was forbidden by the rest of the White Pantheon, ultimately resulting in Alarus's execution. Enraged and grieving, Nyaxia had broken away from the other gods and created vampires—a society to rule all on her own. Now, the gods of the White Pantheon despised her. Acaeja was the only exception—the only god who tolerated Nyaxia and the vampire society she had created.

It was not up to us to judge our conqueror.

But I wanted to. I wanted to judge him. I wanted to judge

anyone who made a city look like that, feel like that, just as my own home had felt so many years ago.

That made me a poor Sister. I was, at least, self-aware.

It would be one thing to control a facial expression. But like sight, facial expressions were shallow indicators of the truth. I could control every muscle in my body, including those on my face—it was much harder to control the shifts of my aura, more visible than ever here before my Sisters.

Right now, it seethed with anger. Anger at our conqueror. Anger at Asha for daring to claim his killing could be for the greater good.

And—who was I kidding?—anger at Asha for not letting me take that shot.

{Is there something more you want to say, Sylina?} Asha Threadwhispered, and I was so close to snapping back—

{Enough!}

"*Enough!*"

The Sightmother spoke in both places simultaneously—her voice ripping through the air and the threads.

We all went silent. I collected myself.

The Sightmother said, "Sylina is right."

Beneath my blindfold, my brows twitched in surprise.

And satisfaction.

"We know better than any that evil can wear many different faces," she went on. "Yes, the Pythora King is our enemy. But that doesn't mean that all his enemies must be our friends. This conqueror is troubling indeed."

Troubling might seem, to any other, to be a mild word. Coming from the Sightmother, it might as well be damnation.

"Has the Weaver spoken to you, Sightmother?" Yylene asked tentatively.

The Sightmother did not answer for a long moment. Then

she rose, her palms pressed to the salt. "It is too early to say what the Weaver believes. But we all must be ready for dark times ahead. That, daughters, is true. We must look inward. So go now and prepare for evening recitations."

In unified movements, we each drew our flattened hands in a single sweep across the table before us, scattering the salt. Then we rose. I went to follow my Sisters from the room, but the Sightmother said, *{Not you, Sylina. You're coming with me.}*

3

The Salt Keep earned its name due to its location in the mountains of eastern Glaea, a notoriously inaccessible piece of land. The mountains that surrounded the Keep were tall, treacherous, dense, and incredibly effective at keeping outsiders away. Even if one managed to locate the Keep—difficult on its own, given the Arachassen's unmatched ability to keep secrets—the journey over the mountains on foot would be almost certain death. The mountain range was so dense that even most magical travel—already very rare—was impossible over such a distance, and dangerous. Unless your coordinates were very, very accurate, you had a significant chance of throwing yourself into a ravine. Which did indeed happen once, about a century back, when some poor lovestruck sorcerer tried to follow the object of his affections back to the Keep.

Yes, there were many practical reasons why the Salt Keep was built here, right where the mountains met the sea, isolated from the rest of the world. None of them were its aesthetics.

Still, it was beautiful.

When I saw it for the first time as a child, I'd never felt smaller in my life—like I was caught between two godly realms, the mountains to one side and the sea to the other, massive forces that rendered me nothing but inconsequential flesh and bones. It cemented the Arachessen in my mind as a power greater than the sum of its members—something greater than all of us. Of course, I reasoned, the Salt Keep would be the only thing that could exist here, at the apex of these two worlds.

I no longer could see the view as I did then, of course. Not that I didn't see it in my own way—not that I didn't still experience it, maybe even more deeply than I did that day. I now *felt* the world around me in every sense, the presence of the world wrapping me up from all angles. Every jagged plane of the rocky cliffs—grey—the roll of the surf—green—the dusty, dry, shin-tickling grass—dim gold.

I had nothing to mourn. I had gained more than I had lost. This is what I would tell anyone who asked me.

But secretly, in a part of myself I tried not to acknowledge, I missed being able to *see* it. Sometimes, when I'd come out here, I'd try to conjure that memory—the memory of sight, from when I was ten years old.

"You're distracted, Sylina," the Sightmother said, and I snapped my head forward. We walked through the rocky paths along the cliffs, pulling our cloaks tight against the salty wind that stung our cheeks.

She was right. I was distracted.

"I apologize."

I heard the warm smile in her voice. "You don't need to

apologize. Ascensions are difficult. And I know Raeth's has been especially so for you."

This was what I had always appreciated about the Sightmother, from the time I was a child. She was foreboding, powerful, strict—yes. But she was also kind, warm, present. I had so needed that when I met her. I still felt that I needed it.

For this reason, I didn't bother trying to lie to her.

"I've struggled with it," I admitted.

"Raeth is more alive than she has ever been. But I know that you know that."

"Yes."

Ascension, not death. Never death. Arachessen didn't believe in death, only change. Just as the loss of our eyes didn't mean the loss of sight, the loss of a heartbeat didn't mean the loss of life.

Still, it was hard not to mourn someone who existed now only as air and earth and water, which had no room for the memories or thoughts or experiences that made a human a human.

"What's so troubling to you, Sylina?" the Sightmother asked.

I didn't answer, and she laughed softly. "You were always ever the mysterious one. Even when we found you."

"I—" I chose my words carefully. "I felt that Raeth's fate was avoidable, and I've carried bitterness about that. That is my weight to carry, not Asha's."

"It isn't just about Raeth."

I didn't answer. I couldn't think of a way to do so without sounding resentful. Maybe because I was.

"Weaver's name, Sylina, just speak your mind." The Sightmother nudged my shoulder affectionately, shaking her head. "It's no interrogation."

"I don't like to give voice to thoughts that don't deserve it."

"And I'm sure Acaeja is grateful for your piousness. But humor me."

My teeth ground, just as they always did, involuntarily, whenever I thought about the shot I was so close to taking and didn't.

"I could have ended it then," I said, after a long moment. "I had a clear shot to him. I was going to take it."

"Why didn't you?"

I disliked when the Sightmother did this—asked questions she already knew the answer to, just to make us say the answers aloud.

"Because Asha commanded that I return."

"Is that really why you didn't?"

I paused and turned to her. The Sightmother kept on walking.

"Keep going," she said. "Why did Asha tell you to return?"

"She felt we were running out of time to flee."

"That isn't the only reason." Now, the Sightmother stopped, too, and turned to me. "The Arachessen only exist to be architects of the fate the Weaver shows us. We are not judges. We are not executioners. We are followers of the goddess Acaeja's will, and followers of the unknown."

My cheeks flushed—irritated to have this explained, and embarrassed that the Sightmother, who I so admired, apparently felt it needed to be.

"I know, Sightmother. And I'm committed to that."

"Oh, I know you are, Sylina. This is why I'm telling you this. Because you're a committed Arachessen. A committed Sister of the threads. A committed daughter of the Weaver.

And I know you have struggled with this. I think for reasons beyond those even you yourself understand."

"It's—there is so much suffering," I said. "It isn't just about Raeth, or Asha, it's—"

"It reminds you," the Sightmother said, "of your own past."

I was ashamed of the defensive anger that leapt up in me at that.

"With all respect, Sightmother—"

She raised a hand. The movement seemed to erect a wall between us—her presence pushing back against mine. "You do not need to agree with me or argue with me. In the end, it doesn't matter if you think I'm right or not. You have had a longer life beyond the walls of the Keep than most of the Arachessen. I know that has been difficult for you. In some ways, it has compromised your training—compromises that I'm proud to say that you've overcome."

My face was hot. I didn't like thinking about this. It had been a long time since I'd had to defend myself against the many accusations that I would never be a good Arachessen because I was so old by the time I got here.

"Your past has instilled in you a strong sense of justice. This makes you a powerful warrior, strong in your conviction. But it also means that you struggle with the reality that there is no good or evil in this world, just as there is no good or evil in us. Only what is Right by the fates."

I wished I could say she was wrong. I had tried over the years to beat that quality out of myself, the piece that was so obsessed with justice and righteousness. And I'd done a good job of it, for the most part.

There was no moral good or evil. There was only what was fated and what was not. What was Right by the threads our goddess wove, and what was a deviation of what should be. Judging which was which was not our place.

I nearly jumped as a warm hand touched my cheek. The Sightmother's caress was brief and gentle.

"You have a kind heart, Sylina," she said. "That is a gift to Acaeja, even if it is, at times, a burden to you. Temper your expectations of this world. But do not dampen your fire. You'll need it for what's ahead."

What's ahead?

I didn't need expressions to feel the shift in the Sightmother then, a solemn tinge to her presence.

"What is it?" I asked.

The Sightmother pulled away, resuming her walk. She didn't answer for a long moment.

"I peered into the darkness last night."

I faltered.

Peering into the darkness. A phrase to describe the advanced form of seering conducted by the highest ranking of the Arachessen—usually only by Sightmothers. That, then, was why the Sightmother had been absent for the last several days. Peering into the dark was a long, arduous task that left them near-dead to the world for many hours, sometimes days. But the upside was that they came as close as most humans ever would to the gods themselves.

"What did you see?" I asked.

"Acaeja showed me the conqueror. She showed me terrible consequences that would take place if he were to succeed in his task. His actions are not Right. They threaten the realm of Acaeja, and all of the White Pantheon."

My brows lurched.

That was a strong, strong accusation.

I managed, "How? Why?"

I felt her wry smile. "The Weaver, hearts thank her, is cryptic. She shows me only threads, not the tapestry. But I saw enough to understand her intentions. The conqueror needs to be stopped." Her brow twitched. "If you're still regretting that missed shot, you won't be for long."

I couldn't speak for a moment. Then, "You want me to go."

"I do."

"But I'm—"

"We need fire, child," the Sightmother said, simply. "You have it. But if you don't want the task—"

"I do want it."

I spoke too fast. Too eagerly.

I had been given many missions during my time as an Arachessen. All of them I executed skillfully, accurately, quietly. I trained twice as hard to make up for my late start, to make up for everything I knew the others would always say about me. And it had been recognized. I had risen through the ranks swiftly, earning respect if not always affection.

Still, these last few weeks... parts of myself I thought I'd long ago discarded had started nagging at me again. I hid it the best I could, but it bothered me to know that the Sightmother had noticed.

I had seen other Sisters be cast out of the Arachessen. Our goddess demanded discipline, distance. Not emotional volatility.

I had been handed a gift in this mission. I would not squander it.

I bowed my head. "Thank you, Sightmother. I accept the task."

The Sightmother tilted my chin up, lifting my lowered face.

"All deserve another chance," she said, then looped my arm through hers as we walked together.

"What do you know of the Bloodborn vampires? The House of Blood?"

Arachessen extensively studied all the continents and major kingdoms within them. It was hard to learn about the vampire Houses in much detail because they were so isolated, but we had our ways.

"I know enough of their history," I said. "I know of their position with their goddess."

Nyaxia, the mother of vampires, was notoriously protective of her people, lording singularly over the continent of Obitraes for the last two thousand years. But long ago, the House of Blood had questioned Nyaxia and offended her, perhaps even betrayed her—offending her so violently that they were cursed rather than given the gifts matching those of the other two Houses. Few details about the curse were known, only that it resulted in young, ugly deaths by vampire standards. The House of Blood was reviled not only by the human nations—who wanted nothing to do with any of the vampire kingdoms—but also the other two vampire houses.

"Are you aware," the Sightmother said, "that they have a strong affinity for seers?"

That, I did not know.

"They don't make such information well known, of course," she went on. "But all major military operations from the House of Blood are almost always accompanied by one seer, who typically remains very close to the leading general. Their king, apparently, has one who never leaves his side."

Strange, that a kingdom of Nyaxia would be so reliant upon seers. Nyaxia did not offer her followers any magic that could be used for peering into the future—which meant that seers would need to be human, worshipping other gods who offered magic that could be used for such things. Like Acaeja.

"Our conqueror is no exception," she went on. "He has a seer as well. Join him, infiltrate his army, and watch his movements. Should you earn his trust, your position as his seer will give you unmatched insight into his movements and intentions."

"You say he already has a seer?" I asked, and the Sightmother nodded.

"He does. For now."

She did not need to say more. I understood right away what she was telling me to do—create my own opening.

"His forces move north," she said. "I do not know what his ultimate intentions are with our country, but I know that now he moves for the Pythora King. We need to know why, and what else he intends. Accompany him. And then, when the time is right, you will kill him."

Years ago, I might have wanted to kill him immediately. But I knew now what it was to cut off the head of a snake and have two more grow in its place. It would take more than a single dagger to his heart to end this.

Perhaps it could've been that simple when he first landed. Not now, after he'd started laying roots.

"I won't lie to you, Sylina," the Sightmother said quietly. "This will be a dangerous and unpleasant task."

"All tasks are dangerous and unpleasant."

At least this one meant something.

She nodded, understanding me exactly.

"Go now," she said. "Travel through the pools. He moves to the southwest tonight."

I didn't argue. I didn't ask if I could say goodbye. The threads connected us all, anyway.

I bowed my head. "Thank you, Sightmother."

I started back to the Keep. I'd gather my things and go within an hour.

The Sightmother did not follow me.

"May she weave in your favor," she called after me, her voice lost in the ocean wind.

Continue Sylina's story in *Slaying the Vampire Conqueror*.

COLLECT THE ENTIRE MORTAL ENEMIES TO MONSTER LOVERS SERIES!

Read these scorching hot romances in any order for monstrous romance, morally grey leads, and guaranteed happily-ever-afters!

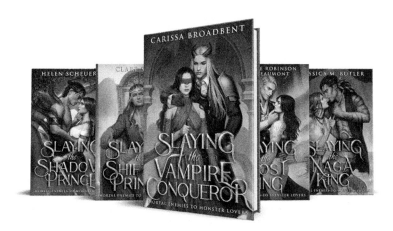

Discover them at www.mortalenemiestomonsterlovers.com

ACKNOWLEDGEMENTS

I've come to learn that it doesn't matter how many books you write, listing those who've helped along the way never feels quite adequate enough in the face of all their efforts. But here we go again...

First, to Clare Sager, thank you not only for offering your friendship, but for inviting me to be a part of this epic multi-author series. I've always wanted to do something like this, and you made it happen for me – thank you.

Next, thank you to my other fellow *Mortal Enemies to Monster Lovers* authors: Carissa Broadbent, Candace Robinson, Elle Beaumont and Jessica M. Butler. It's been such a privilege joining forces with you all, and such a thrill seeing a book of mine alongside yours.

Thank you to the incredibly talented Natalie Bernard for the sensational cover art. Working with you was a breath of fresh air, and the way you brought Talemir and Drue to life was nothing short of inspiring.

As always, thank you to my other half, Gary. For your dramatic reading of a certain passage at a dinner party, and for your unwavering love and support. You bring me more joy than I've ever known. Having you with me for this journey means more than I can say.

Thank you to Sacha Black, voice memo extraordinaire and daily author support person. Your initial reactions to this manuscript not only made me laugh when I needed it most, but also gave me the confidence I needed to take the big swings. Here's to world domination!

Thank you to Claire Wright, for your insightful feedback and epic phone calls.

Thank you to Anne, for your constant cheerleading and your eagle-eyed typo hunting skills.

To my wonderful patrons, thank you so much for your patience and support. I have loved sharing the behind-the-scenes of this book with you.

To the Scheuerer clan back in Sydney, I don't know how you're going to explain this one to Grandma. And it's probably best if you don't mention I borrowed the name 'Starling' from her...

Mum, thank you for proofing the final pages. I hope you got the romance fix you were after, though I reserve the right to reject all related questions at family dinners.

Thank you to my beautiful friends who show their love and support in a myriad of ways: Fay (the art goddess to who this book was dedicated), Eva, Lisy, Natalia, Aleesha, Hannah, Ben, Erin, Danielle, Phoebe, Maria, Bethany, Podge, Joe, Annie, Chloe and Nattie.

More special thank yous to these incredible bookstagram friends: literarycollectors, itsmejayse, bookbookowl, bookscandlescats, bookishbron, leezland, just_perfiction, bookbriefs, balancingbooksandcoffee, joyfulreader, linathebookaddict, labsandliterature, leezland, clareapediabooks, coffeebooksandmagic and devoured_pages.

And as always, last, but never least... Thank YOU, dear reader, for joining me on yet another magic-filled adventure. This certainly isn't the last we've seen of Talemir and Wilder, so here's to the next one!

ALSO BY HELEN SCHEUERER

About the Author

Helen Scheuerer is the author of the epic fantasy trilogy *The Oremere Chronicles* and the *Curse of the Cyren Queen* quartet, as well as the epic romantic fantasy series, *The Legends of Thezmarr*. Her work has been highly praised for its strong, flawed female characters and its action-packed plots.

Helen's love of writing and books led her to pursue a creative writing degree and a Masters of Publishing. Now a full-time author, Helen lives amidst the mountains in New Zealand and is constantly dreaming up new stories.

You can find out more via her website: www.helenscheuerer.com

Printed in Great Britain
by Amazon

47793729R00239